LIGHT
CHANGES
EVERYTHING

ALSO BY NANCY E. TURNER

These Is My Words

The Water and the Blood

Sarah's Quilt

The Star Garden

My Name Is Resolute

LIGHT
CHANGES
EVERYTHING

A Novel

o   o   o

Nancy E. Turner

THOMAS DUNNE BOOKS
NEW YORK

Published in the United States by Thomas Dunne Books, an imprint of St. Martin's Publishing Group

www.thomasdunnebooks.com

Designed by Omar Chapa

The Library of Congress has cataloged the hardcover edition as follows:

Names: Turner, Nancy E., 1953– author.
Title: Light changes everything : a novel / Nancy E. Turner.
Description: First Edition. | New York : Thomas Dunne Books, 2020.
Identifiers: LCCN 2019034037 | ISBN 9781250186010 (hardcover) |
    ISBN 9781250186027 (ebook)
Subjects: LCSH: Young women—Fiction. | GSAFD: Historical fiction.
Classification: LCC PS3570.U725 L54 2020 | DDC 813/.54—dc23
LC record available at https://lccn.loc.gov/2019034037

ISBN 978-1-250-75652-7 (trade paperback)

Our books may be purchased in bulk for promotional, educational, or business use. Please contact your local bookseller or the Macmillan Corporate and Premium Sales Department at 1-800-221-7945, extension 5442, or by email at MacmillanSpecialMarkets@macmillan.com.

First Thomas Dunne Books Trade Paperback Edition: 2020

10 9 8 7 6 5 4 3 2 1

Omnia Mutat Lux
to Janet Ruth Dailey
1939–2017
Amica Vera

There is a stubbornness about me that never can bear
to be frightened at the will of others.
My courage always rises at every attempt to intimidate me.
—Jane Austen, *Pride and Prejudice*

LIGHT
CHANGES
EVERYTHING

CHAPTER ONE

Arizona Territory, Summer of 1907

I blame the beginning of the whole thing on Jane Austen. From where I was sitting on the back of my horse that morning, the only place where I could see anything clear, everything had changed once my Quaker ma found *Pride and Prejudice* under my pillow. Pa was raised on the back of a horse and thought of reading as something only girls did. Neither one of them had ever read the likes of Austen before.

I'd been admitted to Wheaton College without setting foot in a schoolhouse. My aunt Sarah Elliot had a large collection of books that lined every last wall, floor to ceiling, in her ranch house. One day last fall, after having read almost every book there, I was looking for something new and discovered a nearly hidden section of novels on a high shelf. The titles, *Sense and Sensibility* and *Pride and Prejudice*, sounded like essays on principles of virtue and meritorious living. Well, they weren't.

My sister Esther and I used to read these novels to each other as whispers late into the night. Jane Austen's books sure made us dream of finding a handsome man to make our lives good and rich, but this was the Arizona Territory. Most of the two-legged rascals we weren't related to were cowpokes and drifters, so I never looked at any of them to make my life any different than it was. Thing was, I didn't really like the characters or the stories. Just like so many other things I had read, the people were more tangled up about getting hitched and swooning over some lover or other than they were about the lack of rain or the cost of a new saddle. They never did anything actually worthwhile except get dressed up in fancy clothes and go to dances, but it gave us something to do on a summer night when the sun didn't set until nearly ten. I mostly liked real stories about people who did things that mattered. Inventing and discovering, that's what interested me.

Even in the early morning, I could smell rain in the air. Mosquitoes tried to make breakfast of my neck, so I pulled up my kerchief. I had a city bonnet in my parcels, but for now I was wearing what suited me, a new Stetson hat and a split riding skirt.

As Esther read aloud until she fell asleep with the book on her chest, I would lie in bed and wish my life could amount to more than just a romance. I wanted to draw pictures of people and animals and I had a sketchbook that had not a square inch left without a picture in it.

It was a shame that for me to get to go off to school like my brothers had done was about to cost me Ma's scorn in a way that felt as if she'd hate me forever. She'd picked me out a fellow, and I was leaving him as well.

Sprawled on the floor in Aunt Sarah's parlor, my siblings and I were taught the only schooling any of us ever got from that library, and it ran from astronomy and animal husbandry to skinning a snake and zebras on the African veldt. This education got my brother Joshua into medical school. Aunt Sarah's daughter April married young and lives in Tucson, while her two boys went to the University of Arizona to study geology, but dropped out after a year due to "lack of inclination." My brother Clover went to school for two years and he's set on keeping up Pa's pecan farm. My brother Joshua is off to study medicine in Chicago. Besides Esther, I have twin older sisters, Rachel and Rebeccah. Rebeccah likes to cut roses and make grafts of the stems. It sounds unusual out here in the Territory, but pretty much anything with a thorn will grow here, and so she tends her flowers and studies botany. Rachel embroiders. I hate that stuff, and the threads all tangle up in my hands. Give me the back of a horse running hell-bent, and I can stick a post with a knife or a bullet, either one.

I was the youngest girl; always the keeper of Ezra and Zachary, my two little brothers, the rottenest and smelliest little toads ever lived. All my blessed life I've heard, "Mary Pearl, get the boys out of the sugar box. Mary Pearl, change Zachary's diaper. Mary Pearl, mind those boys don't fall into the well."

I wanted to amount to something more than that. I was about to turn seventeen, and it was high time.

Often I felt so thrilled at the thought of going away to school, I could barely stand it. Then shivers would take hold of me as if I had volunteered to walk naked down Meyer Street at high noon. I thought of Ma, running off to marry Pa on their trip here from Texas, when he was just a boy from the next wagon. They'd fended off Comanches on that trip, but her mother had been killed. It was on that trip that Ma laid aside some of her Quaker notions and edged a little closer to Aunt Sarah. Aunt Sarah always carried a loaded rifle and a pistol in her pocket. I'm told, but I don't remember, that she's used them, too. She has a look on her face that even strangers notice and they don't question her. Ever.

My ma has never shot a gun, but she told me once that she was ready to do it to save her children. Those were the days our families would lay down their very lives for each other. So much has changed. My friend Elsa Maldonado's mother died. After that, Elsa spent many days at our house. Her pa tried to woo Aunt Sarah, but when she turned him down, he soured on the whole family. Elsa loved Sarah's boy

Charlie, and we girls thought they'd be a great match together. It broke her heart the way her pa talked about Charlie after that.

A roadrunner skittered before us, shaking a skinny lizard, running alongside on the bank of the road for a good quarter mile. The August sun baked my back and Duende, my horse, danced and jostled high on his hooves. Brody Cooperand rode with us, too, since Clover was coming on the train with me, and so he could drive the wagon home once my sisters were finished shopping in town. He was one of the hands from Aunt Sarah's place, too, and I figured he might be sweet on Rebeccah. We got along down the road and found the summer rains had made the river run, so we rested for a bit at the muddy bank and let all the animals drink while Clove and Rebeccah set up a picnic lunch.

While we got ready to leave this morning, Mama wept in the rocker on the porch, and when I waved my hand, she up and went into the house. I knew Pa was there, and while he wasn't necessarily taking sides in this dispute, he'd allowed me to go and wrote checks for my tuition and my horse's board, joking that said horse had better keep his grades up as well, since he was being sent to college. When Mama fumed over that, he said, "Well, she's got to have transportation."

I figured Ma was actually more upset about Esther than about me.

CHAPTER TWO

Esther was older than me and for all our lives we shared an upstairs bedroom over the kitchen pantry. Many times Elsa, Esther, and I would camp on the floor and read aloud to each other, trying to act out how fancy and often silly those girls in the books were. One day last fall Esther had left *Pride and Prejudice* on my bed, and I couldn't find that book for three days, and then Ma ordered me to return it to my aunt, unread. I didn't have the backbone to admit to Ma that Esther and I were reading it for the fourth time. We knew every line by heart, and though I was ready to get out *Macbeth* just for a change, Esther was as in love with Elizabeth Bennet as if she had been her best friend. I resolved to do a better job of hiding Austen.

It was during Aunt Sarah's cattle gathering last summer that we began to find love notes on the windowsill. Mama reckoned they were put there by some two-bit drifter helping with the gathering. Esther and I shared many a night giggling under the covers and talking about what kind of fellow was writing poetry to us and which of us the notes were meant for. She'd say I surely was the one, but I saw in her eyes she wished the rose petals and hair ribbons were meant for her. Finally, we learned from one of the hands that this Romeo's name was Polinar Bienvenidos. One day just to make her smile I told Esther I hoped his love notes were for her, but she knew right away I was lying. I'd never felt that silly over a cowhand before and I told her I was sorry, but I did have a strange feeling of giddiness every time we found another ribbon.

One night Esther slipped out the window, leaving a letter on her pillow. Papa was angry, but he keeps his fires banked pretty well and was of a mind to let things be since Esther's letter said they would marry when they reached Benson. Mama was beside herself.

A few days later the sheriff tracked down a crazy water witch who admitted that he'd murdered them both for the sake of Polinar's only possession, a white mule. Esther's Bible was still in the saddle pack. Their bodies had been buried in a shallow grave under a mesquite tree. It was more like Shakespeare's tale of tragedy than any of us could bear.

We all mourned, but Mama nearly died of grief.

Not long after, we took a visit to my uncle's house in Tucson. I sat and drew pictures from the front porch while Uncle Harland showed Rachel and Rebeccah around the house. The longer I sat there, the more I heard the sounds of the town and the house and the people in it. I snuggled down in a quilt on the porch and imagined I was soaking in the place. It was a different kind of peace than we had out at the farm. A busyness that seemed alive. I could see myself living in town. Maybe having an art studio. My brothers romped with their cousins and planned to go down to the Santa Cruz River. For once, I didn't have to go along with them. They didn't take fishing poles, just walked off without a care in the world. It was cold but they weren't even wearing shoes. Boys had it so easy. No one had to chaperone them when they wanted to get up to something. "Hey," I hollered. "I'll come with you!" They took off running.

I sat there with a new sketchbook in my lap and four new pencils before me. I sharpened them with my skinning knife. I worked slowly until I could put a nice point on without breaking the lead.

We stayed there two weeks before my little cousin got a fever. Before long, all of us had caught it, Ma and Pa and Aunt Sarah, too. I remember Pa carrying me to the kitchen. I remember a doctor looking down at me and shaking his head. The hours lingered along with the fever, and I began to believe I would die, that it was only a matter of time.

Then one day—or night, I couldn't tell—Aunt Sarah and Mama came to me with an envelope and some papers. "See, here, Mary Pearl," Mama said. "Sarah found this advertisement in the paper that they want girls to go to college back east. A place called Wheaton College. She sent off your picture you drew from the front porch, and they've written to let you come. Please get well, honey, and you can go to school and study art. The price is reduced for girls. Won't you get well now?" Then she waited awhile until I opened my eyes, and gave me the sternest order I'd ever heard from Ma: "I'll give you anything, but don't die, girl!" Then she walked away.

I remember waking up later, holding the envelope to my chest, and looking at it as if it had been a dream. Art school. I let it sink in for a while. It was real. It was only six months away. I held that envelope in my lap like it was a baby, dreaming of the things I'd learn. First thing I did was write a letter to my old friend Elsa Maldonado, who now lived in a convent in Tucson. I didn't know if she'd get my letter, but we'd grown up together, and I wanted her to know I was leaving.

Riding home under a blanket in the buggy instead of on horseback, I thought long and hard about what all this growing up was about. My sisters, Elsa, and I had been so happy, so easily looking forward to spring, or new clothes, or a good pair of gloves. Now suddenly we were "marriageable" and it seemed the world had lost its grip on us. Like we'd become parcels instead of persons. We girls were just things to tack down and hobble, as if the whole family was afraid we'd sally around and act a fool, instead of that we'd grown into young ladies who might have a notion of their own. Made me simmer, thinking of it.

Spring came by the end of February, and by the second week of March the hills were covered with salvia and penstemon flowers in red and purple swords, and over everything lay a carpet of golden orange poppies. It was a fine time of year—still a little cool and downright chill at night, but a good time to open windows and deep clean the house. When Rachel was here, we sisters all complained about it, but now that she was caring for Uncle Harland's children and there was only Rebeccah and me, we helped each other and sang while we worked. The only time Ma fussed at me was to tell me to rest because of my illness a few weeks ago. I felt so good and happy I wanted these days of spring cleaning to go on and on.

One night, I knocked on Rebeccah's bedroom door. A light came from under the bottom. "You awake?" I whispered.

"Come on in," she called. "What are you doing up at this hour?"

"I came to ask you again to go to college with me. You'd like it, too. Besides, I've never gone anywhere except to town."

She smiled, and looked so much like Ma. "Miss Jane Austen believes a girl ought to seek out ways to further her accomplishments in life. It's a chance for you to learn new things."

"Well, come along then. Please?"

"I think I'm bound to be an old maid. I don't truly want to go, honey. But you're more adventurous. You're brave."

I sighed. Didn't feel brave. "Reckon I've been told too many times to be afraid lately. Too many people around that don't belong here in this Territory."

"You'll make friends there in Illinois. It's a real state, not just a territory. They've got more law and order. Likely most girls don't even own a pistol."

"That's ludicrous."

"Mary Pearl, they dress like the pictures in a *Godey's Lady's Book*."

"No place for a gun belt or a scabbard on that rig."

"Nope."

It wasn't many days after that we got a visitor. A man and his grown son came down the road looking for Aunt Sarah's place. They were carting a wagon and in it was a coffin.

Turned out it held my uncle Earnest's remains, brought back from where he'd been buried in Cuba after the war a couple of years ago. The fellows were the Hannas. Said they were looking for a place to settle maybe. Only, the younger one, he wanted to live in town. He made me plumb weary, watching me like a coyote does a rabbit, ready to spring at any second. He was polite and all, and fairly nice-looking, but he was older than my oldest brother Clover, and I was too busy planning my wardrobe for college to mess with him. I thought of the younger Hanna as someone who might take an interest in Rebeccah, and as we held Uncle Earnest's little burial I clung to my sister's arm any time he came near, and I made sure my skinning knife was on my boot every last second.

Then in a couple of weeks, here came Aunt Sarah saying Mr. Hanna senior and she would like to take a buggy ride, and Mr. Hanna junior, Aubrey was his name, wished me to accompany them as the two younger of us would be their chaperones. Ma fetched me from the pecan barn and said to wash up, I had a caller. Pa shut down the rolling machine and put Ezra where I'd been standing at the sorting table.

This fellow I was to sit beside was mighty well-dressed and handsome in a city way. I reckon Ma and Pa trusted Aunt Sarah with their very lives and the lives of all of us, or perhaps things might have been different, but since I'd been asked for, I cleaned up my face and hands and put the work apron on a nail on the porch.

Off we went with a picnic Aunt Sarah had made, and we drove in her four-seat buggy down through the hills to a pretty area where we could see far and wide across the desert. Aubrey Hanna, sitting next to me, said, "Usually it's the young people who get chaperoned," and he smiled with a genuine and pleasant expression. I liked his marble white teeth and his bright eyes.

"That's what I've heard," I said.

"Are you cold? Sit closer to me and I'll cover us with this blanket."

I moved closer, but soon as I did it felt too close. Too near his whole self, as if he'd grown twice the size he'd been.

Mr. Hanna stopped the buggy, then he and Aunt Sarah got out to stretch their legs, walking up a hill. I moved back to where I'd been, but that place had been taken up suddenly by his big arm. Then after sitting quietly for a few minutes, it didn't seem so strange when that arm circled around me. It was nice. Comforting. I let out a deep breath I didn't know I'd been holding in, and when I did, Aubrey took my hand in his.

"I suppose you're spoken for," he said softly, his eyes trained on something in the distance.

"Me? No. No fellas around here to speak of, except my brothers and cousins."

He kept staring off, and I took the opportunity to study his features close up. He had different hair than I'd ever seen and smelled of finery and starched linen. Next thing, he asked me if I'd ever kissed a fellow, of course I told him no, except for my brothers and Pa. He asked didn't I know what he meant and I said I expected so, and so he did. Kiss me, that is. Sort of turned me to face him with that arm wrapped around my shoulders, and planted his lips plumb on mine.

"Cut that out," I said.

"You're the most beautiful girl I've ever laid eyes on, Mary Pearl."

He drew me up closer and did it again, smooching like my face was a piece of warm pie just out of the oven.

"Now, Aubrey Hanna," I said, "you know my mama doesn't allow anything but talking before we're engaged." I meant my sisters and me, not him and me.

"Then we are," he said. "We are engaged. Say you'll be mine. Marry me. It'll make me the happiest man alive. And you can learn to go out in society, and live in a fine house. I'm opening a law practice in Tucson. I'll be sure you wear the best of everything and know how to have the right manners and everything. We'll have a fine address in Tucson. Plenty of children. You'll be a governor's wife before you're old. Marry me."

"Oh, Aubrey, sincerely? You want to marry me?" My heart thundered in my ribs and my throat turned dry as dust. At that second I could see in my mind's eye my mother and sisters, joyfully holding out armloads of gifts for me, the youngest daughter, well-married to this handsome and wealthy lawyer soon to be governor. I'd be appreciated for my fineness of dress and manners, not just my ability to brand a calf and string a lariat. This was so startling I felt as if I needed a walk, too. I wished I'd brought my horse. First thing when we got home, I was going for a long ride. "I don't know why you'd want to marry me. You don't even know me."

"I know enough. You come from a fine family, industrious people with plenty of land. Your beauty makes men faint. You are gentle and polite. The perfect age. There's no woman on earth I could want more."

"I'm going to art school. College. In the east."

"Kiss me."

I'm not going to claim I was certain I liked kissing him, but I sure never had known that strange stirring it caused. I almost felt relieved when he let me go and sort of settled back in place, saying, "Here come the courting ones." He laughed and I felt at that moment the sound of his laughter was music to me. I never expected this to be the outcome of a simple buggy ride. I felt as short of breath as if I were having the ague again.

I couldn't look at my aunt and Mr. Hanna, but luckily for me, they only had eyes for each other. First thing Aubrey did was pipe right up and say, "We're thinking about getting married, too, folks. Miss Mary Pearl says she'll have me."

"Well," I said, "I said Ma would want us to be engaged before—"

Mr. Hanna smiled over his shoulder at his son and me, and said, "Maybe we were the ones needing to be the chaperones, eh, Sarah?"

It was a happy drive home. Aunt Sarah and Mr. Hanna planned to marry. Aubrey and I planned to marry. I made them all promise to let me tell my folks, and not to make a fuss about it until I had done so. The three of them reluctantly agreed, and for the first time in my life I felt as if Aunt Sarah and I were girls, instead of her being the older.

A few days later, I rode Duende to get the mail from Marsh Station. Ezra was perched on behind, and we were both bareback. With the two of us on there, it was hard to balance the crate addressed to Ma from the Park Seed Company. Ma was tickled to pieces and soon as we broke the crate open, she made Ezra, Zachary, and me start to dig up the ground around the front porch. It looked like a box of onions to me. Ma oversaw our digging, and made us fetch the oldest manure from the piles and work it into the soil. While we worked, we sang. And then there was a pause between songs while Ma thought of another one, and I said merrily, "Ma? Aubrey Hanna asked me to marry him."

She stared at me as if I'd told her I had danced on the roof, then her face broke into a great grin. "Is that so?"

"Yes," I said. "I told him I am going to school, and I'm too young to marry anyway."

"Well, well, no, you're not. Plenty of girls marry at seventeen."

"I'll be nineteen when I get home from school. I always figured to marry at nineteen."

She handed me a bunch of bulbs and said, "Put one of these in each hole. Five inches deep. When did he ask you?"

"A few days back. I've been thinking about it."

"You're not going to turn him down, are you?"

"What do these flowers look like? I reckon I can learn to draw all kinds of flowers at art school."

"But you're engaged. Betrothed. You can't leave home now. That's my final word."

"But, Ma, I'm no different than I was ten minutes ago before I told you. You told me I could go to school. Aren't we going to talk it over with Pa?" I asked. "I've been planning on going away to school. I told Aubrey about it. That it was settled."

But right then, Aunt Sarah drove up in her buggy with Granny seated beside her. First thing Ma said was, "Mary Pearl is going to marry Aubrey Hanna. She's not going to Illinois. Isn't that good news?"

My aunt looked surprised and gave me a look I couldn't figure. "No art school? I thought you'd had your heart set on it."

Ma said, "I'm planting daffodils. I ordered five dozen."

"You know the javelina will eat 'em," Aunt Sarah said.

Ma's face reddened. "Spring should be in May, not February. Flowers bloom in *spring*. Here it is March and every night for the last six months I've been so hot I never got to sleep."

"Savannah," Sarah said gently, "Mary Pearl wants to go to college. I see it in her face."

Ma nearly shouted, "She ain't going to college. She's getting married. You children bury those bulbs right where I told you."

"Mama," Zachary whined.

Well, Aunt Sarah said something more and Mama scolded back, and before you know it, Mama blamed Aunt Sarah for turning me into a brazen hussy. Me, standing there in a long-sleeved drab dress that once was Rachel's, my brother's cast-off work boots, and a ragged old sunbonnet, hardly the picture of a fallen woman, unless a person meant she'd fallen down a mine shaft. I'd rarely heard a cross word from Ma in all my days except to scold us children for some nonsense, and it wasn't like her to fume so hard, but she laid into my aunt without mercy, until we all just stared at her like she'd lost her mind.

Granny banged on the side of the buggy with her walking stick and said, "You girls quit fussin' and Mary Pearl come get in this wagon. I've come to get Mary Pearl to take down my words. I've a mind to put down my memories. Mem-wars, you say them."

"Don't you move until you've finished planting my bulbs," Ma said.

Granny just smiled at her and said, "Could be you're going through the change, honey," and nodded as if she'd just proclaimed the answer to Ma's problems. "Take some prickly pear tonic."

Ma put her apron to her face and cried out as if she were stung, and ran up the porch steps to the door. There she turned to me and said, "Mary Pearl Prine, you are not going to leave home and you are not to set foot in Sarah's house ever again."

By then I was crying, too, and Aunt Sarah's face looked as if she was holding back a storm. Only Granny smiled and said, "That's the change, for sure. You, Mary Pearl, you come along tomorrow." Mama slammed the door. Granny continued, "I am the matriarch of this family and I got an inclination to set down my memories and I'm gonna tell 'em to you and you can write every word before I die. Starting tomorrow."

When they drove away, I ran to the barn where Pa and Clover

were stacking burlap bags of pecan shells. Brown dust hung in the air like a fog, and I had to call out to find them. I felt I had to tell my side of the conversation before Ma could sway him into making me get married. I told them everything that had just happened. I told them about Ma having a conniption, too. Finally, I asked, "What should I do, Pa? I sure did want to go to school. Wouldn't a man wait a few months for me to try it?"

Pa leaned his head like he does when he's thinking. "If he loves you he'd wait fourteen years for you. I'll go talk to your ma. Likely she's been working too hard. It's a tedious hot spring, this one."

I was left there with my brother Clover, who'd never paid me more than a passing glance as far as I could remember. He said, "It ain't likely that another fellow is coming down the road anytime soon."

"So you think I should marry right away and stay home?"

"No, you're just a child. I'm wondering why he'd ask you, only having made your acquaintance a few hours before."

"Is that too soon? Ma has told me again and again that all she and Pa had to do was lay eyes on each other and they were sworn for eternity from that moment."

"Well, what do you think of the man?"

I know my face turned dark and I was glad for the shadowy barn. Still, I turned away from him and stared out the open door. Memories of Aubrey's arms around me, and his lips on mine, and the churning of my insides flooded over me like a fever, and my knees trembled. "I . . . I reckon I love him. I'm not sure. He made me feel real strange."

"I'm thinking of inventing a shelling machine that doesn't crack the meats so much. What do you think?"

"That'd be nice, I suppose."

"I'll go to town and ask some folks about him. Sheriff ought to know something. You ain't getting married tomorrow, anyhow. Rest easy and if you love him, you'll figure it out. Plenty a girl has said yes and then had second thoughts, just like Violet McMurphy did to me."

"Well, all right then," I said. "If you think it's all right to wait. Did she break your heart?"

"I reckon. But she went on, and so did I, and why would I want to be married for a lifetime to a girl who took a notion on a whim? She got engaged about eighteen times before she finally threw a noose around one of 'em."

"It's different for men," I said, thinking of the rich fellows in *Pride and Prejudice* who had fortunes I didn't understand, and the girls in the story who had to marry or starve.

"Nah. You've got a home and family and you ain't going bad, long as we're around. You don't need a man for that," he said, just as if he'd heard my thoughts. "Go on to school. You can get married some other time. Maybe to the nineteenth fella. This is only the first of hundreds of boys who'll fall in love with you." He tossed a pecan toward me and I caught it, smiling.

That made perfect sense to me. In just a moment I'd gone from being betrothed with my whole life planned out according to Ma's outline to a free person who could choose something else. I felt such a relief I could have hugged him, but Clover was wearing a heavy apron and even his face was as brown as wood from the pecan dust. When he grinned at me his teeth looked so white and sparkly it made me grin, too. "Thanks, *mi hermano*."

"*De nada*."

The next morning I prepared to take down Granny's memoirs by wrapping white papers and pen and ink into a brown paper folder. Pa kept on saying how his ma was to be respected, even if she seemed addled most of the time, and that she was the boss in her own way, although we didn't usually pay much mind to anything she said. Ma was fit to be tied, and said as much. She wrenched her handkerchief until it was shreds in her hands. I was just about to go saddle up Duende when we heard an awful racket in the yard. The dogs were going after something like it was the end of destruction, and I opened the door to see a herd of probably twenty full-grown javelina, along with eight baby ones of varied sizes, ripping through the daffodil bulbs and tossing dirt all around. Mama cried almost as hard as when Esther had died.

"Everything in this sorry, forsaken place is wrong!" she cried out. "Nothing lives here normal. Nothing grows unless it's covered in thorns. My children won't do what I tell them and my husband won't listen to me and my child is dead and my flowers are gone."

She ran to her bedroom on the ground floor and shut the door. I picked up a rifle from behind the kitchen door, and Ezra and Zack came with pistols. We shot several of those pigs and the rest started running. In just a second, here came Mama and she jerked the rifle out of my hands and aimed it into the scrambling herd. "Ma!" I shouted. "You're going to kill old Jess. You don't know how to shoot a gun. Look behind your target; you could have killed the dog."

She looked so beaten, so sad, I felt my own tears start. "I'm so sorry," she said.

"Oh, Ma."

But before I could say more, she handed me the rifle and went back to her room. The boys and I had to get a lariat and a horse to drag those carcasses away from the house a mile or so, or we'd be set upon by coyotes in a few hours. Ma was rocking in the rocking chair, staring out the window at the ruined daffodil patch, when I went to tell her good-bye so I could go to Aunt Sarah's. She didn't say anything when I left, but Pa came from the barn and asked me where I was headed, as if he'd forgotten.

It took me all summer to write what my Granny had to say. Pure tedium, interrupted by her tears over nothing at all I could see, and a whole lot of rabbit-chasing stories. To hear her tell it, she remembered things back before her great-great-great-grandma came to this country and worked as a servant. She'd weep over heartaches that were not her own, weep for the struggles of members of our family, and then she'd say how one liked his whisky too much.

She remembered the Civil War, she said, and I believe the years are right for that, though she'd have been a child. It was all a great conspiracy against my mother's demand for me never to set foot in Aunt Sarah's house again, so I was all for it. Mama would glare, and I would smile, and Granny would be satisfied that she was getting her words listened to.

Now, I know my ma had read *Pride and Prejudice,* and I believe it changed the way she looked at things. Mama had got the idea I ought to marry Aubrey Hanna from the minute he first looked at me with his big, warm calf eyes. "A young, wealthy lawyer will provide for you," she'd say over and over, with the point of her finger etching the air in front of my face. I agreed, Aubrey was mighty handsome in a way, and the idea of me being hitched to a big-city lawyer made Mama prouder than she'd ever admit. But he was so old. Twenty-eight. More like Papa than my brothers, most of whom—even though I was small in stature—I could still whip, given a notion. It made me wonder if she thought he was one of those passionate-but-caring rich gentlemen in the Jane Austen books.

When I was in his presence, Aubrey made me feel all swoony and silly at once. I was as smitten with him as Ma was, but in a different way. Nor could I explain, even to myself, why I had to leave him. I felt as if the art school in that far corner of the world, Wheaton, Illinois, was calling to me, a plain girl from the sorry end of Arizona Territory, to get across a divide of some sort, some gap between me and my ma and pa, and my passel of sisters and brothers. I tried to tell Ma it was a yearning older than the earth, but she was having none of that. She insisted that Aunt Sarah had put notions in my head of a wild and worldly nature.

So, on a sweltering day in August, Papa gave me money, a bank account book, and a new saddle. My brother Clover and the lot of them set out before dawn for Tucson to catch the train to escort me to college.

By the time we got lunch put away, thunderheads rolled up from the south threatening another wild rainstorm. I loved the summer storms for the cool air that came with the rain, and hoped we'd get cool breezes just in time to get to town. It was a quiet trip except for a few minutes of commotion when Ezra shot a rattlesnake and wanted to keep the skin for a hatband, but his horse wasn't having it draped across the saddle, and that animal like to rolled Ezra and Zack into a pancake getting the snake off. The boys were the color of the road and covered with scratches, not to mention cussing mad by the time Zack jumped up and tossed the dead snake off into a bush. Ezra went and got the thing, and while we watched, he swung it around and around over his head and let it go flying high into the arms of a saguaro, where it landed and stuck in the thorns.

"What did you do that for?" Clover asked.

"To keep from stepping on it, that's what," he said. "We got to get home and it'll be dark. If this rain comes, the wind could blow it right back in the road."

When we got to town, I asked Clover to leave me and my trunks at the depot with Brody to watch over the buckboard, and deliver a farewell letter to Aubrey. My little brothers, Ezra and Zack, disappeared up the street. Clove took Duende and he was back in just a few minutes.

I said, "Did you give Aubrey my letter?"

"Mister A. W. Hanna, Esquire, wasn't in. You'll have to mail it from Phoenix." He shook his head toward our old buckboard as he passed my letter to me. "Where's the little fellas?"

Brody swung up to the driver's seat, while I gave a shrill whistle to call my younger brothers, who came scampering from down the street. Clover loaded Duende into the horse car at the end of the train.

We took seats and Clove let me have the window. We could see the twins fussing over who was to sit next to Brody, and I grinned when I saw it was Rachel. She was the one I figured was eager to set her cap for anything in long pants, and Rebeccah probably would remain an old maid with her poetry and roses.

Everything about the train was new to me and yet old, as if I'd somehow been late to arrive, that something I'd never even dreamed of was already shredded and used up by other people, all the shine worn off and dull metal showing through. I waved to my family, trying not to seem as happy to leave home as I felt.

As the train started to move, I spread the letter on my lap. If Clove could not hand-deliver it, I didn't trust leaving it in the post office in town because I knew the two women who sorted mail were mighty fond of prying open things they could glue shut. Anything I posted in town would be served up on someone's supper table by tomorrow. Mailed from anywhere else, I'd be sure it'd get stuffed in a different box and go straight to Aubrey.

I got out a pen and ink and settled them into a handle on the side. I read the letter for the ninth time to see if anything needed changing. Then I frowned and said to Clover, "Are you going to read over my shoulder?"

"No, ma'am." He leaned his head against the seat and settled his hat over his eyes.

Attention the Honorable Mr. Aubrey Hanna, Esquire.

(Was he "the Honorable"? Not sure.)

Although words have passed between us upon the subject of a promise of marriage, as you said you cared for me and wished to procure my utmost happiness, you will understand my wishes in that regard remain the same except for the time of that event which must not be next month as you requested but rather take place on a later date. I have undertaken to complete all preparations to attend the art school to which I was admitted last winter while being confined in town due to the quarantine for influenza when Ma thought I would perish otherwise she would not have approved. I hope you will wait for me to fulfill those intentions since I have prospects of attending college in the city of Wheaton, Illinois, and have entertained said notion for a matter of years—almost two.

Your very fond and devoted friend,
Mary P. Prine.

Reckon I should add a postscript to explain why I didn't send this in town or tell him in person, because I tried to tell him, actually, only he was more interested in kissing and hugging than explanations, and I swear but twenty renegades would not have got his attention away from that. I read it again. Perhaps it was too grown-up sounding and old-fashioned. He might think Papa wrote it.

I drew a line under the letter and dashed out,

Postscript: Mr. Hanna, by no means did a few kisses on a single afternoon pledge me to a lifetime of wifehood when I am yet but seventeen years old. I had only got quite carried

away by your attentions and you may'st call me a fast girl if
you must but you started it and I was just being polite by not
slapping you into kingdom come. I have made up my mind to
go to Illinois and that's that. Yours sincerely and fondly and
truly, Mary Pearl.

   Post postscript: We can hitch up when I get back. I'll
write.

I felt eyes upon me and glared at my brother. "What're you grinning at?"

"Wasn't grinning at all," Clover said, and yawned.

CHAPTER THREE

I carried my grandmother's memoirs, hidden from my ma and pa and smuggled like molten plans to a revolution, in the bottom of a shabby carpet valise all the way to Wheaton College. It was patched with pieces of saddle leather sewn on with rawhide. Granny Prine had asked me never to share the memoirs until after her passing, so I speculated the only way to obey was to have them with me.

Just yesterday Clover had promised Ma and Pa that he was real good at reading the train tables, and I had to leave when I did, or I'd miss school. When Ma wasn't looking, he winked at me. I wasn't sure why. Ma said he had to be wrong, and a body could get from here to Paris, France, in ten days on a train, and I'd have laughed but for the mood she was in.

Ezra popped up and said, "Mama, the train don't run over the ocean," and got himself sent to his room for that. She was in a state like I'd never seen and scolded us from young to old if we so much as looked sideways at her.

During endless hours in the Pullman coach, when the sights grew boring and conversation with my brother Clover went to the mechanized pecan shelling machine he kept inventing and reinventing, I drew pictures of home on my sister Rachel's gift of a sketchbook, trying to record my own memories, which even now seemed grayed and fading as the lead I used. I hoped they had mountains in Illinois like the Rincons and Catalinas here. What was there to draw if you didn't have mountains?

Sometimes I practiced drawing things from one of Granny's stories, pulled from a memory handed down to her at her grandmother's knees. I drew a girl looking out to the ocean from a castle, and another on a ship. Maybe I'd travel all over the world, painting great paintings and portraits of kings and dukes and great ladies of status. I wanted to be somebody special. Mama was just trying to hold me back. I was going to a place where I would soak the calluses and pecan-shelling brown stain off my hands for good.

"Clover? I don't think I've practiced my Latin enough. I've wasted so much time writing Granny's memoirs."

"Well, it won't last much longer. Do you need Latin to draw a picture?"

"Maybe I'll need it to finish school. What if, what if I could become a lady of letters?"

"They don't give degrees to girls."

"Maybe they will."

"Just don't break too many hearts, that's all. And that includes the professors. When I went to the college in Tucson, one of the teachers married a girl from the class."

"That's . . . that's diabolical."

He just grinned. "I guess she didn't mind. Didn't have to take the final exam since they skedaddled before the end of class."

That night we went to sleep in bunks arranged in the train car, with a curtain for each person. I began to feel lonesome. Scared. Felt like I was about to step off the earth into some awful darkness. Clover slept in the bunk below me, oblivious to my angst. I was a betrothed woman. I was also a girl running away. Naturally, I wanted to marry, but just not this month or next.

I took the sheaf of Granny's papers from their wrapping. I didn't even believe all of it, but I had let her rattle on about our family tree being stocked with brave women doing amazing things, because it was better than being stuck in my room because of Mama's peevishness. The whole family knew Granny was so old her mind was gone, and she'd always had a notion to sit and look gloomily at all of us, and tell us we acted a fool when it was obvious she didn't even know what day it was or whether it was Christmas or calving time. It was too dark in the bunk, of course, to read, too close to Clover to give real vent to my crying, and so I sobbed soundlessly—awash with lonesomeness and longing and fear—into a pillow that smelled foreign and faintly sour, crushing Granny's memories to my bosom.

I mailed my letters to Elsa and Aubrey the next day when we stopped in Phoenix, telling Aubrey Hanna to wait for me. I was sure he'd already be missing me, and there'd be letters from him awaiting me in Wheaton. Probably get his whiskers a notch out of joint, but I expected boxes of loving letters nonetheless. If the letters begged me to come home, though, I might be swayed. At least I could be near home, near my family. What had possessed me to take off like this? By the second night alone in the bunk, I doubted that Rembrandt and Vermeer could fill the hollow left by the lack of Aubrey's arms. And then I chided myself. I reckoned I was just homesick. I wanted to leave, but I wanted home to stay as it had always been, before Aubrey Hanna. Did I love him? I barely knew him. But at least he lived in Arizona Territory.

In the back of the train, two trunks with my name on them rumbled back and forth. They had been packed full of new dresses and books. Ma was determined I should look some combination of stoic matron and innocent child in my leaving home and hearth, and all the outer things were rigidly plain. In the last six days before my departure, a flurry of sewing had taken place in the parlor. She allowed not one flounce, not a line of stitching other than necessary. Lace had been removed. Ruffles straightened. Everything was tight enough to stunt my growth if indeed I might grow another inch in any direction. My new corset was straight as a tree trunk with no room for the natural shape of me. Even the bonnets were severe and drab.

This was about more than my mother's Quaker upbringing. This was about my leaving my betrothed in the flower of his passion to go my own way like a froward hussy. Mama told me every intention of her heart without saying a word in the angry regularity of the stitches, every line of thread meticulous, taut, and stern, like lines drawn on a bit of sand over which I must never step.

I gave up fretting over the ugliness of the clothes. I accepted the stuff thinking of Elsa at the convent wearing hoods and robes. We were both to be shrouded in wool the color of mud for the sin of being young and blooming and independent-minded. I hoped when she read my letter, she would run away and marry Charlie.

I was leaving for Illinois and I didn't care what I had to wear to do it. But here, in the curtained sleeper coach, the blisters on my sides and back had seeped through my chemise and blood dotted my bedroll. I peeled loose the corset, feeling the burn of the skin letting go, and slept bare. That night I tossed about, feeling feverish. At daylight Clover woke me with a gentle nudge, but I cried out when he shook my bunk.

"Get your duds on, Maypole," he said. "Let's get some breakfast. We're stopped for water. Two hours."

I felt like an old dishrag. "I don't like that nickname, Clove. I'm grown up now. First, I'll walk Duende."

"Eat first. You're looking peaked."

I fussed with my clothes in the cell of the Pullman bunk. Finally I said, "Clove, I can't get this cinch done myself. It's too warm in here and I'm all thumbs."

"Now, Mary Pearl, I can't do that."

"Well, I can't eat breakfast like this." I poked my head through the curtains and swung my legs over the edge. "Nobody's around. Help me down." Clover set me on the floor and I turned around, showing him my back and holding out the corset strings. "Tug from the top, backwards of a boot."

"Mary P, you been wearing this the whole time? Are you telling me girls just get used to it?"

I knew my chemise had a row of blood spots on the back of it. "The cords rub me raw. But I can't get the dress closed without it. Mama made it good and tight."

"Well, tight anyway. Wouldn't call this good by any means." He gave a tug and I whimpered. "I can't do this," he said.

"You're my brother. You have to help me."

"I diapered you when you was a baby. I ain't gonna do *this* to you. Wear it loose and put my coat on."

I bit my lip to stop its trembling. "All right."

"You feeling puny?"

I nodded. "My toe hurts."

He made me take off my stocking and show him. My toes were swollen and misshapen but not overly red. Clover brought me oatmeal from the dining car and a mug of cream to pour on it, then left me alone to go fetch a doctor from town.

There was something in the air where he'd been that ever so slightly smelled of home. Sunshine and horses. The never-ending orchards of pecans and peaches. Greasewood. I wished I'd brought a sprig of greasewood with me. I fell asleep on his bunk. I woke with a hiccup and opened my eyes to a short man dressed in an old-fashioned top hat peering at my big toe and holding thick spectacles on his nose, holding my foot up to the light by the heel with his other hand. I collected myself and said, "Hello."

He spoke with an accent thicker than his eyeglasses. "Well, dear. Your eyes is open."

He nodded, shaking my foot toward Clover. "This is how bad a snake is. Not even breaking the skin it infects the nervous system and lymphatic system. But you are going to be well." He opened a canning jar that smelled of vinegar and whisky and pulled out a strand of brown paper. Doctor Herberger put a salve on my toes, and wrapped my whole foot in layers of the narrow brown paper and vinegar. "Rest today and don't eat meat for two weeks. Don't give any proteins for the snake venom to digest."

Clover leaned over me, studying my toe, and nodding. "Thanks, Doc," he said. "And you'll tell her the other stuff?"

"What other stuff?" I whispered. My head hurt, and I was afraid I was going to hear something shocking about my person. That thought was followed by a torrent of guilt. Perhaps this doctor could tell this fever was not about a near snakebite but some aftereffect of kissing a grown man in a buggy with no chaperone in sight. While he talked, he powdered my back with Church and Company's saleratus powder and laid a damp pillowcase over it.

"This notion of women to wear corsets is bad for the healthy movement of internal organs. You cannot hope to enjoy a healthy life with this mechanical deforming of ribs and squashing of organs. You cannot have a *baby* wearing this. That husband of yours is right and you listen to him. Do not wear this thing again." He gave me a wrinkled leaflet entitled *Reformation Underwear for Better Living* and with a nod and a pat on my cheek, he left.

"Clover? Are you out there?"

"Yes, Mary Pearl."

I stuck my head out of the curtain. My brother was standing close and all the other folks had gone. "He thinks you are my husband. He was worried I was not going to have any children. I guess I'm all right. How's Duende?"

"He's fine. You're supposed to rest with all that on until tomorrow."

"My back feels better already. Reckon I have been doctored pretty good. Lectured, too."

"Well. I didn't listen." He looked away.

"Didn't matter. He's just not in favor of wearing corsets. Me, too."

"Well. There's honoring your father and mother and then there's rigging like you wouldn't do to an animal. Stand up on your good foot and I'll lift you back into your own bunk."

He tucked up the covers. Even though I was miserably hot, I let him do it because he seemed to take such care with it all. I'd kick them off after he closed the curtain. "Mama doesn't mean anything bad by it," I said, although it was the first time I'd let down being angry at her in weeks. She'd called me an adventuress. I felt tears burn at the corners of my eyes when I said, "She's trying to do what she thinks is right."

"I know. But it's Papa's word that you can go to school and you ought to give it a run. You're smart as a whip and in my opinion it'd be a shame for you not to try it. I just wish it wasn't so far off we can't see you till Christmas. She's gotten more peevish over the leaving of each one of us, but I reckon she ain't as sour at you as you think. It's mostly because of Esther. Wouldn't want to be Ezra or Zachary now, would you?"

The memory of my littlest brothers' faces, freckled, dirty, and snaggle-toothed, made me smile.

Clover said, "You'll come back. She'll gentle down."

I laid my head upon the bag with Granny's memoirs and looked back at a memory all my own. A week before we left, a three-foot Mojave rattlesnake had sunk its fangs up to its gums in the toe of my right boot. I shook my foot without thinking about the spreading poison, but the hooked teeth pinned him to me. A small rattler can do the same thing to you as the big ones, and then some. Getting him loose might bring worse than I was already in for, so I held on to the noise-maker end and gave him a shave with my skinning knife, close. The head stayed on my boot, eyes glaring angrily at me as I pried the teeth up and out like fish hooks. With my left boot heel I crushed the head into the dust.

My toe was fine, far as I could see, but kind of red, and maybe there was a scratch that some snake spit had got into, maybe not.

When I got home Mama kept me in bed all the next day with cold compresses on my feet and head. She asked me again was I sure it was a Mojave, couldn't it have been a diamondback? I could claim it was a diamondback, but that would have been a lie. A Mojave bite could be a death sentence. Lying there staring at the ceiling boards, I grew all the more certain marrying Aubrey could be put off for a while. That there was something I'd better do, or some kind of notion I had to put to rest before I took up nursing babies and living in town. Much as I still felt drawn to those passionate kisses, it had taken a rattlesnake to make up my mind that life was mine to be lived, not pawned off on the first proposal that came my way. With my toe in a pan of hot, salted vinegar water, I had written two letters to Aubrey that I tossed into the fire before I had written the one that Clover had failed to deliver.

Due to Clover's odd planning, we took the Yuma Pacific all the way to Fort Worth, Texas, and then headed north to Kansas City. In St. Louis we had to pack up and transfer everything as we changed trains again to the Chicago, Alton, and St. Louis railroad. It moved slower, stopping more often, to take on and let off passengers. When we stopped one time I bought another sketchbook. Got so tired of my own imagination that I drew the upholstery on the seat in front of us.

Illinois State was green as an emerald earring I saw once in a store, and full of streams and ponds, thick with trees like I'd never seen except in my imagination. By the time we reached Wheaton, I'd seen more cornfields than I could have ever figured existed in the world. The air smelled of corn. Pollen drifted in swirls on every breeze.

I'd given up my city clothes and corset, and dressed in my best riding outfit so I could breathe until we got to the school. When my brother tugged Duende to where I waited, I said, "Clove, I thought we were going to rent a wagon to get us from the depot."

"Used up the extra cash on the doctor, sis."

"Well, use some of my college money here." I held out my bag.

"Nah. I'm strong enough, except for what two weeks on a train will take out of you."

"String those bags up here, then."

By the time we stood on the mowed grass in front of the college, we were both drenched with sweat. Duende stopped and nibbled the cool grass until a horseless carriage with five people in it, all waving and cheering at heaven knows what, drove right by Clove, throwing gravel and dust and sparks. One of the people tossed a scarf or something at us, and that was all it took. My horse reared and snorted, lurched forward with me on him, my bags whipping away onto the grass, and barreled across the lawn before I could get him calmed back to a walk. Clover was a brown speck across the road from where my horse and I were, up on the stone steps to the main hall of Wheaton College.

CHAPTER FOUR

I sat hours waiting outside the office of a lady wearing a prim shirt-waist. This lady said the dormitories were not yet open for the term. There was no dining room, no staff, and no open doors anywhere for another eight days. Turning her eyes to her paperwork, she said, "Go home and wait until the term starts, dear."

I had to stiffen my lips not to cry, and I feared it showed on my face. Clover had already caught the southbound train. I knew if I went back now, I'd never return. I'd be married in two months for the rest of my life. "I came all the way from Arizona Territory. It took near two weeks to get here. I'll sleep in the barn with my horse and I can work for my keep. I can clean the place and scrape out the stalls. Even cook some. I can't go home."

She finally looked up at me. "The barns are not open yet. Horses are—where did you say you lived?"

My face went to flush, red as a piece of calico. "Arizona Territory, ma'am. Would you like to see my drawings? They said in the letter—I got it right here—that I was good enough to come study art here."

"Girls who know how to follow *directions* will do better in classes than those who do not. Take a look at the third paragraph of the acceptance letter. It gives you the date of Monday, August 26, 1907, as the earliest date on which you may arrive, does it not?"

"Yes, ma'am. How did you know it was there?"

"I typed that letter to every student, including you, on *this* very typewriting instrument. The letters to our probationary students all have the same date. It gives you two days to settle in before classes begin."

"Yes, ma'am."

She peered at me over her spectacles. "Afraid your parents would change their minds?"

"I . . . I can't say, ma'am." I knew what I'd done. Jumped headlong without thinking, into something new and strange, just like promising to marry Aubrey, without any plan what might happen once I hit the ground. I'd shooed Clover off to the station, too, soon as we ate, telling him I could sure enough find the college again as it was just a straight shot down the road. I'd promised myself I was master of my own life now, and didn't need his help. "I was afraid I'd miss the train," was all I could squeak out. I remembered Clover's wink at me about the schedule and felt even more confused, as if I wasn't just fooling Mama, but that people were fooling me.

But while Miss Kotterman seemed stern, she wasn't without a heart, and pretty soon, I felt altogether thankful that Miss Kotterman allowed to let me sleep on a cot in the library storage room. I was to keep it clean, she warned, and no cooking in there.

"Ma'am, you reckon I can read some of those books in there?"

"Yes, you may. Anything you remove from the shelves must be put into the baskets on the end. Our trained staff will replace them. If they were to be misplaced out of order, there would be great trouble replacing them," she said. "You will have to take suppers with different families who have agreed to *temporarily* support new students. I'll

give you a list of names and addresses later. You will be expected to
stay clean of mind and body. There is a washroom on the second floor."

I reckoned that other meals I would have to buy or find, so I
thought I'd just try to get some apples and tortillas, as I know I could
live on nothing but apples and tortillas, long as I find a place where
they know how to make them without too much lard. Duende would
be my responsibility, too, she said, and I'd have to purchase his feed
and haul it myself for the time being and did I have the money for that?
"Yes'm," I agreed heartily. I might have agreed to anything rather than
be told to get myself back on that train toward home for two weeks
then turn around and come back. If I were to land on the front porch
at home, what with Aubrey's now having most likely gotten that letter
of mine, he'd be there waiting with a lasso to keep me there.

Once I got the horse's stall fixed up with some nice grain and
water, I took him for a ride up the center street of town. People stared
at me. First I thought they were just interested in Duende, because he
is a remarkable horse. Then I decided they were city folks and were
just rude. I rode on and quit saying good morning to them all. I found
a ladies' goods store; I could tell because they had a corset right in the
front window. I went in and handed the lady inside the folder from
that doctor on the train, and told her I needed some fitting for my
shirtwaists and all, too. At another place I stocked up on some apples
and peaches, but no one I asked knew where I could buy tortillas, and
acted like they didn't even know what they were.

Before long, I was suited up fairly nice, and I bought some needles
and thread to fix the rest of my clothes. It was much harder than it
had seemed with my ma and sisters all threading needles and snip-
ping cloth at the kitchen table. My stitches were rambling at best, and
pure sloppy in the worst places, where I figured no one would see. I
never had given thought to having to become good at sewing at the
same time as drawing. Meanwhile, I tried to settle into the storage

closet, making up the cot with the two blankets that Miss Kotterman had given me on loan. Night was coming on, and I was expected at supper at some member of the school board's home.

The supper was pleasant enough. The people were kind to me. They were the Jaegers and had eleven children and said they were Lutherans, and served me and all of the children glasses of beer! I had never had it before, and I said my ma would not allow me to taste liquor. Mr. Jaeger said it was not liquor, only beer, and that it was good for me. I had a sip, trying to be polite, but the taste of it was like a mouthful of soap. I finally asked Mrs. Jaeger for water, saying I was only ever allowed water at home. Though the food was simple it was plentiful, but everything was drenched in lard. I tried to smile often and thanked them as earnestly as I knew how. It gave me something to ponder on later, these people who'd never touched a branding iron or a shooting iron, never seen a person with any color to 'em more than they had. When I tried to tell them about the javelina and coyotes, Mr. Jaeger's face got pale. He said with a whisper, "Ah. Wild boars and wolves. Just like in the old country."

"Yes," I said, not knowing if it were true or not, but I'd read plenty of tales about wolves.

He smiled at me and raised his glass of beer. "That's a wild country you have left. I'm sure you are glad to be here."

"Yes," I said again, thinking that I missed the sounds of quail and the smell of creosote.

When I left, the sun was waning and the sky raised a mist just like there had been rain. I marveled again at the smell of corn in the air, especially in light of not finding a single *tortillaria* in this entire town. The barn was dark by the time I got Duende bedded down.

The library had two fluttering gaslights at the front door, but the entrance I'd been told to use was down one side in the dark. I let myself in, feeling the shadowy interior of the room like it was brushing against me. I struck a match from my pocket and lit the kerosene lamp at the borrowing desk. The books, the rows, the chairs upside down on the tables, all had looked so innocent and somewhat welcoming earlier when Miss Kotterman had shown me to the room. Now the enormous ceilings towered overhead, and everything was dark and whispery, as if the pages full of all those stories were telling them aloud to each other at night. I crept to the storage room on tiptoes and slammed the door. Everything heavy I could stack went in front of the door. I heard footsteps as if someone were pacing around outside it. I tossed all night on the cot, now too hot, now too cold. I cried for lonesomeness. I cried for Ma and Pa and my brothers and sisters. It was the longest night I had spent since Esther passed.

At dawn, I gaped again and again at the rows of shelves laden with more books than a person could read in a lifetime. I climbed every set of stairs. I saw at a far wall, a tall clock, its hands motionless, the pendulum still. Above it hung a great painting that filled the wall nearly to the ceiling. It showed wagons crossing a great divide, and mountains both far and near, a river that looked so real I could hear it gurgle in its bed, wide valleys, and people pushing toward some far-off land. Let my brothers moon over machinery or medicine or baseball. This work of art spoke to me, whispering of divine places. I lost track of time, staring until my eyes felt coated with sand.

After I had looked everywhere in the library that I could, I went back to the painting and looked upon it until I could hold no more. I remembered my horse and my growling stomach. There was no time to waste. I wanted to devour the contents of this library, to read every book while sitting under that painting. After I'd fed Duende and gotten some breakfast, I checked with Miss Kotterman for the time. Knowing how lost I could get into a single book, and how I'd been warned they held all the classes by the time of day, I set the big wall clock's hands a couple of minutes beyond what Miss Kotterman had said, pulled the weights, and tipped the pendulum.

Even though I appreciated people being willing to have me to supper with them, I always left early to get into the storage room while it was light. Trouble was, no matter that I piled the boxes of books, a cabinet of drawers, seven brooms and five mops, and a tin bucket against the door, I heard footsteps outside the storage room. I'd lean against the door and hold my breath, and the steps stopped. Then if I went to lie on the cot, I heard them again.

I loaded both pistols and laid them at my sides, slipping the knife without its scabbard under my pillow. When I finally fell asleep, however, I reckon I was tired, for I didn't open my eyes until morning.

I reported the footsteps to Miss Kotterman, but she dismissed it with, "Students often tell me they hear such things there, even in the daytime. I am sure it is a curtain being drawn out a drafty window or something of the sort." That explanation didn't make it set easier with me, but I only had six more nights to go. It might be bats or mice, I thought, but I didn't say it.

With a basket full of apples, raw corn in husks, and small bread rolls, I set about reading. I didn't move the chairs off the tables, except for one I used to reach a book on a top shelf before I discovered the ladders. I read volumes of art and architecture, even one in the section on human anatomy with shocking images of naked people. It made me wonder if in class we'd have to do drawings of bare-naked girls and boys alike. I wanted to paint flowers, and landscapes like the one above my head, and, of course, horses. I brought my notebook and sketchpad along and made lists of the titles and the strange numbers along the spines.

That night, the same footsteps kept me wary until the small hours. At first I felt frightened. Then I felt angry. If someone wanted to attack me—"ravish" was the word I had read in a novel—let them come try it. If someone was walking around to bother my sleep, I'd like to tie him to an anthill.

Next day after breakfast, I searched the building top to bottom, sometimes pistol in hand, trying every door and window, searching for something that might draw a curtain. I found nothing unlocked, no glass broken. That was the day I found the huge cabinet of small square drawers full of cards. I figured out the numbers on the book spines went with the numbers on the cards, and I could locate anything I wanted by searching the cards first. What a joy to live in a palace lined with books.

I moved one of the wooden boxes I used to lock my door at night. Tacks sprang from the side. The contents hit the floor, slithering out like a stack of snake pancakes: old *Harper's Weekly* magazines, newspaper clippings, some handwritten pages, and copied drawings that looked like they'd been traced on something held to a window. One of the magazine pictures was tacked to the wall in my own bedroom. I'd drawn that Remington horse at least ten times.

I took the chairs off one of the large tables, and carefully—the paper was crumbling at the edges—laid out the magazines and tracings and all the rest. Then I picked up the pieces of the crate to take them to Miss Kotterman. She wasn't in her office. I had a supper scheduled with the Jaeger family again, and I didn't want to be late, so I went to get my hat and gloves. The lamp I had left turned low was out, and shadows loomed toward me. It seemed to grow dark so much earlier here in Illinois, I thought. The stack of magazines and papers I had laid so carefully on the table had been strewn here to yonder. Not just tipped over or slid off as if I'd stacked them carelessly, no, there were torn pieces hanging from a chandelier. I drew in a breath to shout something about how I wasn't afraid at all and I would get the person who did this, but I changed my mind. I would set a trap instead.

I begged pardon from the Jaegers' table early, telling them I had studying to do, although I just wanted to get back to my bunk while it was still light. I stood my horse at the side of the building before I went in, loosely tied to a bush, and told him to wait for me and not make any sounds until he heard a whistle. Since I had found several kerosene lamps in my searching, I lined them all in a row and took the globes off so that I could light them quick and easy. In a shadowy place where my back was to a solid wall, I tied the saddle end of my lariat to a pillar that held up the upper floor. Made me a good throwing loop. Stacked up those magazines just as pretty as you please.

Then I got one of the ladders and climbed up on top of the bookshelf. I reminded myself what my brothers had said about hunting. Don't let your legs go to sleep, no matter if your head does. So I sat to wait, boots and all, a pistol before my left knee, my lariat in my right hand. My calf roping gear, three piggin' strings and a leather strap, lay in my lap. The big clock chimed seven. I still had an hour of daylight left, but I didn't have to wait long. I heard the soft click of a key turning a lock. Footsteps. The hairs on my arms raised first, then the ones on the back of my neck.

A man's voice with a peevish whine said, "No, no. You can't put those here." When the footsteps sped up, I hung my first string in my teeth. In a second, out of another shadow, a form lunged for the stacks of paper and magazines, shouting "No!" again. He flung them with his arm, and no sooner had he sent the last piece of paper sailing into the air toward me, than I let go with the lasso and swung myself to the floor by sliding my gloved hands on the rope. He was too tumbled to fight and I whipped his ankles together with the lash I had held in my teeth. I pulled another string from my waist and had his hands tied before he quit rolling.

Well, I don't mind saying that what the fellow hollered wouldn't set down at Mama's table, but I booted him like a barrel and rolled him right up in the rope. I yanked another knot in the lariat before I stood up. "You are *done* stomping around this library all night, scaring the devil out of me," I said. "Get up."

The fellow had bruised his face when he fell. He hollered, "You can't stay here. That room's mine!"

I whistled loudly. The front door creaked open and the unmistakable clopping of a well-shod horse came toward us. I took my bullwhip from the saddle and held it under the man's nose. "I'm going to let loose your one leg, so's you can get on down the road."

"Where do you think I'm going to go like this? Let me go, I say. Let me go." Honest to goodness, the man started to buckle up and cry.

"You're going, all right," I said. I stuck the ankle piggin' line through the knot of the lariat so he had one leg kind of hitched to the middle. He'd go, but he wouldn't be going too fast. Then I took the lariat off the post and yanked it over the saddle horn, and said, "On your feet, sneak-in-the-night magazine thrower. We're going to see the sheriff."

"No."

I snapped the bullwhip at his shoe. I knew he could feel it through the leather because my brothers had tormented me like that once for putting sand in their beds. "I reckon you *are* going."

"There's no sheriff here." He snuffled and then raised his eyebrows. "Who are you, a Wild West–show lady?"

Something about the way he said that made me wonder if the fellow had his senses knocked out of him, so I said, "That's right. You are coming with me or I'll know the reason why."

After that, he came along fairly peaceful. We created a spectacle in the gas streetlights: Duende, who can draw a crowd by himself, me holding a fancy gold-braided lariat with a bread-loafy-looking man on the end of it, his hands tied together, tears on his face, and gimping because of the tie on his one leg. People pointed, gawking and laughing. The man seemed to like that, and started calling out, "I'm in a Wild West show! Look at me, I'm gonna do some tricks."

I pulled my Stetson low, hoping no one would recognize me, but I knew instantly that there was no other woman around wearing a man's roping hat and hauling an overgrown, childish rascal through the street. I'd made myself a spectacle, for sure. They might send me home from college. It had seemed like the right thing to do, to capture someone messing around the library at night, until people were laughing at me. I came to a building marked DuPage County Courthouse and tied Duende to the rail. I didn't have to go inside; several men in black suits came out the door to see what was going on. One of them, I saw with relief, was wearing a badge.

By the time I got back to the storage room bunk that night, I knew plenty about Calvert Mott, the man I had hog-tied and marched down Main Street. He was a simpleminded, much tolerated, overgrown child. To hear the lawman say, he was no more dangerous than a housecat, though he was given to temper tantrums and peevishness. Instead of being locked away, people either ignored him or protected him; fed him, too. But, they didn't always know what he did with himself, especially during winters. They expected he'd freeze to death somewhere in a barn, but he was always there in the mornings, looking for a meal from his usual "haunts." He had a clever streak, apparently, for he'd gotten himself a key and let himself into the library at night through an upper hall on the third floor that connected this building to the classrooms next door. He slept in the storage room, but not on the cot I'd been using, for he preferred his own blanket, he said. When he had found his "bedroom" occupied and the door barred, he'd walked the library floors at night, crying, hoping to come find the door open, though it never was.

In the end, the sheriff and I agreed with Calvert that he could sleep in the jail, unlocked, for the next few days until I was done sleeping in the storage room. For every night he stayed in the jail, I would show him a "real Western rope trick" the following day, like the one I'd used to tie him up. It seemed a small enough trade. I told him I would meet him at the barn of the college, where I knew other hands would be there to keep an eye on him. He may have been simple, but he was a great loaf of a man, and I didn't want there to be a chance for him to get the upper hand.

It was plumb dark as pitch when I got back to the library, but I lit a kerosene lantern and put it on a safe shelf near me, and kept my pistols near as I lay down. It was a quiet night.

CHAPTER FIVE

I'd gotten a bed in a huge room lined with stacked-up beds, and though the one on the bottom was empty, a girl in the bed next to mine told me to grab the top bunk because it was warmer in the winter and cooler in the summer up there.

Each and every teacher had a list of things I had to buy: books, art supplies, paints of every color, and odd things I couldn't even name. I took notes on every word the teachers said. I stared open-mouthed at the drawings on the walls, the lumps of clay that would become busts, and the photographing equipment. By the end of two weeks, I joyously engaged in every class, still trembling with the thought that they'd see I didn't belong and send me home. I was out of money. Pa had expected me to make it last the whole year and I was flat broke. I wouldn't even be able to get a pair of shoes, and they didn't feed Duende the nice hay he was used to getting. I needed a job.

I couldn't say why I asked the head librarian, Mr. Finch, who was Miss Kotterman's boss, about making some small money hereabouts, but when I began to talk to him about the heaps of books that students returned, and how I had learned to make sense of the numbering system, I became employed by the end of the week. He told me to come in before seven and work until a quarter to eight every day, and then after classes until eight at night. As the month wore on, I became pretty fast at restocking the books, and was even allowed to show students where in the stacks of shelves they might find the source they were hunting.

Mr. Finch was not long on praise, but I saw that he looked mighty pleased when I brought to the desk a book on Sir Christopher Wren, and asked might it belong in architecture of the Middle Ages or would it be more modern. Mr. Finch had studied architecture, and longed to talk to someone about the subject. My uncle Harland, I said, was an architect in San Francisco, but after the earthquake and then his wife died, he moved to Tucson to be nearer family. Mr. Finch wondered that there were buildings in Tucson that needed an architect, as he assumed we lived in tents and teepees, he said, adding, "Meaning no offense."

"That's all right," I said. "Tucson is more of a town than that. We have gaslights and a streetcar, paved roads, and two hospitals."

"Hospitals?"

"Tuberculosis." I smiled and added, "And the occasional snakebite."

"Ah. Is it the volume by Rudolf Dircks?"

"Yes, sir. The numbering is worn off the spine. Someone removed the card envelope."

With a roll of his unmonocled eye, he took the book to be repaired. I was not allowed to glue card envelopes into books, yet.

One night late, I came across Calvert slipping through the shadows at the wall toward the storage room. I hollered out that it was me, and asked if he wanted to do some more roping practice.

Calvert smiled. "That was real fun times, miss. Real fun, but I gotta get to bed."

"I work here now, and put books away in the mornings," I said.

"I won't tell anyone you sleep here. But you quit messing things up if I stack them."

"Okey-dokey. Do you want a apple? I got two."

I smiled at him. "You sure you ain't hungry enough for two?"

"I'd rather share 'em with you."

I took the apple and said, "Happy dreams then. Thanks, buddy."

He puffed out his chest, saying, "I'm her buddy."

One of the requirements I had to do was enroll in some classes strictly for academics, not just art. I was glad there were only two in this section. History, which I knew some of, and then I could choose another. I looked over all the courses for something that seemed might be easy. I went to the beginning lectures on five different subjects in one day, and decided to take Latin. I sat down to do three translations with a bunch of nineteen other students, mostly boys. Men, I suppose. Well, they didn't act much like men. That thought gave me to think of Aubrey Hanna, and that I was practically engaged, and I was glad of that. We turned in our written translations to a group of five older students—they called them graduates, but I don't know why if they've graduated they are still hanging around to read our papers— and pretty soon they stacked up the papers. Only ten students had passed and I was one of them.

After that, my course was set. History, Latin, sculpture, perspective drawing, art history, beginning oil painting, and principles of photography. By the end of the first couple of weeks, my schoolwork seemed to triple and then triple again. The big room where all the girls slept was noisy, and I often went to the library to work. Even there, sitting under the beautiful painting I so admired, I felt not so much inspired as overwhelmed by it. How could the history of some old falling down and half-buried building on some island off of Greece, and the shape of its columns, help me to learn to paint? I did pretty well in the history and Latin, though, but all the art classes were harder than I could have imagined. I thought I had been pretty good at penciling down a likeness, but I soon learned I was at the bottom of those classes.

The days grew cold, colder than I could have imagined this early in the year. I determined that I'd save up money and buy myself one of those fur muffs the girls wore around their hands. Until then, I wore my leather ranch gloves, but I found myself hiding my hands under my books when other girls were around.

I didn't try too hard to make any friends, because I had so much work to do, and so my letters from home seemed to be my only connection to anyone still alive. All these artists were dead or not even named.

Elsa wrote me that she was planning to run away from the convent, and not to let on in any letters home. It was just between her and Charlie, and as long as no one knew, they thought they could get away with it. I warned her just to be careful for the sake of Esther.

I wrote letters to everyone although they were short, and though I promised myself I'd write every day, that was often the last thing on my mind at night when I closed my books. Sometimes I kept a letter going all week just to give it a few lines every day. I wrote Aubrey most often, of all the things I was doing and learning, imagining him being so proud of me. I wanted to be worthy of him. He must have gone to school for ages to learn law. At least I would be accomplished in ladylike things like painting and drawing. I hadn't gotten any letters from him yet, but I was sure he was busy with his law business, and maybe things got pushed aside or the letters got lost.

On Saturdays, the girls in the dormitory washed their clothes and bathed. It had become the worst annoyance to me to have to always keep fixing my poor sewing. About mid-October on a Saturday, when we were all gathered around the washing—except I, who sat with needle and thread—there was a bitter chill in the air. A small cluster of other girls from another dormitory came to us, giggling to each other behind their hands.

"Go on, ask," one of them whispered loudly.

I knew that bunch. They slept here for the fun of it, but they had families in town and laundresses and maids, and they rode in coaches around school.

"So you're from Arizona Territory?" the girl asked. "That's not even a state, is it? Isn't it because it's full of bad men and Indians?"

"Well, I reckon," I said. I tried to smile but I got a feeling that there was a rustle in those petticoats like a snake under a greasewood bush. They were dressed really fine. All wearing fine white blouses in the latest styles, with lace and brooches of cameos.

Another girl said, "My father said you were a sight. A spectacle dressed like one of Buffalo Bill's madams, straddled on a horse, pulling that idiot downtown."

"Melinda!" her pal exclaimed, elbowing the girl. "That was rude. Saying 'straddled.'"

She didn't say anything about the word "madam" used in the same way. Like I was some kind of low woman. I felt a blush rise. I had grown up on a saddle, sitting like my brothers did, every day of my life. I kept silent.

"Well, she was."

A girl nudged me. "Don't talk to them, Mary Pearl. Those girls couldn't ride a horse without a hoist to get them up there and a gallon of glue to stick them to it." I didn't even know her name, but I smiled at the person who was willing to ride alongside me.

The first one said, "I ride very well, thank you. I have been educated in the finest dressage since I was twelve. On a sidesaddle."

I had seven brothers and sisters and I knew when I was being teased. "Cut a lot of stock on a sidesaddle?" I asked. I wasn't going to be kowtowed to her.

She made a face. "I don't cut anything."

"You must be a load of help come gathering time," I said. "If you're such a smart piece on a saddle, I'll meet you soon as I get my skirt changed. We'll have a race."

"Meet me out back."

I asked, "Dress-ahhhzh? Isn't that where your mule wears lace pantaloons and a bonnet with a flower? I'll bet you could carry a teacup and not spill it from a sidesaddle."

"I could, actually. I ride a show horse, not a mule. You probably smoke cigars and drink whisky like a man."

I laughed, and a couple of the other girls did as well. I smiled at the girl. "I also eat cactus for breakfast and stir my coffee with a branding iron. Can't wait to see your pony. I'm sure it's the finest piece of mutton on three hooves." I figured she'd laugh, and I knew when I cut my eyes just the right way that both my dimples showed to their best advantage. However, my attacker, whose name I didn't even know, had quit making fun and turned bristling and red. "One hour from now we will meet at the back of Wilson's Dry Goods and see who the better horsewoman is." She stomped away, followed by her pals.

I said, "What do you reckon got under her bonnet? Hornets?" No one answered.

By the time we got to Wilson's Dry Goods, a crowd of students had gathered. One of the boys called out for us to start at the corner of the store, loop around a light post at the far end of the road, and come back to the starting point. I paced Duende a couple of times around the loop, feeling him shiver with excitement, like he knew what was coming. I was thinking it was going to be hard to get him to stop on that short a run, when here came Miss Fancy Duds, all set up proud and haughty in some kind of tight black jacket, riding a leggy dark horse with a sleek rump and a high neck. She held a short whip in her right hand, her knees up to her waist, and her curls had been pulled back so she could wear a gent's top hat.

We set up at the starting point and I got low over the saddle horn, then some fool spanked both horses on the rump. Duende leapt forward, but so did her gelding. The girl looked like she'd topple off any second. I urged Duende to do what he did best of all. The cheering from the side just made it more fun. We made it to the light post neck and neck, but I rode all my life with my brothers and I was forked on like a saddle tramp, and cut that corner brushing my knee against the metal post. From then I was so far ahead I couldn't even hear her horse's hooves but I heard the crowd gasp. I looked back and pulled my horse up short and swung off. The girl lay sprawled in the dirt, her hat gone and her saddle flopped down on the side of the worried-looking mount.

"You all right?" I said, and pulled her up by one arm. She jerked away from me. "Suit yourself," I said. Then I turned to the horse she'd been riding. I tugged his head down and gentled him, crooning to him, "*Calmar, buen muchacho, calmar. Tu chica fino.*" Then I straightened her saddle up and tightened the cinch. "Want to call it a draw?" I asked over my shoulder. "It ain't fair if your cinch slips."

"Where's my hat?"

Plenty of others were gathered around by then. I pulled my glove off and held out a hand. "Mary Pearl Prine," I said. "I come from Arizona Territory to go to school here. Nice to meet you."

She looked pretty glum, but then started to grin. "All right. You won. This time. I'm Prairie Amelia Longmore. Is my horse all right?"

I pushed my Stetson back on my head and smiled. I liked anyone who cared about their animal first. She hadn't even brushed the dust off herself. "He's fine. A bit skittish since you went flying off him. He probably feared he'd killed you."

"I . . . I don't know how you can ride in that getup, Miss Mary."

"I was thinking the same thing about you, Miss Prairie." She and I both laughed, and she put out her hand and shook mine.

After that day, I felt as if I fit right in with the other students. I hadn't even realized that I had been lonesome for friends, but I sure noticed now that I had them in good numbers, packed down and overflowing as they say. Now, folks said hello to me as I shelved books in the library, and helped me carry my photographing boxes and jugs of developing fluids around. I had been so busy, so preoccupied with learning everything I could as fast as I could, and writing letters home, I had ignored everyone around me. I felt much happier now that people spoke to me and I could walk to classes or eat lunches with other girls.

When I wrote home, which happened fewer times every week, I imagined Elsa Maldonado reading my letter, or Rachel and Rebeccah reading my notes aloud to Ma and Pa with Ezra and Zack at their knees. I had so much fun I quit looking for letters from Aubrey every day. They never came anyhow. I kept writing him, and I pictured him nearly aswoon with passion and longing, but I had not a single letter from him in all this time.

Prairie and I worked on our projects together, ate together, and sometimes, we went riding in the beautiful wooded avenues around the school. I'd never seen so many trees, and they were all decked in colors of red and orange. Grassy lawns and bushes lined every street. It was a sight to behold, greens and golds and plants still in flower.

"And, is there law and order? I mean, police? What do you do if you need an officer?"

"In Tucson there is. Out where we live—" I had to pause. Taking old fat Calvert to the sheriff was nothing. Where I lived, the law was what you made it. I remembered our near war with Elsa's pa, *el Señor Maldonado, el pinche Pendejo,* who poisoned Aunt Sarah's well, ran guns to Mexico, and was once a suitor to that same aunt. "We have Arizona Rangers, sometimes Texas Rangers," I said, thinking that the gap between right and wrong out in the desert was measured by a length of rope or a well-aimed bullet and often men's fists. "Where we live, there are good people and bad ones. You get to know pretty quick."

"But what could your parents be thinking, raising a daughter in such a place?"

"I suppose they didn't guess beforehand I'd be a girl. I had three older sisters. Two are left."

"One got married?"

"She did. Then she got killed. You get used to carrying iron wherever you go. Looking under every rock for a rattlesnake."

"Iron? Whatever would you do with an iron? Hit someone?"

"I don't mean a sad iron. I mean a shootin' iron. A pistol."

Horror flooded Prairie's face. Then she tilted her head toward mine and whispered, "Do you have it with you now?" looking up at me with a sparkle in her eyes like I've seen in Zachary's when he's got a mouthful of sugar stolen from the pantry.

"Well, of course. There might be snakes in these woods."

"May I see it?" The look in her eyes was like that of a little kid, too giddy, too tickled. Just the kind of person who'd accidentally shoot a hole through someone's house or someone's dog without even knowing they'd pulled the trigger.

I lied right to her face. "It's hard to get it unhitched. It's under my skirt, just for emergencies. You can see it some other time." I grew up around guns; a loaded rifle stood ready behind every door. There was a pistol in every room, one in my pocket while I rode, and two by my side when I traveled. Once we were past the age of ten, there was always a gun ready if you needed one, and sometimes you needed one. I felt safe knowing that everyone around me respected them and knew the use of them. I didn't want Prairie or anyone else having themselves a tinhorn lesson on gunpowder.

"If you were my friend you'd let me."

"Honest to blazes, Prairie Longmore. It's not a test of friendship. It's not for foolin' around, neither. Ask me sometime and we'll plan a day and get way out of town and I'll show you and let you shoot. Let's ride back to school. I have to get to the library pretty soon."

Once we parted company, I stopped at the hardware and bought myself a padlock and a chain to keep the key around my neck. I would store my "irons" in a locker near my bed, same as before, but the question of whether Prairie actually liked my company or was simply curious about me, as if I was still a spectacle in her mind, made me wary.

Prairie wasn't so easy to find for a few days after that. I reckoned she took offense, but if she wouldn't talk to me, how could I explain? I found her one day with that same bunch of girls and offered to go find a good place for some target practice, but she was too busy having a party every single day, she said.

"Suit yourself then," I said, though I felt a little raw over her snubbing. I wrote all about her to Elsa Maldonado, and then to Aunt Sarah, the two people most likely to take my side in any situation.

I loved my studies. I wasn't necessarily good at them, but I practiced. The hardest thing for me was mixing paint, because all I'd ever had was a pencil. There were all kinds of things to do to get colors, and mine were never right. Nearly every morning before chapel I ran up the stairs to stare at the huge landscape painting on the third floor. Every time I messed up yellow ochre and raw umber and tried to fix the difference between crimson and cadmium red, I admired that artist even more.

Getting to class on time was torturous, because these folks did everything by the chime of a clock and all I'd ever used before was the angle of the sun. Here the skies were gray, and I began to listen for a clock to tick even in my sleep, and I'd dream of running in late to class without my work finished and without my boots on or my hair done.

We went to hear the school chorus sing some songs, and the underclass orchestra tried their best. We girls applauded, but I didn't think I'd like to hear more. We also had to see some dancing called a ballet, and it was embarrassing watching all those men and women tromping around in their tightest underwear and spinning and leaping with their legs and arms held out peculiar. I expected any second that someone would split their britches and all kinds of buck-naked silliness could follow, but it didn't happen. Prairie wanted to stay and sketch the dancers, but I told her I was going back to the library to study, because I'd seen plenty of boys in underwear at home.

At the library, I straightened a stack of scattered newspapers. I read the headlines just out of casual curiosity, and I was startled to find an article that mentioned Mexico. "President sends advisors to Diaz to forestall war." War? I read faster and faster. "Met with resistance . . . Lieutenant Ramirez . . . head of operation Colonel Hagenmeister . . . Germany . . . denies all claims yet forward observers . . . troop landings . . . Veracruz . . ." I read the article again. Looked at the date. Yesterday. I started to tear out the article by folding it along the lines, but instead just took the whole section to a table near the window where I could read it again. Then I had to find a map to locate Veracruz. It was a long way from my family, but we'd seen so many wagons driven south by blond-haired men, I couldn't help but guess they were from the German government. They were certainly not Mexicans traveling to Mexico, we'd all known. I took the piece back to my dormitory to mail home to Pa.

We went to Chicago on a train one morning for a look at an art museum. We had to make notes on seven different pieces and I nearly twisted an ankle as I scrambled through the place, trying to find the most elegant and beautiful art there. I left all my girlfriends behind and hurried, like I was looking for gold. Being in that place filled my heart with what I can only call *duende*, the spirit after which I'd named my horse. It was a sort of joy and anticipation and excitement along with a feeling that I'd never measure up to the paintings before me. I floated from exhibit to exhibit, admiring, and then I found myself in a room filled with statues of old generals and some Roman or other, and some of the boys I'd seen at school were gathered before a wall of photographs. Under one, a label said it was "President Theodore Roosevelt and his Rough Riders at San Juan." I peered closely. "That one there is my uncle Earnest," I said to no one.

"Shoot fire, really?" a boy said. "Oh, sorry, miss. I didn't mean to swear in front of you. Which one again?"

I pointed.

"That must have been a great time for those boys. All that gunpowder and glory. Riding hard through the jungle and coming back with a chest full of medals. Look at those photographs! Imagine being right on a battlefield with a camera and twenty boxes of plates. 'And gentlemen in England now a-bed shall think themselves accurs'd they were not here . . .' I'd certainly like to take some plates of that. Glory and bloodshed in a fight for the right."

"Uncle Earnest came back with a chest full of lead in a pine box soaked in mud and ten kinds of corruption. There ain't no glory in gunpowder." I winced inside at my use of slang, but there were some things that proper English didn't cover.

His mouth hung open. "I'm sorry, miss. I didn't mean anything by it. You're that girl from Arizona, aren't you? I heard you'd shot three people before you came here, and that you carry six-guns everywhere you go."

"You heard some leg-pulling tall tales then." I walked away from him. I wasn't dressed in my riding clothes, and I wasn't carrying pistols. There was a glass on the wall before me and I could see that he was behind me, following, looking like a calf that just got its head banged by a bull.

"Miss. Oh, miss. Let me apologize. My name is Nation Hollings-worth. I'm *so* pleased to meet you. I have heard about you, you know."

"*Vete.* Just go away." I wished Brody was standing there with a machete. Prairie was in another room with her circle of girls, and I swooped into the midst of them, caught her arm, and whispered, "Are you still mad at me?"

She smiled, but there was ice in her eyes. "Whyever would you ask that? We are the best of friends."

I lowered my eyes. "You're not convincing *me* and I've never even been to one of your folderol parties where you learn to trick people with your words. Look me in the eyes."

"I am mad at you."

"Not believing that, either. Whether you are feeling like you've got a bur or not, we are all in this class together and I'm trying to get shed of a horsefly wearing long pants." The girls around us gasped and looked in different directions. I shrugged and added, "Have you seen the Dutch masters' room yet? We have to write a paper on one of them. Might as well pretend to actually earn one of those straight A grades you girls get for doing nothing. What's wrong, didn't you know every-one sees that you don't turn in papers? Come along, ladies." They let themselves be led by me, it seemed, even against their own wills. I shook my head. Bunch of ninnies without a backbone among them. By the time I was done taking notes, I had been occupied long enough that the girls had slipped away, leaving me alone. I didn't see that cay-use named Hollingsworth when I got back to the photography room and I was glad. I just wanted to be left alone to see the art and photo-graphs. The museum had magnifier glasses hanging by every plate and I used them until it was time to leave.

The very next day I finally got a message from Aubrey. It was not just a letter but a packet, a wide and thick stack of something, wrapped in twine.

Dear Mary Pearl,
Enclosed you will find a gift for you, and a sum of money in a
bank draft to help you in your studies.

Very fondly yours,
A. W. Hanna, Esquire.

He mentioned nothing of missing me or loving me. Fondly yours? What kind of note was this from my betrothed? I sat on my bunk in the dormitory with all the girls around me chattering about their class-work or some fellow they fancied, and read it again, my heart pound-ing. At last I set down the note and looked at what was beneath it. It was a bank draft on his account in Tucson for two thousand dollars. It was enough to stay here for ten years and I'd never have to sweep another floor or sort another Dewey decimal number. Under that, in its own blue card stock wrapper, was a stack of papers titled "Deed." It outlined a section of property giving all the metes and bounds in henceforths and thereuntos. Six hundred forty acres. Then I saw the name of the previous owner and I knew where it was. My heart soared.

He had bought the Wainbridge ranch for us to live at. Next to Ma and Pa! And there I'd been, thinking I'd have to be stuck in town the rest of my days. My mind raced ahead at the horses we'd run, the cattle. Probably get the old-fashioned criollos from Mexico, because they did well on the scrub grass but if we get a good well, we can bring in Cha-rolais. Chickens. I'd want some good heat-sturdy stock. Aunt Sarah said she'd been thinking of getting sheep, what a thing! Of course we'd build a house. A big, fine, two-story house with a cupola on top of the third story to pull out the heat. I read the deed again. It was in my name alone. Aubrey's name was not on it. I reckoned he meant for me to know it was mine for the having and he'd add his name when we got married. I just wished he'd spent a bit more time on his letter to me. It was mighty slim on words, from a fellow that I'd written to nearly every day confessing my longings for him.

I locked all those things away. I didn't do well on my test in art history later, with my mind set square on six hundred-odd acres of desert land a long way off. He could have at least written "dearest" instead of dear. I wrote home to Ma and Pa, telling them of the gift, all the while wishing Prairie were still my friend so I could tell her in person. But I figured owning land still wouldn't make me good enough to go to her tea parties.

I packed my camera gear into a box I had had made by a carpenter in town. Everything fit really well, and I could keep ten plates in one side of it. The only thing was, I couldn't get Duende to let me hang it behind the saddle. He didn't like the thing banging against his backside. I asked him how was I going to go out and get the pictures I wanted if he wouldn't haul it? But the horse just turned his head back at me and showed me his upper teeth. "Varmint," I said. Finally I went and got a sheepskin and had the man nail that, wooly side down, under the camera box, and then that snorty cayuse let me pack it on him.

That afternoon, as I was walking him around so he could get used to the idea of being both a saddle horse and a pack mule, Prairie rode up on her sidesaddled cayuse. "Ho, there, Miss Mary!"

I had to grip Duende's halter. He got to sniffing her mare and put his ears back and forward real quick about five times. "Back up, Duende. *Alto*. Hello, Miss Prairie. Are you done attending all those parties so now you can talk to me?"

She stiffened. "It isn't like that. Ma makes me go to cotillion lessons. Dancing and social graces. It's not a party for fun, it is lessons in deportment and fine dining. Elocution and refinement of one's public bearing and demeanor. Dreadfully boring. Anyhow, I'm really sorry."

I kneed Duende to get up beside her horse and we walked on. "I've never been to a party of any kind, except roasting a beef quarter in our fenced yard. Everyone brings cake or beans and salad or some tortillas. How do you have an elocution party for refinement and demeanor?"

"Everyone dresses in their best. We sip tea and eat petit fours. I have had to have fittings for four new gowns. It takes forever. And Ma bought me three fans, but one wasn't the right shade of rose to go with my cream and amber gown with the embroidered sash, so we had to take it back and order another. New hats and fascinators in the latest colors. The hairdresser! Oh, I could tell you things that would give you nightmares about having to sit still hours for her to do my hair."

"How do you keep up your schoolwork, doing all that? Or is that why you don't really *do* the schoolwork?"

"The teachers all understand the strain we're under. Besides, school doesn't really matter, honey. Cotillion practice is the key to my future. I'm just here until I find a husband. You're lucky, you've already got one waiting."

I was ready to brag to her, "Aubrey bought me a ranch," but I reckoned I'd keep quiet for now. I remembered Aubrey saying how he'd teach me to go amongst the finest societies. How I'd learn to dress and talk refined, so I asked, "If it's so all-fired important, can I come along and learn it, too?"

"Well, well—well, your parents have to arrange for it. You'll have to take music lessons. Do you play the harp or the piano? Violin? Do you speak French? See, you have to start sooner. There's dance steps, and singing, and the great works of art and composers from the Baroque period. You have to quote poetry."

"I'm pretty good at *listening* to music, although I've never seen a harp in person. I speak Spanish pretty fair. And I'm getting better at

Latin. Why don't you teach me some of that society partygoing, and for trade, I'll teach you to shoot a pistol?"

She looked positively skittish, her eyes scanning the corners of the earth like I'd laid a snake in her lap. "I don't think I could."

After a minute I said, "And you ain't inviting me to the lessons, either, I see."

"You see, it isn't up to me. It's all arranged by the society—"

"I can pay for it. I've already got a handle on the great works of art. Even some of the naked ones. Let me see your drawings of the ballet dancers."

"Oh, Mary Pearl. There are tests. At each party there are tests. They have a person, or an incident arranged. It's always to see how a girl reacts. Every moment you are watched and judged and graded. If you were to come, you see, they'd be watching you, too. You see, it is . . . I like you, Mary Pearl. I love you like a special sister."

"My clothes aren't right?"

"It's not *just* that."

I stiffened. Did she mean my clothes weren't right, and then some? These were the best dresses I'd ever had, never mind they were made over a bit from letting out that corset. I kept them clean. I patched the holes and I washed my hair regular. Did up all the buttons on my shoes without fail. Ironed my hair ribbons. What could she have meant, "special sister"? Was I an oddity she didn't want her fancy friends to know about? "What is it, *just*, then?"

"Oh, I don't know."

"If you don't tell me what I'm doing wrong, how can I fix it? My betrothed back in the Territory expects me to come home with some fancy ways, I reckon. I can take a test. I got into a class only boys were in, I reckon I can learn that stuff, too." As I heard myself say those things to her, I hated Prairie Amelia Longmore for making me beg for her knowledge. I decided that instant to write a long, long letter to Elsa, a girl like me, who I could pour out my thoughts to. And Clove. And the boys. And Pa and Ma. I didn't need one speck of Wheaton's foolish harp-playing cake-eating folderol. Prairie stayed quiet for a long while. So I said, "Well, then if you got nothing to say I reckon I sure do understand," and kneed my horse ahead of her and took him into a canter. I didn't expect her to push up next to me again, but she did.

"No, you don't. You see, you're different. You say 'reckon' instead of 'believe' and you stride straight into a room as if you owned all the air in it, instead of tipping in demurely as a lady should. You'd not fit in with the other girls and it wouldn't be because you were there to learn things. They wouldn't *give* you a test because they'd think you *were* the test that day. The girls would be expected to react to you, be polite to you, and treat you as if you were some low sort of person who'd stumbled into the wrong door."

I felt like she'd just slapped all my teeth loose. My chin hurt from trying not to cry.

Tears slipped easily down her cheeks. She said, "I don't want you to be hurt. It's all silliness and etiquette, but my mother sets a great store by it."

"Your ma seems to like me all right when I've come to supper."

"She does, you see. But the other ladies, well, we know their sort. They're dreadfully judgmental about the ladies with whom their daughters associate."

"You make it sound like you only 'associate' with me same's you would some orphan in bare feet at a revival meeting in a bean field. My pa calls that 'love 'em with a stick.' You're building up a fine herd so's you feed 'n water a stray and then drive 'em out from your fence before they have a chance to get served by your prize bull."

Prairie clamped her hand across her mouth. "What a thing to say."

"Well, don't forget I pack a shooting iron and talk with an accent, too. I have homework to do. Reckon you'd better just get along now."

"Mary Pearl? Please don't be angry. I just didn't want you to think it was because you aren't welcome. It's because the others would treat you poorly." Tears flowed in earnest down her face.

I stared hard at her. "I don't understand you at all. I know when I've been insulted, though. I've got family. I've got a fiancé. I own a section of land all to myself, one hundred percent. I don't need any blasted electrocution lessons."

She looked at me, real startled. She smiled through her tears. "It's elocution. *Electrocution* is when someone touches a wire and there's a spark of electricity that kills you."

I didn't smile with her. "I'm not a low person."

"I know you're not. You are just different. I liked you the first time I met you. My mother and father do, too, and they think *I'm* destined to be a wild hooligan. They tell me you are more ladylike than I am, even though you speak differently. I used to slide down the banisters in my drawers and once I put a whole box of salt in my bathwater to play that I was in the ocean. It plugged up the plumbing for a week."

"That doesn't sound so wild."

"I bit my piano teacher when I was eleven."

I stopped feeling bad for a minute, and almost laughed. "Why?"

"He kept reaching over my shoulder and smacking my fingers with his pointing stick. He had body odor that made me ill and he reached over one too many times."

I didn't laugh, but I didn't feel like crying anymore. I added, "My cousin Charlie put glass eyeballs in a skull and wired them up so the jawbone laughed and the eyes rolled when a telegraph came to the stage station. Then he stuffed his old shirt and pants and used it to scare the lights out of my brother Clove."

"What about *you?* Didn't you ever do anything sassy?" she asked.

I thought a bit. "I got bit by a rattlesnake once. Lived over it. Worst thing I ever did was coming here. Ma didn't want me to come. Pa said it was fine, though."

"That doesn't seem so wild, either."

"When I was learning to brand, a couple of times I got the iron upside down. Pa said that cow had better learn to sunfish so the neighbors would know it was ours."

"How does a cow go fishing?"

This time I laughed right out loud. "It's when a horse jumps up so much his belly gets more light than his back."

"Let's go riding."

"I have schoolwork."

"Can't you leave off it for now?"

Against my better learning and all my inner leanings, I agreed and rode to the surrounding farms alongside Prairie, her on a sidesaddle, and for a while I thought of breathing in all the air just like I owned it. That part she said, well, if it were true, I was glad of it. I knew where I wanted to go, a place we'd seen before, where I could set up my camera and get a couple of plates of the trees all turned colors. There was one already bare that seemed to reach for the branches in the others, the way it sat all black against the bright leaves. I liked the stillness of it. The lonesomeness.

Prairie came along and just handed me things and moved a rock when I saw my camera was off-kilter. We didn't talk much. I had to figure things out. I didn't feel angry so much at her as at the way of life here. What a wagonload of nonsense was life in this big city. Not a speck of interest in where their water came from, nor whether there was enough for their neighbors to eat. Just busy with doing things and having things I wouldn't even know I didn't have, which included crystal punch bowls and harp lessons.

We turned toward home when the sun was getting low. She had

another event to dress for and I had lessons to write and plates to develop.

I loved my photography classes. I stayed busy studying and developing pictures. Next semester we would learn more developing techniques, the teacher said, that would correct the lights and shadows. It was turning fall, some said, and the trees looked like they'd caught fire. If only the plates could catch that color. I knew the only way to get that was to study harder on my colors and painting. Someday I'd figure it all out and be able to paint it, too.

I wrote Aubrey and thanked him for the money and the deed to the ranch. I assured him I would keep it safely under lock and key. I sent him prints of my best plates. I wanted him to be proud of what I could do. By the end of the month there was a snap in the air, and it wasn't even November. People burned leaves and it made a dreadful smell, yet girls all around claimed they loved the scent of it. To me it smelled like my cousin's Grandpa Chess's old cigar with added mold.

Prairie invited me to go with her friends on a horseless carriage ride. That boy Nation Hollingsworth jumped on the running board on my side and hung there like a mail sack the whole time. Every now and then he'd have to get a better grip because we bumped along some rutted road or other, and when he did, he always managed to brush the back of his hand against my arm. I had on a nice coat, but I felt the touch of his arm through it, likely because the intent behind it was to get his hands on me. I reckoned—I *believed* I wasn't sure whether that felt like a compliment or a pestilence.

The end of the first week of November, there was snow. It was so beautiful; a dust across the land, like when Ma sprinkled sugar across doughnuts or cake. If only there was a way to paint the trees, still holding tightly to their bright leaves in all the colors I could imagine, and include the sugaring of snow. I was struggling with colors in class still. I just could not figure how you could mix one red with blue and get purple and another red with blue and get brown, and still another red with another blue and get black. I painted and painted. We had to do two small works every week and turn them in, even if they were horrible. It was a blue ribbon day for me when one came back with a C- on it, instead of D or F.

The painting teacher fussed at me for outlining things because there was no black in nature, but I've seen a black horse and a black dog, and Duende's mane was blacker than coal, so I felt as if he was not looking at color the way I was. The fact remained that even though at home among my folks I seemed to have a hand at drawing things, like my uncle Harland used to do, getting a rein around theories of colorization and shadow, mixing paint, sketching perspectives and all was not as easy as I had imagined when I signed on for this schooling.

The second week of November came with more snow and a blistering wind that made riding a chore. I hated the way the snow hit my face like needles. I spent two dollars each on new blankets from the dry goods store but still shivered at night. I got up several times two nights in a row to put more coal in the heater.

I got another package from Aubrey. Inside, a stack of envelopes, all sealed and numbered. The number one envelope held a train ticket. Round trip. Leaving here on November twenty-third. It included a paid pass for a stage from Benson to Marsh Station near our house. The second envelope held three hundred dollars in cash. The third held a handwritten letter from him.

> *Dear Friend,*
> *It is with great joy as well as tender sympathy that I write to inform you that your sister Rachel and I have found ourselves becoming the dearest and closest of friends. Since your first letter gave question to the breadth of your devotion to me, I discovered that Rachel and I share a likeliness of mind, of*

heart, and of intellect, and maturity. We have agreed to marry.
She has made me that happiest of all men in accepting my suit.
I trust you share in our felicities with the joy of knowing that
as you have chosen a different path in your life, so I have found
one that I believe is also right for me. I will make your sister
the most blessed and cherished of all women. I pray you at-
tend our wedding November twenty-sixth with nothing but joy
for us.

I have found a train route to bring you home for a week's
visit that will include Thanksgiving Day on the twenty-eighth.
If you can find someone there to take you the hour's carriage
drive to Chicago, in less than two days you will ride from Chi-
cago to Santa Fe. Your connecting train will stop at Benson.
From there the stage will get you home. It will also allow you
to attend our most blessed event.

Your loving brother now and always,
Aubrey

It must have been noon when I quit crying. I remember hearing
a bell. I'd missed lunch and my class in watercolors. My toe was throb-
bing. I felt sick like I'd taken quinsy in an hour. Loving brother? Now
and always? The train ticket was crushed and sweat-soaked. Prairie
came in just then with a tray holding a bowl and a pitcher.

"Oh, you're awake? Here, I brought more cold towels for your
head."

"I'm not sick."

"Yes, you are. Heartsick is still sick. I apologize but I couldn't help
but read the letter when I picked it up off the floor."

"I need to take off my shoes. I accidentally bent my knee under
me all this time and my foot is swelling up."

She looked puzzled, but helped me with the buttons. Two of them popped off by the time we got it off and my ankle was red and leathery-looking. "Oh, my goodness. What is wrong with your foot?"

I stared at my blasted toe and said, "That snakebite I told you about. I believe it will pain me all my life." I turned to the mirror at the end of the dormitory and leaned my head toward it. "Prairie Amelia Longmore, my friend, I need clothes. New clothes, really nice ones. Where'd you come by that outfit you're wearing?"

Prairie laughed and repeated, "Outfit? It's called an *ensemble*," then took my elbow and spun me around. "My mother will help us. I know just how you feel. Like you'd better go there looking gorgeous as a Greek statue and he'll come to his senses."

"Not exactly. I'd be glad to look like a Greek lady, but I don't want some fellow who don't want me."

"You don't want to make him jealous?"

"I want to make him sorry, and her, too. Just sorry as the day is long." I didn't know who'd be sorrier, though, them or me. I wanted nice new dresses because I wanted to look like a gloriously grown, wealthy, educated, and modern woman, so I could sneer at Rachel's nearly an old maid, pecan farmer's daughter's clothes. I had money to spend and spend it I would. I asked her, "You've got classes later, don't you?"

"That's all right. Let's go to town. Will your horse take two?"

"If you can straddle him in that skirt."

That night after we shopped and shopped and I bought things off the racks because nothing could be made fast enough, I'd written Rachel a quick note, like you'd send congratulations, but it was just four words. What do you say to a sister who has schemed and twisted the heart of your betrothed away from you?

You wicked, conniving wretch.

Didn't even sign it. She'd know. I had to go to the library diction-
ary and be sure I wrote the proper kind of wretch, the vicious "scraped
from a cow stall" kind, not the "hanging over a rail" one. I mailed it
in the morning, then I went to classes feeling haughty and brimming
with righteous indignation. I wore new clothes and the other students
noticed. Professors held doors open for me, and boys turned red in
the neck when I passed them.

Today I felt sorry I'd sent it.

CHAPTER SIX

I spent the night at the Longmores' home the day before leaving Illinois for home and left my horse with them. Mr. Longmore said he'd drive me to Chicago to catch the train. I felt haughty and I liked it. I wished that bumpkin brother of mine, Clover, had owned any notion of how to read the train schedules and maps. Then, instead of taking me ten days, it would have only taken two to get here. But, then, if he'd known it was so quick, and had told Ma and Pa, I'd have had to stay at home longer and, I thought with a catch, I'd probably have gotten married and never come. I knew in my heart it wasn't that I *never* wanted to marry Aubrey Hanna. It was just that I wanted him to wait for me to go to school. I'd never been to a real school before, and it was all I imagined and more. I loved this place. I would be glad to go home and take up being a wife, if only he'd have waited for me.

Instead of having to work my horse every stop, I simply strolled and stretched my legs, tended my foot, and primped my hair. I spoke to no one but other ladies on the train and to Mr. Washington, the conductor, a prim-looking black gentleman. I felt safe speaking to him, and once when some other fellows took it on themselves to address me directly, Mr. Washington told them to leave me be or he'd get the engineer to throw them off in the desert. He told me this train went right up to Tucson, but Aubrey had calculated well, and it would be closer to get the two-hour stagecoach in Benson than to rent a horse and ride the seven hours home from Tucson. Of course, I kept my pistols with me, hidden under my handkerchiefs in my valise. I wanted to look like a lady, but I wanted to get home safe, too. What little I slept on the trip, I dreamed of being surrounded by snakes with only Mr. Washington between them and me.

When I got off the train and he wheeled my new trunk to the depot, I tipped him a ten-dollar bill, and he slid it into his pocket without even looking at it. I made a note of that; if somebody gives you some kind of bonus, take it gratefully and without counting.

The stagecoach stopped at Marsh Station, and just like I'd never missed a moment of time, I asked Señora Algodon for mail for Prines or Elliots and anyone else out our way. Shouldn't have been surprised that she handed me my own letter to Rachel along with an implement catalog and a small box addressed to Aunt Sarah. As I rode in the coach the rest of the way, I imagined handing that letter to my sister and watching her open it. Imagined the hurt on her face. Venom filled my heart and tears filled my eyes. I wanted to watch Rachel crumple to the floor and weep for hours as I had done.

Tears dampened the front of my starched, white lawn blouse. At last, I tore that letter into bits smaller than a dime and dribbled them out the window. I had a trunk full of new or borrowed clothes, some taken in, some let out. I'd also brought three famous-looking hats with high feathers and broad brims that nearly touched my shoulders, and a fistful of footlong hat pins to keep them in place. I'd be doing no riding or working other than laundering all these fancy clothes while I was home. I had five pairs of new dainty gloves, a hairpiece with framework to balance the hats, an ermine muff with little black tails on it, and a fine trunk to carry them all safely.

The stage driver knew our place and knew our family, and when he saw a boy on a buckboard by the road up ahead, he pulled to a stop. There sat my littlest brother, Zachary, playing with a return-wheel toy off the side of an old swaybacked dray. Why on earth had he hitched up old Buster, when any of the younger horses would have been a better choice? Zack liked Buster, though, and used to play under his huge feet almost daring the horse to step on him. He didn't even look up until the dust settled. I stepped out and the men on top handed down my trunk, a leather valise, and three hatboxes decorated with wallpaper and ribbons almost as gay as the hats inside.

"Zachary?" I called.

He looked up. "Hey, that's me."

"Well, help me with these bags," I said.

"Lady, I'm awaiting for my sister from back east." Then he jumped off Buster's back, dropped his toy in the dirt, and whipped his hat off, covering his belly with it. "Wait a minute. Balderdash and Caledonia! Ma and Pa'r sure gonna be horn-swoggled. That ain't really you, is it, Imp?"

"If you call me Imp ever again in your entire *life*, Zachary Prine, I'm telling Pa that you swore 'Caledonia' again. Just because you didn't add 'dammit to hell' like usual, doesn't mean it's not swearing. He's going to tan you good."

"Well you sure enough look like a lady, not like any sister *I* ever saw."

I smiled at him. "You don't look much like any conductor I ever saw, either, Zack. We'll need one of the big boys to get this trunk up there."

He tugged at the trunk. "What you got in here, Maypole? Half the rocks in Kansas?"

"Illinois, not Kansas. Don't drop it. It's full of glass photographic plates." I took off my fine gloves and helped him hoist the trunk, and hiked up my skirt to climb into the old buckboard. I wished he'd brought the family surrey instead. The seat looked dirty, and I could just imagine my smudged backside when I stood again. I settled my hat and pulled the gloves back on. "You drive, please. How do I look?"

"Too fancy. I want you to drive. I got this wheeler-upper to show you." He pulled the wheel from his pocket and, pulling a string over his middle finger, proceeded to make it whip up and down on its own power. "I can do it all the way home without rewinding."

"I promise to watch you do it this afternoon, and I'll help you with your chores tomorrow, if you'll drive. I don't want to spoil my new gloves."

He let out a long breath. "City girl now, reckon."

"Just drive. Drive or I'll kiss you."

"Dammit to Caledonia."

Mama kissed me and declared she had thought she'd never have seen me again, that I was running away for good and all. Pa just patted my shoulder and smiled. Rachel hugged me and I patted her on the back, but I didn't return her kiss on the cheek. She said she was glad to see me, had been afraid I wouldn't come. I couldn't speak to answer her, and I smiled but not at her.

I felt Rebeccah's hand on my arm as Rachel squeezed me to her bosom. Beccah said, "Come and turn around for us. You sure look different. All grown in just a couple of months. Where did you get this lovely gown? Did you make this? Tell me what you're studying. I can't wait to hear it."

Rebeccah held my hand or petted me, staying close as can be even while I watched Zack showing off his returning wheel toy. Then he and Ezra helped me get my camera unloaded, along with the three dozen silver plates I'd brought, so we were occupied quite a while with that, and explaining it. Mama was amazed and kept looking at me as if I'd put on a mask and a costume. I suppose in a way, I had indeed. I practiced saying "I believe," instead of "I reckon," and the word "ain't" was long gone from my use, too.

The next morning, Aubrey showed up in a fancy new carriage pulled by a team of four. He brought his pa and Aunt Sarah, and her boys rode horses, so the house was packed to the rafters with folks. I was glad for the noise. Glad to watch from a corner. I told them I was looking for a good time to take a photograph, but I was really trying not to lay eyes on that villain Aubrey Hanna or that evil snake in the grass, Rachel.

Pretty soon they held hands and said some vows to each other. Promenaded around the room kissing everyone in turn. I managed to hide behind first Rebeccah then Aunt Sarah, then Ezra, and I stayed busier than I needed to; if Rachel came near me I always thought of something I needed to check right away, so I wouldn't have to pass words with her. I slipped into the kitchen saying, "I'll get Ma's cake."

They ate cake, but I stayed behind my camera. I finally told the whole family to hold still and look toward me. Mama was beaming. Pa gave me a wink. Clover said he had to get some work done and I scolded him to hold his head right up. Just as I touched the flash, Mama said, "Is that going to burn a hole in my rug?" and so her mouth was sure to be blurred in the photograph.

"No, Ma, this is the low-flash kind."

I had been warned by my teachers that it is nearly unheard of to get that many people to hold still for ninety seconds. Under any normal situation, though, there wouldn't be a single photograph, or maybe just one of the married couple after they'd taken up house or had a child.

After a while of it, I felt so tired of hiding and smiling I could barely keep from sobbing in front of them all, and I decided to take my camera equipment to the outside of the house. I loved this house, and maybe I'd take a good plate of it, and maybe when I was done with school I'd use Aubrey's money to build me a house just like it next to Mama and Papa on the Wainbridge land.

Clover stood by my side, asking questions of everything I did. Then he said, "Want to see my new shelling machine? It'd make a fine photograph." He carried my camera under one arm and a box of plates under the other. "You spent some cash on this stuff, didn't you?"

"Some fool sent me some. Bought me off."

"No, it ain't like that."

"What do you mean?" I squinted at his face. "You knew he was courting our sister, and that he planned to send me money?" He looked purely ashamed. I asked, "Is Rachel having a baby?"

"What a thing to say about your own sister."

"I got plenty of other things to say about her. Why else?"

"I'm just saying, take what comes. Don't fight what is already done. It ain't our way."

"Your way, you mean. You older ones got all the lessons. All I got was 'Mary Pearl, mind Ezra. Mary Pearl change Zachary's diaper. Mary Pearl, the boys are in the sugar barrel.' Anyhow, I'm *not* fighting it. If he wants a wretched hussy who'd steal her own sister's beau, he can have her and I'll have no pity for either of them." My chin hurt with the effort of holding tears back.

Clove looked at the floor and breathed in and out loudly. "Take a look at my machine here. I was hoping you'd make a plate of it." He started up the sheller, and the air filled with brown haze and the smell of pecan shells that had perfumed my entire life.

At that moment I realized how far I had traveled away from this place. I couldn't get a photograph of the machine while it was running so I made only one plate and said, "Clove, you better apply for a patent. I'll send you a print so you can." He grinned as he shut it down.

"Leave the box here and tomorrow I'll take another when the light comes in that door. The sun's going down. It's dark and I'm low on flash powder."

When he left, I walked through the place, looking at the places where my own boots had worn many a step into the floor. I slipped off my lacy gloves and admired the whiteness of my hands, and carefully chose a couple of freshly shelled pecans to eat from the bottom of Clove's machine. Brown stain touched one nail and I licked it clean. Then the tears overwhelmed me.

After a few minutes, the door squeaked. I held my breath, waiting for some voice to call me to the house. I used my clean gloves to dry my face, thinking I was glad I had more than one pair, surely surprised to see the man standing there. "Aubrey. What do you want? Rachel isn't out here with me."

"I just wanted to tell you we are leaving soon."

I waved my hand, turning away as I spoke. "Well, then. So long. Happy trails. Good riddance. Watch your back. All that."

"I had to see you before I leave."

"You've seen me. Get on down the road. I just came in to hunt something I lost." I looked toward an upper window that let in light and breeze, if there were any. In that moment he closed the distance between us.

"Did you find it?" he asked.

"What?"

"What you lost. My God, I forgot how beautiful you were." He had me in his powerful arms, his lips upon mine, searching just as ardently as he'd done before.

I felt myself sway toward him, and then every last nerve I owned hit sparks. "What on earth do you think you are doing?"

He kissed me again, and not sweet but rough; his hands bruising my arms. "I know you still love me as I love you."

I jerked my head away from his mouth so he only kissed my neck. "You don't love me, and don't try to lie to me, you, you *cabrón!*"

"I sent you the deed to the land. When you come back, I'll build you a house there and we can be together—often."

I punched him with all the power I had, feeling the lack of strength from sitting in classrooms. "Take your hands—let go—get off me, you buzzard." At last he complied and I stepped away. "Together? What are you thinking? That I would go behind my sister's back? Get out of here before someone finds us together and thinks the same thing you're thinking. *Pendejo. Cabrón!*"

He grinned and winked at me, replacing his top hat. "Plenty of spitfire left, I see." He went out the side door with a saunter as if none of this had any meaning at all to him. As he disappeared in the dusk, I dropped my face into my hands, and heard another door opening. This time I couldn't hide the tears.

It was Aunt Sarah. She ran to my side, held me to her, and I sobbed so hard I wrenched my sides. Finally she said, "Now, you've gotten it out of your system. You probably needed a good cry. Don't go letting anyone else see you like this. Just remember he's chosen Rachel, and surely she's a better match for him. Quieter, more steady. Older. You'll have many more chances than she will; you wouldn't want her to be an old maid, would you? He's just what she needs, and they'll be happy living in town. You've got a ranch here now, and we'll help you get up a herd when you're done. Come on back to the house now, and have some lemonade and quit taking pictures so you can just set and eat cake. Aubrey and Rachel are fixing to drive off. You say so long to them, put him behind you, and get on with your studies."

"I can't begin to tell you," I said. Fresh tears fell.

"Now, listen to me. You've been jilted, sure, but many a girl has gone through a dozen fellows before she settles on the right one. Be glad you aren't caught in a marriage where he mighta been eyeing Rachel all through the years. It's better this way, I promise you that."

I could still feel his kisses on my face and neck, and I brushed at them with the back of my arm. She didn't know what he'd said and done, and I was determined at that moment that no one would. Only Aubrey and I knew. It wasn't better this way. This was far worse than Rachel stealing him away. I pressed my damp face with the hem of Prairie's borrowed skirt.

Aunt Sarah said, "There, now. No more tears. It's done and gone. Hold your head high and let your family love you. We've all missed you mightily. You took all the spunk in the house to Illinois. The boys are running wild without you watching over them like a governess, and your ma is fit to be tied. Come on back to the parlor. Now the wedding's over, we've got a present for you."

Ezra was under the kitchen table, tickling people's ankles with a piece of straw from the broom. Zack nearly dropped his pie plate and Aunt Sarah scolded them both. Ma came to me and patted my cheek, hugged and kissed me. "You've been crying," she whispered. "It's going to be all right, honey. Come see what we got you for your horse."

I felt sorry to leave them and glad to go at the same time. I carried my new Indian horse blanket in my arms to Illinois. It was too thick to fold into the trunk, so I settled it in my lap. Old now, and hardened by heartbreak, I made myself smile at my family outside the window. I'd managed to make Granny mad at me for not carrying her memoirs with me here and there, because she'd ordered me to carry them until her dying day. I told her they were locked up in my dormitory trunk, but that didn't settle her and she called me a will-o'-the-wisp, which is right up there with ne'er-do-well in my family's book of insults.

At least at school I could just think about composition and lighting, and colors and shadows, and making prints of all the plates I'd exposed. At least at school I could sit with girls like me who meant to make something of themselves, who had talent and cared about learning instead of marrying. Ma's last words to me as I waved through the window of the train were, "Don't worry, another fellow will come right along," and it took the made-up smile right off my face. As if that was the only thing missing from my life. She was waving her handkerchief with all her might. I started to say something back, but at that moment the train let out a whistle and a belch of steam, and I settled into the seat, satisfied to only frown at the knees of the man sitting across from me.

How could I ever go home again? Did I have to stay away forever because Aubrey Hanna would be waiting there? How could I tell anyone why I'd run away? I decided to write to Rachel and let her know what she had gotten for a husband. I'd mail it to my folks' house so he wouldn't get it. What would hurt them less, to know the kind of man he is or to never find out and have me stay gone? How could I have thought him manly and handsome? I took out a pencil and went to borrow paper from a porter. The moment I touched the point to the page, all the words I might have written flew from my mind like fluttering birds.

I turned my face to the window and closed my eyes, trying to sink deep into my own skin where I could think and not cry. I'd never felt so alone, but it wasn't like going for a ride out in the desert to sort things. I was in the middle of a car full of strangers. On top of everything else, it dawned on me just then that no one had suggested I needed Clover or anyone else to chaperone me back to college. I was tossed out with no care at all, now that *somebody* had married themselves a lawyer. Lands, but I felt I understood my own ma less than any human on earth, with the exception of that citified skunk Aubrey.

"Miss Mary Pearl? They're stopping for water. Would you like me to fetch you something to eat? The sign on the depot said they had boiled chicken dinner."

Sitting straight across from me was Aunt Sarah's cowhand, Brody. He held his hat in leathered hands, pressed against his chest. My mouth hung open for a couple of breaths. I had not seen him at all. "That'd be real nice," I said. As I spoke he was already standing, settling his hat, heading for the end of the car. "Thank you, Brody," I called. Brody stopped in his tracks and half turned toward me. Red-faced, he nodded with a snap of his head.

I stood up, wishing I had gone out myself just to stretch my legs; I thought how I shouldn't be treating him like he was some kind of servant. I made sure no one was around and stretched my arms and legs, then started for the door. There he was with nothing in his hands but a dish towel held up like a bag.

"There's nothing but some biscuits. Reckon they ran out of chicken dinners this morning at sunup."

Even the biscuits tasted like they had been made two days before. "Why aren't we eating in the dining car?" I asked him, after sipping from his canteen.

"I didn't know there was a dining car."

"We can go there this evening then."

He just nodded.

"How come you're coming with me, instead of one of my brothers?"

"I asked them the same question. Told them to send one of the little fellers. Reckon your Aunt Sarah, I mean, Miz Elliot, had a reason, getting you outta there."

It took a second to let those words sink in. I was beginning to feel like nobody wanted me around, including my own family. "Getting me out?"

"Mind if I play my guitar? I brung it along to pass the time."

"Why did they want me out of there?"

He picked a few notes and seemed to be concentrating with all his might, staring at his left hand as it searched for fingering. "It's complicated. They're keeping you out of sight."

Did someone know what I had done? Did someone see Aubrey kissing me in the barn? "How complicated? I have a mind. How complicated is it, Mr. Brody Cooperand? There's something you're not telling me and I think I have a right to know."

His eyes never left his hand. Cold steel fingers ran up my back. He said, "Figures to be a range war opening up. I reckon I'd do better there. They shoulda sent yer little brothers both with you and you could keep 'em with you until this blows over."

"Range war? What range war?"

"There's some kinda mess with the railroad. Took your granny's land. The smugglers have picked up and don't stop night or day, heading to Mexico, and a couple old boys took some potshots at me when I got too close to 'em. You already know somebody's poisoned your aunt's chicken yard with salt, and one of the wells, too. I ain't too clear on what's back of it all 'cept I should be there instead of here."

"Well, just get off at the next stop and go back. I'm fine on my *own*. I got here alone, didn't I?" He strummed a few chords and then began to play a tune. I stewed with anger. His playing got softer and slow, as if he'd come to a part he didn't know. I seethed. "What do you care? You're not family. Get off and go to Oklahoma for all I care."

He stopped playing and his face reddened again, but there was a distinct bristling about him, lowering his brows and eyelids the way a wild dog will do just before it rushes for your throat. "I ride for Miz Elliot."

That was all it took. I knew his kind. Ride for the brand. In cowhand lingo, we were his family and I'd as much as told one of my brothers he was an unwanted stepchild. I felt sorry I'd said that. Now Granny was angry, and so was my escort. Wonder who else I could rile before I even got back to Illinois? Still, he was sent here and there like a lackey. A fellow ought to have more pride. Most lonesome old cowhands either settle in or take off, and this one had stayed for years. I wanted to know more about why he thought I was actually being sent away rather than going off on my own to study art, but I snapped my lips shut and turned toward the window. I said softly, "I'm sorry. I didn't intend being so mean."

The train swayed and Brody played the strings. I stared out the window and let the songs wash over me, bringing tears. Such nice music. This was the sound of home, not the brassy stuff from the college orchestra. Not the huge swell of the college choir. A single guitar in the nighttime was the sweetest sound on earth to me. The feeling of pain within my ribs swelled to a roaring ache. Was this all growing up was, feeling more and more lost and unconnected? No wonder some girls just jumped at the first fellow that asked them for their hands. I felt so very *single*. Alone, unwanted. If there was some kind of problem going on at home, why didn't anyone tell me? Eventually some man in a bowler hat came to him and told him to quit playing, that he was irritating the man's wife. Brody put the instrument down at his feet and leaned it against the wall, saying, "Mighty sorry, sir."

"You should have told him to mind his own business," I said. After a while I added, "You're kind of *güero* to play guitar like that."

He lowered one eyebrow. "You don't like it, either?"

"I like it real fine. Better than the stuff at college. That fellow isn't the end-all of good music. I only heard the other men play it Mexican style, that is. The caballeros."

"I picked it up a long time ago, watching them fellers. Look out, next I'll yodel for 'em," he said, and grinned. "My grandpa was Swiss."

Despite my pain, I grinned, too. This time when he caught eyes with me, Brody's face reddened and he turned away, sheepish. After a while he asked, "You like going to that school up yonder?"

"Yes, I do. Only, not everything is easy. In fact, nothing is easy. I work and work and some things I just can't figure out. Everything runs by a clock, and you can't just work until the work is done, you have to do it before the clock strikes. Some of the other students are nice, some are not. Some just hard to figure."

He nodded and said, "That's pretty much the way of it anywhere, I reckon. Couple of the fellers on the ranch I wouldn't give two shakes for. Some's real good people. I watch how a man treats a horse first."

It was my turn to nod in silent agreement. I thought to lighten the mood, and asked, "You can really yodel?"

"Nearly."

"Show me sometime?"

"Nah."

"I'm sorry I fussed at you."

"Still ain't gonna show you."

CHAPTER SEVEN

I made a dismal showing on my first-section tests at school. I was called into the dean's office and told I was only being "retained as a student" because my work before the wedding was "superior." I didn't even know what that meant. My colors were always terrible. I had no eye for perspectives. I couldn't compose a single apple on a table. Next term was going to be much more difficult, they said.

Apply yourself. Apply yourself.

By the time he was done fussing at me, I wished he'd send me home instead. I was ready to leave that very afternoon.

I wrote a letter to my older brother Joshua. I hadn't seen him in three years. He was in medical school in Chicago, only a few miles from Wheaton. I begged him to come with me and let's go home.

On the day I returned the two borrowed dresses, clean and ironed, Prairie remarked that I seemed so sad, so addled since I'd returned. I told her almost everything that happened down to the last supper dish I'd washed. I left out Aubrey's forced kiss and his horrible proposal. It made him seem so much more innocent to leave those things out, I realized, like skipping a chapter of a novel, and you wouldn't know what a skunk this Mr. Wickham was in truth. She asked, "Was he that madly in love with your sister? Didn't he even notice you or say he was sorry?"

"He noticed me, all right."

"Well?"

I couldn't say anything. I felt struck dumb. "B'lieve they're on their honeymoon. They'll be buying a house in town. Be all settled in by Christmas. With any luck I'll never lay eyes on either of them again."

She clucked her tongue, then said, "You're lucky to be rid of him, I think."

"Let's go riding," I said at last. "I feel like skipping some classes." We did. In an hour, the cold air turned to piercing wind, all brittleness and gloom, and a light snow began by the time we got Duende back in the stall and Prairie left on her mount for home. As she left, I felt envious of her ease at getting through school, not caring whether she even showed up, still certain to make top marks.

I barely made it through the semester's final exams. I felt weary and cold and I learned to love hot mulled cider and hot coffee with cream, which we never had at home. Cows weren't always giving milk, and somebody had to go fetch it, so we didn't have cream except for a couple of months of the year. After all the tests—and thank goodness for my Latin score or I would have been expelled—it was time to pack and get ready for home. There were just a couple of days, and at last, I got both a letter from Joshua and a telegram from home. I needed Joshua, so I opened his letter first. Joshua wrote that he could not leave school until February, but then he'd be a real, certified doctor and surgeon. He hoped I would attend his graduation, but he knew I'd be in my studies as well, so not to fret. He wished me merry Christmas and enclosed a length of yellow velvet ribbon. Next, I opened the folded telegram.

CANNOT SEND ESCORT STAY PUT SORRY. STOP. PA.

Well, I'll be. Why did he think I needed an escort to come home? I'd done it on my own for the last trip. If I didn't feel like I'd been tossed out like a hank of worn-out rope before, I sure did then. All it would take was Clover or one of the boys to come here. The very idea, not to come home for Christmas? Tears filled my eyes. I thought of asking one of the boys at school to see me home, but I'd seen enough of them, and gone on enough horseless carriage rides with all the kids, to know that these city people had a different idea of folks depending on one another than I did. Why, back home I could ask someone like Brody Cooperand to ride to California with me and he'd think nothing of it. But to these fellows, asking for an escort home would be the same as a marriage proposal to the rascals. How could I ask a professor? They'd all have families and want to be home for the holiday. Finally, I decided I would just go by myself. I had to get Duende back to the ranch. It could be cold there in December, but no worse than here.

That day, all we did in class was clean up the art rooms. I took out some anger on paint-splattered tables and dusty corners in the mixing lab. They let us go early so those who needed could get their tickets home, as we'd only have lodgings another day or two.

The very last day of classes they handed out assignments and enrollment forms for the following section, but by then I'd already made up my mind to give away my paints and pencils and sketchbooks, take my horse and my camera, and head home to the Territory and never return. I said good-bye to all my friends, and since only photography class was left, at lunchtime, when they served a nice chicken dinner, I headed back to my dormitory to pack. Halfway there, I remembered I had left some prints hanging in the lab. They weren't any good, so I didn't care about taking them home, but I also didn't want them to be used as an example next section of what not to do. We'd all had to endure the humbling experience of having our work held up before the room and criticized.

The professor was giving a talk. I slipped in late, and sat in the back. I took in the smells of the place, sad to leave. Capturing my vision with a lens was so much more satisfying than trying to draw it. At least with a camera, I could really preserve an image of what my eyes saw. He was talking on and on about next term. We would learn to use shadows that make highlights stand out. Exposures used to their best effect, to produce more than just a record, but a real piece of art.

Someone up front asked him if there would ever be colors in a photograph and I rolled my eyes. I couldn't bear to have to get the colors right on a silver plate, too, unless the camera itself produced what I saw before me. Then he said, "All of you who finish next term with passing grades"—and he looked straight at me, which caused some heads to swivel—"will be invited to accompany myself and the rest of the class on a trip to one of the scenic wonders of the world. We will travel by train to the Grand Canyon. It has been arranged every other year to visit a known site and spend the last week of school at a challenging and satisfying location. Please take this paper home to your parents. This gives them all the information you'll need. Costs, equipment, everything is there on the form. From that point in Territorial Arizona, you will depart for your homes. We'll have time during next term to make all the arrangements. Those of you with either horses or horseless vehicles will have to make your own arrangements to get them delivered, because you will not be taking them along."

Someone asked him if they'd need to fight Indians along the way, so I didn't even listen to the reply. The Grand Canyon. I'd heard about it. Seen a print of a painting by Thomas Moran that I'd tried to copy. I might like to see that. To take that trip. Imagine, me, a traveling lady, single and with camera in hand. If my family didn't want me home for Christmas, I'd make another way for myself. I might just make a career. I could be another Nelly Bly. That's what my future looked like, and it raised my spirits just fine.

That evening the last of the students gathered in the main hall, sang carols, drank tea, and ate cakes. I got overwhelmed from the students in the photography class with silly questions about Arizona. No one had the slightest idea what could be in store on such a trip. Truthfully, I had not been in that part of the Territory, either. We'd certainly want water, I said. I told them all to bring a couple of canteens each, and heavy boots because of rattlesnakes. Maybe we'd need a couple of Arizona Rangers for safety, although when I said that you'd have thought I had guaranteed they'd be needed.

"Don't worry," I said. "Maybe I can ask one of my brothers or my cousin Charlie to come along. He's a good hand with a gun." I could only guess there might be desert to cross, and in May it would be hotter than blazes. A boy asked me why it would be so hot in the springtime. I laughed. "Spring is in February. May is just a foretaste of June. June in the Territory is halfway to perdition." The whole crowd hollered with shocked laughter. The boy fell off his chair.

The more the students talked about the trip, the more I wanted to go as well. I told Prairie I'd see her again after Christmas, and on the spot as I spoke I changed my mind and told her I would make a try at the second term. She cried and hugged me for joy. "I'm going home by hook or crook," I said. "I'll be back in a month. I'll bring canteens for both of us for the trip to the Grand Canyon."

Her pa was there with his carriage, drove me back to the dormitory, then waited to take her home. She gave me a top hat for riding, with a silk ribbon and cockade. I gave her a set of fine leather gauntlets to keep horse grime off her sleeves. I felt pretty sure both of us would rather have had what we gave the other, but even if I never wore the fancy riding hat, I'd always treasure it.

Next morning Prairie's father again arrived with his carriage and we tied Duende to the back. He asked me if I had a chaperone, and I assured him I did, glad he didn't ask for more information. I had Duende in his stall and laid an extra old blanket on top of his new one. Snow packed against the windows while I waited for the train.

I eyed all the folks around me. I wished I'd dressed the way I had when I first arrived here, pistols and all, instead of a nice ladies' traveling suit. When at last we boarded, I was so happy to see Mr. Washington I could have hugged him. "Mr. Washington!" I called.

"Is you traveling alone, miss?" Mr. Washington asked, his voice a bare whisper.

I nodded. "I suppose I am."

"Just you be satisfied I'll watch out for you. Just take your rest easy."

"Thank you, Mr. Washington."

"Ita be my pleasure, miss. Rest easy."

I was sorry to leave the relative comfort of the train, drafty, smelly, wet, and dismal as it was, for the hard seat of the stagecoach in Benson. I tied Duende to the back, angry that I hadn't dressed to ride him like I'd done before. The stage was packed two deep, and I had to hold a cantankerous child on my lap, which wrinkled my skirt because he wouldn't be still. I got so tired of that boy I whispered in his ear that if he didn't quit kicking my legs, I was going to throw his shoes out the window. Instead of him being quiet, he set up a raging howl, and his mother gave me a bawling out. I arrived at Marsh Station two days after my trip had begun, alone, freezing cold, and hungry.

There was no one there to meet me. I had to leave my camera and trunk at the station. If I was going to ride home in the dusk on Duende, I wasn't going to do it in this skirt, so behind the waiting stalls I changed into my split riding skirt. I strapped my gun belt on as well. I had it in my mind to tell my whole family just what I thought of being left high and dry a week before Christmas, and that I was plumb fed up with being treated like this. Going to pack up what few things I had left there and leave them for good and all. I rehearsed the words. "Stay put. Sorry." Then I headed for home.

I wasn't halfway there when I heard hooves behind me. The sun had dropped early. Shadows grew long until they merged with everything around, and Duende startled a rabbit. He made a regular cloud of steam around his nose. The rider behind did not come on nor drop back, just followed. I kicked my horse into a lope. Holding one hand on the reins, I felt for the pistols, unsure whether I had loaded them. I loosened the bullwhip from the piggin' tie on the side flap, and held it in my right hand. Then, just as I came to our familiar gate, the hoofbeat sounds behind me dropped off and faded or the rider had stopped still, watching.

I didn't knock on the door, but pushed at it to open it. The door was barred from the inside. Only one window held a light, and it looked to be far inside, probably in the kitchen. "Mama? Papa?" I called. "Clover? Rebeccah! Ezra! Zack! It's me. Mary Pearl."

There was a clattering and rattling, and at last the door was opened and a hand swept me inside, closing it and barring it again, before a figure came from the kitchen carrying the kerosene lamp. It was Ma. "Mama?"

All at one time the room filled with them calling my name. Mama grabbed hold of me and crushed me to her, crying, saying, "Oh, my baby. My precious girl. Oh, my daughter. *Why* are you here?" But everyone crushed me so I couldn't answer; all the boys, even Zachary, had tears in their eyes. Last I was passed to Pa, who held me, shaking like a leaf. "Didn't you get my telegram? How did you get here? Who brought you? I warned you not to come. Oh, kitten, why didn't you stay?"

"Is someone sick?" I finally got out. At last I was able to tell them about my journey, but as we huddled at the kitchen table, with Ma never letting go of my hand, and the boys telling me how brave I'd been, and Rebeccah wrapping me in her own shawl, I began to get used to the dim light and the looks on their faces frightened me. "Why is there no Christmas tree? Why aren't there any candles? Someone please tell me what has happened. Is it measles again? Typhoid?"

Pa hung his head. Finally, Clover said, "War, honey. Range war."

Ma shook my hand with one of hers, and pressed her other palm against my check. "Sweet Elsa is dead, along with her unborn child. Killed by her own papa, as she ran between him and your cousin Charlie. The railroaders were gunning for your granny. Shot up Sarah's house real bad." I gasped. "Granny's all right. Your cousin Gilbert was shot, too. He's not going to pull through. The doctor said his lungs have collapsed and he's got no air. Grandpa Chess had a heart attack. And. And—" She put both hands to her face and sobbed, unable to speak.

Rebeccah finished Ma's tale. "Aunt Sarah went to check on Uncle Harland in town, and found our tiny cousin Blessing sick, but there was nothing they could do. She took pneumonia and was buried two days ago. She died in Aunt Sarah's arms. Uncle Harland hasn't been right in the head ever since."

"We wanted," Pa started, with a tremble in his voice, "we hoped you'd stay there with your friends and have a happy Christmas. I sent a telegram telling you to stay. You must not have gotten it. The weather's been drear. Maldonado had declared—" Then his voice caught in his throat. I stared hard at my pa. I couldn't see his face at all. He'd shrunk into the shadows.

"I'll stay here and fight with you," I said, but my voice didn't sound as firm as the words did. I squared up my shoulders. My voice might falter, but my backbone did not.

There were a few moments of silence. At last Ezra, fourteen years old now, and gotten all long and gangly, said, "Old Mr. Maldonado said he was gunning for you, Mary Pearl. He laid it was your letters that sent Elsa out of the convent and married to Charlie, and got her killed even though it was him put a bullet through her back." He sobbed and wiped at his eyes indignantly. "Poor old cousin Charlie. Right in front of him. He picked her up but she was already dead."

Elsa. All we'd ever done was braid each other's hair and tell each other secrets, laughing about boys as we grew up. Now she and Esther, the closest girls I'd known all my life, were gone, for the sake of what? They'd died because they'd loved someone? I was only a witness to their hearts, me, the girl slightly younger, caught in the middle, the holder of their secrets, and the only one left alive, other than Rebeccah who stood behind Ma. The only way I knew it was she was because I saw the glimmer of tears streaking her face. "How is it my fault?" I asked, knowing there was no answer. All of this, less than four weeks since Rachel's wedding to Aubrey? I began to weep, as well, and we huddled together for a while. I tried to put all this in place. "What about Rachel?" I dared.

"She's in town," Rebeccah said. "She's fine."

Zachary climbed into my lap and strung his arms around my neck, saying, "But you *are* home, Mary Mary quite contrary Maypole. Safe and sound. You are here with us, and you are safe." Even Ezra wrapped his bony arms around me. I thought I heard him say, "I love you," but I couldn't be sure, mumbled as it was into my shoulder.

For a while, everyone in the room shrank into their own thoughts as if even a prayer was too much to venture. Pa said, "Mary Pearl, that's twice you've come home alone. I don't want you doing it again. It's too dangerous. I know you feel like you're grown up, but don't do this again. Promise me."

"All right, Pa. I promise," I said. Tears fell unstopped then, I was so overcome by all the sorrow and misery I faced. My poor family. And there I'd been, dressed in a nice gown, closest to the heater in the classroom, fussing about whether Roman sculpture was copied from the Greeks or the other way around while people I loved were dying.

At last Ma stirred and asked, "Are you hungry, Mary Pearl?"

In the broad light of day, we traveled to Aunt Sarah's place and I heard more about what had happened. Sarah prayed over Gilbert, lying on the kitchen table, blood splattered about him on the floor. A young doctor named Pardee had come to tend to him, and Rebeccah was trying to do a good turn helping out. I couldn't stand to see it, but I hugged Aunt Sarah, and then Ma and I did some washing, trying to soak the bloody sheets from all the horrors. I cried without a moment's peace, and after a while I had to go into the book room and curl up on a stuffed chair and pour out my sorrow on the arm of the chair. Rebeccah brought me a quilt, and then Ma came in with coffee. She set it by me on the floor and then just wrapped me in her arms and we both rocked and wept. I'd never before known I could feel so grieved, and when I said that, Ma said, "Just give vent to it, honey. If you try to hold back the tears they will get stuck in your heart and make you touched all your life, like my sister was." By the time I quit sobbing, my coffee was cold, but I drank it anyway, and Ma went back to Aunt Sarah's side in the kitchen with Gilbert. I couldn't bring myself to go back in there, and to me, the whole house smelled sickeningly of blood. I was a long, long way from Wheaton College. Couldn't imagine ever going back.

Later, the boys showed me Grandpa Chess's grave. Said he'd been digging it for Gilbert so it only seemed natural they laid him in it, and dug another for his grandson who was not yet ready to pass over. Ezra told me that the doctor had been worried Grandpa might have taken morphine to make himself die—something none of the adults had mentioned at all—but all the pills were accounted for, and so the doc concluded it must have been his heart.

Zack said, "Do you think my heart will give out, too?"

"No," I said. "Does it hurt you?"

"Mine does," said Ezra.

"Mine, too," I added. Grandpa Chess Elliot was my cousin's grandpa by birth, but mine by choice. I felt misery take hold of me, deep inside.

The day was cold and drizzly. We stood there in silence for a few more moments. Then I heard careless footsteps behind us, and turned to see Brody standing there with an ax. He said, "I'm splitting firewood. Wondered if you boys'd help stack it by the stove for the ladies."

"Yes, sir," they both replied.

"Miss Mary Pearl, your mama wants you to come back to the house, too, if you will. Says she's worried you'll take another chill like last year."

"Sure," I said. "I feel fine, though, except this—" and then I couldn't get the words out.

"Yes, ma'am," he said.

"What's wrong with your hands?" I asked. "Your gloves are torn apart and there's blood."

"Dry mesquite. It's the very devil to split. Sorry if that ain't polite talk."

"I see that. Pa and Clover always did it at home, and I never knew it could cut you up so bad. You better come on in and get some salve on it."

On the way back to the house he held back a tree branch for me and I saw he had on heavy chaps, too, so he could stand in the dead and frozen chaparral and make a path for me. Even as we walked I hoped he wouldn't ask me to clean the blood off his hands. I just didn't think I could take any more blood. But he stopped at the door and went to the bunkhouse. In a while he left there and went back to the woodpile, wearing heavy gloves.

For the next week I moved through all the people, stunned. I suppose since they'd been here, they had taken it in as it came, like having to be dosed with bitter medicine day after day. For me it was a rock slide of bad news, and I forgot for two days about my things back at the stagecoach station. Finally Charlie and Clover took me up there in a buckboard, bristling with rifles and shotguns, and we brought back my things. The boys were purely edgy, and jumped at every jackrabbit. I asked them where Elsa was buried and they told me that in the fury that followed, with guns blazing every direction, El Maldonado's men had taken her body and she was buried on his place. I was warned by both my parents at the top of their lungs not to try to go there, and I knew they were right. Instead I said good-bye to my friend at my sister Esther's grave, and imagined that someday I might paint a picture of the two girls, the same ages when they left this earth, walking hand in hand in heaven.

When next we saw Uncle Harland and his little boys, it was Christmas Day, and they came with a couple of wooden tops for my brothers, and Zachary gave Honor and Story his Yo-Yo, the toy he called a "wheeler." He said, "I'm sorry, but there's just one. We ain't been able to get to town. You fellows can share it, can't you?" It was tragically sweet.

Uncle Harland had had a memorial portrait taken of Blessing, laid out in a new dress in her bed as if she were asleep. "It's called memento mori," I said. Someone had curled her hair and put flowers in her hands. She had been only six years old. I studied it a good while. Seemed to me I would have used brighter flash powder. But, perhaps it was one of the things we were to learn next term—brightening and darkening that happens in the developing room. She looked sad and wasted. I felt something sweep over me, as if I could have done better, not just for my grief and this dear loss, but that I might have soothed *his* grief just that tiny bit more with a better photograph. If I could learn enough, study hard enough, I could give people something to remember their dear children that would not look so grim. Oh, but what if I couldn't go back and learn that? If they needed me here, I had to stay. Our lives were a thousand years and nearly two thousand miles from Illinois. Perhaps we were ruffians. We were the people they were two or three generations descended from, the ones who'd fought and clawed their living out of that land of cornfields and trees. I wanted to go back but I needed to stay here. I would wait until I could talk to Pa and Ma in the peace of some coming day. I handed the card back to him and said, "Thank you for letting me see this."

We had no Christmas tree and no gifts. We gathered all the relatives, even Rachel and Aubrey, along with Aubrey's father Udell, who'd been courting my aunt Sarah—my, how long had that been going on?—and shared a quiet meal at Aunt Sarah's ranch house. It gave me a shudder deep inside to see the bullet holes across the doors, and rags stuffed in all the broken windows. Poor cousin Gilbert was not able to come to dinner, but he'd at least moved into his bed so we could use the kitchen table, which had been his bed for a week. His girl, Charity, had come from town, too. I listened carefully to the sounds and rhythms of their talk without adding my own voice.

For a gift I gave them the prints I'd made of each person during the wedding. To Ma and Pa, I gave a set of each of their children, except of course Esther and me. Mama looked up at me and turned her head to one side. In the slanted light, she looked older than I'd remembered, and tired. Lines crossed her face and creased deeply at her eyes and mouth. "Mary Pearl? Come into the book room with me and set awhile." Once we'd sat, she said, "When you go back to school after Christmas, would you please, *do* have one of the others take your likeness as well? I want to have all my children's likenesses."

"Sure, Ma. I didn't think about it before."

She stared at her hands, rubbing the back of one with her thumb. "We didn't get a good crop of peas this year."

"Oh." I looked over the shelves of books. They seemed so small, now, compared to the grand library at Wheaton. And Mama seemed purely addled, talking in bits about one thing and another just like Granny always did. Was this what age did to women? Or was it shock and death? What if Granny wasn't addled but just sad? I felt as if I might stay sad forever, too.

"Rebeccah's friend. That doctor. Dr. Pardee. He's taking good care of Gilbert. Reckon he'll be coming back this afternoon. Maybe we can have beans instead of peas. Sun's going down early. Mary Pearl? You didn't really come all the way from Illinois by yourself, did you?"

"Yes, Mama. I didn't have any choice. And I've done it before, don't you remember? By the time Pa sent the telegram I'd already bought the ticket."

Mama grabbed hold of me and like to squeezed the life out of me. "Oh, honey. Don't you have any idea how dangerous that was?"

"Apparently not as dangerous as staying here. Are we still in danger, or is it finished?"

She mopped at her face with her apron. "I haven't been so afraid since we crossed the desert to come here. Comanches and all. My ma died on that trip. I know our days are counted, and known, and numbered by Providence. It's just that a body never expects so many to leave at one time. Your cousin Gilbert, I don't think he'll make it."

"Aunt Sarah said he's doing better."

"He's her littlest boy, never mind he's twenty. She's wanting to just will him better. Your littlest boy will always be your boy. Just like *you* are my littlest girl. I'd perish if anything happened to you."

"But then why were you so upset with me? Why did I get sent away? Why didn't anyone tell me the whole Territory was about to explode like dynamite?"

"At first I thought you'd be safe in town, married. Rachel has nothing to worry about there, except the usual things of housekeeping. She even has maids to help with that."

"It seemed like everyone here knew about them courting, Mama, and didn't confide in me. As if you were all in cahoots with him. I wish someone had told me what was happening so I would not have been so surprised and, well . . . hurt."

"I'm sorry, honey. We didn't mean to be. We could hardly get the mail, what with smugglers and bandits stopping everyone on the roads. If one of the boys rode across the desert, they'd be followed by men, and we've heard of some being waylaid and killed or robbed. I wanted to tell you, but by the time it was certain they were to marry, we were cut off from all trails to the mail at Marsh Station. And then, I thought you would be safer far away from it all. If we all perished, you'd be able to go on. It was only that Aubrey wanted you here so bad. Rachel, too."

"Ma." I felt tears welling and near to spilling over. A bitterness came, too, with her words. The knowledge that Aubrey and Rachel had cared more for their wedding than my safety.

"I ain't saying it's sensible. I'm just saying what I speculated. You and the little boys, you could take care of things. You're mighty capable."

"I don't feel capable. I was so sad about what Aubrey did, when he'd promised to marry me, I couldn't study. I tried so hard and worked so much I didn't even notice you hadn't written. I've failed some subjects. I am all but expelled for my poor schoolwork."

"You'll catch up with the others. I know you. You've got more gumption than Clover and Joshua put together." She gave a deep sigh, patting me again. "For myself, I'm going through the change of life. Felt addled as Granny all those months. You know how she bursts into tears all the time? That's how I feel, even now."

"I've taken down her memoirs. She cries all the time, but it's not from that, Mama. It's from true sadness. While she was remembering, she cried for her sadness and the sadness of people who died long ago, when she was telling me about their sore trials and tribulations. At first I thought it was because she had turned to a lunatic, but I think it was as if she was living it over, even though some of it happened long before she was born. She could just imagine how sad things might be and cry for them even though the people were gone. She's got all these stories about the old days. She said it was important for me to know I come from a line of women who took a stand. You see, Mama, I didn't mean to buck you. You were just so sad about Esther—we all are—it seemed like you wanted to lock me in a trunk. I thought I was taking a stand. I was just putting off getting hitched for a couple of years. It was Aubrey all het up about being married so fast. He made me scared."

"Well, Rachel was glad for his intentions. Afraid she'd be an old maid. Beccah doesn't mind though. Said she'd rather be single than sorry."

Rachel's going to be sorry, I thought. "You don't mind if I go back again, just this next session, and try again? I want to go. Even if I don't go next year and finish the art certificate, I want to go this spring. I feel like I should stay here, but my camera might give me a way to make honest money for myself, if I never marry."

"You're a smart girl. But you're too pretty never to marry. Did I ever tell you, you take after my sister Ulyssa?"

"Yes, Mama."

"Well, you do. She was so pretty some men couldn't look at her without falling down. You look so much like her some days I think I see her in the parlor and it's you."

"I like that I look like her," I said. I liked that I could flash a little smile and know my dimples caused men's hearts to flutter, but I wouldn't say that to Ma. Aunt Ulyssa made 'em weak in the knees, I thought.

"Made 'em weak in the knees," Ma said.

I chuckled a little. Then I leaned against her shoulder as we sat on the settee. She wrapped her arm around me and said, "You go on back if you want to with my blessing. I never imagined what might come of it, you studying art. I never imagined what it would mean to me to have a picture-photograph of my own children. Reckon I had the notion that I could put you safe in a nice homey nest, and you'd never have any problems like I've had. You being my littlest, I wanted to save you from every trial coming your way." I nestled in Ma's embrace in a way I hadn't in a year. In those minutes, it felt as if the weight of the Wheaton library lifted off me.

My reverie was broken by the Yo-Yo flying through the air over our heads, landing smack through a window glass across the room. The shattering noise crackled like lightning. In two seconds, four boys ran through, looks of horror on their faces. Ezra hollered, "The string broke! It was wore out! Oh, Mama, he didn't mean to let it fly, honest. I played it too much."

Ma just shook her head. "Well, one of you go tell Aunt Sarah we've got another broken window to fix. At least it's not a bullet hole."

While the little fellows were hunting a piece of string, we cleaned empty dishes and got ready to head for the house. Rebeccah would stay at Aunt Sarah's to help nurse Gilbert. Mama and I made eyes at each other, watching the sparks flying between Rebeccah and Dr. Pardee. It felt so good to have a secret between Ma and me. Funny thing was, I didn't see any sparks between Rachel and Aubrey, just what I'd call courtesy. They acted as if they'd been married twenty years and it was only a few weeks. They were helping us carry things to our surrey, and Aubrey bumped into me once, and then handed me a crockery bowl, letting his fingers touch mine. I felt repulsed, like I'd touched something filthy. His face showed no feelings at all. Anyhow, since they'd have an eight-hour drive back to Tucson, he and Rachel were going to stay at our house, in Rebeccah's room, probably for a couple more days.

When I got home, I found a key for my door, which I'd never used before, and made sure to lock it when I went to bed.

CHAPTER EIGHT

Brody rode to our house from Aunt Sarah's the next morning, when the sun was at about ten o'clock. He swung off his mount. Pistols hung on both sides of his belt, tied low for easy pulling. He was knocking on the front door as I watched from the barn where I brushed Duende, getting ready to saddle up for a ride. Pa warned me not to set foot off our land, even to Aunt Sarah's place, which we could see from here, without an armed man along. When I was a kid, I used to ride eight miles down to Maldonado's place to visit Elsa. Times were just too troublesome now. Mostly what was on my mind was getting away from Rachel and Aubrey, who were making pleasant small talk in the parlor.

Mama came to the porch and started ringing the dinner bell, too many times, so that we all knew there was some kind of news. I took off toward the house, aware that Duende was following me, like he'd felt put upon to have his morning gallop interrupted.

Brody said, "The whole Maldonado clan has taken up lock, stock, and barrel and gone down to Sonora, Mexico, according to their head-man. Their cook and the headman are living in the great house. I asked them when Maldonado was coming back and they said he never was. Miz Elliot said those servants would live there until Maldonado comes back or the railroad came through the kitchen, but anyhow, she sent me here to tell you folks."

Pa said, "Let's ride over there, Clove. You boys come, too, but everybody bring a rifle."

I said, "I'll come, too. My horse is ready and waiting."

"I'll take your horse," Aubrey announced, taking three long steps ahead of me toward the door. "Good thing he's ready. You women wait here for us."

"I want to see Elsa's grave," I said. "Besides, Duende doesn't like men riding him. He's only well-behaved for me." It was a lie, because my little brothers rode him all the time, but I took in all the faces in the room in a couple of seconds. They seemed tense but no one spoke up to chide me, either. In just a minute, all the fellows were out the door and headed to the barn, except Brody, who held the door for me. "That horse is going to throw him," I said, hoping it was true.

Brody's eyebrows rose. "Yes, ma'am."

"Don't let him pull his mouth."

Aubrey, in a three-piece suit and derby hat, had climbed into my saddle, not even realizing that the stirrup straps would be too short for him. His knees were shoved up to his chest like a jockey and Duende's ears were pinned back like he was ready to unleash demons. He wheeled and reared and within a flick of his tail, he unseated that city lawyer, who landed, sadly, on his feet like a cat, still holding the reins. He proceeded to jerk the bit and slap Duende's face with the tails of the reins. He growled through grinding teeth, "I'll teach you some manners."

Thankfully Brody had sized up the situation before Aubrey hit the ground and with a good cutting horse under him, wedged between Duende and Aubrey. "This horse ain't for that kind of ridin,' sir," he said. He whipped the reins loose and slung them over the other side with a soft whistle. Brody's horse circled Duende like he was a lost calf, allowing Brody to catch the loose reins, pulling him toward me. Without any change of his face or tone of voice—which surprised me because I was gritting my teeth and ready to tear Aubrey's hat off and slap him with it—Brody said, "We'll get you a horse from the barn, sir. This here's a lady's horse. Ain't your fault, sir. Some are just not cut out for men to ride, no matter how big they are."

I was furious at him for slapping my horse in the face, but anybody with some know-how could ride Duende. He wasn't wild, just too smart. My mind whirled back to Prairie Longmore saying the girls had to learn how to handle difficult people in strained situations, keep polite, and speak softly and clearly. I set to wondering what kind of tea parties Brody had been to. In a heartbeat I was on Duende's back, my face in his mane, murmuring to him in Spanish and peeking through the black hair to the two men there.

I thought Aubrey would simply accept the change of horse, but instead he came to my side—reached up and patted my leg!—saying, "Hop down there. No reason I can't ride this one if I change the stirrups. You stay here with the ladies, dear. Wouldn't want you to get hurt."

How dare he put his hands on me! I tapped Duende's flank with my heel and left Aubrey standing there, wheeling that horse around at the gate to face the others.

Pa shoved a rifle in Aubrey's hands before he could come after me, and said, "We need someone to stay here and protect the women. Zachary, you stay by your mama." Zachary groaned for a moment, but he checked the breech and slid in a bullet, mumbling his agreement.

Pa, Clover, Brody, and Ezra caught up to me at the gate. Pa said, "You hang behind us, Mary Pearl, but not so far I can't hear your horse."

"Yes, sir." I felt I'd won that battle, and I was willing to do as I was told.

We stopped at every rise and hill, scanning the horizons for any movement. The only things moving were coyotes and a few quail and rabbits. At Aunt Sarah's place, my cousin Charlie, Aunt Sarah, and a couple of the other hands joined us. Sarah dropped back beside me, and the lot of us rode quietly toward the Maldonado hacienda. The reports were correct. A few chickens scattered as we entered the yard, but nothing else moved. Charlie led the way to the corrals and barn, and found two cows, one followed by a year-old bull calf.

A woman came to the door, waving, smiling. "*Tortillas? Tienes hambre?*"

Pa and the others spoke to her while I pulled my hat lower, urging Duende toward where Charlie stood in his stirrups, getting a look over the top of the house. "*Dónde está la tumba de Elsa?*" Elsa and I always spoke to each other in Spanish. I forgot I didn't need to now.

Charlie Elliot looked fifty years old. My twenty-two-year-old cousin was ragged with grief. He must have really loved her. "Yonder. They built a fence. But they didn't put my name on it, and we were sure enough married. Her name is Elliot, not Maldonado."

"I know."

"I ain't staying around here."

"No?"

"Gil was supposed to go to West Point like our pa. Only, he's too beat up now, even if he lives. He'd never make it through. I'm going in his place. Only—"

"Only you were thinking about revenge, first."

"Stayin' here is killing me. I figure I could get to Mexico and back in four days. How did you know, Mary Pearl?"

"Because I see it in your eyes. I got some revenge of my own I'd like to do, but you've got far more reason for it."

We dismounted and stared hard between the iron curlicues at the name on the monument. It was too far in to so much as touch it. No one was allowed to caress even the cold stone.

Charlie's voice was raspy, but he said, "Yeah. That fella Aubrey done you wrong, sure enough. His pa ain't like that at all. He says Aubrey takes after his mother, and blood will tell."

Blood. Crimson and cadmium and burnt sienna. I could imagine Elsa's best sprigged muslin dress splattered with it, without any coaxing at all. But Charlie meant relations, not paint. Tears ran down his cheeks, unwiped, unnoticed. To bring my thoughts away from his pain and my shock, I thought back to that buggy ride where Aubrey had kissed me while Aunt Sarah and Aubrey's pa Udell had taken a walk. I asked, "His pa going to marry your ma?"

"Soon, I reckon."

"Then you're going to West Point," I said without asking. "You're going there and not Mexico. Please, Charlie. I can't even imagine how terrible you must feel. Nothing that bad has happened to me and I can bear my broken heart. But if everything I've heard about the German army and all the guns they've sent is true, you're going to run into war down in Sonora if you head down there right now. They're landing troops in Veracruz. Smuggling trainloads of cannon through Naco. It's in the papers that we get at Wheaton."

"I read those articles you sent, all three. It's sure enough happening right here under our noses. But I'm having trouble with my eyes so I don't believe I can pass. I tried to read a book this morning and my eyes aren't clear."

I dusted his shirt with my Stetson hat. "Pish. Sure you can pass. Your eyes will clear up when you get done weeping for Elsa. Ma told me that. I remember your pa. He was a soldier through and through. Everyone says you're just like him. Aunt Sarah's the smartest person anybody's ever met. Gilbert's the one I couldn't picture being a soldier.

He takes after our side of the family. Farmers. So, he's going to marry that girl Charity, and your ma is marrying Udell Hanna. The angry neighbors are gone south, and everything is settling in. I'm going back to school, too. This time with Ma's blessing. I'm going to become a photographer." I hadn't actually decided it until it came from my own lips, but I felt joyous about the decision. It was the right thing to do.

"A lady photographer. Well, that's something."

"Yup. It's all about getting the lights just right, and keeping shadows off faces, and whatever you want to portray—well, never mind." And then, I thought, I won't worry too much about oil painting and watercolors.

He said, "I sometimes get a hankering to try one of those flying machines. Wouldn't it be something to take a photograph from up in the sky?"

"Sure would. I'd go up in one just to do it. If you fly one, I'll go up and bring my camera."

A shrill whistle from Pa brought us up. We mounted and I said, "Just so you know. Aubrey Hanna sent me the deed to the Wainbridge place. Part of his buying me off. I figure to sell it. If you hear of anyone—"

"I'll let 'em know."

At Gilbert's wedding, Rachel said in front of everyone how she and Aubrey "coveted" my presence at their new house. She said I would be better off to say farewell to the rest of the family here, and drive to town in their buggy with them. Then after three days' visiting, they'd see me to the train, direct to Illinois. I tapped Mama's wrist and shook my head, but there was no getting out of it.

Mama just whispered, "Forgiveness, Mary Pearl. Practice forgiveness. It will deepen your spirit and strengthen your heart. She's your sister, and she means to love you. Please let her."

And then, there were just four days left before I had to take the train back to Wheaton. Ma, Rebeccah, and Aunt Sarah helped me launder my clothes. I was leaving Duende behind. It made me sad, but at the same time I felt packed a bit lighter. I would have another two hours every day to devote to studying instead of to the horse and all it took to care for him. Ezra was chosen to be my escort this time. He was pleased to be riding on a train for the first time. Zachary was mad that he wasn't going along, and sulked for two days.

Later that afternoon, after I'd carefully laid all my clean clothes in the compartments of the trunk, folded everything in paper around the two hats I was taking back, my Stetson and a fancy bonnet, I went to say farewell to Granny.

"You carrying my memories yet?" she asked when I came in the door.

"Yes, ma'am. They've traveled the length and breadth of this country by now. I brought 'em home, and I'm taking them back."

"You read it again yet?"

"No, ma'am, Granny. I've had too much studying to do."

"Well, you ain't studying on the train. Best you read it again whilst you ride to Kentucky."

"I'm going to Illinois, not Kentucky, Granny."

She peered at me as if I'd been telling lies to her, like she was sorting me out. "Illinois. Is that a state, now? It wasn't used ta."

"Yes'm."

She held forth her hands and took mine, wrapping her tiny, bony fingers around my hands. "Not Kentucky? Fetch me some sassafras tea, Mary Pearl. And put some honey and some o' that whisky in't. I think I'm catchin' a cold."

There was a jar of dried sassafras leaves on her shelf. Her cookstove was near out, so I stoked it up and filled the kettle, and sat with her to wait for it to boil. Now that Ma didn't feel so peeved at me, I felt less peeved at the whole world. More patient. "I promise you I will read them over again, starting on this trip north."

"And don't you spread word around, nor leave it where your relations can read it."

There was nothing in her memoirs that to me seemed a scandal, but I wasn't about to argue because in truth, I barely remembered any of it. It was just her droning on and on as I took notes. "Yes'm." I made her tea, and put a stiff dollop of whisky in it. It was no secret she used it almost every day for her aching joints. A bit more to soothe her lungs if she's catching cold would not hurt. "Here's your tea."

She took a sip, smacked her lips, and said, "That's mighty strong, child. You think I'm a drunkard?"

"No, Granny. You said you were catching a cold."

"It's good," she said, taking another sip. "Don't you let them read my memories, now. Wouldn't want anyone to know their granny's kinda wild. 'N don't you go actin' wild, neither. Just you take a notion from the lessons I learnt."

"I will, Granny." I kissed her good-bye, and left her wrapped in a shawl, sitting up in bed. As I closed the door, though, it came back to me how the losing of loved ones could happen anytime. I wished I had taken another plate of her. Now my things were all packed and she was sick. It would probably trouble her to take a plate while she was ill in bed, but I knocked on the door softly and told her good-bye one more time. "Take care," I said, "and get well soon."

When I walked back to the house, Aubrey and Rachel were in the parlor, reading books. Mama was mending the knees of Ezra's second-best pants. "Do you want me to let down the length of these sleeves?" I said. I knew how to add a new cuff, so when he was wearing a coat, the shirtsleeves would look fine. No sooner had the words come from my lips, but we heard a tumbling and bumping from upstairs that shook dust down on us.

Voices in a loud whisper—we couldn't tell whose—said, "I can't find it! I can't find it! Why did you put it in there? Where did it go?" And pretty soon, "Ouch! Knucklehead! It's going to fall! Look out! I got him. Why did you—where did he go?"

By that time Mama and I headed up the stairs. In my bedroom, Ezra and half of Zachary lay in a heap of my clean clothes with the trunk on its side, leaning against the bed. The top half of Zachary was under the bed, and as Ezra looked up at Mama in horror, Zack yelled, "I caught it! I've got him!" and wiggled out from under the bed with a rat-sized, hissing mad gecko strung on all four feet with dust balls and cobwebs dragging a couple of dead bugs. The animal made a terrified shriek, but at least Zachary was able to hold on to it. Until it bit him. Then he let it go, Zack hollered, and the creature scrambled under the chest of drawers. Zack brushed at his hands while he looked accusingly at me and asked, "Mary Pearl, why don't you clean under your bed once in a while?"

"I've been gone," I started to explain.

Mama lit into him, scolding and fussing, but then Ezra interrupted her, and said, "It was me that done it, Ma. I didn't know I would get to go along—"

I went from amused to angry, just like that. "You put a lizard in my underwear, and you only took it out because now you get to go?"

"Well," he said, "I thought it would be a good surprise when you get to Illinois."

Mama looked like as steamy as Granny's kettle on the boil. She put her fists on her hips and said, "You two are going to do something you'll hate worse than a whipping. You are going to straighten and fold and nicely pack every last stitch of your sister's underwear. All the corsets and camisoles, all the drawers and stockings, every chemise and petticoat. Every skirt. Every blouse. Don't you dare make a wrinkle in those tuck-front shirts I just starched and ironed. Don't you let one crease get into the hair bows. Straighten every last piece before you leave this room, or I'll get the strap and I promise you neither one will sit down for a week. Ezra, you will have to ride to Illinois standing up."

"Mama!" they said at once. "No. Oh, no."

She glowered at them and they quit wailing. In our house it was better to take your scolding with no back talk or whining or you'd rue the day.

They hung their heads, and both said, "Yes, ma'am, Mama."

"Get busy!" Mama pushed me out the door and closed it behind her, then turned and yelled through the door itself, "And find that lizard before I do." Then she wrapped her arm through mine, leaned close, and said, "Boys!" in a whisper. We giggled at each other all the way down the stairs.

At supper I said that I had something to say to everyone. "I'm asking you, please, to hear me and know that I mean this. Next time, or if something dreadful goes on here that threatens life and limb, please let me know. Or come get me. Don't tell me to stay in Illinois, because I won't do it."

"It was for your own good," Pa said.

"I know. But I'm part of this family. If it happens to you, it happens to me, too, only it adds guilt if I'm not here to help out. This schooling of mine is only temporary, and it's not as important to me as this family is."

That night, as I finished my last packing for town, I unwrapped Granny's memories to retie them. A page fell open and it reminded me I'd promised to read it again. I sat on the bed, sure if I just looked at a single paragraph, I would have fulfilled my promise.

Don't think everyone you meet with a pretty smile and cunning talk means they're a friend. Why, once when your great-grandmother was a girl, and her parents had died, people took her in and told the authorities they would be good parents but they treated her like a field hand. She worked dawn to dark, nor never got a bath nor food, yet she grew up smart and even though she married young and died young, she left a girl named Truly Myrtle Bayless. That girl Truly was one of the nurses in the Andersonville prison and she helped that famous nurse Clara Barton. Then she married a coal miner and had five children and four lived to grown. And her brothers all had to work in the mines too, but they made a living, and Truly was known so much for tending folks they wrote a pamphlet on her life and put it in the county courthouse. I'm saying good people don't talk. They do. And they do *right*. My pa lived in Arkansas a while. By then we had sheep and goats and two mules.

It was all like that, just rambling thoughts about this person and that person and some of them overlapped with what she'd said her real life had been. That was why I couldn't take it seriously. Seemed like a made-up story. I tied up the pages and put them back in the bottom of the trunk.

CHAPTER NINE

I never felt as stiff in all my life as I did trying to sit up in a corset and blue traveling coat in the back of their carriage all the way to Tucson. I carried my camera in my lap. My trunk was upended next to me, and it banged against my shoulder the whole way. Rachel kept trying to keep up conversation, but I'd only answer part of the time. Otherwise, I hollered, "What? I can't hear," and that kept me from having to talk to her.

Ezra rode on one of the carriage horses up front, which Aubrey didn't like him doing, but it couldn't be helped; there was no room for him in the carriage. I have to admit, Aubrey Hanna was as polite and courteous to my sister Rachel as any man could be. He smiled at her opinions, asked about her comfort, and stopped the carriage partway there so she could walk around. She took my arm and we headed for some ironwood trees where we could rest, as the two fellows went the opposite direction. As if we'd planned the exact moment of return, all four people claimed their previous positions. If I let myself think about it, my toe hurt.

It was eight hours' driving to get to Tucson, but I couldn't do any sketching on the way for the bumpy road and crowded seat. Out of pure boredom I began to think about my granny's memoirs on that ride. All those women from days past, who'd withstood and held firm against far rougher times than I'd ever see, she'd said. Women who drank their own tears to sustain themselves. It was as much as like she was telling me a story rather than her own memories. Still, it was nice to put order and names to some people I'd heard about around the dinner table, because she had all the generations in her head. All my life I'd grown up thinking my grandma was addled beyond repair, but all these years she's had all that stored in her head behind all the crazy things that come out her mouth. Always wanting to go to Kentucky. Always thinking there was soldiers tromping through the house. Always waiting for someone to come home that wasn't coming, either because they were dead or maybe had never been alive. Some days, as she was talking, she'd lose track of where she'd been, and we chased a good many rabbits with her making me go back and find a page about someone and add a note in the margins like, "Dorcas smoked a pipe on Sundays in the evening," but mostly it seemed pretty clear.

I was supposed to admire Rachel's house and all the bits of lace and china figures on the mantels. I told her it was right sparkly. She sent a boy to take my trunk up to the room set aside for me, even though Ezra was sturdy enough to do that. He had his own room as well. She sent a lady to fix us supper, too. I didn't tell her my friend Prairie lived in such a sumptuous house that Rachel's whole place would fit in the Longmores' parlor. At supper we heard about all kinds of folks Rachel wanted to introduce me to. I was mostly glad to have a bath and crawl into bed.

Sometime in the night I woke up hearing my name called in a whisper. The moon was coming in the window, and I could make out an outline of someone in the doorway, where the door stood ajar, not closed as I'd left it. It couldn't be Ezra, because he'd stomp right in and yank my covers to wake me. It couldn't be Rachel, because she'd come with a lamp. It made me shudder. It couldn't be Aubrey, I told myself, holding very still, pretending to be sound asleep.

"Mary Pearl?" It was a man's voice. It was Aubrey. If the house was on fire, he'd come ayelling. I laid still. In a few moments, the door closed. I could hear the tiniest click of the latch and footsteps as he walked away down the hall. I turned up the lamp by the bed and eyed the furnishings in the room. I took a chair and pushed it hard under the doorknob where there was no key to lock it, and then balanced a mirror off the dressing table on the chair legs. If anyone pushed it in or forced the door, it would break and make a nice racket.

It was well after daylight when I woke, kept deep asleep by a sore and rasping throat and a feverish feeling behind my eyes. There was a tray on a table in the hall, where a teapot of cold tea had waited for me. The house was quiet. I pulled on a wrapper and stuck my head out the door. "Rachel?" I called.

"She went out to the garden," a different man's voice said.

"Ezra?"

"Yup."

"Your voice is low all the time now."

"Sore throat."

"Me, too. I think I caught Granny's cold. Are we all alone in this house?"

"I reckon. Breakfast was a while back."

"Listen, I don't want to sleep in this room. I want to sleep in your room tonight, and don't tell anyone."

"Scared of the dark?"

"Sorta."

"There's only one bed."

"I don't care if I sleep on the floor. I'm not sleeping in here again. I'll just come upstairs after everyone goes to bed. We only have two

more nights. I'll rest in here during the day. I'm sorry you caught this
cold from me."

"Want t' trade? Your bed looks soft."

"No. I want to be with you. Upstairs."

"Ghosts and boogermen?"

"Something like that. Don't say a word to Rachel."

"I'm headed down to the livery and hardware."

"Before you leave, would you please put some water on to boil? I
want a hot bath and more tea. There's a pot here, but it's gone cold."

He rolled his eyes as if I'd asked him to climb me a mountain,
but I knew he would do it. Later Rachel came in and brought me more
tea while I soaked in her lavender water soap. I felt even worse afterward, and spent the day in bed. She was mighty disappointed to have
to cancel her ladies' luncheon. I didn't apologize for that. "I'm sure
they'll be glad not to all take the ague home with them," I said. Then
I took a long nap.

Supper came to my room by way of a maid, without a word from
Rachel or Aubrey. I believe she was peeved. She didn't even come to
say good night. So, it wasn't any trouble at all once the lights began to
go out, to carry a couple of blankets and a pillow up the stairs to where
Ezra was bunked on a cot in what he said was usually the maid's room.
He complained that it smelled faintly of naphtha soap, but I didn't
mind. Of all the smells that *might* be in a house, that wasn't bad.

Late into the darkness, my throat hurt and my head ached behind
the eyes. I tossed around on the floor. I thought I heard footsteps on
the stairs. I listened and then drifted into sleep, then woke again, listening intently. At last I saw sunlight through the dormer and rolled
up my bedding and trudged down the stairs back to the bedroom. I
straightened it all on the bed and listened to the sounds of the house
waking up. The flue rattled with the stove heating. Aubrey was hum-
ming something from the bathing room directly below my bedroom.

I smelled shaving soap and steam, and studied the floor a bit. The cracks in between the boards were directly over the bathing room! I could see him and he might see me. I pulled a rug from where it lay under a chair at the window, over the boards above the bath. I had this chilling notion that he was down there being *aware* of me and every move I made. Perhaps I was the one aware of him. Perhaps both. I laid my head again on the pillow and closed my eyes. My arms and legs ached. My eyes burned. That bed was both a comfort and a torment. I wished I could rest another three days until this cold was past, but I also wished I could get on the train this very day. When I awoke, the house was again quiet. Only one more night to stay here.

There was no teapot outside my room that day, but I didn't give that any mind. I felt a bit refreshed by the nap. I pulled on a wrapper and, listening for voices, made my way down the stairs to the morning room. Rachel was sipping coffee at the table with a piece of some kind of cake before her on a plate. "Morning," I croaked.

"You're still sick," she answered with a frown.

I ignored the hurt I felt at her attitude. "Is the coffee hot? Any left?"

She didn't answer, so I poured myself a cup and sat a couple of chairs away from her. "I hope you don't catch it," I offered.

"Ezra's sick, too. No doubt the whole house will be down any day now."

"Well, I didn't *plan* it. Unlike some people who are good at scheming ahead of time."

She sipped her coffee again. "I will be canceling the dinner party for this evening. Unless you think you'll be able to get dressed by eight."

"Is that all you do here in town? Have parties and teas and folderol?"

"I have a position to maintain in society. You wouldn't know anything about that, would you? That, Mary Pearl, is why Aubrey chose me. You had your chance. He realized how immature you are after that stupid letter you sent him."

"I wrote you one, too," I said, but regretted the words as soon as they passed my lips. "You won't be getting it, though. I believe you're clever enough to guess."

"Don't be so childish. Are you still leaving tomorrow? Ezra said his head aches, too, but he's not lying about all day."

"I know. He told me he doesn't feel too bad. I'd like another hot bath. Wouldn't want to take pneumonia on the train. Go ahead and have your dinner. I'll eat a cold plate in the bedroom."

"That won't do. Everyone in town knows you're here. I invited all the important people. They'd expect to see you. I'll send Dorothy up with towels and some Epsom salts."

I paused at the doorway with my coffee cup, remembering what it was like at home. If someone was sick they received extra kindness, not snubbing. Tears blurred my sight. "You've got no reason to be cross with me. I'll be gone tomorrow before noon. Ma's real happy for you, you know. All rich and married and happy. I always pictured we'd be glad for each other, like the sisters in a Jane Austen novel."

"Decent people don't read novels. Want to tell me where you were last night?"

"I slept with Ezra, on the floor in his room."

"Why?" She set her coffee cup on the saucer a bit too hard.

"How did you know?"

"Aubrey checks the house each night. Makes sure the doors are locked, looks in on every room. It makes me feel safe here in town. He's very thoughtful that way. He told me you'd gone . . . *out*."

"Out? I had a bad dream. Figured I'd sleep better hearing at least one of our brothers snoring. I always have bad dreams when I'm sick. What did he mean, out? Do you believe I went out at night like some harlot?"

Her face changed from bitter to softening. "Well, no. I told him you wouldn't. I thought I might be expecting a child. I . . . I found out this morning that I'm not."

"Oh. I'm sorry. Likely this isn't a good evening for a party anyhow."

Rachel nodded but her own eyes filled with tears. "Go on back to bed. I'll send up Dorothy and she'll call you when the bath is ready. She'll bring you some breakfast, too."

"Thanks." Since she said nothing more, I went back up the stairs.

I have asked myself a thousand times since that morning if things might have gone differently, had I not had another bath. Not been sleepy from sickness and not gone back to bed. Not fussed at her. Not been so independent. Not agreed to stay with them. Not been too shy to tell Rachel I was afraid to be alone in her house. But I did all those things. All the things I wish I hadn't done. When she told me, after bringing the breakfast and her maid Dorothy coming in with Epsom salts, that she and Dorothy were going to walk up the block and deliver her cancelation regrets in person to a highly important lady, I had shrugged and wished her well, told her not to strain herself, and sat to eat the breakfast she called "coffee cake" along with a fresh cup of coffee.

After the bath I slipped on a warm flannel gown and my wrapper and house slippers, and carried my things upstairs to settle in bed. I felt warm and drowsy.

A hand reached out of a dream about riding Duende through a field of corn up in Illinois, caressing my face. I heard my name. A cold wind through the cornfields touched my hair, called me. Whispered sweet words filled my ears, words in a moment more, as I came awake, that filled me with terror. I brushed at the hand and it resisted. Then it clamped hard over my mouth. He was strong and he was heavy, and he'd been ready before I awoke. Every horror I had ever been told about, every warning for every young girl, every nightmare came alive to me and I was flattened and torn asunder under an unbelievable weight and I choked and vomited coffee and cake as he groaned and I tried to scream for the pain and then fought to simply breathe and then my right hand seemed to find inhuman strength and tore itself from his grasp and reached under the pillow where I slept upon a single pistol and the deer hunting knife I kept always at my side. The horrible weight and pain abruptly rose up off me and I slashed wildly with the knife, aiming first at the source of my agony, and swinging upward toward Aubrey's once handsome face.

He swore.

His look of shock was not enough for me. I wanted him dead. He backed away, jerking up his pants, swiping at his chest and the blood flowing freely from a vertical cut like a whip line that stretched from below his belt to his left eyebrow. His mouth agape, I screamed at last and reached for the pistol, but he was gone from the room before I could pull the trigger.

I heard Rachel's voice below in the parlor, calling up the stairs, "Aubrey? Why are you home in the middle of the day?" and then just as quick, the sound of glass breaking in their bedroom, and his voice moaning.

"Rachel!" he called. "I had ink on my shirt and I came home to change because I have court at one. I bumped the mirror and it broke. Fetch a doctor."

I cried and sank to the floor, wailing, but she could not hear me over her own cries. "No, he didn't!" I called. "Rachel, Rachel."

I dropped the knife on the floor and hurried back to the bathing room, sinking into the cold water, nightgown, wrapper, and all, sobbing and curling over my pain so that I nearly drowned. Rachel screamed from the bedroom, but I could hear him asking for towels and a clean shirt, then her light steps hurrying down the stairway.

Dorothy knocked on the bathing room door and brought in more towels and a steaming kettle. I was shaking and blue. My fingers had gone "all to raisins" as Ma would say. She said she'd cleaned up the vomit in my bed, and I could go back to it now. Said she'd left a bucket there in case my stomach came up again. Said not to worry about the blood on the floor, that "the missus sometimes had a flow in bed, too, although not so great an amount." When she saw I'd gotten my clothes wet, she quietly disappeared and returned with something from Rachel's closet.

Once I was suitably returned to bed, my hair stringing and my tears unending, Rachel came into the room. "Aubrey's been terribly hurt," she said, tears streaming down her own face. "You're so kind to weep for him, too."

I stared at the coverlet. What could I say to her? I wanted to kill him and her, too. My own sister. Where was my hunting knife? "Go away," I said.

"Fine."

She was at the door when I gasped out, "Rachel? He came in here."

"Why didn't you tell him I was paying a call? The poor man, he's been gashed by that huge mirror that hung over my dresser. He was just looking for me."

"I was asleep. Rachel—"

"He'll likely have a scar. It's terrible. For a prominent man who appears in court all the time. A scar on his face like a brawling cowboy! He had to have stitches on his—his person. They had to continue his case because of the accident. Of course, I canceled our formal dinner. You didn't want to have it anyhow."

"Rachel, will you listen?" My mouth only moved silently then. "I couldn't—" Couldn't what, fight? I was angry and devastated. There were no words to utter what I felt. I thought of the pistol under the bed and imagined a bullet rattling in my head, back and forth like a pebble in a jar, bouncing though my own skull, cauterizing my brain, and shutting out this day for all time.

Rachel smiled sympathetically and said, "Get some sleep. You look terrible."

After she left, I cried new tears though I could not have imagined there were any left to cry. At suppertime, Dorothy brought me beef broth and toast, glancing into the bucket in case it needed cleaning. Ezra came in, sneezed a dozen times, and asked, "What is the ruckus downstairs?" His voice sounded far deeper than it had been yesterday.

"Ezra, you're really sick now."

"I sound bad, but I don't feel it much."

"I was hoping you wouldn't mind to pull me another bath."

"Take it quick and I'll have one after you while the water's still warm."

I nodded.

He said, "We'll be good and shiny for the train ride."

I wanted to blurt out things to him, things a boy of fourteen shouldn't hear. I wanted to plot with him to kill Aubrey Hanna. I wanted to send him to fetch Ma and Pa and all the men from Aunt Sarah's place. I wanted an army to surround this house and burn it to the ground. I felt so aching, so beaten, and bruised. Worse than being thrown from a horse. Tears filled my eyes again. If only, if only we hadn't stayed *here*.

Ezra wrapped his arm around me, then pinched my shoulder. "Don't worry, sis. I'll get you to college. I'm not as sick as you got."

Later, when he came from the bathroom smelling of lavender and Epsom salts, I stopped winding my hair in rags to get my reticule. I gave him ten dollars. "I want you to buy Zack a new wheeler toy. Get one for yourself or something else you want."

"Golly. I'll buy Mama a new kerchief."

"Whatever you want."

"You want to sleep in my room again?" he asked.

"Why don't you sleep in here instead? This big bed will hold two people easily." I shuddered when I said that.

He didn't even ask why I pushed the chest of drawers in front of the door and hung my pistol belt from the bedpost. Nor why I found my hunting knife with a rim of brown on the blade under the bed like it had been kicked there. He just spit on it and wiped it on a dripping towel still wet from his hair. "There. Towel was too wet to dry it. Don't want you to rust up," he said, drying the blade against the sleeve of his nightshirt. "Old Rache is gonna fuss over that stain."

"I don't care."

"Me, neither."

I felt beaten. My jaw hurt when I moved it, like someone had nearly torn it off my face. "I'm real tired. You want to sleep feet to feet in the bed like we did when we were little?"

Ezra laughed and his eyes crinkled like Pa's. "You ain't more than a mite, sis, but first thing you know I'd have my big toe in your eye. I'll take the floor like you did." We lay there in the dark.

After a while, I said, "I wish we'd brought Zachary, too."

"He'd have had a good time, sure enough."

"Yes," I whispered. "Maybe he would."

CHAPTER TEN

It hurt to walk for three days more, and although my cold was better, after I got to Wheaton I stayed in bed a day, claiming it was the ague. I didn't write my family as soon as school started, like I'd done before. I hadn't read Granny's memories on the train, either. I just wept and wept some more.

When classes started I felt better, and right away I took to target practicing in a field. I'd gotten permission from Miss Kotterman, who seemed to know everything there was to know about Wheaton College, and who to ask, what to ask, everything. Prairie Longmore came along sometimes, clapping her hands when I hit a bull's-eye or broke a bottle. Sometimes she brought her other friends to watch her take shooting lessons from me. They were impatient and whined about the cold, and pretty soon they all found reasons to go on home. I could see that Prairie wanted to go with them, like they were a string of quail, all following the leader. "Grip down," I said. "Pay attention; don't watch them leave. Now, do it again but don't let the barrel fly up before you even pull the trigger. Expect it to rise and grip down hard."

"We're doing the debut in two weeks."

"That so? That the final exam for all the dancing and folderol lessons? Watch my hand. Grip down and don't let up." I pinged a bullet off a branch that sent splinters flying through the air.

"I wish you could come but—" She stopped.

"But my family is not from here and they'd have to be old money and plenty of it, and I'd have to talk more citylike and stop carrying a pistol."

"Well, yes."

"Well, I'll never *not* have a gun in my hand as long as I live," I said. "So that's that. I don't really care to be invited and I don't care to match all you young ladies like we were nuns in a convent. I don't match anyone and I like it that way."

She studied my face for a while, then said, "Well, don't fuss at me. There must have been more trouble when you went home. You haven't told me anything about your visit, and I've told you everything I did over Christmas holiday. We had the gayest times. What happened there in Arizona? You just aren't the same."

"There weren't any parties," I said, then I could only breathe slowly and stare down the front of my skirt. I pulled my empty pistols with both hands and twirled them forward and back and dropped them back in the holsters slick as any gunslinger. "Nothing like a little practice," I said. "My cousin Gil got married. I don't care about parties that much. If you're cold we can go in."

"All right. I'll be really busy for the next couple of weeks, but I'll see you in class."

"I'll see you."

"Won't you tell me what's wrong?"

"Someday. Not today, though."

As I practiced shooting every afternoon, I prayed. I never stopped praying, even in classes. Angry, frightened tears often filled my eyes while I prayed, as I shot out Aubrey's eyes with every bullet that hit the hay bales. While I bathed and looked I prayed for signs I was as barren as Rachel. I wished I'd made a steer of him when I'd had the chance. But, I reminded myself, girls carrying babies were often sick and tired, and I was neither. It couldn't be. It couldn't. Please.

I also took to reading Granny's memoirs as I had promised. There was a story about a woman who "carried messages for the Union Army against the Confederates," another who "carried money to the CSA baked in a pie that she even served a piece to some Yankee without giving him the part with gold in it," and yet another who "carried messages for George Washington against the British."

On the day Prairie and all her friends donned their white gowns and went to their ball, I found this passage:

If you ever find yourself in real trouble, you do what thousands of girls have done since Noah landed that boat. You just hold up your head and buy yourself some widow's weeds and a weddin' ring. You put on that ring and pull down your veil and move to a town where no one knows you nor the name you give 'em. You make a way for yourself seamstressing or making hats or gloves. Don't hang your head to no one. Don't use it as no excuse to go into that business, neither. Ain't no woman in our family ever been in the streetwalking trade. There's fine sewing in your blood just like that black hair of yours and those fine teeth. And that will make you a life along with your poor child.

My stomach lurched and my heart felt as if it turned black and leaden with fear that Aubrey's attack would lead to my needing that advice. I went to bed that night, but slept very little.

At least in classes, I could forget for a while.

Some of the girls wanted to go to a melodrama and through whee-
dling and begging got me to go along. Being lonesome for some girls
to talk to without Prairie, I went along but at the doorway, I stopped,
afraid to go inside. All my life I'd heard how theaters were places where
the lowest of all people worked, that it was the devil's own nest of iniquity. I said to one of them, "I don't think Wheaton girls are allowed
in here," but she just laughed and pulled my arm. We went through a
dark maroon velvet curtain where it parted, and were engulfed in
smoke and black smells, far worse than my picture-developing liquids.
I jerked my arm from her grasp and dashed out the door, holding my
hand over my mouth. It didn't help, though, because the smell stayed
in my head and I was sick in the street. I looked around and no one
seemed to have noticed, but I ran for the dormitory in the last light of
the evening and immediately got into bed. I felt as if I'd stepped into
the doorway to perdition, and I shook with the shock of it, telling myself that I would have been sick no matter what and that didn't mean
anything. I was only sick because I entered that parted curtain where
the air swirled with a blue haze of tobacco smoke. I felt as if I'd touched
evil. As if Aubrey Hanna had been waiting in there. I pulled out Granny's wrapped memoirs and the small Bible Ma had given me and
clutched them to my bosom for comfort. I was glad no other girls had
gone to bed yet. Under the warmth of those words and without reading any of them, I fell almost immediately to sleep.

In this term's photography class, our new assignment was portraiture. We were to sit for each other and take plates, and practice
shadowing and lightening in the darkroom with tools over the papers.
One day when I'd agreed to sit for the students, nearly every person
there took my image. I wore a nice hat and a fascinator I borrowed
from Prairie, but she declared it looked so well on me, I should have
it. Now that her debutante nonsense was finished, she'd been more
friendly and made every effort to include me or sit by my side in classes.

I suppose I should have felt flattered, but I just do not understand a friendship that changes with the weather.

The day when it was my turn to pose, everyone had their own opinions about the numerous lamps and reflection panels, the flash pans and powder. I put all my effort into composing my face so that it seemed at rest, not angry, not tearful, although that was how I felt. It was exhausting and all those lamps made the room so hot, but I promised myself it was nothing like summertime at home in Arizona, so I kept the sweat off my forehead with a hanky, and looked this way and that as each student requested.

Finally the last boy, Nation Hollingsworth, announced, "Fellows? Give me a hand, will you? Take away all but two lamps." Those he placed both on my left side, and said, "Look toward the clock, there, in the corner, please. No, that's too much, look at something on the wall closer. All right." He moved a lamp. "You look tired." He sounded as if I'd disappointed him by being exhausted.

"This has been going on for three hours," I said.

"I want you to close your eyes. Please. There. Now remember the happiest time you can think of, the best day of your life so far. Go back to when you were little if you must. Now raise your right arm and place your fingers against your cheek. Then, when you lower your hand again to your lap, open your eyes at the same time and imagine that memory right there on the wall. Don't smile. Just imagine. Okay. Now."

Well, it was mighty strange, but I was so tired of all this, and feeling my stomach riding uneasy in the warm room, I did what he asked without another thought, just wanting to be done. I imagined it was three years ago when Duende's reins had first been placed in my hand by my pa, putting my face against his neck and breathing in the tangy scent of him, all of two years old and full of beans. Nation took that photo with the smallest amount of flash powder you could use, the kind you might have to use at a funeral or in a church.

All total, Nation Hollingsworth took seven plates of me. I never was one to spend much time in front of a mirror, but after that afternoon, I sat down with one to study just what it was he saw in me that I'd never paid attention to. At first, all I saw was plain old me. I practiced smiling and watched the dimples flirt on my face. My skin was smooth. That was good. Some girls weren't so lucky. I hoped I always kept my teeth. They looked pretty good for now, and none of them hurt at all. On the whole, I looked something like my sisters and a bit like Ma, who always said I was the spitting image of her sister Ulyssa, long gone before I was born. I never did anything but wash my face and clean my teeth. At last I put the mirror down and shook my head. I concluded my face didn't seem unusual at all, but I would certainly ask one of the students for a copy of their prints to take to Ma, if any of them came out well. Meanwhile, I had my own prints to develop, so I put on my shabbiest old dress and an apron and gloves and went to the laboratory.

Four weeks later the students were to present their developed photographs and describe the processes they'd used to achieve each effect. Most of it was pretty boring. I'd taken as many plates of horses in the barn as I had of people, and I preferred talking about them, so I did.

Again, Nation waited until he was the last to present his work. When he put up his assignment, I gasped. He had taken no other faces but mine. He'd done thirty prints. All of them were shadowy and some muddied with his attempts at dodging. The last he pulled out from carefully laid protective papers, and smiled at everyone before turning it around, letting his eyes linger on mine. He lifted the tissue paper off and people moved and made noises. Some moaned with joy, some more sympathetic girls made gasps of shocked anguish. It was colorized with great skill, making my lips dark as cranberries, my cheeks deepened with rouge, and my eyelids smoky and heavy with desire and passion; the face of a painted woman.

I stood immediately, as did all the others in the room. I forced out the words, "You've reddened my face until I look—like a trollop! I've never worn a speck of face paint or lip rouge in my life! Give me that this instant!"

"Nothing doing," he said, stepping between me and the horrible portrait. "I captured what I saw, nothing more."

"I am not a painted woman!" I turned to the professor and said, "Make him take that down. I don't look like that! I've never looked like that!" I felt bitterness welling in my eyes, and an anger that bordered on murderous. Nation had charged his coloring brush right into my heart where I already felt both guilty and wronged, fallen and abused. I watched the teacher's face for sympathy, but saw none, for he was staring at my portrait as if Nation had just brought in a live, naked girl.

Nation was smiling proudly at his creation. "The eyes. The anger. The angst. I have caught a depth of soul more tragic than anyone here even knows. You are an artist's dream, Mary Pearl. Beauty and pathos and longing. The fire of a passionate woman's heart. Look, ladies and gentlemen, Professor, at those eyes."

Some male voice behind me said, "I'd kiss her *any*time." And another one said, "I'll kiss her for you, so she'll know she's been kissed." The boys around us chuckled, and one made as if he'd nearly swooned. Some went red-faced and sat abruptly. The girls all looked peevish, but murmured sympathies for me. "He shouldn't" and "That's dreadful."

"I am not like that!" I felt the pistol hanging under my apron. Sadness and anger overwhelmed me. I sank in my chair and wept openly. "Please make him tear that up. Please, someone. That's *not* me."

Then the teacher gave us a lecture in honest portraiture, which meant capturing the person's likeness, not changing it to be what you want it to be. He cleared his throat about a hundred times during it, like he was coming down with the grippe, and though he addressed the class, he stared at the colorized print. "You might be allowed to shade a tree or a carpet, but never a face," he said. "That will be all for today. Pick up these printed sheets about our upcoming field trip to the Grand Canyon on your way out the door. Mr. Hollingsworth, the portrait in question, please. I'll have to have a consultation over this," and it was handed over with much scowling and grumbling. But he didn't tear it up. He laid it in the top drawer of his desk. I hoped he planned to give it to me to destroy. But he did not, even when I asked him again. Said he had a meeting to go to, and shooed me out the door. Nation was waiting in the hall, but I kept my eyes forward and didn't speak to him, although he interrupted my steps four times.

Friday afternoon I went to the teacher and asked for that colorized portrait to be given to me, not to Nation Hollingsworth. He promised he had "disposed" of it. Then he handed me the papers of information about the class trip to the Grand Canyon. Said I'd missed picking them up when the papers were handed out. Wanted to know if I'd be going.

"Sure," I said. "I've always wanted to see it."

"I thought with you living there, you'd have seen it already."

"Arizona Territory is easily twice the size of the state of Illinois and then some, and I haven't seen but one small corner of it," I said. "There's a girl in my dormitory that'd never seen that big lake outside Chicago until we went."

"Do you have enough money for the trip? The train tickets are nearly four dollars each way. There will be food expenses and you'll want plenty of Eastman plates. Then you'll have to get home, too. Most students are coming back here."

"I can get off in Albuquerque on the way back, and go south from there to Benson. It's not direct, but it gets me home." As I spoke I was considering my remaining money. There was surely enough to get home, but I hadn't worked at the library in a couple of months, and I'd paid out plenty for those hats and dresses I'd bought. It would be easy enough to rein in my cash.

"Miss Prine, I know you were upset by the unauthorized doctoring of your photograph by Mr. Hollingsworth. That makes it all the more difficult and, well, complicated, to ask you my next question. I was hoping, wondering, that is, I'm wishing to ask you, if you'd sit for *me*, as a portrait study. Privately, of course. I'd like to put the faces of our students—"

"No."

"—in a magazine or a gazette. I have a publisher who's done other work of mine and your portrait—"

"Only mine? No."

"Won't you think it over? There's nothing to gain by being obstinate."

"Obstinate? Does that mean the same as not saying yes to your request? Why don't you give me that print you took from him? Or did you return it to Hollingsworth? Did you really dispose of it as you said?"

"He came for it. I couldn't see keeping it when I can easily take another. If you will pose for me, I can arrange for your fare on our excursion to be made gratis."

"By posing for you? *Privately?* You're not family, and that wouldn't be for a class grade. That would just be for strange men to admire. I don't need your money that bad."

"Bad*ly*. Have you ever considered going on the stage? You saw how the students admired you. Why, with your face and your figure, you'd be welcome in any theater and my photographic portraits could pave the way for you—"

"Theater? What is there about me that makes you think I'm that sort of girl? You know there are plenty of men who see a dimple and think it's put there just for them to admire. They see a smile and presume that it's theirs to own. I'd never go into a theater, ever, and I'd certainly never stand upon a stage to be ogled by strangers. I pay my own way. I won't owe you. I'll pay my own way," I insisted again. It took every ounce of control I owned not to look in his eyes with the venom I felt for the man. I walked to the door of the room and turned. I felt my backbone stiffen and my shoulders settle into place. With it came some vocabulary words I'd only ever read in a book, never used myself out loud. "What you've proposed, sir, I am quite certain, is outside of the intention of this institution according to the policies pledge I signed. You tell Hollingsworth to give me that print, and I'll think about not going to the dean." The heels on my fancy city-girl shoes made loud clacks against the floor.

I met Prairie and some girls in the hall. My voice came out shrilly. "Sweets, are you going to the Grand Canyon on the class trip?" I asked. I was flaming hot, my fists balled up like I was ready to punch anyone who looked crossways at me.

They all said they were, and Prairie added, "I planned to go. Why?"

"I'm going, too, and I want us to bunk close by, and stay close by, all the time. Will you do that for me?"

"Of course, Mary. Of course. Let's go get some supper. You seem so, well, out of sorts. I'll bet you're hungry. My mother won't mind me bringing you along."

All through that supper, I counted the months. Counted again. Checked my calendar and felt of my sore bosom. I couldn't cry. I've never really known the word "forlorn" before, although I have certainly felt grief and sadness, but I believe I was truly forlorn. I remembered Granny's warning, and suddenly the word "Albuquerque" echoed in my thoughts. It was the right place. I had no other choice.

Late in the night, I awoke and lit a lamp, sitting at a small desk with paper and pen.

Dear, dearest Ma and Pa,

How can I tell you what has happened to me? I want to come home but I believe with all my heart that I must leave home for good. I can't stay here, either. After much thought and prayer, I have decided I shall live in Albuquerque by making photographic prints for people. When my photography class returns from our trip to the Territory, it will be a natural stop for me, and no one at the school will have any knowledge that I did not come back to you. Nor will anyone in Tucson know that I have not stayed in Illinois. It is the best I can do, and I will only be one day away by train. I promise with every fiber of my being that what has happened was not my doing. I was small and unaware in the presence of someone large and strong and violent. I know my shame grieves you sorely. If you can forgive and accept my new life, I shall return to you in a couple of years, a widow,

Then I added *and a mother,* and felt as if I would faint.

I opened the grate to the heat stove, threw the letter in, and stood there until my feet went numb from cold, watching the fire consume my words. With those words, the family I loved would never have had to sit across a table from Rachel and Aubrey knowing he'd ruined me. They'd think it was someone here in Wheaton. I decided I would write it again, and do it sitting at the post office, so that no one here might see it. I'd post it as we left for the Grand Canyon, just like I sent that letter to Aubrey, and my family would get the news after I was out of reach by letter or telegraph, too late to change my mind for me, or come get me. *Like I'd done to him.* That was the first time I'd felt ashamed of doing that, but this was different. This time, I had to escape this way, for their sakes.

The next day I pulled out Granny's memoirs and went to the library.

There's a place in Kentucky on a hillside, where my life changed forever. That was where I saw my pa hanged and my papaw shot down. You see, we had kin on both sides. Some was for the North, some was for the South. I tell you what, though, if President Lincoln hadn'ta been killed, things wouldn't have been so bad for us up in the Kentucky hills. Them patterolers quit looking just for slaves and went to looking for sympathizers, or anybody who hadn't carried a gun in the war. I knew my pa had robbed a Union Army train. It was war. Everyone did what they could to help what they thought was their side. He admitted it, too. Hoped for mercy. There stood this fellow I was sweet on. Watching. He lifted nary a word to Pa's defense. Stood by doing nothing. There ain't nothing worse'n doing nothing. Stand for what's right, girl. So I went on, acarrying his baby, and took off to the Oregon hills where I met your grandpap on the way. 'N he said "Will you?" and I said "I will" 'n we walked together more'n thirty years after that.

Even though I'd taken down those words as she spoke them, the truth was slow in making a bed in my mind. My pa wasn't the child of his own pa. He was someone else's, a man who'd stood on a hill and let another man die without raising a word. I knew enough about breeding horses to know one leggy one doesn't always mean a stable full of them. Pa's sister, Aunt Sarah, was no taller than Ma, and while Clove was tall, Joshua barely met Ma's height, and Rachel and Rebeccah had been only a little taller than me. Descended from that grandfather who Granny had married secondhand. He'd died of a bullet wound that festered, long before Ma and Pa were married. So I actually had some other grandpa than the Comanche-killed one. Still, Pa was my pa, and he was good and steady as a rock. This was just *some* of what Granny didn't want known through the family until she had passed away.

"Hey, there, buddy!" The voice stirred me from my reverie.

"Hey, Calvert." I could ask him to deliver a note to Nation. Cal would never know what it said. "If I give you a note to someone, can you take it? Do you know the students?"

"Only the teachers. I know *them*."

"Oh." I'd have to think of something else. "Good night, Cal."

Through the first half of April, I stayed so busy studying that there were hours and even whole days that I forgot my predicament. I never felt sick anymore so that much was easy. Letters from home seemed pleasant enough. Ezra wrote that he and Zack were riding Duende to keep the horse's spirits up. Spring had come and gone and it was hot there, whereas here in Illinois we had a late snowfall. After his graduation, Joshua had returned home briefly and then moved north of there. He was planning to set up a medical practice in someplace more in need of a doctor since Tucson was brimming over with hospitals and the like. He set up in the area near Phoenix, out by Fort McDowell. Ma wrote that Pa was not pleased, as he said that little old rut in the road called Phoenix would never make more than a two-bit town. I wished he'd go to Albuquerque, but I didn't want to hint of my own plans.

As our Grand Canyon trip neared, the students had come upon the library's book about Thomas Moran, who'd visited there and done many paintings and drawings. If it weren't for the lending limits, I'd have hardly gotten a look at them.

I was coming out of the developing lab with a broom in my hand, and Prairie pounced on me with a sparkle in her eye and a grin like a cat. "Mary Pearl!" Then she dropped her voice to a whisper. "I'm engaged! Look, look, look!" She pulled a chain from her collar and showed me a ring with a large emerald stone and two smaller white ones. "Come to the engagement party, please say you will. Everyone will be there."

"I wouldn't have the right things to wear."

"You are the first of my friends I've told! Please, please come. It's April eighteenth. I'll send a carriage for you to the dormitory at eight. Promise you'll be ready!"

I wore my best dress, happy it still fit, and yet glum because I felt like a saddle tramp compared to the lace and satin gowns swirling all around me. I was asked to dance, though, but I felt like a loose steer in a horse corral, and couldn't manage some of the steps very well. I knew some dancing from home, but not these big swooping waltzes. Nation Hollingsworth was there. When he asked me to dance, I asked him to fetch me some punch instead, and we sat on the porch—it's called a veranda—while he peppered me with questions about Arizona. Reckon he was going to the Grand Canyon, too, so I'd have to put up with him that whole way. I even got to dance with Mr. Bradenton, the famous fancy-pants cattleman from Chicago who'd gotten Prairie's parents' approval to own her heart, mind, and body. He didn't look like anybody I'd want to be saddled with the rest of my days, but to be honest, he seemed like a nice enough fellow, and he was surely smitten with Prairie from the look on his face.

At one point between dances, she whispered in my ear, "We're going to Niagara Falls on our honeymoon, and then off to Italy for a month."

"Aren't you going on the class trip to the Grand Canyon?" I asked. "Please tell me you will."

"I can't say yet. The wedding is not until June, but there is so much to do."

"I need you to stay by me," I wheedled. "There are a couple of fellas

I want nothing to do with who'll be coming along." The professor himself came to mind.

"I'll tell Mother again that I promised you. They think of you as so capable, though, you don't need me. Mother said you were sturdy stuff. Pioneering spirit and all. I have to get the trousseau fitted and my gown. Oh, wait until you see it! Why would you need me?"

"Because you're my friend."

"I'll always be your friend," she said, while admiring the ring on her finger.

"But you'll live here. We'll likely never see each other again. It's only a six-day trip. We'll remember it. We'll have photographs of each other, and of the canyon." And, I thought, I need to take spectacular photographs of every angle of that canyon so I can promote my photography business in Albuquerque. I didn't want any boys hanging around me. "I'm just flat afraid to be alone," I added.

"That's just silly, Mary Pearl. You're the bravest, strongest girl I've ever met. Listen, there were two men over there admiring you. I'll tell them to ask you to dance."

My heart gave a thump. To be touched by a strange man! Just the thought of it made me feel like gagging. "No, that's not needed. If they have to be prodded, they aren't likely my sort of fellow. I'm not interested in the likes of those two. Don't like either one. What is wrong with city men? They are all so odd I can't get a rope around any of 'em." I was aware of eyes following me from the direction she'd waved her fan. One of the fellows looked well built and tanned from being outdoors. I thought it might be nice to talk to someone who didn't live inside a building every day of his life, but even my horse didn't have to be asked to come to me. He just came. Then it turned out the outdoor-looking fellow shied off in favor of a refreshment table, and the pale, narrow-faced boy wearing a pound of hair pomade came and asked me to dance. I did one turn around the floor, cringing the whole time from the smell of his hair. Once the waltz had finished, I slipped into another room. Men. Seemed the ones I didn't want showed up like rattlesnakes, and the ones I might have had a talk with didn't have any interest. Finally the happy couple posed for a photograph, and Nation was there, arranging the flowers at their feet, popping his head under the black sheet, making sure everything looked perfect before he flashed the pan.

The very next day, Nation came to the dormitory waiting room to call on me. He'd brought a bouquet of flowers, and even though it was cold outside, and there were still patches of snow under every tree and bush, he wanted to walk in the garden. He handed me the roses.

"No, thank you," I said.

"Please. They are the color of your cheeks. You must take them. They cost dearly this time of year."

"Leftover from Prairie's engagement?"

He looked genuinely angry for a moment. "Not at all. I paid for them and I have the receipt. I have come to *call*."

"Well, at least you have some honor. Thank you for the roses. What's that flower?" I pointed next to the walkway.

"Ah, I think it's called daffodil."

"I'll come back and sketch it, and paint it for my mother." No one here called their parents Ma and Pa.

"Would you please sit here, on this bench?" he asked, then pulled out a paper from his coat. There he read to me of his earnest fondness and kind regards from a piece of notepaper, and asked me to marry him. I put my fingers to my lips. Marry? Could I marry someone instead of moving to Albuquerque? This was a solution I had not thought of. That would change everything. My eyes settled on the yellow flower just opened amid a handful of spearlike leaves coming from the ground. Almost every one of them was swollen, pregnant, ready to blossom.

I swallowed hard. Studied his face. He wasn't really bad-looking, though his hair needed combing every time I saw him. I told him I would seriously consider it. I realized, too, that I didn't really hate him. I just wanted my portrait to represent who I was, not some made-up version. It would mean lying to him, but I would be saved from any reproach. Plenty of babies came early. No. I couldn't do that. I might accept his offer, but he would have to know why I did; I vowed that much to myself. "Give me one week for an answer. But," I said, "I hardly know you. I want to know what you will do with yourself. What plans do you have for the future? Are you rich? All the rich fellows were at the Longmores' party last night. Do you have a job? What do you do besides take plates of people and floozy up their looks?"

He laughed, a sound that warmed me, and said, "I borrowed that dinner jacket and pants. Honestly, I don't have a cent. My folks both died a few years ago and I live with an aunt who likes to write stories under the pen name of Milton Barnes. She's going to introduce me to her editor at the *Trib*, and I'm going to sell my photographs to all the newspapers in Chicago. It's a great start on a real groundbreaking career. They're starting to print photographs in all the big papers. I'll be there and drive a horseless carriage to every big scene. Fires, murders, bank holdups, you name it." His eyes lit up as he spoke of it. "I'm not rich, not yet, but you and I, we'd make a swell time of it."

"Where do you plan we would live?"

"With my aunt at first. Later, we'll get a little apartment right downtown. Right in the middle of everything."

The image of my baby growing up in a busy, dirty corner of a bustling city, her father always dashing out to photograph some tragedy, filled me with sadness. My baby. I had to protect her from the world he described. "I thank you for the compliment of your offer," I said. "But I don't need to consider for a week. My answer is no. I already have other plans. I believe I'm not in love with you."

He looked truly crestfallen. "You're not? I'm quite lovable. Everyone thinks so. My ears don't stick out, much. Are you still engaged? I heard that was called off."

"It was, truly. It's not that," I said with a little laugh, "but I'm very practical. I have plans. Plus, I'd like to feel more than fondness for the fellow I marry. And a sense that my life will be settled and, and, will you be so kind as to give me the plate you took of me for class? Why don't you give me that print where you colored my lips to look like rouge?"

He smiled. "Well, no. That one is mine. If you'll marry me, the print and the plate'll be yours, though. And you said you *are* fond of me."

I didn't smile in return. "Most people who pull a holdup use a gun." I handed him his flowers. "Believe those roses cost you something, getting them this time of year. Take them home to your aunt."

"That's your final word?"

"Yes."

"I'll give you the *uncolorized* portrait of yourself. I need the colored one for my portfolio."

"You want to show people you take pictures of scandalous women?"

"Gorgeous women. You don't look scandalous. You look gorgeous. And, well, *com*plicated."

"Give me one of the plain ones, then, for my mother. She has a photograph of everyone except me. Then we'll at least part as friends."

He smiled, the real, genuine kind of smile that came from his eyes as well as his mouth. I was beginning to see what I'd missed about people, especially men outside my own family. That there was a deeper quality I could read better if I watched with the eyes of an artist. Maybe he hadn't meant to be mean after all, the way he'd done my portrait. Nation said, "Friends, then, forever," and bowed, then reached into his ragged satchel and pulled out the print I'd asked for.

"You carry it with you?" I held out my hand, but he held the print right above my grasp.

"You know I love you, don't you?"

"It's called 'being smitten.' You don't know me enough to love me. I've been smitten before and no good comes of it."

He bent his head close, placing the print in my hand. "It's true no Aphrodite could compete with your features, 'a woman's face with Nature's own hand painted,' but I feel the fire in your eyes like hot coals in the depths of my soul. I'll spend my lifetime learning, only let me sit at your feet."

Shakespeare. He'd quoted Shakespeare to me. My resolve was softening. "I can't ever tell when you are just pulling my leg, Nation Hollingsworth. Do you mean to court me?"

"I do," he said. "Don't let those two words give you any nuptial ideas, though. I'll carry this photograph of you with me my whole life." Then he laughed, tipped his hat, bowed, put the hat back on his head at a jaunty angle, the roses over one shoulder, and went whistling down the garden path. At one point he turned and called out so loudly that people turned and stared, grinning at the two of us. "'Mine eye hath played the painter and hath stelled, Thy beauty's form in table of my heart'!"

Well of all things. I felt a blush rise as I turned to hurry away, for I had wanted him to stay and keep on talking love to me.

Over the next few days, I made many sketches and watercolors of the little stand of daffodils. Along with that, I began to look at every man I saw as a potential husband. Standing in the darkroom one morning, I thought, I couldn't force myself to feel attraction just to get me out of a fix, and I still couldn't stand the thought of one of them touching me. Quite obviously, even a rich, educated man can have the heart of a rattler. No. I would not marry someone I hardly knew just to save myself the hard road I saw ahead. Nation Hollingsworth looked better every minute. Living in cold Chicago in a cramped apartment with some other woman and a crying baby did not, however.

It was April twenty-fourth. Less than a week until the trip. That afternoon, mail was piled on a table by the door of the dormitory. There was a letter from Ma. Before I opened it, I thought of the letter I intended to write to her, to let her know I would never come home again and why. How it might break her heart. How it might shatter all my dear family's love of me. I might be forever banned. But I would think about that later. I would concentrate on doing everything I could with my plates of the canyon. That was my future. I had to succeed at it. If Ma would accept me a year from now, I could visit her from Albuquerque.

1908

Dear Mary Pearl,

Your Aunt Sarah and I are coming to get you. I am aware your school year is not over, and I am sorry. Be ready to travel by April 28, and meet us at the depot. The train schedule says we arrive there at 11:45 in the morning. We will take the next train south that same afternoon. Please arrange for your ticket. We have already got round trip fares. Your Pa will fetch us in Benson.

Very sincerely, your ma

No, no, no! screamed my heart. I gasped so loudly that other girls in the dorm looked up. I had to get to Albuquerque. I wrote her immediately.

Please wait until after the class trip. Please tell me what is wrong. Please tell me who has died. Please just another couple of weeks. I have a plan for my future that depends on taking this photographing trip. I can't leave yet. Let me do this. Please. Just a little more time. A few more days. Please.

Had I mailed my note that very instant, I knew, they would be on the train before it reached home. There was no reason for me to post it. Her letter gave me no escape. Something had happened, something now so dire it could not be written in a letter. No one had written to me of my cousin Blessing's death. No one had told me to come home because Elsa had been killed and Gilbert was shot. What could be worse than those things? If Ma herself was coming, was it Granny who had died? Even with that, I decided, Ma would have waited until I arrived and shown me the grave. Had Pa died?

I told Prairie I had to leave in only four days, but I didn't tell her why. She didn't ask, either, only said, "Oh, dear, before my wedding?" dabbed at her eyes, kissed my cheek, and then asked me if I'd still go with her to choose some dishes for her new home.

"Aren't you going back to classes at all?" I asked. "School's not over until the trip."

"Oh, it doesn't matter now. I'm leaving all that behind me. So tell me, did Nation ask you? What did you say? He's terribly taken with you. Although, well, he dresses quite shabbily."

"Taken with me? I don't think he knows me at all." I didn't want to talk about Nation Hollingsworth.

"You're blushing," she said with a giggle.

"No. He's a nice man and all. I don't care about shabby clothes." But he'd quoted Shakespeare. There was more to him than his ragged clothes and wild dreams, just as there was more to me than a set of dimples. I wanted to turn the conversation elsewhere. "Well, do you think married life will suit you?"

"Oh, certainly."

"You know, he's going to want children."

"I can't wait." She squeezed my arm and her face flushed. "You know."

"I grew up on a ranch, so yes, I've always known about that." We sat silently for several moments, and I felt ashamed that the image of Nation came to me then with more than a little urge to have him kiss me. Wasn't there a sonnet about "cursed desire"? And how could that be true and lasting love?

Prairie cleared her throat demurely and whispered, "Do come with me downtown. I want to show you a pattern of china."

"No, I have work I haven't finished. I need to take my rig home with me."

"That's all right. I'll get Rosalee to come. I do hope you and your mother have a nice trip. Maybe you can get back here in time for the Grand Canyon. Write me! Oh, I'm so thrilled for the both of us. Tell me all about your wedding plans, when you make them, and I will come, I promise!"

"Sure." Where did she get the idea I was making wedding plans? With Nation? I didn't correct her because she'd already flitted down the boardwalk, just happy as a robin.

And that was it. All our days and weeks of friendship seemed to have dried up in one small conversation. From the way things had gone, I could see her mind was buzzing like a bee tree full up with wedding plans. If I wasn't available, Rosalee was just as good. I felt glad she was so cheerful. Still, I'd lost so many loved ones, it hurt me even more to watch her saunter happily away. The thought came to me, then, that I shouldn't dump sand in her beans just because I was disappointed. I had six dollars left in my pocket, although there was more in the bank I had plans to use, and took five of them with me downtown. There, I bought the prettiest petticoat I could find and had it wrapped and sent to Prairie for her wedding trousseau. I added a note that said, "I hope you're as happy as you can be, forever." In the depths of my heart I was saying good-bye forever as well.

The next day, I hunted up all my teachers and explained I'd be leaving, except for that scoundrel in the photography department, and the ones I couldn't find in person, I left notes for. I thanked them all for helping me learn so much. Told them I hoped to use my learning in the future, but I was leaving for home before the end of term. Told them how glad I was to have gotten the chance to live at this nice college and hear about artists. To my drawing teacher I added that I would continue to practice my perspectives and shadows. He seemed truly concerned, but I said it was a family emergency and I didn't have any more information. Then he smiled and said, "You have come a very long way in this class. Made a great deal of progress. I'm very sorry you have to leave. Give my best to your family, and my sentiments for whatever trials they are facing. Do keep at it, dear." That made me feel very nice indeed.

Later, I moped for wanting to see the Grand Canyon while I sorted and packed things. I believed I was showing the tearfulness of carrying a baby. I remembered Ma getting just tore up over dropping an egg on the floor when Zachary was coming. I supposed that canyon wasn't going anywhere. I'd go by myself, someday, if I had to. Because I *had* to. I had to have a set of fine pictures to hang on the walls of my photography business.

All I had left to do, I did alone. Every person there was in their own whirlwind of motion, and I don't think a soul realized I'd be gone. I had to pay a buggy company to carry my things to the train depot, and I rode away without even waving, as if I'd never been there, and would not be missed.

CHAPTER ELEVEN

I sat at the depot waiting for the train, shivering in my shawl, imagining that it was probably hotter than Hades back home. My belly was round enough that I could feel it pressing my clothes, now, although no one had guessed. What was I going to tell my mama? It had seemed like the right thing, to just carry on, go on to school, keep quiet, to protect everyone from what had happened. Seemed the only person I couldn't protect was myself. I should have written a note and explained. Run away. Married Nation Hollingsworth. Only I hadn't. Here I was at the depot waiting for a train that was three hours late. Maybe I wouldn't tell anyone. Maybe I could still make it to Albuquerque.

At last, some boy who'd been listening to the tracks with his head laid on them hollered, "Here she comes!" and I settled my hat at a nicer angle and waited.

Soon as I saw Ma and Aunt Sarah, all three of us said as one, "What is the matter?"

Ma grabbed me to her and said, "You look so worried, honey."

"I am, Ma." Both the women looked haggard and gaunt, as well.

Aunt Sarah had her arm through Ma's elbow, and we went to wait for their bag—a single valise shared between them—so we could make sure it got right back on the train to head home. The outbound southern was due to leave in only forty-five minutes.

"Train was slowed up by the weather a hundred miles south of here," Sarah said. The look in her eyes scared me more than any snow.

"How is everyone at home?" I asked.

"Not until we're on board," Ma said. "Do we just get back on the same train?"

"No, ma'am," I said. "It'll be headed to Chicago and then New York. Other side of the depot is where the southbound goes out. The switchman will make sure it comes up next to the platform."

Ma stared at me. "You seem like you've grown five years older in such a short time. Not my little girl anymore. Well, no longer a child, at least."

I clung to her as close as I could, allowing that we could both walk, wishing she'd see there was still some little girl left in me. "It's only that I've learned to get along here," I said.

It took some trouble to get my trunks loaded. The second, a new one, was entirely camera equipment. I had decided to invest in a good trunk to carry it all, since it was to be my livelihood. I had four boxes of Eastman's dry plates to take home. Large jugs of chemicals and mixing and rinsing pans. I also had a carpetbag and three hatboxes, two valises, and a small reticule stuffed into a large one. At last we sat on a pair of facing benches. Aunt Sarah leaned forward to take my hands. Just as she did, another woman came and looked as if she might want to sit with us. Sarah shook her head and the woman moved on, but only sat in the very next bench behind Ma.

"How is Gilbert?" I whispered.

"He's doing just fine. He's been riding fence for a month. Nothing like being young to heal up quick."

"And the rest? Pa? Granny?"

Both Ma and Aunt Sarah nodded. "Fine. They are fine."

I waited for someone to say something. Finally Ma said, "The day I wrote you, Mr. Maldonado sent us this." She began unfolding a telegram which she'd pulled from her drawstring bag.

I watched the lady behind her twist her neck like an owl, so I said, "*En español. La gente nos escucha.*" Then Ma handed me the paper instead of reading it out loud.

BOYS UNHURT. SEND FIFTY THOUSAND DOLLARS US.
SEND ONE PERSON. NO RANGERS. NO DEPUTIES. CASH. CARRY RED
FLAG. FRANCISCO WILL MEET YOU IN AGUA PRIETA JUNE 1.
ASK FOR SR. AGUIRRE.

"What boys?" I asked, trembling violently as I handed back the worn paper. "Not our—*tienen los chicos?*" No one needed to say more.

Mama dropped her face into her hands, shaking with quiet sobs for a few moments. Then she whispered, "Zachary and Ezra had ridden down to Benson, following Doctor Pardee after he'd come to tend Gilbert and pay a call on your sister Rebeccah. Ezra said he wanted to buy me a kerchief for my birthday. They didn't think anything about the sun going down. They didn't have any reason not to ride home in the dark."

"My brothers? Weren't they carrying a rifle? And why?"

"Maybe he just needs the money," Ma whispered.

"But that's fifty years' worth of pay," I said. Fifty thousand dollars. Did they think we were the Vanderbilts?

It only added to the sadness to find out Zack and Ezra had been on my horse Duende when they'd been kidnapped. I looked at Mama's face, her eyes scanning the scenery, and said, "We won't get there until tomorrow, Ma. Our stop is after Deming and Lordsburg, so if you watch for those towns, you'll know we're close to home. We have hours to go. Do we have a plan? Do we have *any* money?"

Aunt Sarah reverted back to Spanish. "Maybe eight thousand."

Ma said, "We'll sell the farm," as if it were already done, and it shocked me just to hear the words. "You did ask us to come get you if something happened, remember? I'm sorry about taking you away from your schooling."

I couldn't hide my disappointment. "It's all right. The boys are more important." Tears filled my eyes and I turned to the window, wiping my face on my sleeve. I turned back to Ma. "I have the deed to the Wainbridge ranch land. Sell that."

Suppertime came and we went to eat in the dining car. Ma could hardly swallow, she said. We slept in our seats, heaped together. I woke once to observe Ma and Aunt Sarah, their arms linked and settled together as if the sore feelings between them were gone and forgotten. I imagined the whole thing as if it came to me in black-and-white moving images on a screen. My proud stallion, the two rascals perched on him, and that familiar road to Benson from our place. That curve where the sandy hills gave way to red rock and granite-lined arroyos where we used to pick up Indian arrowheads. So obviously a place for an ambush. Two silly young boys on a single horse would have been arguing or laughing, poking each other, shooting at ground squirrels with a slingshot. Bandidos would have had no trouble, waiting with guns drawn, to force them to hand over the reins and lead them to the Maldonado's place. Having my brothers taken felt as if part of my very life had been severed somehow. Were they scared? Did they fight? Were they hurt or killed? Surely, surely, Elsa's papacito would not harm them. Surely he would remember our childhood friendships. I watched Ezra's eyes widen with shock and Zachary's mouth contort in pain, perhaps beaten, perhaps hungry and cold.

"Mary Pearl, why are you crying?" Mama asked.

"*Temo que están muertos.* I'm afraid they will die."

She said nothing, but turned to the window for a very long time.

In Benson, just as promised, Pa was at the depot with a wagon. Two Rangers, wearing badges and bandoliers of bullets, scrutinized everyone who got off the train. To my surprise, though, we did not go home but stopped first at Udell Hanna's place, now my aunt Sarah's ranch. There were more Rangers there, a deputy from Sheriff Pacheco's office, most of the hands from her ranch and some of ours, plus my brother Clover and cousin Gilbert. Cousin Charlie was conspicuously absent, but he'd sent word that he was going to come home from West Point and enroll again in the fall. We left Aunt Sarah at her door, then Pa drove Ma and me home.

Next morning, the kindling lit and crackled right away as I started the morning stove for Mama, put the coffee beans in the roaster, put on the water to boil. Even fire started differently here than in Illinois. I let out a sigh, standing there over the coffee beans as they began to give off their aroma, staring at Ma's calendar that hung next to the flue pipe and the shelf of dried herbs. I figured we'd be riding out as soon as Pa had breakfast, but he said no, he was going to town, just for the day, be back after midnight tonight. Ma didn't ask why, and so I wasn't free to ask, either, but later she told me he meant to mortgage their ranch and try to sell mine.

Since I'd come home, more than a week had passed and we hadn't done a blessed thing, but we'd had another note from Maldonado's people. They lowered the money they wanted to twenty-five thousand. No soldiers came with word about our boys.

By then, all the other students who'd signed up to see the Grand Canyon and take photographs of one of the great wonders of the world, were already on their way home. I had paid my money and lost it. And it had been at my own insistence that I be brought home for any emergency. Ten days had passed and I could have gone on the trip. Could have seen the Grand Canyon instead of sitting here waiting. Not that my brothers weren't worth missing something for. Not that I didn't love them. It was just that I felt this terrible dragging of my soul, as if I'd lost more than the photographs I might have taken. I'd lost my plan for solving my bigger problem and my little brothers were still just as gone as ever. It was so frustrating I wanted to holler.

Rachel and Aubrey were coming for a visit sometime that day, going to spend a couple of nights. I felt cranky. My skirt was too tight. My chemise, too. Granny hadn't seemed angry or surprised, but she was not Mama, and I woke up thinking about girls I'd heard about who'd been thrown out of the house, long before they could manage on their own. If only I could have taken the photos at the canyon, I could leave as soon as my brothers were safe at home, and go live in Albuquerque. I spent an hour writing a letter to Prairie. That was, after I started it and accidentally wrote, "Dear Elsa," at the top. I had to fold it and tear off part. Back at school I'd have gotten a new sheet of paper. Here in the Territory every scrap was precious, and you didn't waste an inch of it. Using my art paper was out of the question, of course. I don't know why I felt I had to send a cheery note to my friend, but I felt as if it would be my "last known correspondence," and perhaps if I perished soon, she'd keep it as a remembrance.

When I came downstairs I couldn't keep my face from carrying my peevishness, I suspect. All through breakfast, Mama was watching me overmuch. Finally, as we did the dishes with Rebeccah, she asked, "Mary Pearl, are you feeling poorly? You look peaked. Have you been working too hard?"

"No, Mama, I'm fine," I lied. "I don't sleep well worrying about Zack and Ezra. When are we going back to Mexico to get them? Why doesn't Pa decide?"

"No," she said, "I don't sleep well, either."

I wrinkled my nose, smiled, and made a humph in my throat, trying to keep myself from tears, adding, "I think I have a touch of the vapors from all the red chili I ate yesterday."

Rebeccah said, "Oh, look up the hill. There comes Rache and Aubrey. They must have left before dawn!"

"How nice," I said.

Ma frowned at the expression of disgust I couldn't hide. "Don't look a gift horse in the mouth. Maybe he's sold our land."

"Too bad they can't buy it outright. Aubrey and Rachel. Then they could hold the note and sell it back to Clove."

Ma hugged me. Then she looked into my eyes and frowned. "Something's different about you, my girl. You're *too* worried. We'll get them back. I just know it. I have faith. You must turn to faith."

I turned away from her gaze, afraid that any moment I'd blurt out what I'd been hiding. "I want to go for a ride," I said. "Don't worry about me. I'm going to ride part of the Wainbridge place." I smirked. "I guess it's the Mary Prine place, now."

By the time I got a horse picked out—there were only a few left on our place, most of them waiting at Aunt Sarah's, ready to take off to Mexico—a dust trail appeared on the road behind a buggy. With a little hurrying on my part, I could miss saying hello to them for a couple of hours.

I mounted the mare and planted myself on a beat-up roping saddle. After that big stallion, Duende, this mare felt little and placid, not fiery and bold. She moved pretty smooth, though, and didn't take more than a nudge to know what I wanted of her. I tickled her sides with my spurs and we took a good run until I was out of sight from our farm.

I rode across the Wainbridge land, studying every saguaro, every cholla with the ownership I felt. It was my place now. Got down to the cabin, thinking, watching for rattlers and coyotes. Occasionally I looked around to see if anyone followed me or watched from a hill-side. On the way there, I felt a rumbling in my belly and guessed I'd be having some wind later, and like a tick of a clock, I pulled the reins. The bubbling feeling was in the same place as before, not moving naturally. I gulped.

It was the baby moving.

The horse stood shorter than Duende. I slid off and hit the ground hard and my ankles stung. All I'd ever done, good or bad, as well as everything I'd dreamed of for my future spread before me, as if I could see my entire life laid here in the desert sun. Burnt and curling at the edges. Wasted. This child I carried could be the death of me and I've only just begun, I thought.

I walked to a fallen fence, brushing through brittlebush and prickly pear, feeling but not flinching from the thorns that poked through my brother's old pants. That horse just stood where she was, docile and drowsy. I stomped back and grabbed her reins, marching uselessly around the outside of the cabin, and she followed me with a sleepy look in her eyes, as if the hot sun were lulling her as it was baking my brains. She just didn't have half the spunk in her whole heart as my Duende had in one hoof.

I knocked my boot against the porch and heard a clunk inside. This had been a place that for all my memories had been banned for us children. Never to step on this land nor enter this house. "Well, it's my house now," I said aloud. I kicked open the door. It swung in on creaking hinges, barely enough wood in it to call it a door, and when it hit something inside, buckets of dust fell from the rotted timbers. Either a foot or a cannonball had gone through it, and several bullets had peppered both the door and the walls beyond. There wasn't one whole piece of glass in any window. Cobwebs draped every corner, and a funnel spider had tied a fallen-over chair to the hearth with the biggest spider tube I'd ever seen. In another corner a pack rat had built a mound of cholla burs and corncobs four feet across and two feet high. The people had left behind curtains, an old bedstead, a tin pan worn through the bottom, and a man's plaid coat hanging on a peg on the wall. I recognized strips of it in the pack rat's nest, too. I never knew those people, the Wainbridges. They'd left before I could even ride.

There were only two rooms. Sky showed through the walls. The back room had a fireplace instead of a cookstove. This room wasn't so shot up, but some kind of critter had left its lifeblood and bones in the middle of the floor, along with tufts of black hair and a skull with jagged teeth. Might have been a skunk, but I never knew anything desperate enough it would eat a skunk. I heard another clunk behind me and drew a pistol. I turned around. Glaring at me as if I were the intruder, a half-grown bobcat sat on his haunches. The iguana in its mouth gave a wiggle and he shook it. "Go on and eat it," I said. "I didn't come for supper."

I backed away and as I did something crunched under my boot. I kept the pistol aimed at the bobcat, but bent to see what I'd broken. It was a wheel, come off an axle, the kind on the bottom of a baby's roll-around toy. I looked around again, looking for some other clue. Diaper cloths coated in dust hung in drifts from the ceiling, and strings laden with them had fallen to the floor. A child had lived here! Some poor woman had brought a baby to this. Had it always been a filthy wreck? Maybe the child died. Maybe that was why they gave up and left. "Only things Aubrey Hanna ever gave me is this rattrap old shack and this baby. This land is mine and this child is mine." I stepped onto the porch and the cat leapt through a window, hightailed it to the chaparral, and disappeared.

I stood in the doorway imagining that mother long ago looking over the desert shimmering with heat waves, hoping some cloud would drift by, a little rain, something to cool the air. Oh, lord, is this how a mother feels? I'd watched over Ez and Zack all their lives, but I knew they weren't my children, they were family, but it wasn't up to me to teach them right from wrong, just to keep them safe and relatively clean enough to eat at the table. I would protect this child, I vowed to myself. And love it. Her. Him. I would choose a name from bold names I knew, and I would carry on and raise this one to be good. Honest. Decent. Nothing like his father.

After I got back on the saddle, I turned the mare and stared at the place. I said to the horse, "I'll bet Aubrey got this for about six bits. It's hotter than a devil's frying pan, not a speck of wind, and the only thing any woman could do to this house is to burn it down and save ol' Beelzebub the chore."

I headed home, a bit concerned when I saw a rider all in black making fast tracks away from the house. Pretty soon Pa came out the front door with a rifle and shot at the man! I was pretty sure he didn't hit him, but this was not like Pa. Ma wasn't at his side, so I kicked the mare into a gallop and didn't stop until I slid from the saddle at the front porch. Pa's gun had smoke still curling from the barrel. He had tears in his eyes.

The rock that had crashed through the biggest glass window we had in the kitchen was inside a note tied around with string.

Written in ragged hand unlike the neat printing of the first note, it said,

Be sad wen tu ninos starf to deth. Com soon or next mesig will contan hand of chico.

Mama bent over her arms on the supper table, wrenched and wailing while Rebeccah sobbed, her arms wrapped around Ma's back. I didn't feel like wailing. I felt stiff and angry and determined to set this right. I felt again that strange strength in what my friend had said, that I could swallow all the air in the room, and that it would hold me up against everything else.

Pa hadn't had any luck getting a mortgage on the ranch. The banker had told them in no uncertain terms that the place was worth more than a hundred thousand dollars, but their income from selling nuts and fruits wouldn't pay it back for forty years, and he didn't expect them to live that long. No one had wanted to buy a piece of it, either, he said, calling both their spread and mine worthless desert, fit for nothing but snakes and lizards. There was no extra money beyond what Clover had scraped together selling the red-wheeled buggy he'd bought last year to go courting in, to—of all people—Aubrey and Rachel.

That was what they'd arrived in, just as haughty as you please.

By that evening everything and everybody was settled. Of course, Aubrey and Rachel had no money to contribute to the ransom. Nope, everything was "tied up in bonds," he said. "Not liquid," he said. I couldn't understand what that meant, but I saw the face he made when he explained to me that, no, he didn't keep his money in a jar. That meant it was untouchable. "Liquid assets," he said haughtily, "are things like a checking account, or"—he cleared his throat—"your pocket change or pin money." I had a bank account. He didn't have to look so smug.

They begged Ma to come with them and be safe, but she wanted to be home in case the boys got loose and came on their own. The time had come to act, money or no. We'd take what we had for bargaining, and the rest we'd balance with lead.

Mr. Hanna senior put in some cash. All he had without going to town, he said, was five hundred dollars, but we believed him. I didn't know him well personally, but if Aunt Sarah thought well of him, that was enough for me. I studied his face a bit, trying to see any of Aubrey's features in him. Far as I was concerned, the less anyone looked like Aubrey the better. And then it came to me, a realization that might explain everything about that, too. Maybe Mr. Hanna only thought he was Aubrey's father. Maybe he wasn't. My own pa wasn't the son of the pa who raised him. Well, I'll be. Surely, a sorrel horse isn't going to produce a buckskin. Plenty of mares jumped fence. I hoped that Aubrey was not really kin to Udell Hanna. That made it easier for me to be courteous to him. By marriage, he was now my uncle. I looked right at him and said, "Uncle Udell, how come Rachel and Aubrey aren't coming with us?"

"Aubrey'd not be any use in a gunfight. Reckon his wife might be too delicate for this riding." Ah, I thought. Maybe she was at last going to have a baby.

Aunt Sarah whispered to me, "Never mind about them now. We don't want to have to take care of a tenderfoot with more brass than sense."

A large remuda of horses milled in the front round corral. Several of the hands were there, too. Brody sat on a hay bale, a dog at his feet. Now and then the dog would move and he'd pat its head.

Aunt Sarah and Udell served us steaks and beans with fried eggs and tortillas. There wasn't room in the house for everyone to sit, but the food was brought to big tables in the yard. By the time we'd finished supper we had almost everything planned. Mama would stay at home, just in case the boys got loose and came home. Gil and Charity would tend Aunt Sarah's old ranch. Granny was staying at the Hannas' place, where Aunt Sarah had made her a room of her own. They told me she'd have only some hired hands for company unless I stayed with her.

"I mean to come along," I said. "I've planned it ever since I knew."

Pa looked at me like I was a four-year-old, and Clover shook his head like I hadn't a brain in my skull.

I stuck out my chin. "Well, if you don't let me ride with you, I'll wait back and follow behind." Everyone's eyes rolled, except Brody's. My skirts still fit. They were tight, but they fit. There was no reason I couldn't go along. I felt just fine and no one knew the truth. "I'll do what I'm told. Besides, no one here speaks the lingo better than I do."

Granny raised her head from over her plate, and said, "Little Gilbert and his wife can keep me company. I'll be all right. You fetch those boys."

Gilbert cringed at being called "little," but he nodded.

"The deputies are already headed down to the border," said Brody. "They're waiting for us there, and they can't cross but we can. Maldonado wants one person, but he knows everyone here, so if he sees two or three he knows, he won't be too surprised. Then we'll split up and let the rest follow. If eight or ten more are behind, they'd come in handy."

"That's exactly what I thought," I said, although even *I* didn't believe I'd had that in my head before he said it.

Pa said, "I want the shadow bunch to stay at the border. Just me and Clover will go to Agua Prieta."

Aunt Sarah said, "Should be me and you, Albert. Clover is a good man, but I shoot better than you do."

Nobody was of a mind to argue. They knew it was true. My aunt Sarah stacked the dishes and then brought out her gun-cleaning rags and rods. As we worked, nighthawks started their evening swooping, trying to get the mosquitoes before the bats came from their caves. Their trills came from the air around about, echoed from hills to the east, and an owl crossed us overhead on silent wings. Coyotes sang to the moon, a sound that gave an eternity to the place, that life would remain the same even though it wasn't. How could I have grown up in this land, thinking I was safe and that Pa provided for us, never hungry, never afraid, rarely sick, and the worst thing Ma worried about was a few daffodils? I breathed deeply of the creosote-laden air. Watched a tarantula scaling the water trough near my brother Clove. He picked it up and sent it on its way so it wouldn't drown.

I watched the people around me with the interest of an artist, composing the scene, trying not to think that we could lose anyone else. Certainly not Pa. No one spoke for a good while. I wished I hadn't spent Pa's money on college. I wished I hadn't bought hats and dresses and all that camera equipment and the new trunk. I thought about its gleaming leather straps and buckles, filled with costly gelatin plates and stands, but I still had money left from the two thousand that Aubrey had sent. "I brought the deed to six hundred and forty acres, next to Ma and Pa's place," I said, breaking the silence. "Can't we add it to the money?"

Clover sat up straighter. "I was fixing to ask you if I could buy it, on time of course. I'd be paying you for ten years or more. There'd be no cash in it."

"Well, it's got to be worth something. I'd like to wait on you, Clove, but we have to get the boys back. I'll give the rest of my money. I've got nine hundred and thirty-seven dollars."

Pa said, "It wouldn't be right."

I stood. "It *is* right. I don't see why I can't give my money."

Aunt Sarah spoke. "Trying to sell land could take months. Even when I knew the railroad wanted Granny's land, it took a month to get the cash. We don't know anyone itchin' to buy any of our land. I've got six thousand, three hundred, and nine dollars in cash." She took a deep breath. "It ain't twenty-five."

"I've got a hundred and eighty dollars," Clover said. "Mary Pearl, would you write down what everyone wants to put in? You have a faster hand than the rest of us put together."

In a few moments of flurried activities, a lamp appeared on the outside table, bringing with it a storm of moths and other bugs. By the time I'd taken every name and every amount down, we had a total of nine thousand and sixty-seven dollars.

Ma said, "Clover, you stay home with me. We'll load up the wagon and drive to town. We'll sell the furniture on the streets if we have to. Take everything in the house. The dishes. Every last curtain. Together it ought to bring another two thousand dollars. Maybe."

In the middle of people mumbling and talking, I felt like I'd got my back up, hearing her say that. "Wait just a minute. Why do we have to pay him at all? If we've got a couple score of deputies, some Arizona Rangers, and the dozen or so of us, and we aren't fools with a gun, any of us, why are we counting up wages and cash holdings and furniture? What's he got down there, an army?"

Pa replied, "The Rangers thought so, Mary Pearl. He's at least got a dozen or so men, and you don't know what a gun battle could be like. You don't know what it's like to shoot at someone who's shooting back at you. You aren't a fool with a gun, but you aren't a soldier, either."

Aunt Sarah patted my arm, her face grim and dark, saying, "It'll make you old, real quick."

Gilbert said, "I don't see why we don't just ride in there and shoot them to blazes and take the kids." That started a whole new round of talking. I held back and listened. It seemed like I'd left a home I knew and come back to a strange place filled with familiar faces, but everything around was upside down and distorted. Dangerous. Out of focus. My head ached. For a few moments, fear overwhelmed me. I wanted to get on my horse and ride, ride far and fast, and to come home again and find it as I'd left it a few months ago. Even a year or so ago. Before Aubrey Hanna had come into our lives, before the railroad and greed had turned our good neighbors, the Maldonados, against us.

The advent of a single day had turned my life on end again. *If only* echoed through my thoughts, yet I wasn't given to wishing on stars or thinking a bent twig or the flight of an owl had meanings other than the bird was on its way and some cow had stepped on the twig. I meant to live my life taking hold of the reins, not drifting in a breeze like a seed.

In the end, long after deep darkness had settled, long after the sky filled with stars, the moon rose, and the coyotes started a new distant chorus, we simply drove home. There was nothing we could do that night. Nothing. I had been ready to saddle up and ride south at midnight. This doing nothing left me feeling like a loose wheel, purposeless.

At dawn I was up again and kissed Ma good-bye, taking some cornbread in my pocket. I picked a good mule to ride bareback to Aunt Sarah and Udell's place. Bats fluttered through the air as we loped along. I was filled with joy to see my granny sitting on their front porch in the half-light, rocking in a chair, wrapped in a shawl against the last coolness this day would hold. "Granny, it's me. Mary Pearl."

"I knows you, honey. You back from Kentucky?"

"Yes, ma'am, I'm home."

"Sit with me a spell?"

"That's why I came." I pulled my legs under me and sat on the porch at her knee. She rested her gnarled hand on my head a moment, then let it settle on my shoulder. After a long while, I said, "So much has happened, Granny. I feel like I should never have gone off to school. If I hadn't done that, none of the bad things—"

"You reckon you'da stopped the kidnappers, single-handed?"

I had only been thinking of my predicament. My *embarazada* situation. I brushed away the thought. "Well, I might have been riding with the boys, and I pay more attention to things than they do."

"Reckon they will from now on."

"Granny? You know you've asked me to keep some really big secrets. Suppose I can ask the same of you?"

"What is it, girl? You got you a fella?"

I told myself, Stop being so teary-eyed. Stop flying off the handle. But tears filled my eyes anyway. "No'm."

After a long silence, she asked, "Some man take advantage of you?"

I put my head on her knee.

"Look up here at me, Mary Pearl."

I did. Her eyes looked opaque, soft, the lenses indistinct, but staring as if she could see into my soul.

"You carrying a babe?"

"Please don't tell anyone. It would hurt so many people."

"That's what comes of a girl going off on her own. What you plan to do? Run away?"

"After we get the boys home."

At that moment Udell Hanna stepped onto the porch with two cups of coffee in his hands. "Granny, I brought—oh, well, here, Mary Pearl. I'll go get another for myself."

While he was gone, she put her lips next to my ear. "You cain't hide it fer long."

"I know. Everything was all planned. I was going to Albuquerque as a widow when I got done with school. I even thought of getting married quick to someone else. Anybody. But who knows what kind of fellow that would end up being."

"Whose baby is it? Someone we know?"

Udell returned, letting the screen door bang behind him. He had to turn quick and open it again because Aunt Sarah followed him carrying her own cup of coffee.

I couldn't answer so I looked toward the hills and said the first thing that popped up under my hat. "Sometimes nothing's better than coffee on a porch. Smells better than in the house." The three of them looked at me like I'd said something foolish. "Sorry. I suppose I'm feeling dreamy."

Aunt Sarah set her cup on the porch rail and said, "Time to mount up."

No more dreams. This was an awe-filled, terrible morning. I felt I could hear Ezra calling me and Zachary crying.

Pa and Clover rode up. My pa looked like a man I hardly knew, his face crossed with lines and his lips turned in so his mouth was but a slit in his face with bandoliers crossing his chest, one of them full of shotgun shells. An owl hooted from the corner of the roof. Then out of the door came my cousin Charlie.

"Charlie! You're here," I called, as if he needed announcing.

We had five Arizona Rangers riding ahead of us when we started south. I wore Clover's old clothes and my Stetson work hat so I'd look like a man. A small man, for sure. I was going to wear Joshua's things, but he'd left home before he was fully grown and they were so tight they actually made my round shape look rounder. I used Josh's boots, though. My heart pounded so loudly I could hear it over the hoofbeats as we rode. I liked being included with the men and my aunt. She wore her usual split skirt and a wide black Stetson. Aunt Sarah and Pa, Udell, Charlie and Clover, Brody, the Rangers, and two other hands plus myself made fourteen. Brody's dog, Checkers, followed him everywhere, and he trailed behind us, out of the way of all the hooves.

We split up the money we came with into seven different saddlebags. It made eleven thousand dollars, total, because the hands all pitched in their pay as well. We also had three mules loaded with camp gear and two more loaded with dynamite sticks and blasting caps. The Ranger boss had made a big speech about who was to do what, and he assigned everybody a job. I know he frowned when he saw me. He figured, I believe, that I was either a girl who'd scream and faint or a boy without any mettle.

With hard riding it would take two days to get to the border, and another day and a half for Pa and Aunt Sarah to reach Agua Prieta. I knew that the main reason I had been allowed to come along was that I could speak the lingo like a native, but I hoped to be of help in other ways. Silly thing was, you'd think a girl would be assigned to cooking, but that was not the case. One of the Rangers was their cook and they made me second wrangler alongside Brody. I figured he'd probably want to be boss, but I didn't care. This was about anything I could do no matter how small, to get my brothers home.

By midafternoon one of the hands declared his horse was played out and lame. We found a spot by a dry creek to camp, but Pa wanted to push on. He and Charlie got to bickering about killing the horses by hard riding against killing the boys by resting. Charlie could see my pa was just plain rattled by the whole thing, but he said another few hours in the heat of the day wouldn't change anything that happened tomorrow. Brody took a shovel and began digging under a paloverde, taking turns with Clover, and before long what had only been a damp spot became a small pool. We let the horses drink first, in case there wouldn't be enough, but thankfully it kept running and I was purely happy to have a fresh, cool canteen of that little well.

Just as I was about to take a drink, Aunt Sarah snatched it from me. "Boil first," she said. "Always boil first. You know that. We've got the fire going and the tub is ready. Pour that in it and Oscar will tell us when it's hot enough. What's wrong with you, Mary Pearl? You look plumb wore out already, like you softened up sitting in a classroom."

"Just tired. I forgot about water. I just wanted a cool drink; it's so blessed hot."

She looked at me with suspicion, asked, "They don't have typhoid in Illinois?" and I turned to settling the horses and pulling up feed bags.

That evening, the sun seemed to never set. We were all steaming with sweat, but we lit a fire and boiled drinking water, and some drank it warm. It made me feel sick, as if it would come back up. Around the

beans and tortillas, without even a grain of salt for flavoring, we talked
awhile as the shadows lengthened and a few of the men put out bed-
rolls. I laid mine between Pa's and Aunt Sarah's, because I could tell
by the stares I got from some of the men that they'd figured out I was
a girl and were none too happy to have me along. Voices stayed low.
No one brought out a guitar and settled the sun with a song. This was
unlike any herd-gathering or ranch work, where we'd ride fence all day
and settle in on the ground until sunup. A soft rhythmic sound came
from the Rangers' campfire, and when I asked Charlie what it was, he
said they were sharpening their knives. In the somber shades of dusk,
serenaded by two packs of coyotes in opposite corners of the world,
we quit talking all at once, and everyone crept into their private
thoughts.

"Aunt Sarah?" I whispered.

"Yes, honey."

"Why did Pa wait so long to come down here?"

"He was trying to get the place mortgaged. He sent a man to Maldonado's old place and told them to carry a message to him in Mexico, to please wait. That day he drove us to town to catch the train, he
sent two telegrams as well."

"I think we should have all gone down with the soldiers."

"Soldiers have a different way of doing things. So do the Rangers. They are going to hold back and let your pa go ahead and try to
reason with them. Albert is hoping Maldonado will listen to him, since
we'd been friends for so long."

"You and I are the only ones who talk the lingo good enough to
know."

"Well, Rudolfo Maldonado speaks plenty of English, too. I reckon
your pa can make his point."

"Why do you think 'El' turned so mean?"

"Don't know. Reckon a man that's got everything he could ever buy, sometimes wants things he can't buy. Power. And maybe he went crazy with guilt after he accidentally shot Elsa."

"I suppose."

"Are you feeling better? You seem out of sorts."

"Do I?" I inhaled. Was there some way I was behaving that would give away my secret before we got home? "I'm fine. Do I look sick, or something?"

"No. Pretty as ever. Maybe it's the men's baggy clothes on you. I'd gotten used to seeing you looking all grown up with a nice figure and all those pretty dresses from Illinois, and here you are dressed like a down-and-out caballero."

I touched my belly. It was only slightly more rounded than usual. "Ma always said I looked like her sister Ulyssa. Do you think so?"

"You resemble her quite a bit. At least, from when I first knew her."

"How come Mama doesn't ever talk about her except to say, 'God bless her soul, the poor thing,' and then go on about something else? I figure she did something sinful Mama doesn't want to recall."

"No. She never did anything wrong. She had some trouble. Then she caught the consumption and died."

"Trouble like in school?"

"Mary Pearl, let's don't talk about it."

"See? That's what Mama always does."

I could hear a noise, a shuffling. Then I saw my aunt's eyes reflecting the last glimmers of the firelight. She'd rolled over to face me and had to prop up on an elbow to see over Checkers's back. "She was set upon by two men who left her no choice, and it destroyed her mind."

I stifled a moan, wary of the night air's way of carrying sound. It was some minutes before I could talk again. "The poor girl. Did she give them any justice?" I pictured Aubrey's blood running to the floor.

Felt the knife hilt in my grip. Heard again the crash of the mirror he broke to hide his cruelty. Wished again I'd killed him.

"I shot 'em. Now, go to sleep."

"Yes'm." I thought how she'd said that killing a man made you old before your time. Saw again the startling face of the bandito with the red dot between his eyes. I thought what it would be like to actually do it. To carry the knowledge that you'd deprived a human of life, just like you'd butchered a calf. I'd never even stayed around for that. Always hid in the house until it was time to hang the meat. I didn't mind meat. Just didn't want to see the calf killed. I wondered if I could pull a trigger if I needed to. I marveled that my aunt had, and more than once. I guess I could have killed Aubrey after he hurt me, and I was mad enough to do it, but I didn't have heart to do it now. That was murder. Surviving things, though, that's what made a woman tough like my aunt. It wasn't that long ago that the family had fought Geronimo and Ulzana at every turn.

This being on the tear with a neighbor wasn't near so bad. Surely we wouldn't have to actually shoot anyone. After a while, I said, "You've shot a few in your time."

"Go to sleep, Mary Pearl."

Maybe I wasn't a strong person. Maybe I couldn't stand up to things any better than Ulyssa had. Maybe I'd lose my mind. Maybe Ulyssa had a baby after what happened, and that caused her to be touched. I reached out and petted Checkers and he startled. I kept my hand still, though, so he'd know it wasn't a threat. The dog turned his muzzle toward me and dropped his head back on his paws. "Good dog, Checkers." I was glad to have him lying there, but I stayed awake a long time, thinking about what it might take to lose a person's wits.

Breakfast was cold coffee, cold beans, and tortillas, and the riding was quiet, steady, and long. It was near dusk when we bedded down near the border. We'd gone toward Benson and past Fort Huachuca, then skirting south of the mountains of Bisbee, we'd made camp in a narrow bosque just into Mexico. I was exhausted to the core. My baby wiggled all day long, but had settled in, probably tired, too, as I fed the horses. My feet felt swollen and sweating in my boots, and my backside felt like it would be shaped like that saddle for the rest of my life. I made sure the horses all got an equal drink, but I'm sure they'd all wished for more, same as we did.

That night, the Rangers camped among us, the men talked more. Much as I wanted to hear, I couldn't keep my eyes open, and I slipped into sleep before I'd finished my cup of coffee. In the morning Pa and Aunt Sarah left early with Charlie, shadowed by the Rangers, to drift east into Agua Prieta a rider or two at a time, where they would try to locate Señor Maldonado or any of his bunch, along with the place where my brothers were held. I, along with a couple of hired hands and Clover, were to stay put in the bosque.

With them, it seemed, went all the determination I'd carried with me. I had wanted to pull my *pistolas* and watch their men cower. I pictured that we'd confront Maldonado and demand our boys, and he'd see the lot of us carrying pistols and rifles, and then he'd feel pity and fear, and just hand them over. Brody had told his dog, Checkers, to stick by me. He did. Like a shadow. He watched me with coyotelike eyes that missed nothing, every muscle on him ready to spring, as if I were a cow or a sheep that had to be kept with the herd. Checkers was bigger than most cattle dogs, too, probably crossed with a shepherd dog of some kind. Supposed I was expected to share my supper with him, too. I did without hesitation, though. He took each bite as politely as a dog can, and didn't nip my fingers.

I held all my thoughts to myself. There wasn't near as much to do, so after feeding our horses and the mules, I ambled a ways into the ravine, admiring the cool air coming up from the damp ground. Birds made a colorful web of sound in the air around me. Lucky for me, I found a small stream of water. The underground flow that had turned this area green came up by some rocks and dribbled slowly back into the earth, forming a pool. I went back to the campsite and brought back the horses in pairs so they could each have a good drink. Then I loaded up a bucket and took it back to camp, too, and filled every spare pan we had that could hold some water to boil it for humans to drink. I kept my eyes sharp for any movement, chased away a rattler, startled a covey of quail. All that watchfulness made me purely touchy by evening.

The next night we cooked a small supper—beans again—and bedded down early, because there just wasn't anything to do, and we all agreed to keep talking to only things of necessity. The night got cool. I laid there watching overhead, counting shooting stars, thinking of my brothers. I wondered if they could see the stars I could see. I wondered if they saw only walls of a jail cell. Or perhaps something worse, like the lid of a coffin. As we made camp and bunked down, the darkness came down like silky sheets, humid and smelling of creosote and damp soil from the lower ground.

We camped there another two days before at last a man named Buck came from the Rangers. He was nursing a knife wound and was going to keep with us, while one of the hands here rode south. Brody volunteered to go, and I wished he wouldn't, but I could not have said why. One of the hands and I cleaned Buck's wound and bandaged his side while he told us how he'd gotten separated and ambushed, stuck and left for dead by the time the other men found him. It looked like an angry opening, but we didn't have anything along to sew it up with. Another man said it didn't smell as if it had hit any organs, so he should recover if he kept it clean. Meanwhile, Buck said, orders were for everyone in our camp to hightail it back over the border and get north as soon and as far as possible. The rest of our bunch were coming, and a pack of *Federales* were only a few hours behind him.

I tied the mules carrying our packs in a string. I made sure that everything was comfortable for them, but no matter what I did, something rattled, and I felt like quiet was the best thing to be. It wasn't long before my pa and Aunt Sarah, Charlie, and all the others joined us.

Charlie shouted, "Hell for leather," and the whole bunch rode as fast as we could for a few minutes. Then we got behind a hill and he held his arm up like a military salute. From there, Aunt Sarah wanted me to lead the way, and the rest of the bunch would follow with a man riding drag a few yards behind. "Just keep the sun on your right shoulder," she said, "and pick a trail, any trail north."

Pa came up beside me and I asked, "What happened, Pa?"

His answer struck fear deep into my bones. "You're to lead, Mary Pearl. I'll take the pack mules. You ride as fast as your horse will go, as long as you can without killing him. If you hear shooting behind you, ride for home and don't look back. Got that? Don't stop, don't turn, and don't look back. Get home."

The ground got increasingly rough, and I was certain we hadn't come down this way. We crossed a moving stream and filled canteens to boil later, but after remounting we hadn't gone a hundred feet when my horse shied hard to the left. I heard a rattlesnake in the brush. Pulled my pistol. The snake was on a rocky ledge at the height of my ankle. I put a bullet through his head.

Buck came riding hard up to my side. "You knothead. You just told everyone within a hundred miles where we're at."

"I didn't think of that," I said.

"Your horse was already wide of the snake. All you had to do was ride around it. I'll ride point from now on."

"Fine," I said. The buzzard. See if I would help patch up *his* skin again. Later as we rode along, I realized he was right, but I still felt slighted by his scolding. We were coming to the top of a ridge, and I remembered the looks of it. That made me feel better, because we were so far out of my usual range that nothing looked familiar. Out of the shady trees and into the hot sun, I pulled my hat lower and kneed my horse to keep up with Buck. I started to cross that stream, but thought to water my horse. I'd already pulled reins and gotten down when Aunt Sarah was right behind me, and said, "You should not have stopped here. This is not traveling, this is running for our lives. Get that animal out of that water."

After a while we were out in the open desert. I could see that fellow Buck up ahead. He went straight and then shifted to the right where a dry wash with some creosote and mesquite hid him from our view. I looked behind to see my aunt and the men were all following me, and we kicked our horses into a run.

As I headed down between the thorny mesquites into the wash, out of the corner of my eye to the left I saw six mounted riders, charging straight toward us. They didn't have the look of uniforms. I didn't see Zachary or Ezra with them. Buck was ahead and I had figured he knew the way home, at least the way north. I followed him farther into the wash and our group came right behind me. In the bottom of the wash, Buck's horse stood and the sign on the ground was that he'd come to a quick halt. It wasn't just an open wash, but an arroyo with a floor like a dry river bed; we were in the mouth of a box canyon. High walls on three sides with a path into it but no way out.

Three men strapped with bandoliers and holding drawn pistols waited on their horses, all their guns aimed square at Buck. Behind them, a cooling fire pit and some clothes hung on bushes showed they'd been there awhile. The rest of our bunch followed and in a half a shake all our people were gathered under a paloverde tree, facing the three pistols. The others were coming up behind us. I heard a shout.

Pa, Clover, and Brody had been bested by the Rangers all bristling with shotguns, and Aunt Sarah and Buck and I stayed frozen in place between them and the banditos. Buck told the pistoleros we were hunting a wildcat that was killing our stock, but no one answered and I believed they didn't speak English. I was just about to holler out in Spanish for them to put down their guns because we were just passing through, but I heard a movement behind me. One of the Rangers spoke real good Mexican lingo, and while pushing his mount to the front of our bunch, asked them why they were stopping us, and to please just put down their weapons as our bunch had taken a wrong turn. I suspected they might either be *Federales*, gunning for anyone on their side of the border, or else Maldonado's men, hunting only us.

As they were talking, Aunt Sarah wedged her horse up so close to mine she could have been wearing my stirrups. Real low, she said, "Anything breaks loose, you make for home. Don't stop and don't turn and look." Then she shoved up so that my horse could only step back.

"I wish I had Duende," I whispered.

"You do like I tell you."

"I could—"

"No. Head for home and don't let anything stop you."

One of the banditos urged his horse forward toward the two of us. He got close to me on the other side, and tipped his head down and grinned at me. His teeth were mostly rotted and his face was laced with scars like he'd lived through the smallpox. He licked his lips and I imagined his jagged teeth might cut his tongue to ribbons. "*Este pequeño hombre es una chica.*"

He could tell I was a girl? "*Yo no,*" I said, trying to lower my voice. I ducked my head and pulled my hat down.

When I dared to peek from under my hat brim, he had raised his pistol and pointed it at my head. I felt as if a cold iron bar had laid against my backbone.

Then he turned, addressing Buck most directly, as if he were the leader of our bunch, and said in Spanish, "We have heard that a band of outlaws from the north have come here to take that which is not theirs. We also have heard that these filthy robbers have taken money from His Excellency, Señor Maldonado, who only wishes to live in peace."

The Ranger said loudly, "Maldonado has kidnapped two boys. These people are their family."

The man surprised us by speaking English next. "I have not heard of two boys." He rubbed his grizzled chin and upper lip with his left hand. "*Ha secuestrado?*" He stared hard, straight into my eyes. I could see the lust that glowed in his eyes turn to a greater hunger. Greed. "Who carries the *dinero? La chica? El dinero del rescate?*"

I heard hammers nock all around me. I was smack in the middle of a true standoff, and I stood to take the most lead if something happened. I felt my baby wiggle. Everything got hazy and gray, and I gripped my horse tight to keep from falling. She jerked against the reins, not sure what I was trying to get her to do.

Pa said to me, in a voice too animated, too forced, "Give him the money, son. You have *all* our money. Give it to him."

I only had about eight hundred dollars of it. Everyone, even some of the Rangers, had bits of it in their saddlebags. His calling me son was to save me, I knew, from atrocity, but what hit me like a brass clanging was that I should never have come. I thought I'd been helping our family, but images flitted across my mind like the flickering of camera flashes, that to save me, others might die. Pa kneed his horse again, shoving himself right between the bandito and me.

"I . . . I'll have to get down." My hands shook worse than Granny's as I stepped to the ground. My knees buckled. I reached for the saddlebag straps, and all I could think of was that I wished I'd gotten to see the Grand Canyon before I died here, sweating and trembling, at the hand of some *cabrón* bandito. I wished I'd gotten to see my baby's face. I felt the babe move again. This man could not be allowed to harm my child, I thought. Anger and determination stiffened my legs and my resolve.

While he kept his pistol aimed at me, so close to my eyes I could see that three bullets were already missing from the cylinder, I fished in the saddlebag and came up with the packet of money. It was in paper bills, folded around with a page from a Sears and Roebuck catalog, tied with string. "*El dinero*," I said.

"There's more than that," he said, leaning down, breathing in my face so that I wrinkled my lips.

"*No mas*," I said with a shrug.

Granny's memories had several pages about a great-great-grandma, who'd faced right up to British Regulars and lied and acted like a fool, all the while carrying uniforms for the Patriot army under her big skirts. I thought of that woman, small of stature like myself, wondering if her lovely, sturdy name of Resolute made her brave, and if a girl with a frilly name like Mary Pearl could do the same.

This time I spoke English, loudly. "Take it and rot, *pendejo. Los Federales* are almost here. You won't go far." I braced my shoulders.

He laughed, his face registering surprise, and grabbed the package, motioning with his pistol for the men to ride away. "*Gracias, mis amigos!*"

But I had been correct. More riders came at a gallop, five of them, all uniformed up and bristling, their saddles and bridles heavy with carved leathers and conchos. They drew weapons and spread out like a pack of coyotes, my family members in their sights, the Rangers whirling to take aim, myself in the middle, standing on the ground, Buck and the banditos beyond me in the box canyon. Everyone seemed to hold their breath. No one made a move, but from behind me, I heard the unmistakable nock of a hammer on a heavy bore.

The Mexican federal troop leader, a miniature man with a regal bearing, holstered his pistol and drew a sword. It made a chilling sound of metal against metal, sweeping from the scabbard. He held it upright against his chin and said loudly in Spanish, "In the name of His Excellency, the emperor of Mexico, I command each person here to lay down his arms. Pronto. You are all prisoners of Capitán Miguel de la Lopez de Obando. I will not repeat my order."

I watched Pa and all my family comply with his orders, slowly, slowly, putting away our defense. The banditos, on the other hand, had not lowered their guns. In fact, the laughing face that had taken the money from me had darkened to purple with rage. I didn't feel brave. All I could think of at that moment surprised even me: My mama. If this scene exploded into a hail of gunfire and we were all shot to shreds, Mama would have no one left. I'd never see her again. Only Rebeccah had stayed behind. I was the only person on the ground. Everyone else still sat their horses. Even the Rangers had complied and we were all quiet, like animals awaiting their slaughter.

The leader of the outlaws said to *el comandante,* "'These are my prisoners. I was bringing them to *you.*"

I looked from him to the soldiers. The officer in the middle whispered, "*Bajen sus armas.*" The four soldiers raised rifles at the bandits, who did *not* put down their guns, with us in the way and me on the ground. Mama. Oh, Mama.

At last the banditos lowered their guns. Old pistols, mostly, although one had a rifle under his leg in a scabbard on his saddle. The bandit leader said, "Oh, it's nothing, señor. You see, these *norteamericanos* have crossed our borders. They are prisoners, we turn over to you." He grinned again, trying to look innocent, maybe, and foolish, as if it were all just a mistake. The same look I was hoping to achieve but all I'd done was appear wide-eyed and terrified.

The *comandante* looked everyone over and chose my pa to speak to. "You, señor, *adonde,* where is your home?"

"A ranch. *El rancho.* In between Benson and Tucson."

"And why are you riding with *guardabosques de Arizona* here, this side of the border?"

"A man named Rudolfo Maldonado has sent us word that he had taken my two youngest sons. He wants money to get them back. We went to Agua Prieta to find them but no one there knows of them—"

"Stop. Didn't he tell you to come alone? That is how it is done."

"I'd go to him alone, sure enough, sir. But to travel all this way, with bandits everywhere, it isn't safe."

The *comandante* eyed the banditos, nodded, and lowered his sword at last. "And these men, *estos rufiánes*, they have stopped you from saving your sons. I, too, have sons. I wish to see them grow to men."

He looked back and forth between every face there, and before he came to me, I stepped sideways behind the rump of my horse. He dismounted and walked to where our bunch was separated from the banditos. There he made a line in the dirt with the point of his sword. "I think this is the border of Mexico. You are all on the north side. Go home, gringo, and I will make inquiries for you."

The banditos stirred their horses at that. I felt bitterly angry. "*They took our ransom money*," I said under my breath.

"*Qué?*" he asked. "Come out from behind that *caballo, pequeño soldado.*"

I kept my hat down but spoke loudly as I pointed my arm at the bandit boss. "He stole the ransom money, *él tomó el dinero, por mi hermanos.*"

El comandante urged his horse past me and straight up to the bandit so that their knees were touching. He held out his hand. "*El dinero.*" The bandit reached into his shirt where he'd stuck the paper packet of bills. Without having untied it, all of it had to be there. I smiled. I felt very proud of myself for speaking up and getting our money back. *El comandante* took the packet and opened it, throwing the wrapping paper and string to the ground. "*Cuánto?*" he asked the bandit, who had sweat running from his face.

"I think eight hundred, they said. Yes, that's it. Eight hundred dollars, American."

El comandante drew his pistol and fired on the bandit, point-blank between the eyes. Without even a change of expression, the man stiffened and leaned sideways, falling from the saddle and startling the horse of the man next to him. The remaining two banditos held their mouths open in surprise, but remained very still and quiet.

El comandante flipped the bills, counting. Then he pulled out two hundred dollars and handed them to me.

I kept my face down as I mumbled, "*Gracias.*"

I hoped he would give the rest to Pa, but he passed the money out to his men, counting, "*Un montón*, one hundred, one hundred, one hundred." He rolled the remaining bills and rammed them behind his uniform blouse. "This, *damas y caballeros*, is the cost of doing business, and will pay for me to find your sons. But I have never heard of Señor Maldonado, although I know of a *rancho grande* only twenty miles from here. That may be his. Perhaps not. Since I don't know this haciendado, it may take me a long, long time. Go to your home and do not come so close to the border again." He saluted us with his sword again, turned his horse, and galloped away, followed by his men. The two bandits that remained bolted past us and charged off in another direction, as if they were glad to get away with their lives. All of it couldn't have taken more than five minutes, but it was the longest five minutes of my life. I sighed, feeling as if I'd faced down an army all on my own.

Brody galloped toward me and lifted a whirlwind of dust as he hit the ground right in front of me. "This was a big mistake, letting you come here. A big mistake! I'm—I'm just *fit*, that's what. Fit to be tied. What do you think you are doing talking to that man? Don't think for one minute he couldn't tell you are a girl!"

Pa and Clove came up behind him and dismounted, too. I thought they'd take up for me and tell him to pipe down, but instead Pa said, "Yes, it was a mistake. Mary Pearl, I want you to go home."

I said, "Why are you mad at me? All I did was try to get the money back."

"If you'd kept quiet, he might not have killed that man," Clover said.

"Are you telling me you wouldn't have said anything?"

Pa raised his voice, and the anger on his face cut me to the bone. "We are lucky to be out of here with our skins. I want you to get on home. Leave the pack mules here. It's a day's ride and Clove can go with you. We'll make another plan with the Rangers and head south again from Sarah and Udell's place."

I could hear him muttering the word, "Trouble," as I swung into the saddle with one move. I was beginning to like riding in pants, for sure, but here was everyone mad at me again, as if *they'd* never have spoken up for our money. Now we had even less to get our boys home and we'd wasted another whole week. Ezra and Zack could be long dead by the time we found them. "Fine then," I said. "I'm going home." I kicked my mare too hard and made her swing her back hooves up. Without a word to anyone, I started north. Soon enough I heard horses behind me.

I shouted, "I don't need you two sorry cayuses following me. Get on back there."

Clover didn't rankle easy, but he looked red in the face. "I just hoped you would sit quiet and let the men handle things."

"I didn't see any *men* handling anything," I said. "And you, Brody Cooperand, what makes you think I need you along?"

"Everything I've seen you do since you got back from that eastern girls' school, that's what."

"Oh, my lands. The two of you." I galloped ahead so they couldn't hear what else I was saying. I'd heard my aunt Sarah let out with some spicy words now and then, when she was peeved beyond containing, but this was the first time in my life that they came to me as naturally as if I had always been used to airing my lungs like a mule skinner.

CHAPTER TWELVE

"Mama, I'm home. Mama?"

She wasn't in the kitchen or in the bedroom. I found her out watering the garden wearing a wide straw sombrero. "Oh, Mary Pearl! Have you come with the boys?"

I fell into her arms. "No, Mama. Only Clover and Brody. We couldn't find Zack and Ez. Pa and the Rangers went clear to Mexico and no one heard of them." I hung my head. "It was a terrible time, Ma. We got captured. This general from the Mexican government shot a man standing in front of me right in the face. He shot him for stealing our money, but then he stole the money from the bandito. Everyone was mad at me, and wanted me gone. All I wanted to do was help."

"Ah, honey. Sounds to me like they couldn't do any good, either. Better you stay here."

"Mama, you're so skinny."

"No one here to cook for. I just pick at things. I never had no one to cook for before. Granny's going to come live here for a bit, so both of us won't be so lonely. I'm trying not to give up hope but I don't feel like eating."

I collected myself for a spell, just being quiet, the way she liked to handle things; thinking and praying and quietness was what she lived by. After a while I said, "I want to take a bath."

"Look on the kitchen window first. There's a letter for you from a lady in Illinois."

I left Mama in the garden and walked through the kitchen. It usually smelled like supper of some kind, but today it only smelled of desert heat and dust and tired, old, wooden furniture. The letter was from Prairie. They'd gone to Niagara Falls and Rome for a honeymoon. She was setting up house in Chicago in a good district. She went to the symphony every month and she had two maids. Bully for her, I thought. It all seemed too far away to imagine I had been for a while in a college in Illinois. I had thrown snowballs and here it was 112 by the thermometer nailed to the door out back. I had learned to compose photographs and develop prints wearing protective aprons and gloves, and I had dreamed of traveling more and wearing city clothes and riding in buggies to the symphony. The letter closed with, "Write back and tell me of your adventures. I hope you are having a lovely time and that you are as happy as I am."

Disheartened and angry, I dropped the letter on the table and went out to the screened-in bathtub room behind the house and started pumping water. I had to pick a skinny tarantula out of the bathtub. Poor thing was nearly starved from being trapped in the tub with no scorpions to eat. I set him down by the door where he could easily crawl away, since I'd already stripped off my dusty old clothes. I stepped into the water, cool from the earth, and covered myself with Aunt Sarah's homemade soap. Then I cried and cried as if I would spend my last breath doing it.

I had ruined everything. I gave away our place by shooting that snake. I cost a man's life by asking for our money. Maybe he'd have died anyway. Maybe we wouldn't need the money the officer kept.

Maybe it was too late to save my brothers. My own life was a mess, too, and all I'd wanted to do was find our boys before I ran away from home to have a baby in Albuquerque and never see my family again. Everything was a disaster, and I was the biggest landslide in the middle of it. Prairie's letter only confirmed how different our lives were. How tidy and sorted out it had seemed in Wheaton, and how rambling and dusty and dangerous it was here. I wished I'd married Nation Hollingsworth and stayed in Chicago.

Yet all this would still be happening. They wouldn't have told me or come to get me. I just wouldn't have been here to help. Or likely, I wouldn't have been here to make a mess of everything, shooting at snakes and having to see a murder less than six feet from my face. That was different than being shot at and shooting back, like Aunt Sarah had warned. That was just murder and it made me want to vomit. I wept so violently I nearly drowned from bobbing my face in the bathwater.

I heard Clover call out. Since the bathing room had only got walls halfway up and screen on the top half, it was our rule to holler forth if someone wanted in, so they didn't alarm anyone who might be in there. "You drowning in there?"

"I'll be out in a minute," I croaked, and sucked down my tears.

That evening, Clover and Brody ate supper with Granny, Ma, and me. Ma declared she was happy to have someone to cook for, but I can't imagine why any woman would welcome standing over a hot stove in the summertime. I listened as the men talked about everything on the farm that had gone bad while we'd been off on a wild-goose chase. Then they talked about where Maldonado had gone and where our brothers were.

Then Brody looked straight at me and said, "You look like you've been crying for days."

My lips started to tremble again. I felt very aware that my skirt waist was hiked up in front a bit, and that I'd gotten round. I only said, "I've never seen a man shot through the head only six feet away from me. Even if he was bad. I've never seen that before."

He turned away, shaking his head.

Mama sighed. "No, of course not. I thought times had changed, but not so much. Up to now, honey, you've been spared many things I grew up seeing."

I stared at her a moment, my mouth hanging open. I'd heard all about their struggles. I knew Pa's face sagged on one side from being shot across the skin above his ear, but I never had imagined what it looked like before then, or what it might have been to witness such a thing. I'd never imagined a gun pointed at my head, or thought that I could die any second before I'd even begun to live my own life. I said, "I'm not cut out to be strong as you, Mama."

Granny looked up from her plate. I thought she'd fallen asleep. "Ever' woman has her troubles. Is it Comanches?"

I heard a buggy pull up outside and voices. Mama said, "That'll be Rebeccah and Dr. Pardee." While she left the table to go to the door, I stared at my plate, and when I looked up Brody was staring at me like I'd grown two heads.

"Something on your mind?" I asked. "You look like you've got something stuck in your craw."

"I would just like to know why you're so all-fired set on acting like a man."

"Don't be silly. I'm not."

"Prancing around wearing men's pants. Riding out like a wet-eared boy trying to do a man's job. What's got into you since you went to that college?"

"Nothing—well, nothing. What's it to you? You think you have something to say about my life?" I drank some water.

"I can tell you *one* thing—" and then he stopped because Rebeccah and her fiancé, Dr. Pardee, and some old woman came into the room with Ma.

I was looking hard at Clover, sitting there, not minding at all if this hired hand talked to me like a child needing a paddling. Clove at last caught eyes with me and his brows flew up, he stifled a grin, and stood, welcoming the ladies to the table. Brody muttered something about washing up outside. I frowned and stuck my chin at him, but he wouldn't look my way again.

Mama said, "Mary Pearl? Say hello to Miss Flanagan, Dr. Pardee's aunt, who came along as a chaperone for them," and she was giving me a look as if she'd already said it once before.

I said hello, and dished them up some supper. Staying busy with my hands was a good way to swallow my sadness. Wasn't there something in Granny's memories about that, too? Maybe that was why all the women in this family worked so hard.

In just a little while, the sun's angle was no longer striking the front porch and we took coffee out on the chairs set all around. I told Mama I'd wash dishes, and soon as I said that Brody stood up and started for the kitchen, too, but Rebeccah said she'd help, and he turned right around and went outside. Soon as we were done, we joined the rest of them, but just as I sat down Clover disappeared into the house. I could hear him going up the stairs the way he and my brothers always did, two or three at a time. He came right back down with Brody's guitar and handed it to him. Not a word of why it was in our house, but there you are. Always felt lately like my brother was up to something.

Brody picked some tunes. Rebeccah and the doctor, whose name was Robert, made moony eyes at each other, and Ma and Miss Flanagan talked about cabbage. Cabbage soup, cabbage fritters, boiled with onions and potatoes. My best opinion of cabbage is that chickens like to eat it and the more they eat of it, the less I have to.

"Well," I said, "I'm tired. I'm going in to bed."

Brody kept on playing, but he looked toward me for a moment, and just for a split second, he didn't look mad but kindly, with gentleness in his eyes, which was the first time he'd looked like that in a hundred years, I'd bet. Then, what did I care? Just another pair of big stinky feet around the house, that's all he was. Him and Clove caught eyes together and then he turned back to me with a little smile and a flush on his face.

Clover announced, "Me 'n Brode are gonna sleep out here on the porch. Doc, you can join us. It's cooler than the girls will have upstairs."

"My room is just fine," I said. "Third floor pulls all the air up the stairs and it's plenty nice. Rebeccah can sleep in Esther's old bed in my room. We'll make up a bed for you in the twins' room for privacy, Miss Flanagan." I didn't say the rest of what I was thinking, which was that now we'd have to wake up and share the outhouse with just as many people as usual, and one of them was that Brody Cooperand and why in blasted cow pies didn't he just ride on home to Aunt Sarah's bunkhouse where he belonged? What was he doing sleeping on our porch? Then, I thought, perhaps, just perhaps, the banditos followed us. Or the *Federales*. Of the two, the last was the most frightening.

Once I remembered that, I guessed I didn't mind the men being there overmuch. At any rate, by the next morning I didn't remember my head hitting the pillow. It was full light when I woke the next day. Rebeccah's bed was already made and the house was silent. I knew chores started early, and I felt ashamed of sleeping so long, but even with the guilt, a lingering drowsiness kept me moving slowly. I didn't even dress, but put on a wrapper and went downstairs to find some breakfast. I found the coffee gone cold on a sideboard, next to some sliced bread already curled up and dried. I doused some milk in my cup and dipped bread in the coffee and milk mixture, and it struck me how it was sparse fare, but so much more to my taste than what we'd had on the trail. I reread Prairie's letter while I ate.

I found my family sitting on the porch. That alone was so unusual it gave me concern, but everyone smiled and greeted me. Pa had come home during the night, but Dr. Pardee and Miss Flanagan had left at first light, they said. Brody had gone back to Aunt Sarah's since she'd be home now. His guitar still leaned against a wall behind a pot of aloe.

Ma had a Bible open on her lap, but her arms were crossed, as if she'd already said what she'd meant to say. Clover spoke up first, saying, "I never could have guessed we'd come to this. We have to get the boys back."

"Where did all the Rangers go?" I asked.

Pa said, "They said they were sorry, but there was no trail to follow. If we get another notice or other information we should send them a wire. That's all they could offer." He walked to the far end of the porch, then came back and put his hands on my shoulders. "I know you want to help, Mary Mine, but I fear for your mother home alone. Heard you popped a snake with a hip shot. I need you here."

"I want to find my brothers, Papa," I said with tears again filling my eyes. "If it's the last thing I do."

"This is how you help us do that."

Mama at last turned to me and said, "Please, Mary Pearl?"

"Yes, ma'am, Mama." I wanted to say, "But you'll have Rebeccah here for company," although I knew in that same instant that company didn't mean safety, and that Rebeccah had never in her life pulled the trigger on a gun, and so maybe Pa wasn't just being protective of his women. Maybe he really needed me here.

Pa and Clover set out for Aunt Sarah's house. They were planning to collect Udell and Charlie, and head south to the Cochise County sheriff and see if they could raise either some information or a posse. They took all the money with them.

Mama watched them ride away, and said, "Mr. Hanna will be good help."

"No telling," I said. "If he's like his son, probably not."

"You're sure sour on Aubrey, aren't you?"

"I have my reasons."

"Well, Rachel wrote that they are going to come visit again next week. By then the boys will be home. We're going to want to set up all the summer beds on the porch while they're here. I have new potato sacks that I want you to thread on the rods for cooling. Beccah will help you."

I stared at her a moment, wondering if she'd lost her mind, but I said, "Yes, ma'am." I should write to Prairie of my lovely adventures. Seeing a man shot between the eyes and hanging hemp bags on wires to pour water over, just to try to get a night's sleep. Sometimes we even wet down our sheets, just so we can escape the roasting temperatures. I wished I was back in Illinois. Wished I was at the Grand Canyon. Or Kentucky.

While we worked on hanging the curtains and making beds, I asked, "Ma, is Brody going down with them?"

"I don't know, honey. Why do you ask?"

"Well, Aunt Sarah would be all alone then. She should stay here, too, until all the men get back."

Granny walked out onto the porch and took a rocking chair. "Come over here, girl," she said. We all took notice but I moved toward her first. She reached for my hand. "I want to add something to my memories. You got 'em hid, like I told you?"

I bit my lip. "Yes'm. I didn't tell anyone else."

"*I've* let the cat outta the bag," she said, pursing her lips with a frown.

I nodded. "I'm sure we can trust Mama and Beccah to mind what you ask." They smiled and nodded as well.

I sat for an hour and wrote her words while she went on about how to cook a wild rabbit so you don't catch rabbit fever. Granny fell to sleep in the middle of her last sentence. I just set the pencil down on the papers near her, and put a rock on the stack so it wouldn't blow away.

Rebeccah leaned in close and whispered to me, "Why doesn't she want anyone to read her memoirs?"

I thought a minute, struggling with telling an outright lie and finding a way to smooth out the truth. Then I said, "There's nothing in there except a person getting on through a hard life. You know she was young during the big war. I reckon she doesn't want to answer any questions. She had some things to say, that's all. You know how Granny will say things that don't fit what's going on, or seems like she's addled? Well, after listening to her tell me all these tales about her life and things her granny and great-granny told her, and putting them all together in light of what's happened at the minute she decides to say something, what I believe is that her words are coming from some distant time, and seem out of place the way we hear it, but all her life is one huge supper table, and it's her going around taking a bit of that dish and a bit of this one. Some of it is sweet relishes and some is bitter and harsh. It goes together, but not in our listening order. It comes out in her tasting order. She ain't addled at all. Her table's just full." My words surprised my own heart. I hadn't ever put into a statement what had become my inner knowledge. I felt proud.

Rebeccah stared at her hands, then looked up at Mama with tears in her eyes. She kissed my cheek and the tears spilled over onto my face. She wrapped her arms around Granny, as tenderly as if she were a dried leaf that might crumble. Rebeccah whispered again, "Granny, you are so dear. Please don't ever die." The older lady didn't wake.

Then my older sister looked at me and said, "I've never been jealous in my life before. Not of anything or anybody. But right this minute I'm jealous of what Granny gave to you."

"I understand, Beccah. I'll let you see it when the time is right. I promise. For now, as she says, secrets are heavy things to carry." With that, I thought how I treasured Granny's memoirs, too. I vowed to read them over again, soon as I got some daylight and solitude, even if I had to go sit in the henhouse.

Nights on the sleeping porch were my favorite place to be. It was warm, sure, but on our side of a hanging blanket it was just us women there, and we slept in our thinnest cotton gowns with wet burlap curtains hanging everywhere. With a little breeze it got so cool I pulled a quilt over me. Hard to see stars through the screens and waving burlap bags. But the moon was full and I heard coyotes on a distant hill and a puma roaring somewhere. An owl sat on our chimney and hooted three times. Moonlight hit the side of the house and I felt filled with contentment. The sounds of the desert and home. Sure, we were missing our fellows, but they'd return, I just knew it. I simply claimed it as fact, with nothing to prove it. I figured they'd come up from wherever they were being kept like a picture comes up on a paper after a time in the developing. The time would come when I'd have to leave. Maybe I'd have to tell Mama and Papa why. It would break their hearts, but I'd leave so as not to shame them. Maybe if the boys get home I'd light out of here before I had to tell them. Before anyone could see how my body was changing. For I could see it every day. Plumped all over like a ripe little hen. I repeatedly told Mama I was hot and wanted to wear my big sisters' baggy old shirts and skirts.

The sky had started to green in the east and the moon hung like a beacon in the morning light, brighter than ever. Someone banged on the screen door post. A dog barked. "Hello, the house," a man's voice called. It wasn't sharp and frightening, but in the stillness before dawn, it seemed loud. "I've come for Miss Mary Pearl. She out here? Checkers, be quiet."

"Brody, is that you?" Ma asked. That startled me because I hadn't known she was awake.

"Yes, ma'am. There's a problem. Gil and I were out all night riding fence."

I stood in front of him wrapped in my quilt, my hair hanging down, not even braided. "Why do you need me?"

Brody ducked his head, embarrassed. He wouldn't look at me. "We think we found your horse, Duende. He's alive but bad. If I didn't know who owned him, I'da put him down, but since the animal belongs to you, you should decide."

Brody had saddled my mare. I didn't ask questions. I followed him, so thankful he'd found Duende, and yet terrified of what I would see. Checkers wove in and out between the horses' hooves for a minute, then ran wide of our path. Our horses kept up a good lope for several miles and then Brody slowed. He got off his mount and walked slowly down a steep sandy canyon, picking his way in the dim light.

A dark form writhed in the shadows. The dog came running back and Brody pointed at the ground. Checkers immediately got in his herding position and got quiet. I had to trot to catch up to Brody; he was walking fast then. I heard a horse whimper.

I'd like to say I knew it was my horse, but honestly it was just a horse in pain. I'd never heard Duende make that noise. Brody said, "Climb up here," and held out his hand. I took hold and leapt onto the boulder. The sun had cleared the hills enough that it showed the sight below the boulder. Struggling just lower than our reach, my magnificent stallion lay, bloody and trapped. His nose was bound to his foreleg with a strand of barbwire that disappeared under his belly. The leg, the only one we could see, looked broken. The shoe was almost off and the hoof had a crack. The rest of his body was caught between the large boulder and another that must have come down on top of him.

Brody had helped me up on the rock, but he had not let go my hand. I was glad. I squeezed his hand with mine for a second and tried to look closer. He looked full in my face with real sorrow. "Can we get him out?" I asked.

We crept closer, and the pearly green daylight revealed what I hadn't wanted to see. The horse was sorely wounded, flesh hanging off his back. Duende murmured and breathed hard, every movement a fight against agony. The signs of large claws and teeth tearing at his neck told a tale of a big cat. A trail of blood and torn-up ground led from about ten yards away where a stand of trees had made tempting shade as well as a trap where a mountain lion could wait. Looking down at this tortured animal that had been my pride, I felt hard and cold. It was our way never to let an animal suffer, but he was mine and I wanted him. Against all warnings that he was too much horse for me, that he was too big and wild and beautiful, he was mine and I wanted him and I would not shoot him until I knew that there was no hope at all.

I dropped Brody's hand and found a hefty branch to pry away the stone. Brody took hold, too, yet when we heaved on it the branch broke in half. Duende moaned. Then he began to fight and writhe again. To me it tore my heart like a scream.

"Here comes Gil," Brody said.

Gilbert showed up sitting on the back of a huge draft Belgian and had brought a stack of blankets and ropes, things I hadn't even thought to bring. He got that old Belgian up on a slope and threw Brody a rope. I helped him get it around the jagged boulder that was pinning Duende in place. With a simple "hup," the massive horse started to pull, and the stone rolled away. It kept on tumbling, and to keep his horse from going with it, Gil cut the rope.

When I saw the rest of Duende's wounds, I thought my heart would quit beating. He was trying to stand. Brody and I rushed to him with blankets to cover his skin and to shield ourselves from the barbwire. It cut through, anyway, piercing my sleeves and my breasts. Brody spoke in words so soft I almost couldn't hear. "Take his head. Hold him as still as you can. I've got wire cutters. We'll get his head free from the leg first."

I felt as if my heart was banging in my brain by the time we got him standing and quieted.

Gilbert looked mighty sad. I turned to Brody and asked, "Is he going to live?"

"I don't know."

"If this was any other horse would you shoot him?"

"Yes."

I breathed in and out slowly. "But might he be saved?"

"Mary Pearl, you could do everything humanly possible for this horse and a year from now he'd fall over dead. I'd say he's got a small chance."

I raised the pistol from my right holster.

"I'll do it," he said.

"No. He's my horse." Then I put the gun back in the holster.

Gil stepped in closer. "My ma's place has got a rig for a broken leg. If we can get him there, I'll sling him up."

We put blankets under Duende's belly and cut holes in the corners of the blankets, threading them through with giant stitches of rope. We tied the ropes so he was lying in a sling and only had to use his three good legs. I tried to hold Duende's nose and put a soft bosal on him. I walked between Gil and Brody on their mounts, Duende hobbling.

"Where are we?" I asked after a while.

Gil said, "You're west of Maldonado's place. I forget the name of the gorge. We have about seven miles to go."

I stopped and turned. "We're past Maldonado's? What were you two doing riding fence down here? Your ma doesn't have fence down here. I'm sick and tired of people lying to me."

At last, Brody said, "Following buzzards. Looking for your brothers."

"Ah," I said. "I hadn't thought of that."

My cousin Gil looked sad but not sheepish. "Any answer is better than no answer, Imp. I saw buzzards and heard a puma this morning early. Thought it might be them."

"Let's get this horse home," I said. There was nothing else I could say. They'd put into action what I'd thought without saying. That my brothers could be long dead, lying in a shallow trench, eaten by animals and their bones picked by buzzards.

Later, Gilbert left Brody and me in the barn and rode off to tell everyone. It was under a mile. It wouldn't take long. We spent the afternoon trying to soothe him and wrap the wounds.

Charity came out to the barn saying Gil got back and was eating supper. She was carrying a pillowcase full of clean clothes along with a basketful of biscuits, a jug of hot pinto beans, and a bowl of cut-up tomatoes. I told Charity thank you, and decided she wasn't a complete ninny after all. But then she insisted I come into the house and sleep with her and let the men sleep in the barn with the horse.

"No," I said. "Duende's my horse. My responsibility. If he's going to pull through I want to be here. If he isn't—then I want to be here."

"You can't sleep in a barn with a strange man."

"He isn't a strange man. He's Brody." It didn't dawn on me what she was inferring until I said that. The shadows lengthened and my resolve crumbled as I watched her walk away carrying the dishes. Brody was washing his face in the horse trough, mopping his wet hair with his handkerchief. "I hope you don't think I am, well—nothing. Are you a strange man?"

"Nope. Kinda regular, I 'spect."

"That's what I thought."

"I'll watch first. You can lay that blanket there on the hay."

"Call me, if anything."

"I will. You'll have to take a watch sooner than you hope, on accounta I'm tired to the bone, being up all night last night."

"Then you take the blanket. I mean it. I feel wide awake and full of starch. I stink to high heaven." There was no sense in washing up just to lie down in a stall.

He seemed to be thinking it over just a bit, then nodded. I don't know what he was agreeing to—whether it was the smell of me or his need to sleep—because he didn't say another word. Just curled himself on the blanket and dropped off. Checkers came into the barn and it made Duende uneasy. I let him lick out my bowl of beans then led him over to where Brody was deep in sleep, and told him to lay there. That dog did just what I said as if he could understand every word. Gilbert checked on us before going back in the house, but he'd be out again if we needed him.

I lay next to Duende and put my head on my canteen with one hand on the horse's neck.

Morning came and Brody was up, changing a bandage when I awoke. "How is he?"

"Holding on."

Duende looked pathetic. The broken ribs were so obvious, caved in on his side. His breathing was shallow. Other bones made outlines on his skin, too. He was starved. I asked again, "Are we doing the right thing?"

"If you came upon this horse in this shape, and he wasn't yours, what would you say?"

The horse was fluttery. In pain. I said, "I'd say I gave him that name because I thought he was grander than any horse ever was. I'd say I've figured out that I can't give any man nor beast a heart and soul just because I wish it on him. He isn't ever going to stand on that leg proper. He may never get his wind back. But I don't mind feeding him the rest of his days. I won't give up on him, even if he's not like before, but he's a horse. I don't aim to be childish about it. I want to do what's right for the animal."

"Then let's give him a chance, and see what tomorrow brings. Decide every day if it's fair to him. Maybe every hour."

"Would you spell me awhile so I can go home and clean up?"

By the time I got back, there were other voices coming from the barn. My cousin Charlie had showed up. I said, "I'm glad you're here. I want to see if we can backtrack Duende's path before he fell. If he had that split hoof before the puma jumped him, and he escaped from whoever has the boys, we should be able to track it easily."

Charlie exchanged looks with Brody and said, "She's smart as a whip."

"Only you aren't going to do that," Brody said to me. "You're going to stay here and Charlie and me'll go."

Charlie pulled his pistol and blew through the barrel before he reloaded it. "I'm ready. Gilbert's wife a good cook?"

"Not bad," Brody said.

"We'll take anything she's got ready and light out now while the sun's got a good angle for tracking."

But then Gilbert came to the barn and offered to sit with Duende until we came back so I could go with the men. Charity said she'd walk back to my house and tell Ma what I was doing. "That okay with you boys?" I asked. I believe they couldn't grudge me coming along, because they just nodded.

We found the boulders easily enough. Trouble was, on so much hard rock there wasn't much track. We kicked our horses up a trail and got to the top of a hill. It grew steep the last twenty feet or so, and we had to lead our mounts and go on foot. I was proud of myself for thinking of this, and prouder still to be the first one to spot a large cat's paw print. Before long Charlie had found horseshoe prints, heading toward the steep area. From the edge we could see a definite track where the horse had tumbled once the cat had him by the neck and back. It must have sprung from some brush and ridden Duende down the hill. Might be that the tumble dislodged the cat, and otherwise the horse would have been dead already.

We spent the better part of three hours on foot from there, and walked down and up that hill a dozen times apiece. In the distance a line shack seemed a likely place to hide a horse, but we rode up to it and there was nothing to see. It stunk like the drifters who might have spent a night there were none too particular about how they used the place, either.

Charlie whistled long and sharp, like you'd call another drover.

"You see something?"

"Riders."

Brody said, "Let's get on back to the house. They look like our people. There ain't nothing here."

The riders turned out to be a couple of Rangers, just out poking around. They'd seen nothing, either, they said, except for a trail of moccasin footprints from that little shack back to Maldonado's old hacienda. They'd snooped around the place, even shot a bullet through a window and disturbed nothing but spiders. They'd eaten tamales from the old woman at the hacienda. She told them that she and her man kept some shovels and tools in the shed, and they'd just come to retrieve them so they could put up a garden. It was harmless.

We headed home.

That night I spent with Duende again. He was fevered and you could just about feel heat coming off him like he was on fire inside. What else could we do for the poor animal?

The next day, Ma walked down to Aunt Sarah's barn, and Gilbert and Charity came. Brody and I stood by Duende, holding his head. The horse breathed shallowly, and kicked up with one hind leg, trying to roll or to stand or something. His eyes were all sunken and sick. Funny thing was, even though I knew what the answer was, I looked to Brody for some kind of hope that there was a choice.

Brody said, real softly, "The leg would heal. But the missing skin on his neck, all the cuts on his back, everything's festered. If you feel him there, the heat has given him the bumps." It was true. Small mounds of infection had risen on his legs. I didn't know what they were called, but I knew what it meant.

Aunt Sarah said, "I rinsed it with salt water while you were gone yesterday. But, Mary Pearl, it's gone bad."

The horse grunted and snuffled, whining in pain. "I'll do it," I said. Gilbert took my pistol from me but I grabbed it back. "I said I'll do it. He's my horse. If . . . if someone else could handle getting him out of here."

"It isn't your fault," Brody said.

"I know it. This is at the feet of whoever stole him. Look how skinny he is. They didn't take care of a fine animal, even before he made a break for it. You all go on now. I don't want anybody to watch."

Everyone except Brody did as I asked, filing out of the barn to stand outside in the blistering afternoon sunlight. I walked around Duende, petted his nose. His eyes stayed closed but his ears went back. Tears overwhelmed me for a moment. "There ain't nothing for it; we've done all we can," I said to him through grimacing lips.

I stood up and drew a deep breath, but someone pushed my hand down. Brody took the pistol from me. Looking into my eyes, he pushed my shoulder and turned me, then pulled the trigger close to Duende's head. The sound made me shake all over. Soon as they heard the sound the whole family came back inside the barn.

Brody said, "You go wash up. Me and Gil and some of the hands will take care of it."

"All right."

Ma said, "Come on home, honey."

Later that afternoon after I'd changed, I walked alone down to Cienega Creek and hung my feet in the water. I dipped my handkerchief in, too, and wrung it out and mopped my face. I didn't cry. I just felt old. Old as the rocky bank I sat upon. Old as time. I heard a horse whicker somewhere off, and my heart pained on the hearing of it, just like I imagine when people say they have heartache. Now I knew what that felt like. I knew animals having to be put down. Any ranch or farm is full of that. I just always believed that horse would live out his days in a pasture. I laid back and looked through the leaves of a mesquite where it tangled into a cottonwood tree.

I pulled on my stockings and boots, and picked up a handful of rocks. One at a time I let every one of them fly into that creek, some close, some far. When I got to the last two, I thought of Ezra and Zachary. I squeezed those two little stones. Then I wrapped them into my kerchief and tied a knot around them and tied it back around my neck where it gave a cool, soft comfort.

CHAPTER THIRTEEN

Rebeccah had some kind of stew cooking on the stove, by the smell. But she was on the porch along with some grizzled old fellow we'd never seen before.

"He doesn't seem to speak a word of English," Rebeccah said. "I offered him some water, but he didn't want it. Can you talk to him, please?"

Mama just looked sort of helpless and questioning at the man. "*Que es?*" I asked. "*Que paso?*"

"Teen tou-sand doe-lors. Quick, quick. Teen tou-sand. *O los chicos están muertos.*"

Ten thousand dollars. It didn't take a translator to understand that. "*A donde los chicos?* Where are they?" I demanded. "Wait a minute. Have I seen you somewhere before? Weren't you with those banditos on the road to Mexico?"

The man flung something dark and shriveled like a large dead bat at Ma's feet. She screamed and clasped her hands to her face, reeling against the door jamb. It looked like a human hand. He said, "Get money *o los chicos* will hang. *Llevarlo a la estación de Marsh. Cinco.* Five days."

He got on his lathered old mule, a ragged-eared, U-necked critter barely standing, and rode south.

Rebeccah was the first of us to get hold of her senses. "We have that much, Mama. We have ten thousand and a little more. We can get them." Mama teetered back and forth as if she was faint on her feet. Beccah said, "Come on in the house, Ma. Come sit. Pa will be home soon."

When the men got back from burying Duende, they were sweating and ragged themselves. I was thankful they hadn't asked me to take part in the shoveling. Charlie, Gilbert, and Brody all had helped, making up a family that felt as close as if we were brothers and sisters.

Charlie was the first one who got the gumption to pick up the hand and look it over. "This," he declared, "is not from a boy the size of your brothers. This is an old man's hand, mummified, the way they get, buried in the hot Arizona sand." It was true. I've seen a mummified cat and a pig, all shrunken, black, and shriveled, but every inch of skin intact, heated and dried like raisins or prunes, like you could add water and plump them back to life. The hand was not Ezra's or Zachary's. I spread my fingers wide, knowing Ez's hand was the size of mine, and this hand was as big as Pa's. Charlie took the thing in a bucket and said he'd go bury it with the horse, because the caliche had been broken up and he didn't relish digging another hole tonight.

I don't know if anyone slept that night. The talk went on until just ruminating set in, then people would talk some more. Finally Rebeccah went to bed and Mama lay on the settee in the parlor. I knew I wouldn't sleep. Couldn't. I strode the floor of my room, restless and hotter than I could ever remember being before. My baby wiggled in different places now, so that I could imagine tiny feet and hands. I had to tell them or run away soon. I'd wait another week until the boys came home. Or if they didn't. That's all I had. I decided to pack.

I opened the trunk with my camera and all the plates. There were some good ones in there of Duende. Maybe I'd take a few hours to develop some. I'd take more photographs. Five days. My little brothers. They'd probably have changed. They'd been kidnapped for six weeks now. Probably not fed well. Hopefully not mistreated in any other way. Oh, please, let it not be in any other way. One thing was true, though. I felt, or believed, that now I could not just up and leave my family and home without telling everyone why. I pictured it would break Ma's heart anew.

I'd be strong. Determined. I'd make a way for myself. Even without the Grand Canyon, I could take a few more plates here. The summer thunderstorms should start any day, and clouds made nice backdrops. Almost anything would make a nice scene well lit and developed. All we had to do was take ten thousand dollars to Marsh Station where everyone in the area picked up their mail, five days from now. I figured then, the boys will be home, and I'll wait just two or three days longer and confess my situation, and get ready to leave. They might disown me. I'd take my camera and my plates and make a life. That's what. I already felt determined.

Toward sunup, I heard distant thunder. The rains were coming at last. That meant an end to cool breezes in the morning and stifling humidity all day. It meant roaring thunderstorms and sometimes wildfire. It also meant no more carrying water to the garden, and instead hoping the vegetables didn't drown or wash away. It meant streams would run, and blood would run down your face and arms from mosquito bites. I dressed carefully, and wore my heaviest boots and widest hat. I packed ten plates in my camera box and carried all of the equipment downstairs a few at a time.

The house was quiet and the storm was miles away. Hopefully I could get out and back before they rose. After all, I doubted anyone slept before midnight and it was barely four forty-five. I left a note for Mama.

All my developing chemicals were in our barn. I'd set up and make some prints when I got back. I saddled the little mare, Fixie, and tied everything down just like I liked it, well-balanced, not likely to make a slip. At the last second, I saw my pistol belt hanging in the barn, and I strapped that on, too. Never know when you'll meet a snake out in the desert.

I rode south for half an hour, turned my head so as not to look upon the disturbed mound of Duende's grave. Thunderheads gathered in the distance and orange lights flicked at their centers—lightning that circled the clouds and didn't come to earth.

Farther up a steep slope, I stopped at the top. From there, the thunderclouds appeared to be closing in. Mighty unusual to come in the morning, too. They were some of them a dark blue, some tinged with pinks and golds. In one place the whole sky became a color that reminded me of a piece of turquoise stone under water. A bit too blue. Lightning shot from cloud to cloud and forked across the sky. Oh, how I wished I could photograph the colors. My poor skill mixing paints would never capture what I saw. If I tried it would look ridiculous and no one would believe the colors of this sky or the straight shaft of a cloud burst of rain drenching the land below it miles from where I stood. I set up the camera and studied carefully, held my breath. Hoped for lightning. Opened the aperture. Counted. Closed it. Pulled the plate and put a second one in. I moved the camera a few inches to the right. I waited and a bright streak of light filled the sky, accompanied by a rumble of thunder like distant cannons. I opened the aperture just a half a breath too late, I was sure. When I pulled out the plate I put my head under the shade cloth and turned the camera on its tripod to where down below stood that old shack. It made kind of a lonesome-looking thing, desolate in the desert. So I put in another plate and focused the lens.

I wasn't thinking about lightning, but the *lighting*. I was too far to use a flash pan. Shadows were good as long as you don't have too many. I opened the aperture. Counted. Waited three seconds longer. Just as I began to close it, a streak of light crossed the sky and the thunderclap made Fixie jump and stir. She whinnied. "Oh, all right," I said. "We'll go home before you get wet." At least she was docile. Not given to Duende's fits and starts. "Imagine," I said to her as I packed up my things, "imagine a horseless carriage running right up beside you and a girl throwing a scarf, and that set you to running right up on the granite stair steps of a college. Imagine you were such a grand horse that you ran like you had wings. Imagine you could be Pegasus. What would you think then?"

She stirred sideways and I knew I had to get her home before we got caught in the fracas. I kept her moving easy, though, back down the slope and across the flat of Maldonado's land and by the big ocotillo cactus that marked the boundary to Aunt Sarah's place. We got to the house just as the clouds passed overhead. A cool breeze came with them, breaking the wall of heat in the air. Hares scattered before me as I rode up to the barn to put Fixie in the corral and go to the house. I left the camera in the barn.

Ma was in the kitchen, washing dishes. "Where did you go, honey? I needed you to milk the cow."

"I'm sorry, Ma. I went for a ride." How could I tell her I wanted some landscapes to fill out a portfolio? How could I explain to her what a portfolio was, and why I needed one? "Did Beccah do it or is Skeeter bawling out there?"

She gripped the back slats of a chair before her. "Help me to the rocker. I can't catch my breath this morning."

"Are you sick, Ma?"

"No. I'm sure it was just the wind, stirring up dust. Makes it hard to breathe. I'll rest a bit and I'll be fine."

"Where is Beccah now?"

"In the parlor. Writing a letter to Dr. Pardee."

"That's sweet, the two of them."

Ma smiled. She breathed heavily, slowly, and for a moment I thought she'd gone kind of gray. "It is."

"Do you feel all right? Should I bring you some lemonade? Where's Pa?"

"He rode your aunt Sarah and Granny home in the buggy. Then he said he was going down to Marsh Station to see if there're any hooligans waiting around to pick up money instead of mail." She coughed lightly, and patted her chest with her fingertips.

"Before I set up my developers, do you mind if I take one more plate of you?"

"Not in this old housedress. Let me put on something nice."

"You are already perfect, Mama. I want a plate of you just like this." I almost said that I wanted to remember her like this when I left, and stopped myself. "You look like a portrait of a mother. It's gentle. The light from the window is coming in just right on your hair."

"It's gray."

I smiled. "It's golden, the light is. Like a halo in some old paintings by the Renaissance masters."

"I don't believe in such things as halos."

"I know. Just sit there a minute more. I'll be right back."

I ran to the barn and retrieved my getup. Set it up in the parlor where I could see Mama sitting at the kitchen table. She was sitting so still, I had another devious idea, too. I opened the aperture without telling her. Then I closed it. Then I said, "All right. Hold still." She turned to me and straightened her shoulders. I counted and tapped the box with my fingernail. "All done. Thank you, Mama."

I got out my tubs and the clay jars of liquids. One of them really fumed when I pulled the cork. I decided right then that I had better print up all my exposed plates and dump the chemicals way out some-place flat and dry.

I set to work, laying papers out on bales of hay, and setting up on a table outside. I fetched three cans of water from the well. I stretched a string and added clothespins. I pulled out sawhorses and put boards on them for exposing the paper to the sun. In the heat of the late morning, the air stopped, as if the sky were holding its breath. It seemed to suck the very breath from your lights, making you feel dried and shriveled. Up from the south I saw thunderheads forming. Those would make good photographs. In a little bit, Clover's courting buggy with red wheels came up the road. It had to be Rachel and Aubrey.

Happily they went into the house and didn't come bother me at all. The very first print I made was of Mama sitting at the kitchen table. Next I did my landscapes, and one of Duende. Last of all I put into my exposing frame the one with the stormclouds and the little shack.

I stared hard as the paper took some shading. Hard to tell what it was before rinsing, but it looked like the glass had cracked. I checked my plate but it was not cracked. "Lightning!" I said aloud. I'd caught lightning on a plate! To capture lightning was something people tried forever with no success and I'd gotten one at only eighteen years old. My baby wiggled.

I rinsed and washed, setting the image onto the expensive paper. Finally I hung it on the string and clipped it with three clothespins. With all the care I knew how to manage, I put the precious plate be-tween two pieces of heavy paper and strapped wood shims around it, then tied them with more string. That plate would make my reputa-tion in Albuquerque or anyplace I decided to live.

As I'd imagined, it only took a few minutes for the first papers to dry. I took them down carefully, placing them between other papers in case there was the slightest bit of dampness. How could there be, in this desiccated air? When I stood before the last print, with the lightning, I looked upon the paper hanging from the line with pride. The lower right corner was damp. I blew against it. And then I screamed. I threw my hands across my mouth, looked at the page again, and screamed again.

I ran for the house. "Ma!" I shrieked. Holding the upper corners of the paper in both hands, I kicked open the screen door, scared the porch cat out of eight of his nine lives, and nearly tripped over Aubrey's big feet. "Ma! Oh, Ma. Oh, my soul."

CHAPTER FOURTEEN

Mama, Rachel, and Aubrey were sitting in the parlor, sipping lemonade and fanning themselves with card fans. They looked at me in that huge tarry milking apron as if I'd come to the house to throw manure into the room.

I tried to speak, but I could only shake. I stammered. I broke out in a heavy sweat from running. "The lightning did it, Mama," I finally got out.

"What are you talking about, Mary Pearl? Is that any way to come into the house? You came in here like a hooligan with no more upbringing than a banty hen—"

"But, *Ma*," I interrupted. "It's, it's Zachary's face! I'd stopped to take a plate of a nice landscape. The lightning flashed. I thought it was great that I caught lightning, Mama, but it lit up inside the shed through that window and Zachary and Ezra are in that shed. We looked around it and saw nothing, but they could have been moved there or threatened to be quiet or were too sick to call out. Look in the window of this photograph. Isn't that Zachary?"

Mama dropped her best teacup. It shattered to crumbs on the

hard floor. Only the handle remained whole. The lemonade ran down her skirt and onto her shoe.

Aubrey snatched the print from my hands. "I don't see a face. Show me where you see a face." He sported a finely trimmed beard and side whiskers that almost hid the scar that I'd left him.

I jerked the paper right back and handed it to Ma. Rachel and Rebeccah came to her. I said, "Look in the window. Look what the lightning did."

Ma cried out as if she'd been whipped. Then she moaned, "My baby."

Aubrey immediately said, "I'll take charge of this. I'll get the buggy. Where is that shed?"

I didn't have time to tell Aubrey what I wanted him to do was twist on a spit in everlasting perdition. Instead, I said, "You can't get there with a buggy. Take your rig to Aunt Sarah's place and fetch any men you can find around there. Gilbert and Charlie, too, and Brody. Tell Charlie it's the shed and he'll know. If whoever has got 'em is in cahoots with the Mexican Army and Maldonado, this could go parlous."

"Mary Pearl, you mustn't go!" Ma said.

"There's no time to get help. Only people besides me who could find that shed are Charlie and Brody. Beccah, won't you and Rachel get me a parcel of food? Blankets and slickers, and plenty of food for Zack and Ez. Something they can carry in one hand like biscuits and a jug of milk. I'm going to change my skirt."

It didn't take any time at all for me to get changed and saddle Fixie. Then I strung on another two horses, one to hold the goods my sisters were bringing, and the other the Belgian just for a spare so the boys could ride. If the boys could ride.

Let me tell you, there was plenty of squalling from my sisters about me going alone and sending the only man in our parlor in a buggy to find my cousins. The only person who didn't think I was dead wrong was Mama. She took me by the shoulders and kissed my cheek. She whispered, "Don't let anything happen to you. Don't try to be daring. Get them but get them safe and don't let me lose you, too."

"Yes, ma'am," I said. "I love you, Mama."

"Godspeed, daughter." She looked into my eyes like she was seeing something deeper than what color they were. I was hard put to keep eyes locked with her, so knowing was her stare, like all my secrets were hers to hold, now.

"I'll come home with them, Mama." I buckled my gun belt and slid my skinning knife into the scabbard in my brother's boots.

I took off on Fixie, moving fast as I dared to do. It felt like the horses' hooves were carrying dead weight. What was that verse about feet of clay? Mama would know. Granny would know. Why on earth had I spent so much time learning about dead painters when I should have learned scripture verses? Wouldn't that help more now?

I trailed with my horse string until the boulders were too rough beyond the hill where I'd taken the photographs. I got off and went on foot up the steepest side of the hill. Just below the summit I stopped and tied Fixie to a mesquite branch.

I watched the shed for several minutes. A heavy woman came from it with a bucket. It was the old lady who'd been at Maldonado's house and who had asked me if I was hungry. There was a man with her. He looked to me like the old peon who'd dropped the mummy hand on our porch. A burro brayed raucously next to him, but the man just leaned against a piece of corral fence, scratching his back on it like a bear would do. He swatted at flies near his head. The woman spoke to him, but he didn't answer. Any minute now, I thought, Charlie should be coming up the hill.

I watched the old woman and the old man collect their things and take the burro's bosalito in hand. They started back up what looked

like a trail toward the old Maldonado place. Would Maldonado himself come over the hills with an army of vaqueros? Would they fight
my cousins, and would some of us die?

Or was this whole kidnapping plot something stewed up by those
two? It couldn't be. Why would they tell us to go all the way to Agua
Prieta? Or were we to have been intercepted by that small band of banditos? The old people moved on up the road that stretched back to the
Maldonado hacienda. They walked like people used to the trail, not
looking around or back, not expecting to be dry-gulched by a girl on
a little mare, confident they had the upper hand. Behind me, in the
south, clouds grew higher and white, like great anvils in the sky. If that
bunch let loose, we'd get a gully washer this afternoon. I left my horses
tied where they were and crept down the hill toward the shed. I walked
all around it like before. The window where the face had shown in the
photograph was dark. I tiptoed to the front where the door was, and
lifting my boots so they made almost no sound, I stepped inside. There
was no window on any wall but there had been a window outside. That
meant there was another room behind this one. A false wall. Oh, why
had we not thought of that!

Granny's memoirs were so clear and plain, like I could hear her
voice at that second thundering in my brain:

And one of my great-grandmothers hid in the secret room
behind a room, where her husband had built them a wall. It
didn't matter if it was soldiers nor Kiowa Indians coming up
the road, she was safe, and there was food down there and a
water trickle, too. Don't ever live in no house without there's
a hiding place to go to. Make sure you've got a secret place.

The bright sunlight outside played tricks on my eyes in the small
room, and it was dark as a cave. So I stepped to the back wall and saw

where there was old tack and discarded feed sacks against it, a pack rat's nest in a corner. But there was one opening, about three boards wide, where no trash lay against the wall. Three boards was enough space to get a bucket through.

I knocked on the wall. "Ezra? Zachary? Are you in there?"

Silence.

"I found you. Nobody is around but me. Speak out. It's Mary Pearl."

"It ain't," a voice said through the wall. "You don't sound like Mary Pearl. Anybody comes here messin' with us, we're gonna get shot. You ain't Mary Pearl. Or if you are, tell us the name you said we weren't to call you ever again."

"You called me Imp. I hated that name, remember? And Zachary says 'dammit to Caledonia' when he gets riled." As the two of them hollered with joy, I put my head near the floor, sprinkled with mouse droppings, and called through it, "Can you crawl through here?"

"No. There's barbwire all hammered in on this side. Iron bars like a jail."

"I didn't bring an axe or anything to tear down boards. I'll get a horse and we'll pull down the wall."

"I'm telling you, this place has got parts of an old jail cell on this side. It's iron everywhere. If you pull down the wall it will crush us to death."

"Who's that talking?" I asked.

"Ezra."

"What's wrong with Zachary?"

"He's starved. He cain't eat the trash they're feeding us. He ain't dead, though, are ya, Zack?"

I said, "I'm going to go get a rope. Don't give up now. I'll get you out." Even though I said that, I had no idea how I would. I scrambled back up the hill and fetched two good long lengths of rope and the lunch pails Rachel had packed. I passed them through the opening. "You boys want this?"

"Yes! Oh, yes. But you be careful, Mary Pearl. That woman only left here a minute ago, did you see her? She'll be back in a little while with our supper. She brings some slop in the morning and some other at night. She just come to get the bucket. Expects us to eat from it like hogs. They'll be back."

"Make sure you hold it with the paper it's wrapped in, in case you have some kind of filth on your hands from being dirty. I know you're hungry, but eat it slow."

I studied the room inside, then walked around the outside of it. I took the butt of my pistol and broke out the glass in the window where I'd seen Zack. I heard them cry out with glee, and sigh for the open air. A wretched smell came from the open window, and I began to wonder if they had any other opening where air could move through. Why, they could die of contagion in their own mess kept that way. It wasn't fit for any animal. "What's your ceiling like, boys? Is it iron bars, too?"

"No, but it's too high. We tried to reach it already. They caught us once, getting away. Beat us pretty bad. They said they'd visited Ma and she'd agreed to send the money to get us home. But no one came. Zack's real sick, too."

I gulped. "What's wrong, Zack?"

A voice said, "Just can't keep my dinner down. Ever' time they bring us something, I can't eat it and if I do it comes back on me."

Shuddering with sadness, I said, "Pa's been trying to find you and pay money for six weeks. The whole countryside went all the way to Sonora hunting you."

"Really? These people told us today Mama had changed her mind and now no one was coming for us. That we were their slaves from now on. One day they tell us we're saved, the next that we're doomed.

They're gonna hang us if they don't get some money or we don't starve first."

"I'm going up the hill to get my horses. Don't give up now."

I pulled the string back and chose a larger horse, the one I'd left without a pack for the boys to ride. Buster had been sired by Aunt Sarah's Belgian. He had sturdy legs and a big chest. We'd had to have a large saddle made for his wide back and I was glad I'd brought him then. I pulled him and Fixie followed obediently, without even being tied. When I got the horse next to the shed, I hitched a loop in one of the ropes and caught that ridge pole coming off the shed with it. First thing I did was climb onto the saddle and stand up in the seat of it, trying to see as far around as I could. The old couple were headed this way, him on a burro and carrying a shotgun slung over his back, her running alongside carrying a bucket. She had a rifle as well, strapped across her bosom like a bandito. I said, "We don't have much time. You boys cover your eyes. I see a pole coming out of the roof. When I get this tied, you get up against the back wall."

Without another word I dallied the lariat to the saddle horn and started edging Buster to pull. Buster tugged and I heard wood creak and splinter. Pretty soon, that pole and half the roof came off in a dusty explosion of flaking wood and dirt. I stood as tall as I could in the stirrups to see. Now the old people were running this way. But they were both slow and plump, limping, but still coming. The woman threw the bucket aside and shouted something.

I ran to the shed. "You boys hurt?"

"No, Imp. Toss that rope down here. I'll tie it around my waist and carry Zack. I'm so skinny I could slip through a knot without Zack sitting on 'er to plug the hole."

That was my brother. Ever telling a joke or pulling my leg. I pushed Buster back to the shed and threw the rope down inside. "Holler!" I shouted. "Move, move, boys. They're coming for us!"

"All right, pull!" Ezra said. I patted Buster's rump and he moved forward. The hardest part was to keep it slow so he wouldn't just pop them out of there and yank them to the ground.

In almost no time I saw Zack's head at the top of the wall. He looked gaunt and thin, and his hair was long and filthy. I smiled from ear to ear and tears streamed down my face. "Come on, hurry. I'll get you down on this side." I tethered Buster to a rock. It wasn't heavy enough to hold him, but long as the horse thought he was tethered, that's all I needed. Then I ran to the shed and held up my arms.

"I'm mighty stinky."

"I don't care. Put your feet on my hands here. That's as high as I can reach." I heard the shotgun blast, but they hadn't hit any of us. Zack swung his bare feet over the edge. I caught him clumsily and eased him to the ground just as a clap of thunder reminded me to look toward the southern sky. "Rain's coming boys. Come on, Ezra!"

By the time they were both on the ground, I was so happy I could burst. They drank my canteen dry. Poor Zack really looked bad. Ezra offered to ride Buster and help keep Zack in the saddle with him. "Come on, boys. I'm going to circle way around. That hill is faster, but you'd have to walk down the other side and it's perilous." I didn't wait for any answer. I pushed on ahead pulling the pack horse and Ezra had enough gumption to keep up.

When we got to the side of the hill I could see a shallow arroyo we could cross to get up the other side. I turned and looked behind me. The old woman saw the shack in shreds, then took the rifle off her shoulder. From the south the wind began to blow. It smelled of rain. From the north, here came Papa along with Clover, Charlie, and Brody. From the east, a band of vaqueros Mexicanos on black stallions rode hell-for-leather toward us.

For a second I couldn't speak. My throat had gone to cotton and my breath was stopped. The old man fired the shotgun again and I felt something whip at my skirt, but it didn't hit my leg. Still, I was frozen stiff. I thought I'd died in my saddle. I looked back at the old woman, who was taking aim toward us with the rifle. I saw the sick hate in her eyes, and called, "*Abuela!* Don't shoot! *No dispares!* I'll give you money. *Tu dinero! No dispares!*"

Charlie must have heard my words, for he kicked his horse into a reckless gallop straight for us.

Lightning forked across the sky, filling the heavens with an unnatural yellow light. The thunder came right upon it, deafening us and making Fixie jump sideways. I circled her around and clapped Buster on the rump soundly. The old man held up a machete as if to throw it. I sent my hunting knife in his direction, fast as the snap of a whip. It found purchase deep in his right leg.

I drew my pistol, planning to fire toward the old woman if I had to.

I didn't hear it.

The rifle she carried already had a trail of smoke streaming from the barrel. I saw Ezra slump and slither from the saddle like a loose sack of beans. Zachary screamed for all he was worth. Even though Fixie was dancing all over, I could see red spraying from Ezra's skull.

"*Mujer del diablo!*" I screamed. "Devil hag!" I kicked Fixie so hard she bolted forward. I ran her straight at the demon holding the smoking rifle. She was raising it again, pulling back the bolt, aiming. I fired three times. Fixie like to chucked me into a prickly pear for doing it.

I got off the saddle and stood there, flaming heart and all, ready to pull the trigger again. The pistol felt warm and alive, powerful like nothing else ever had, like a piece of my arm I'd never known was there. The old man, walking with my blade sticking from his thigh, threw down his empty shotgun, ripped the rifle from under the fat carcass of the woman and raised it, but fumbled trying to aim. In a heartbeat I heard gunfire behind me and the old man rolled to the ground on top of the woman.

Charlie's horse stopped behind me so hard he might have been bulldogging a cow, for his hooves shot gravel and dirt all over me.

Pa met me at Ezra's poor form. "He's breathing!" Pa shouted. "He's breathing."

I could hardly bring myself to look at the wound. Part of my brother's skull was blown away over his left eye, and the blood shot up like a fountain.

Zachary had finally gotten Buster to turn around and came back with him, slid from the saddle to the ground and wailed, his face buried in his filthy hands and his hands in the dirt. He raised his head and dirt fell from his mouth, but still he screamed and wailed on.

Charlie looked like a man possessed. He mounted up and rode out to meet the Mexican *soldados* or whatever they were. Clover followed him, whipping his horse in a fury. Brody's eyes went from me to Ezra to Charlie making dust. He stayed.

Lightning flashed again overhead, and the air took on a steaming breathlessness. The sky inhaling, getting ready to unleash a great storm upon us. "Blankets," I shouted at Pa. "I have blankets?" Nothing made any sense. Ezra didn't need a blanket. Pa said something and I saw his lips move, but I couldn't hear. My mouth hung open. "What? What!"

Pa shook my shoulders. "Get the blankets," he said slowly, very loudly.

I ran to the pack horse. Pulled everything loose so it tumbled to the desert floor. "Cut this and wrap him. Wrap his head."

Pa already had his knife ready. He made wide strips and as I carefully lifted Ezra's head, Pa wrapped his wound. He said something to me again.

"What, Pa? I can't hear you. I can't hear you."

Thunder banged overhead. I heard that. But Pa's voice, right in my face, made no sound. Ezra breathed. Zachary's mouth was open, but if he was crying I heard nothing at all except a buzzing like bees on a swarm flight.

Pa shouted, "We are closer to Benson than to home. We will take him to Doctor Pardee."

"Benson," I said numbly. "Yes. Pardee. Is that what you said?" I stood.

I saw Pa's mouth moving, but I couldn't hear him. Was it thunder? Gunfire? Papa shook my arm and with his face close to my nose he put his hands on both sides of my head and looked directly into my eyes. He hollered at me, but all I heard was silence.

I sat back at his side. "This is my fault. I should have shot first."

And then I could hear him. "You couldn't. You sit here with him and I'll kick some boards loose. We'll have to sort of tie him in place. Papoose-style."

"Papoose. Ezra, don't you fear. You're a long, skinny papoose and I have lost my mind. I'm deaf. Oh, mercy, I'm stone-deaf, Pa." I covered my eyes with the heels of my hands and rocked back and forth, sitting there in the gravel and thorns next to him. I wasn't crying. I couldn't. I was just trying to block the image of Ezra's open, bleeding head, but it was burned onto the backs of my eyes like a brand that will never go away nor heal.

Something landed, heavy, on the top of my head. Water. Rain. Where was my hat? Zachary was holding it, crushed, to his face. Arizona rain was the kind of rain I never saw in Illinois. This was the front of the storm, where the drops fall large as a hen's egg, ten feet apart. Huge blobs of water clopped on the dirt, making thunking sounds like the very ground was a hollow drum. Fixie messed around and shied; didn't like being socked in the eye with an unexpected slap of water.

Pa laid boards and wove my ropes through them as if he'd been doing that all his life—making baskets out of boards. We strung them to the back of Pa's saddle. The breeze cooled. The rain might not come this way. We were just about to return to Ezra's side to raise him onto the basket when a loud voice called, "*Alto!*"

We were surrounded by the Mexican caballeros. They wore expensive sombreros and saddles with silver conchos and jingles. Their boots glistened in the shadowy broken light from the sun poking through the clouds. Pa didn't look up. I stood, expecting to face an army with drawn weapons. No one was aiming at us, however.

"Señor," a man called. "What are you doing?"

"I'm busy. Go away," Papa said. "Mary Pearl, you get his feet while I steady Ezra's head." I ignored the Mexican men and did as Papa said.

On some signal the whole bunch of them dismounted. They walked toward us. Where were Charlie and Clover? Had they been murdered and left in the desert, too? I held Ezra's legs while Pa tied him gently, using the blanket under him for a padding, and we got him mounted on there and strung up like a roasted chicken so he wouldn't tumble off.

One of the Mexican men came toward us. "Señor, if you will permit. The end must be wider. That is too narrow. It will tip and drag him." He gestured as he said, "*Compadres, aquí.*"

The men pushed me out of the way, but not roughly. Pa stood, tears on his cheeks. Two of the men got more boards and used their own lariats to tie a wide runner at the foot end of our travois rig. They were right, I saw. If we'd moved him at all, the one Pa made might have rolled over and dragged Ezra face down. These men knew what they were doing.

My face hurt, but I didn't weep. I went to Brody. "Where's Charlie? Dead?"

"No. He went to fetch your ma and sisters." Thunder interrupted him for a moment. He spoke into Zack's ear. "Hold on there, buckaroo, you're sliding." Then he talked to the rest of us. "He and Clove'll bring the ladies to Benson in a surrey and meet us there at Pardee's office."

I eyed the sky. "It'll be dark or pouring by then."

"Likely."

"Pa, let me set this slicker over Ezra's face," I said. I fixed it over him, but there was nothing to tie it on with that wouldn't press down on him. Ezra was still breathing. I pulled the pins from my hair. I bent them into hooks and rings and poked that slicker, looping the rings around the ropes of Ezra's papoose carrier. My hair fell down my back in front of all these men, shameful as a hussy, but I didn't care.

Brody said to me, "You want me to see you home?"

"No. I'm going with my brother."

"All right. What about this one? He's wore to the bone. Sound asleep."

"He can ride with me. I'll hold him in the saddle. What about all these men? They look like they're here for business."

"I'll tell you on the way, but they're all right."

When the caballeros were satisfied that Ezra would travel as safely as possible, they all mounted up. Pa did, too. Brody held my horse's reins and then passed Zachary up. I held him facing me and he slept, smelly and bony, against my swelling body. I still didn't know exactly what was going on, but the band of men rode up ahead of us as a group. I rode drag with Brody at my side.

Turned out, Pa going to Marsh's Stage and Mail Station was what saved the day. The stationmaster had seen that old man hanging around every other day. When Pa asked about him, the stationmaster knew how to send a message to Maldonado, who was not in Agua Prieta at all. He was living on a ranch in Sonora, Mexico. Most important, he had nothing to do with the kidnapping or ransom requests. That was why he sent this string of *compadres*, his fellows, to assure us he was busily conducting farming and mining in Mexico. This whole plot was cooked up by the cheerful old couple squatting in the Maldonado hacienda and their greedy sons, who were the ones waiting on the road to Agua Prieta for the money. The oldest son was the one the *comandante* had shot. They had followed us back, but had not jumped us because they didn't expect we'd have come in such numbers.

"Do you trust them, Brode?" I asked.

Brody twisted his mouth a little. He needed a shave. I'd never seen him looking so ragged. "'Bout as far as I could throw 'em. But we'll watch and see."

It took nearly two hours to reach Benson. There, Maldonado's men saluted us, and one of them crossed himself and said he would pray for Ezra. We dragged our papoose through the streets of town and asked for Dr. Pardee from everyone we saw. Finally we found a sign for Dr. Pardee's office and I groaned aloud to see it was up a flight of stairs over a store. That didn't matter. The men untied the wide runner at the foot and raised Ezra over their heads, keeping him level. They marched him up the stairs and Brody, first in line, hollered through the door. I followed.

Inside was a storm of its own, for people had been there waiting to see Dr. Pardee for first one thing and then another. They all scooted out when they saw our bloody procession.

"Bring him this way," the doctor said. Zachary followed like a dirty old caboose as we all trailed into the treatment room. It smelled of ether and alcohol and plenty of other sharp chemicals.

I marched right in with the rest of them, and helped with unwinding all the wrapping of blankets and ropes. Finally, the doctor raised the wrapping off Ezra's head. I reached over and held Ez's left hand.

"Papa, he squeezed my hand," I whispered.

"No, I'm sure he didn't," the doctor said.

I frowned. Squeezed Ezra's hand again. Felt him squeeze back. Glared hard at Pardee, who'd lost plenty of footing in my estimation by calling me a liar. I looked toward the door because I heard some racket outside. In came Mama, Rebeccah, Aunt Sarah, Charlie, Clover, Rachel, and Aubrey.

"Folks," said Dr. Pardee, "I'm sorry, but you all have to leave. Immediately. Everyone go. If you care about this boy, find a seat in the other room. No one in here but my nurse. Go on, please. Wait with the others."

"But he's my brother." I held Ezra's grimy hand to my cheek and whispered into his fingers, "Stay alive, brother. I'll take care of you always." My anger at Pardee flared into pure hatred.

When at last I entered the waiting room, our family filled it to overflowing. I stood next to the door to the treatment room and held on to the door jamb. I started to shake all over, hard, harder than having a chill. My teeth chattered and my knees felt weak. My sisters all looked so clean and perfect. So . . . not murderers. I'd pulled a trigger on an old woman and shot her dead. Put a knife in an old man. I'd never in my life have thought older people capable of evil like those two were. I just figured by the time you got gray hair and grew wide in the middle, you softened up and quit being vile and horrible and cruel.

Even Maldonado had softened in my mind. He had not been the one to take our boys. He had not caused Duende's death. He was just down in Mexico farming. No longer a threat. At least we knew he was not coming after us. He'd sent these men to straighten things out. I would never, ever forgive that old woman for shooting my brother. If I knew her name I'd find a *bruja* to put a Mexican spell on her. I hoped she turned on a spit in hell for eternity, that's what. This Territory was full of motherless, blasted, blackhearted, mean—

"Mary Pearl?"

"Hmm? What, Mama?"

"Aunt Sarah was speaking to you. Don't be rude."

My face felt as if it had turned to stone. I stared at my aunt and my mother as if I were invisible, no more alive nor capable of rudeness than if they'd asked a question of the door jamb that was serving me as a spine. "I didn't hear you," I said. "What? I'm only just now able to hear at all. Please repeat the question."

"I thought I'd rent us a hotel room. Maybe two, if they're small, and get you a bath. Why don't you come along with me? There's plenty of people here to wait for Ezra."

"No, thanks. I'll stay right here."

Rachel offered, "Mary Pearl, you look exhausted. I know you'll feel better if you clean up and rest."

Aubrey brightened at that and added, "I'll see you to the hotel."

I glared at him as if he'd proposed to assault me right here on the floor. "I don't need rest," I said. "You go to a hotel. I'm staying with Ezra. Where's Zachary?" My littlest brother was sleeping in the corner of the room, just leaned against the wall. He did, at least, have a dried mustache of milk around his mouth, so I figured he'd gotten something decent in him at last. "I'll sit here by him, then. We aren't in your way."

Rebeccah looked at me with sad understanding in her eyes. "Mary Pearl, honey, you and Zachary are filthy dirty and you're covered with old blood. You both need a bath in hot vinegar and salt water. As long as Ezra is still breathing he has a chance, but if infection sets in, he won't last more than a couple of hours. We have to clean this room and that means the people in it, too."

When she finished talking, I felt as if someone pulled the corners of my mouth into the saddest face in the world. "I can't let that happen."

"Please go with Aunt Sarah and clean up, honey."

"I have no clothes to change in to."

"We brought plenty. Search through anything of mine, too, if you want. All kinds for Zack, too."

"What about Ezra? He's the dirtiest of all of us."

"The doctor will cleanse the wound area and all around it. Ma and Pa will sponge him off when the doctor says they can. The hotel is only one door down on the right. You won't be far."

I bowed my head. Then I jostled Zachary. "Come on, Zack. We're going to go take a bath."

"I hate baths," he said, without opening his eyes.

"I know you do. But give a hand here, stand up, and I'll carry you. I'll buy you some candy when you're clean. Then we'll have a nice dinner at a table, and Mama will sing you to sleep. Come on. Stand up. I can't lift you off the floor."

To my amazement, Zachary stood up like he was sleepwalking, raised his arms, and clung to my neck.

Brody tapped my shoulder. "You can't carry him down those stairs. Here," he said, and pried Zachary from my arms and took him. Brody wasn't a tall fellow but he had wide shoulders and he was strong from working horses his whole life.

Aunt Sarah led the way. Brody went ahead of me down the stairs. I followed into a drenching rain. As they moved across the street, I lagged behind. The rain felt good. As if the sky were weeping the tears I couldn't shed. I turned my face upward and let it wash over me, felt the drops hitting my eyelids, realizing how hot and blistered they felt with tears unshed.

By the time I entered the hotel lobby, I was more drowned cat than human. My long hair hung like a mat against my back. The bulky chaps I'd pulled over my split skirt were heavy as lead and seemed to stretch downward, making me stumble as I walked. Aunt Sarah turned to me and held forth a key. "The maid will pull you a bath in room two, down that hall. Clover will see to Zachary in bath number one.

You go ahead, and I'll bring you clothes in a while. Take all the time you want. Can I help you take off the chaps so you can walk?"

"No, ma'am. I believe my legs will show, I'm so wet." Silly to worry about public decency after everything else, but I did.

The hotel maid looked me over with no expression whatsoever, not even a sneer at my dreadful appearance. Her arms were laden with a stack of towels and a new bar of soap, plus a jar of something blue I couldn't identify. Brody walked behind, carrying my little brother. Clover followed him with towels and soap for Zack's bath. I had to do some talking to convince the maid I didn't want her help undressing. I knew it would be hard to pull off the wet things. I knew how to get in and not slip. I knew how to wash my own hair. Finally, I said, "I'll give you two bits to go away," and she left.

I peeled off my clothes and sank into the warm water. She'd poured the blue stuff in, and it smelled like flowers. The soap was fancy and really hard, not like the soft homemade kind we used. Once I felt like I was clean, I just leaned back and stared straight ahead at the edge of the tub, listening to the rain outside. Strange how a warm bath was nothing like being drenched with rain. Strange how everything felt different. Like I'd changed into another person and was watching someone named Mary Pearl sitting in a tub. Strange how I'd had a bath almost every day in Illinois and now I was having a bath in a place where I didn't live and it felt unnatural. I was losing my mind just like my dead Aunt Ulyssa.

A knock on the door and Aunt Sarah entered when I said, "Come in."

I stood and began to towel off; she had her back to me, setting out petticoats and a camisole, drawers, and stockings, even my best shoes with thirteen buttons up the side and kid leather ankles. She even brought a burlap potato sack to put my dirty things in.

Then my aunt turned around. And then her mouth opened in shock.

My hand went to my rounded belly.

"Mary Pearl!"

"Yes. What you're wondering, is yes. I am."

"Merciful heavens. Are you secretly married?"

"No. Not even openly married. The only thing I ask you is to give me until Ezra is well so I can tell Mama and Papa myself. It should come from me. I can't wear that corset. I'll leave my dress open and wear a shawl and a slicker for the rain. Would you please promise to let me tell my folks? Please?"

"I won't ask you if you made a slip at college. Sometimes girls do if they reckon themselves in love."

"I didn't make a slip. I wasn't in love and I wasn't persuaded. I didn't have any choice. Just like you told me about my aunt, Ulyssa Lawrence, I was set upon while I slept."

"Oh, no. Oh, child. Why haven't you told anyone?" She handed me my drawers and camisole.

"Because I was planning to run away. I meant to leave college and go live somewhere else. I can make my living taking photographs. Mama and Papa would never have to know. Never be ashamed of me. But I couldn't leave without knowing Ezra and Zack were safe. Now, I suppose, I will go once Ezra is out of danger. Ma and Pa will probably want me to go."

Aunt Sarah sat down, hard, in the chair she'd laid my things on. "Oh," she said, and stood again, lifting the petticoats to her lap as she sat once more. "I don't ever keep things from your ma and pa, you know that."

"I know. But this would be a terrible time for Mama to find out, with Ezra at death's door. If you won't keep my secret just a bit longer, that's up to you. Granny knows, too."

"Hmm. Life has thrown some hard stuff at you, hasn't it? That explains why your ma told me you wanted to go live in Albuquerque. You were going to have the baby there?"

I felt my lower lip tremble. Perhaps the tears would fall at last. I couldn't even nod. I felt like a stone had replaced my whole body. "I believe so."

"I'll keep your secret, I promise. Until or unless your mama asks me straight out if you are carrying a child. Long as she doesn't ask, I won't reply. Let her worry over Ezra for now."

"Thank you." After a pause, I said, "I *will* tell them."

"I know you will. Here. I'll fix the back of your dress loose. It really doesn't look like anything if you're wearing the slicker, and maybe it will keep on raining."

Back in the waiting salon in Dr. Pardee's office, I entered and took a chair next to a window. Raindrops still rattled the window glass and a dribble of water came down inside the room from the bottom of the window frame.

We changed watch as regular as soldiers on a wall, waiting around the clock for Ezra to either succumb or wake. During one of my times to sit by him, I kept my face toward the wall as Pardee fastened a curved bowl, a dish formed of flattened silver dollars, on to the bone on his skull. I moaned and hid my face against the wall while Ezra cried out in pain as Pardee used a hardware store screwdriver to fasten that down.

Pardee sewed the skin shut over the plate, and Ezra quit hollering. I wept buckets when he was quiet at last. That doctor had done all this with his other nurse and, of all people, my sister Rebeccah helping out, while *I* stared uselessly at the wall and cried. I ain't any good with that kind of patching up, and I don't pretend to be, nor would I ever want to be. It's the sort of thing I'm very thankful for: that there's doctors and nurses, and even more thankful that I'm not one of 'em. Surely, I have gone lunatic.

Three weeks we waited there in Benson. The day came when

Pardee said we could carry Ezra home; that he wasn't in any more danger of dying now than ever, and had wakened up that morning.

I was swelling like a mare. My secret would not be secret much longer. My baby wiggled all the time. There were too many people around to think I could keep this up until I could run away, and it didn't rain enough for me to keep the slicker on day in and day out. Everywhere I went, I carried bundles and baskets draped with blankets or sheets, piled with food or something I could carry, just to hide the shape of me. Plus, it was hotter than blue blazes and I wanted to lie in a tub of cool water, not dress in a rubber raincoat.

Of course, Rachel and Aubrey had returned to Tucson. He couldn't stay away from his practice for weeks on end, he'd claimed. Rachel said she might be expecting a child, so she, too, needed to get home to rest. Aunt Sarah, Aubrey's father Udell, my cousins Charlie and Gilbert, and sometimes Brody came and went and, of course, they had a ranch to run.

One day it was my turn to take watch and Zachary came along with me. On our way there, Zachary looked at me with his head cocked to one side and remarked, "You're getting fat."

"Well, that is rude of you to say."

"'S a truth."

"Maybe so, but some things a person has no control over and those things are not polite to mention."

"Yer my sister and I can tell when yer fat or not."

"What's got into you today, Zack?"

"There's nothing to do here, no one to play with, and Ezra just lays there dying. I want to go home and I want him to get up and act like a brother again. Why's he got to die? No one shoulda shot him in the head."

"True."

"You sure popped that old lady fer it."

"I didn't want her to shoot you, too."

"I'll tell you sumthin'. You got no call anymore to tell me yer gonna squeal to Ma and Pa about me saying words like 'dammit to Caledonia' when I get mad. Not after what I heard you saying that day. Not even cousin Charlie ever cussed like what you said."

"You best forget what I said."

"Cain't. You done, like Ma always says, 'left a *impression* on my mind.'"

I stopped on the boardwalk in front of the doctor's office stairs and turned to him. "I'da done anything to save you. Are you saying you don't appreciate it because I let some hard words fly while I was in high oats?"

"No, ma'am. Just that I see you different now. Used to think you were kin to the Virgin Mary. Thought that's why they named you that. Now I see yer just kin to me. Kinda ornery."

"Reckon the Virgin Mary woulda got you out of there?"

"Reckon not. Least not with a lariat and a pistol."

"Then stop being so cranky."

"If I feel like it." He bolted up the stairs ahead of me. "I got sumthin' to say to Ezra Nehemiah fiddle-faddle Prine, first."

Ezra looked just as unconscious as he had the whole time he'd laid there. Every single day, every one of us patted and hugged him, but he didn't move. At least, I thought, he no longer looked pale and sunken. We'd been feeding him teaspoons of beef broth and strained vegetables. It was Rebeccah who first saw him try to chew the vegetables. Yesterday, Mama said she was certain Ezra had pointed to his head with his left hand. His right hand didn't move at all, except for a twitch now and then. Mama whispered to him, sang to him, mopped his face, and fed him. I believe she changed his diapers, too, but none of us were around when that was going on. For now it was just me and my two younger brothers, like always.

Zachary asked Pardee, "Are you sure he's awake? He don't look awake."

"The patient is responding in obvious ways to stimuli. He's able to move his left hand, and seems alert. Now you two sit here with him while I see another patient in the next room."

I hated the way he called my brother "the patient." He was a real boy with a name. Pardee stepped into another room and we could hear him talking to some other patient.

"Hmm," Zack said, then went to his brother's bedside and shoved Ezra's arm, and asked him in a loud voice, "Hey, Ezra, you smelly old galoot, did you take my wheeler? I can't find it. I'm tired of waiting for you to wake up. If you took my wheeler I'm gonna knock you into next Thursday."

Ezra's lips curled into a smile on the right side.

The left side, under the bandages and padding, was still. But the right side of his face smiled. He moved his lips. We couldn't understand what he was trying to say, but he was trying to say *something* and that was all we cared about.

Zachary wouldn't let up, though. He leaned close to his brother and said, "You don't stink as bad as you did a couple of days ago. Did you know Mama and Papa together gave you a bath, buck nekkid, right here in this room? Girls was looking in through them windows. You better wake up or they're gonna do it again. I'm gonna sell tickets. It was a comical opera like they tell about in the papers. Open yer eyes, knothead."

Clear as day, Ezra said, "Tell Mary Pearl we got loose."

Zachary, with the vinegar of a little boy not given to indulging his brother in any way at all, said, "She knows it. She's the one pulled you out. Then she took care of business, just wait until I tell you. She's sitting right here. Everybody's been waiting on you for days and days. You been lazying around in bed like you think yer some kinda king.

I'm telling you, here comes Mama with a bucket and lye soap and she's gonna scrub the fur off you with a hide brush, like a dirty old chair."

"Zachary," I said, "what's got into you?"

"I'm sick and tired of him just laying there like a lizard all day. Get yer hide up from that bed, Ezra."

Ezra raised his arm up and said the distinct word, "Help."

I took his hand. Felt the pressure of his fingers clutching my own. "Zack, run get the doctor. Ask him if it's all right if Ezra sits up."

Zack's face lit up like he'd been offered a thousand new toys.

When he came back, Dr. Pardee in tow, I asked Zack, "What on earth made you talk to Ezra like that?"

"'Member when I had measles and Ma made me lay in bed in a dark room for two weeks with a blindfold on? I thought I'd been stomped by a horse and I was dead and closed in a coffin. I didn't realize I was alive 'til I heard you 'n Esther having a set-to over a hair ribbon."

"You hollered 'shut up' at us."

"But I wasn't dead. Seems to me old Ez here needed some fractiousness to know he's alive."

Pardee grinned and said, "Help me get him sitting up here."

In another few days, Pa had rigged up a wagon bed with a sling in it, tied to all four corners of the wagon bed much like the way we'd carried Duende, so that it was a gentle riding bed for my brother to lie in for the twenty-five miles to home. Pardee gave us plenty of instructions, and declared he would only let us take Ezra because Rebeccah was there. That he'd visit every week on Sundays. We'd have to spend the night on the trail, but everyone was exhausted. We'd been in Benson for so long.

I offered to ride drag position, just to be out of sight of everyone there.

Along the whole way home, I rehearsed telling Mama and Papa about my situation. How I had planned to take off, so they wouldn't have to tell anyone in town. I practiced everything but the truth. I wanted to make it sound as if I'd been caught unawares, which was true, but by someone I didn't know, which was not. So far it hadn't actually been that hard to ignore Aubrey. I pretended he was invisible or, even better, nonexistent. Mostly thought of my sister Rachel that way, too. It hurt to think of her in the same way as him, but I'd heard of families who didn't all get along. I had just never imagined ours would be one of them. I figured my brothers and sisters were closer to me than any other person could ever be. Hadn't we all died a bit when Esther died? But this was different. I wished it had been Esther who lived and Rachel had disappeared. Try as I might to excuse a person swaying the mind of a man who'd claimed to love me, I couldn't do it. If he'd really loved me, I don't believe she could have changed his mind. No, Aubrey was a certain kind of polecat. If he didn't wear that fancy suit he'd a been called a back shooter. Or worse.

I'd seen enough of animals giving birth to know my days were coming. By the time we reached our front door, I'd settled on a plan with a couple of variations. Shades, you might say, of choices depending on their reactions. Mama and Papa might sweep me into their arms and exclaim how sad they were that I'd been mistreated. They might pledge to love and raise my child as one of their own. That would leave me free and unattached as ever. But, even in my own eyes, I saw that as wrong.

From one point of view I'd been headstrong and belligerent, leaving home to study art and photograph-taking against Ma's wishes. They might slap my face and call me a loose harlot, a slattern, a trollop. They might chase me from the house with nothing but the clothes on my back. I remembered that print that Nation Hollingsworth had made of my portrait, darkening my lips and cheeks as if I were wearing lip rouge and face powder. They might see my predicament as the natural consequence of playing the harlot while I was away. If they ever laid eyes on a likeness of me looking like that, they'd never be convinced I was anything but a Jezebel. They might throw me out to the coyotes and I'd have to turn to a life of harlotry to survive, just as I'd read in some book. Everyone around Tucson knew, although no one spoke openly of it, that those girls who led that life mostly died young, either at their own hands or those of some brutal man. What was to become of my child, then? No, I could not fall that low. Not ever, I swore.

It still seemed to me that my only choice was to go to Albuquerque.

CHAPTER FIFTEEN

Evening settled in, damp and cloying, and the air felt still, that notion of the sky holding its breath, waiting again to unleash a storm. There were clouds but no lightning. Ezra sat in a chair on the porch, motionless, but present, and now and then he grunted some word that didn't fit any conversation. Rebeccah sat with us. Zack tossed pebbles at a ring he'd drawn in the sand. Granny was gone back to Aunt Sarah's place. A horse snorted in the corral. I drew a deep breath and asked, "Mama? Papa? Do you think Ezra is going to live?"

"Seems like it," Papa said. "He's getting better every day. We'll work on things like he was a child again. Teach him to walk. He's trying to talk all the time."

"Well, then. I have something important I need to tell you."

Mama looked up from her lap, where she'd been staring at her hands. She does that when she's praying sometimes, or just thinking, too. "We already know, honey."

"Know? Know what, Mama?"

"Sarah got it from Charlie that you killed that woman who was holding the boys captive. She said those Mexican men buried the bodies and are taking back Maldonado's place. They'd just been squatters anyway."

Pa said, "We want you to know it's all right, honey. This is a hard country. Things happen, and you did what you had to do. There's nothing to be ashamed of for killing her."

I started to cry. I'd never given that incident another thought until they brought it up. Perhaps I *should* be contrite over it. Or concerned for my eternal soul. Or something. "I wish I had told you this before now," I said. "It didn't seem right with Ezra being so bad off. It doesn't seem right now, either, to say what I have to say."

"We understand, honey," Mama said.

"I don't think you do, completely, Mama. You can't. I haven't told anyone, but a couple of people have guessed. Aunt Sarah knows, but I swore her not to tell you. Granny knew before anything ever showed. It's my place to tell you, and my responsibility. I don't want you to think I'm laying this on you. This is my problem. I know it."

Pa said, "I can't think of what you're talking about, Mary Pearl. It's the kind of speech a girl would make if she was going to have a baby."

My face felt as if every muscle under the skin had clenched into a knot on my skull. My jaw hurt. I squeaked out, "I am. Going to have a baby. I am. And soon. In a month and a half, or two. All I can say right now is that I wish I'd never had to tell you these words."

Mama said, "No. How could you have concealed that all this time?"

"No one was paying attention to me. All month, all eyes have been on Ezra."

After a very long silence, during which Zachary quit throwing pebbles and came and sat on the steps near me, Pa asked, "Were you— were you playing fast and loose?"

"No, sir. Just like what happened to Aunt Ulyssa, I was set upon in my sleep. I couldn't fight back. I had no choice."

Mama cried out as if she'd been slapped. She bit her finger curled up against her lips.

"Who? Who is the father?" Pa asked.

"Well, Papa, can it really make a difference, now?"

"Yes, it does! Was it someone here?"

"No."

"Someone you know? They can be called to account."

Mama dropped her hands into her lap. "Away at school. I knew no good would come of that place. I knew it was a den of iniquity. A nightmare waiting to unfold. I'm going to write to that school in the morning and tell them if they can't guard a beautiful single girl who attends there, they should—"

Pa interrupted her. "You said Sarah knows?"

"I begged her not to say until I could. It's my place to tell you. That's all. And, Mama, there's nothing wrong with Wheaton College. It's a lovely place."

"Don't worry, Maypole," Zachary said. "I'll help you take care of that kid."

And then my tears for my predicament broke through a dam they'd been pushing against for seven long months. I leaned against the porch post and gave vent to every sadness that had welled up in me since I left home last Christmas. Mama wept, too.

Pa said, "This isn't what we expected of you."

I raised my swollen face to look toward him. The sun was long gone and the moon obscured by clouds. "I never expected it, either, Pa. It wasn't even at school. I was, well, trapped in a situation by someone. He overpowered me. I left a mark on him, but that was after."

So many thoughts rushed through my mind. As a young girl I thought I knew Aubrey and wanted to marry him. But if he was the kind of man to do that, I didn't know him at all. What a horrible life

Rachel would have with him, if he were forever preying on young girls who couldn't fight back.

"I want you to go to bed, now. I want to talk with your mother."

"Yes, Pa." At the doorway I stopped and said, "I'll go away. Either before or after, if you want. I have my camera and some money left from Aubrey's jilting me, that we didn't use for ransom. I have some photographs and I can go to Albuquerque as a widow and set up a studio. I'll take pictures of people for money. I can do that and live and you don't need to be ashamed of me. If you never want to see me again, I understand."

I could hear Zachary crying, saying, "No, Imp. No. Don't go away. Don't go away."

"Mary Pearl, please just go to bed now. I want to talk to your mother."

"Yes, sir. Good night. Zack, come up with me. You can sleep in my room."

Upstairs in the room that had been mine and my dead sister Esther's, and which felt like it belonged to neither any longer, I opened both windows. Zack crawled onto Esther's bed and closed his eyes almost at once. I wept slowly but not stopping, listening to the soft music of my parents' voices. Mama cried sometimes. I heard the screen door open and shut a couple of times. Might have been Clover going to bed, or Papa bringing Ezra in. Ez could lean on him and drag his right leg, sort of walking into the house where he had slept in the parlor for a few days until they brought his bed downstairs into the kitchen near the back door. At least, I thought, I have done the painful telling. It was no longer before me. The consequences lay ahead, but I was thankful for the dark night and not being able to see their faces. I believed I'd shattered my parents the way Aubrey had broken the mirror to cover up the scar I'd given him.

As I lay there, staring at the ceiling and hearing their talk go on and on, I believed with all my heart and soul that I never meant to become the person I'd become. How does a person have honor and convictions like Ma and Pa? Where does one find right and wrong? I'd lived on whims, tossing around in any breeze that stirred me. No thoughts about consequences, just running headlong into my desire to be independent, to have some education about something no one else here had. How would I ever raise a child to be anything other than a vagabond hellion, if I had no virtue of my own?

I wanted more than anything for Ma and Pa to think I was as special as my older brothers and sisters, and now all I was, was worthless. I fell into a pit of pity and moroseness. Mama probably wouldn't shed a single tear if I were to succumb in childbirth. I was ruined beyond all hope. All because of something I *didn't* do. Couldn't do. Fight back. I sank into sleep, certain of my fallen status. I was, as Granny said—oh, she was so wise, how could she have known me before I knew myself?—a will-o'-the-wisp. A human wreck.

In the morning when I dressed, I hitched up my skirt and wore a loose shirt hanging over the front. No longer putting on aprons or coats and carrying baskets of things to hide my shape, I felt freer as I went downstairs. Ma, Pa, Clover, and Rebeccah were on one side of the table. Zachary sat on the other by my empty chair. Ezra lay on his bed in the parlor. I sat in my chair before an empty plate and stared down at it. "Good morning, everyone," I said quietly.

The silence made my ears ring.

At last, Mama said, "I wanted a different life for you."

I looked up at her. "I know."

"But we love you, honey. You are our daughter. We don't want you to go away and try to live alone. It is too hard. No one hates you. No one is ashamed of you."

Pa said, "I want to know the man responsible."

"I can't tell you, now, Papa. I just can't. Maybe someday I can. I don't want anyone to go and shoot him, and I can't marry him. He's already married."

Pa shook his head. "Married?" and the word came out like an accusation instead of a question. "He could still be forced to take care of you and your child financially. Maybe even go to jail for untoward advances. We could get Aubrey to file some kind of lawsuit. He'd know what to do if we asked him."

"Please don't ask him, Pa."

"Just because a man is in Illinois, doesn't mean he can't be called to account and made to support his child."

"Are you hungry?" Ma asked.

"Yes'm."

Clover said, "I'd like to see him stretch a rope."

I smiled at Clove, because I'd thought of that, too, at the time. I was glad at least that I'd left a mark on him he'd never forget. Mama was dishing me eggs and a steak. I said, "Sometimes I would, too. But I'm not given to revenge." Ma patted my arm, affirming what I said. My heart hurt a little less when she did that.

Papa put down his napkin and walked around the table, sat in Ezra's chair which was next to me, and laid his hand on my arm. "Daughter," he began. "You still have virtue, though you've been abased by some villain. You have courage, as we witnessed when you found your brothers and risked everything to save them. You have ingenuity, learning all the complicated things about your pictures, and hoping to make a place for yourself. This is my fault for not protecting you. I am sorely ashamed and sorry for my lack and I ask you to forgive me."

"Oh, Papa!" I threw my arms around him, clinging to his neck. "I love you, Papa. This was not your doing."

"Oh, my child. My precious child." Pa's neck was warm and the bristles of his unshaven face felt more reassuring than the softest cotton dress I could ever have worn.

Mama joined us and wrapped her arms around both of us.

Clover blew his nose. Zachary just let tears run down his face.

And then we heard the sound. A moan. A guttural grunt. Ezra bellowed, "Spooh!"

We turned to him.

"Spooh!"

I held up my fork. The side of his face smiled. "Poon!"

"A spoon. He wants to eat. Can we get him to the table?"

From that day onward, Ezra improved every day. He walked slowly until Pa made him a cane. Then three-legged Ezra was nearly as fast as the two-legged one had been. He sat at the table. Held a fork and spoon, and hit his mouth with them most of the time. He couldn't say much, but he gestured with his left hand though the right hand remained limp at his side. We learned that he couldn't see out of his left eye.

Then, one day at breakfast, I came downstairs to find Ezra sitting upright at his old place by mine. He was grinning his crooked smile at me. I sat at my place. There was a plate, but no fork or spoon.

"Where's my fork?" I asked Ma.

"I put one there for you."

My plate was distinctly lying at an angle. I lifted it up and there was the fork, under the plate. Ezra laughed and laughed.

"Did you put that there?" I asked him.

"Food you!"

"Fooled me? You sure did. Knucklehead."

He laughed more. "Nuckahead."

"Ma, he's back. He's still Ezra. He can't talk well and he lost an eye, but he's our brother."

Zachary sneered. "He still never told me what he did with my wheeler."

Ezra said to him, "Inna pocket. Inna coat."

"Pocket of my coat?"

"Uh-uh. My pocket."

"Your coat?"

Ezra nodded and laughed again. Zachary ran upstairs and then came down, triumphantly winding the string around his toy.

CHAPTER SIXTEEN

Our brother Joshua came home from his medical practice in Phoenix. He came to see Ezra and give his opinion about him. I'd spent the last few days writing letters to my friend Prairie. I told her about riding fence. About the sound of coyotes. I bragged to her about having caught lightning in a photograph. I didn't mention my predicament. Meanwhile, I was getting rounder by the day.

Rachel and Aubrey were notified of the child by a letter from Ma, and the strangest thing happened. Aubrey drove all seven or eight hours out to our place from town, left Rachel off, and drove home again. That way, she could visit a good long time and he'd just return in a few days, spend the night, and take her home. That was fine with me. Sure didn't need him around the place.

Then I discovered why Rachel came to visit. She had a plan. Since she'd been unable to carry a child so far, she thought she'd just help herself to mine. At least, that's how I saw it. I had a baby and no husband. She had a husband and no baby. Made it look like he wasn't a real man, she said. Made people raise their eyebrows at her. "Well, he isn't a real man," I said. "He's a backstabber. A chiseler. A ne'er-do-well. A walking sack of—"

Naturally that caused her to go squalling to Ma as if we were children and I'd pulled her pigtails. I apologized for telling her just what I thought of her husband. I didn't apologize for thinking it, nor did I have time to listen to her hold forth on all the ways he was a wonderful man. I was busy drenching the burlap on the porch and sitting near it to be cool. I was busy reading a book, or mending Zachary's pants. I was just busy. Too busy for the rest of my life to listen to anything about Aubrey Hanna except that he'd met the business end of a smoke wagon.

She worked on me for three days and when that didn't stand up she started in working on Ma and Pa. She said over and over that a baby needs a *fah-h-h-ther* and a mother, a home, a school in town. Financial support. Strange how she used those same words Pa had said. Finally, one evening as we sat on the porch, she'd got the whole family to pretty much agree with her and she asked me again in very plain words to let her and Aubrey take my baby with them once it came. Would I like to just think it over?

"Someone took these two boys here," I said, nodding at Zack and Ez. "And they were long past being cute and pudgy. They'd got all long and rangy and smelly. I believe Ma could tell you how that felt to have her children stolen away. Why would you think I'd go along with your fool plan?"

"Because it's better for the child," Rachel said. "You'd do what was best for your horse, wouldn't you? Think of the baby."

"If you think you're doing anything of the kind," I said, "it'll be over my dead body."

"Oh, Mary Pearl! What a rude thing to say. I'm surprised at you."

Zachary piped in with, "I'm not. You ain't heard the worst she's got yet."

"That's enough, son," Pa said.

Well, the evening went along after that, and I don't know how other people felt, but for myself I could have slapped Rachel across the face every time I looked at her. She just kept on smiling at me, looking, to my eyes, like the beady grin on a rattlesnake.

When Aubrey showed up the next day, he kept eyeing me, looking too smiley, too eager. Not exactly lustful, like before, but wanting something I had and thinking he'd just grin me into giving it to him.

I told Ma I had a sick headache, and I was sorry but I'd have to eat in my room and Zachary would have to bring me a plate. I planned to stay there until Mr. and Mrs. "Polecat" drove home. I stayed, too. I stitched diapers and little shirts. Made sure my pistols were always between me and the door. Joshua came and asked me a bunch of questions, worried about my condition, and I told him I was fine, that I was only playing possum to stay away from Aubrey. Joshua thought I was a victim of female hysteria, which often "came upon women in the last weeks before delivery."

"Ha," I said, "then let it be, and when you have a wife who's big as a bathtub, you better treat her like a queen or I'll come calling and straighten you out. When you come back up the stairs, bring me some drinking water, please."

"They're leaving now."

With the shedding of Rachel and Aubrey, I returned downstairs. I felt heavy. As if the baby had slid down and made it hard to walk. Mercy, what a load to carry. How did Mama ever have all of us?

I was on the front porch the next morning when another buggy came up the road. I could tell it wasn't those two returning, so I just fanned myself and watched. Turned out it looked like Aunt Sarah's buggy. Some fellow was driving, but he didn't look like her husband, Udell.

They pulled up and the man helped Sarah down, and she told me hello, and went into the house. Right at the doorway, I saw her turn and look at the man with the saddest expression on her face. I thought maybe there was some bad news they had to bring. The fellow stepped up on the porch and took off a brand-new-looking Stetson hat with a snakeskin band on it and a tiny brown feather cocked out of the band.

Standing there, all shined up and shaved, smelling of hair tonic and lye soap, stood Brody Cooperand. He whipped his hat off and held it up to his chest, nodded to me, and said, "Miss Mary Pearl, would you mind overmuch if I were to—that is, I come to—may I pay a call on you?"

I smiled because he looked so pathetic and frightened, like a cat that fell into a washtub. His hair was slicked down and his mustache trimmed too short for my liking. He had a tie around his neck and it was crooked. He wore brand-new Levi pants and had shined the toes of his boots. Just the toes.

For a moment I didn't actually get the notion of what he'd asked. "Well, sure, Brody. Sit down here. I have lemonade. Would you like a glass?"

"Thank you kindly, Miss Mary Pearl."

A long silence followed while he stared at the toes of his boots and I poured the glass full.

"Here's your lemonade," I said. "I can't get up easy. Would you mind reaching for it?"

"Oh, oh sure."

He drank some, then there was another long silence. I said, "So, you came to pay a call? Or were you just driving my aunt over here for a visit?"

"No, I was coming to see you and she said she'd like to ride along. Well, then. Are you feeling well?"

"Oh, yes. Pretty well. I feel fine, but I get tired easy." I glanced around the porch. He was making me feel jittery, too. "You left your guitar here. Would you play me a tune?"

"Sure thing. Sure. It's probably—I'll play something. What would you like to hear?"

"How about 'Red River Valley'?"

"That's a nice one. I'll just set this down." He set the lemonade down and bumped it over. The glass didn't break, but the lemonade made a big puddle. "I'm sure sorry. Sorry, miss."

"Brody? You don't have to be so formal with me. We've known each other more than five years." As I said that, in my mind's eye I stepped beyond that porch as if I were setting up a scene to take a photograph. I knew why he was here. He had meant "paying a call" as in courting.

My baby started kicking to beat the band when Brody picked the tune on his guitar. I fanned myself while Brody sang, too, and the words were sweet and lonesome. This was very kind and dear, but I sure wasn't in any shape to be called upon. I sighed.

He stopped playing abruptly. "Miss Mary Pearl? Would you please think of something I'm about to ask you? And don't say no yet. Think awhile. I ask you to think, but not too long accounta there isn't much time, if you'd consent to marry me. I came to ask you. I'd be proud to have you say yes, and I'd never mistreat you nor be mean. You know me and you know I'm just a ordinary fellow, but I'd be ever proud and loving and would care for you and your baby, and the baby would have a name, and I'd raise him up as a boy of my own. I don't care about that other. It weren't your fault, was the way I heard it. Would you think on it at least? I'd care for you all the days of my life and your baby would have a name and he'd be mine as far as the world is concerned."

"Brody—"

"I would. I'm a top hand. I could get a job anywhere. If you want to run critters, I'm your man. I'd ride for your brand all the days of my life. And I'll tell you, since we didn't pay the ransom and they gave everyone their money back, that I've been working for your aunt almost six years to buy my own herd. I've got a quarter section outside of Springerville. Good water, year-round, and a little bitty house. I reckon it's just a shack, but it's got a window."

"That's probably the most words I've ever heard you say."

"I mean to persuade you, I reckon."

"Want some more lemonade?"

"Yes, please. My throat is dry as cotton lint."

I smiled.

He stood. Drank the lemonade straight down and then sank to one knee. "Would you think on it, please? I'd do for you always. I swear it."

I saw myself nod, and I said, "I . . . I'll think on it, Brody." I was so touched by his romantic efforts I had to smile at him.

"I can buy you a ring, if you'll have it. But, the cows, you know."

"I know. Cows come first."

"I made you this." He held out a sort of string. A heavy, stiff cable-looking thing. "It's—"

"A braid of Duende's tail," I finished for him. "Brody Cooperand, I think that's the nicest gift anyone has given me in a very long time. Thank you."

No sooner had I said that than my aunt came bustling out the door with a basket of quilt scraps and headed for the wagon, sort of like she'd been listening at the door. Brody turned to leave and drive his boss lady home. "So long, then," he said.

"Brody? I *will* think on it. No matter which way I come down, I thank you for the offer."

He nodded so vigorously I thought his head joint shook loose. "Thank you, Miss Mary Pearl. Thank you kindly for receiving my call."

He took the two steps down to the ground and I leaned forward.

"Brody? What's your real first name? I mean, that's short for something, isn't it? I'd just like to know what it's for."

"My first name is Merle. Reckon I been called Brody all my life, though. I had a little brother for a while, and he couldn't say 'brother' so's everyone called me Brody ever since."

"He's gone now? I'm sorry. There ought to be more like you around. Thank you again."

He nodded without looking me in the eye. "So long."

That evening, my brother Clover sat next to me at dinner, though usually he sat across the table, second in line from Pa. He leaned close to me and whispered, "I saw old Brode sitting on the porch, asinging you a song."

"Well, it wasn't any secret."

"He come sparking?"

"I can't say." I touched the braid of horsehair that was hung around my collar and clasped shut with a brooch.

"I thought you ought to know, before you toss him on his ear, that rascal's been longing and thinking of no one but you since you was fifteen years old and he was eighteen. He's a staunch feller."

"You think I should marry him for that?"

"Only if you're inclined. He ain't as educated as us. Don't talk as fancy, or as much."

I almost said it would be nice if someone didn't talk so much, but I just held my peace and nodded. "I'll consider your words," I said.

After I'd thought every way I could about Brody's plan to rescue me from being marked with sin, and rescue the nameless baby I still called "Homer Jane" because it could be a boy or a girl, I told him I wanted to wait. If he still had a mind to marry me, I supposed, when it wasn't some gallant gesture, I'd consider it again. He could adopt the baby or we'd just give her the new name and not mention it was ever different. I simply wasn't going to take the easy way out. Having my child "without a father of record" as Rachel told us Aubrey defined it, in some other state would brand the baby all the days of their life. But in the Territory, no one hardly noticed. Plenty of children came on top of the sheets. No one asked about that.

I think Brody was truly disappointed.

CHAPTER SEVENTEEN

I never had any doubts about the process of bringing a baby, having lived among animals all my days. Saw my baby brothers come. Reckon some girls perish. No one gets through it without suffering, though it was still surprising just how merciless the pain was. There were a few times I was sure I wouldn't survive. Once I considered asking someone to shoot me like a horse suffering too much to live through it. I was glad Mama and Rebeccah were there. Joshua had stayed until my delivery, he said, in case there were complications, but I had none. All went as it should, according to Joshua. Homer Jane became Remington M. Prine, at last. He was all boy, and had a voice on him from the second he was born. He let the world know he'd arrived, all sturdy and vigorous.

Ezra wanted to hold him, and we let him. He was tender and careful, though he only had the use of his left arm. Ez was healing well. Doing better with most everything except talking. Seemed like he wanted to say something all the time, but couldn't get the words out. He rarely left my side.

A month went by, then another. Remington, called Remmy, was

smiling and chubby. Cute as a button. Hungry and growing daily. Christmas was circled on our cow's head calendar—a new fancy one we'd got last February—the kind where you tear away each old month's page, but the colored picture of a Guernsey cow remained above the fresh month. The weather had cooled at last, and one day at noon, here were Rachel and Aubrey on the front porch again.

We'd expected them to come. Papa told all our relatives, and included Brody Cooperand, that we'd have a supper a week before Christmas. This was to accommodate Aubrey Hanna having to entertain important clients and social uppity-ups in Tucson for the sake of his career. Once Christmas Day came, we usually gave small gifts to one another in the immediate family. Rebeccah was making an embroidered kerchief for Ma, so I didn't know what to get for her. I'd ordered store-boughten gloves for Pa. I bought a bridle with two silver conchos on it. I figured it was for my cousin Charlie, but sometimes I pictured Brody's face when he saw it, and I suspected he'd be proud to have it. I sure wasn't in love with him. My only true love now was Remmy.

I ordered a new wheeler toy for both Ezra and Zack. I didn't know whether Ezra could play with it, but I saw him eyeing his brother while he played. Maybe it would be enough if he just had one to hold. Rebeccah was acting all silly and laughing, forgetting things, dropping things. Dr. Pardee was coming to our big supper, too, and she'd say over and over, "We have an announcement for everyone," then she'd blush and take off to another room. I believed they were going to set the date at last to marry.

Just a couple of days before the supper, I thought of a gift for Ma. I got out the sketches I'd done of the daffodils in the yard at Wheaton. I pulled out my best art paper and painted a watercolor rendering of them, surrounded by green fields. I made two larger ones, then added smaller, more distant blooms that represented each member of this family. One was slightly faded, representing Esther. Thank heavens only one was faded. At the last, I added a smaller plant, just breaking the ground, for Remington.

I sent away for a large ceramic-glazed flower pot that came all the way from Holland, with five daffodil bulbs in it, to grow inside the house. For Pa, I printed two copies of the photograph I made of Ma sitting at the kitchen table unawares. I made two so I could practice colorizing. It took me a while to apply the soft powder color mixed just so, and make her look bright and more lifelike without looking painted. Finally, I got one done to my liking and set it into a nice frame from town. I got a matching frame for Ma's painting.

I wanted something special for Granny, and the more I thought about it, the harder it was to come up with something. Some days when Remmy was a bit more fussy or I'd been up all night with him, I'd stay in bed awhile and sleep and read Granny's memoirs.

Don't be free and easy, giving away what's most important to you. Gifts of the best of you have to be given all the time, not just on a date on the calendar. It isn't giving someone a hank of cloth or a new plow or a stuffed dolly. Those things will bring a smile. Save the best of you, your heart's learning, your time, your sympathy, for someone whose heart is as clear as yours, whose intentions are good and whose mind is set on the high ground. Don't take up with no tinkers or drummers out of desperation to get off from home. Learn to size up folks like you'd size up a horse. Watch for meanness and honor. Take time to know their heart before you hand 'em yours.

I was searching through another catalog, and I found just the right gift for Granny. I sent off for a gilt frame with a curved glass front.

While I waited for it to arrive, I cut off a long strip of my hair about an inch wide, and set about weaving her a hair memory. I used pins to hold it in place and little dabs of glue and set the whole thing on a piece of lavender linen. Rebeccah gave me a piece of lace to put around the edge. My nearly black hair in the middle, woven into a basket with a sort of flower petal around the side, looked really fine. I hoped she'd always think of me when she saw it.

The good news about Ezra was that he could walk now without help, and he could get to the outhouse and take a bath regular. He plumb fussed anybody's head off who tried to help him in there. Said he could manage and he "wa'n't no baby." We all believed he'd never be fully right again and it was more than losing the sight in his eye. Ma and Pa both wept over Joshua's tally of Ezra's prognosis. Ma prayed, sometimes deep into the night, but what we saw was that while Ezra just went on living, there was no miracle of returning to who he'd been before. Zachary had suddenly sprouted up taller than me, and I know Ma was making him two shirts, and Pa'd ordered him some genuine Levi's denim pants.

Joshua planned to leave two days after Christmas, he said. He'd listened to my plan of going to Albuquerque, and wanted to take a trip there and see what there might be available for a young doctor to set up practice. When he said that, Ma looked sideways at me, but said nothing. Pa only said that at least he'd only be a day away, and if I was still set on going to that place, well, my brother could do with my help.

That surprised me. Joshua needed *my* help? I believed they'd say I needed *his* help. Even Joshua remarked, "That would be a blessing. It's so hard to get along and keep up on seeing patients at the same time. It'd be a different life, though, Mary Pearl. I wouldn't ask you to study nursing, but just keep up my office part-time. You would have time to set up a photography shop on your own and I could help you financially with that. It'd be the best thing for both of us. Cold up there in the winter, with snow, but I'd love you to come along."

"I've seen snow in Illinois," I said. "It's got some merits I'd heartily prefer over landing in a blistering saddle out in the sun in July here."

We had so many folks in for the supper, we had to have it outside. Hired hands and all, it was a nice time. The men started up a big spit with a crank and they were out roasting a side of lamb all morning, along with cuts of beef laid on a grill, too. The ladies made up biscuits and fresh peas. I sat at the kitchen table with Remmy slurping on my breast while leaning against the arm of Papa's chair, both my hands in a huge bowl of green peas shelling them. Ma and I laughed and talked. Remmy burped and grinned and I accidentally dropped peas on him when I giggled. By the time dinner was cooked, he was ready for a snooze so I carried him to my room and laid him down with a blanket.

Pretty soon, the tables were loaded with food and chairs and bales of hay had been circled. Checkers found himself a good spot under the meat table, just in case anyone dropped a piece for him. I managed to let a bit slide off my plate for him.

We had a fine meal. Every bowl of food was delicious. Brody brought his guitar and Gilbert and Charity sang Christmas songs with him. I'd rather hear a guitar than any of those ragtime tunes the kids at college liked to sing. In my opinion, a ukulele was just a toy for a child, where a guitar had some life in it. The sun settled on a western hill, painting the house and everything east in shades of crimson and ochre. I felt a sort of peaceful contentment wash over me as I sat there.

Aunt Sarah came to sit beside me and laid her hand on my arm. "Mary Pearl? I have been thinking about that book you still have, *Pride and Prejudice*. I have decided since you love it so much, you should keep it. I give it to you for a gift."

"You do? Well, I never expected such a gift, Aunt Sarah." I thought Ma had taken it back to her months ago.

"You keep it, honey."

I smiled, and it took me about five seconds to lower my gaze, then look back at her smiling face. In those moments I figured that she had no way to know I didn't care for that book, and had never thought of it since I'd left for Wheaton, and never intended to read it again. She couldn't know I gave it no value at all; I wasn't much interested anymore in Jane Austen's opinion of the world and how a girl might get along. But Aunt Sarah is not in the habit of giving away books. She'll buy you a china pitcher or a hank of cloth for a new dress and even sew it up for you, but her love of books is deeper than her well. She'd never given away any before, far as I knew. This was something special. This was something she treasured. I said, "This means more to me than you will ever know. I know how you think about books, and it will be the start of my own library now."

She nodded with one very determined bounce of her head and grinned. She was as pleased as I have ever seen her, and I was pleased to have made her happy. That was enough.

Finally, after all had had another taste of pie and Remmy had awakened so I'd changed him and brought him out with us, holding him in a warm blanket, Pa talked awhile about our family and how happy we were to be reunited with Zachary and Ezra. He got Mama's Bible and read the Christmas story. The whole world seemed to settle around the big fire in the yard. Dogs snoozed. Granny rocked in her chair, brought to a warm spot for her. This, I thought, this is what happiness is.

I began to feel as if I had a real place here. That nothing whatever was wrong. That I'd never think of going to Albuquerque or anyplace else. This was my home and the shadows of saguaros and ocotillos framed the sunset in a way I could never catch on a photographic plate.

A couple of other men talked about things. Joshua spoke about how grateful he was to have been able to go to school to become a doctor, and how grateful he was that his family had made it through a rough time without him. Gilbert announced that he and Charity were indeed going to welcome a precious someone to their family come March. When it got quiet, Brody picked on his guitar. I think it was a song called "Greensleeves." Kind of sad and plaintive. I felt each note from that guitar deep in my bones.

Prairie and her husband, William Bradenton, came to see us soon after that Christmas. They were accompanied by the "brilliantly illustrious" international photographer Nation Hollingsworth, who was no longer living in a closet in his aunt's apartment in Chicago, but was traveling the world selling his photographs from every place he went, mostly to the *Chicago Tribune* but also to prestigious magazines, and he was "much in demand." He was on his way to Africa, he said, and the glow on his face was that of a man who'd found and followed his true calling.

Nation came sparking, that was certain. Brought me candy and flowers and handkerchiefs of Belgian lace. He wanted me to travel the world with him. To use our photography to illuminate the darkest corners of the world, places where few people had ever stepped. He began to list the scenes where he'd taken photographs: Morocco, Spain, Alaska, Trinidad, Prague, and more; he'd gotten a few of some Navajo hogans in New Mexico on their way here. We'd go everywhere, he said, in love with each other and in love with the world and our art.

He made it sound mighty fine. And then I looked around me at the hills and the saguaros I knew so well, the people I cared about. I heard Remmy crying upstairs, then quieting, as Ma must have picked him up and changed his diaper. I pictured her in the rocking chair that was now part of my bedroom furniture. Nation said, "Come with me, Mary Pearl. We'll have a grand time. Nothing will ever be boring; I promise you a life of adventures and thrills."

William set his coffee cup down and cleared his throat. "That's hardly fair, old man. You'd best tell her about the quinine tablets and the case of malaria you picked up in Rangoon. Jungle fever. Tsetse flies. Headhunters and slave traders. You can't ask a lady to join you on something like *your* life without a clear image of what she's got coming."

I looked at William with new respect and thankfulness. "You are right. Everything must have balance. Much as the wandering sounds exciting, I'd want to come home after a couple of months." Even as I spoke I knew I was lying. I couldn't bear to be away from my baby for a single day, although I had made up my mind not to mention Remmy to these old friends.

Nation said, "A couple of months? Why, I expect to be gone at least a year this time. I'm headed to Rhodesia and the Zambezi River. Then on to Gaza and the mysteries of Egypt."

I smiled. "Well, then, I wish you safe travels and happy trails. And no more malaria." I felt old. Perhaps "mature" is the better word. Nation looked like a jolly boy, like Ezra before the injury, a boy with the world at his feet and a goal to be won. That would not be my life or my lot, and I was genuinely satisfied that it was not, genuinely glad it was his. I doubted any of his travels and adventures would make time for me if I had a headache or wanted to see my home for a while. "I *am* happy for you," I added.

"Are you truly? Gosh, but you're a swell kid, Mary Pearl."

"Say, I'd like you to take a look at a print I made; wait just a minute." Leaving them in the parlor, I dashed upstairs to get my photograph, the one in which I'd caught lightning on the plate, now framed and hung on a wall in my bedroom. I raised the latch slowly, tipping in to keep from waking Remington. He snoozed contentedly in Ma's arms, and she, too, slept under a quilt and shawl. I so wished I had a camera ready to take that photograph, but then my heart leapt forward. It would look too much like a postmortem, both of them with eyes closed. No, that was a memory to keep, not a photograph to take. I raised the frame from its hook on the wall and slipped back to the hall. Prairie was waiting for me on the first landing, just a few steps below. I smiled and held my finger to my lips, glad for the darkened stairwell, lest my face give away my greatest secret. "My ma is asleep in there."

She whispered, "I won't wake her. I had to grab an opportunity to talk to you alone."

"Let's do it downstairs." How was I going to keep Remmy quiet all night until they left in the morning? I clutched the photograph to my bosom. "We have a little visitor, too," I said. And then I lied. "My sister's baby is a light sleeper." I was immediately mortified that I'd denied my own child to save myself from her condemnation. Who was Prairie, after all? I didn't care what she thought. If she knew the truth, perhaps she'd feel some moral conviction to leave that very moment and never speak to me again. I plastered a smile on my face and held the photograph out, saying, "Here, would you mind carrying this?"

"Certainly. I'll talk to you in the morning then." She smiled and held my arm as we descended the steps. Thank heavens they were only staying one night. Prairie passed the frame to Nation, with, "I'm sure she wanted your opinion first."

He stiffened and stared at it. "Now, I didn't know you could do something like this. Oh, I've got to have you go with me, kiddo." He held it out toward Prairie and William. "Look at this, kids. Lightning." My thoughts left my own guilty deception as I stared at Nation's expression. Prairie and William both gave it an appreciative glance, but they didn't look at it with the admiration I saw on Nation's face. He was a real, published photographer, and he was impressed with my photograph. That was enough. It was, in fact, more meaningful than any teacher's approval. This was a salute from a professional. I'd captured a miracle on paper.

He started to hand it back to me, when I said, "Did you look into the window, there? Did you see what the lightning revealed?"

Nation peered closely. "A face. A tiny face. Is it a reflection in the window?"

"No. It was a boy held captive inside. We saw him in the photograph and saved his life. He's my brother."

Ezra jumped up and stared at the picture for about the ten thousandth time. "That wasn't me now. Now, I was there, but somebody shot me in the brains. That's Zachary. He's okay, though, now. Didn't get shot like me. And Mary Pearl is going to take care of me the rest of my life, now, 'cause I been shot. It's okay. I'm good now. I got two silver dollars in my head now. She made this with her cam'ree."

Nation stared into my eyes and I could vouch for seeing his own eyes fill with tears. "Is this true?"

"Yes, it's true. Just one of many reasons I can't go traveling with you."

"My God. You have such talent. It will be wasted."

"No, it won't. As I said, while your life sounds wonderful, it's not my life. I can hardly wait to hear about your next adventure. Send me some magazines, will you?"

"I will. Every plate I take will be my love letter. You know, kiddo, I'm never going to get over you."

I gave him my most sincere smile. "I think you will, but thank you. You might think about giving me back that tinted print of me."

"Nothing doing. You're going with me around the world."

Late that night, I'd gotten up to feed Remmy, changed him, and put him back to bed, when I saw a glimmer of light coming from the parlor. Our guests were bedded down in there next to the fireplace. I thought everyone had turned in but I heard voices. I carried a lamp down the stairs toward the sound, and rapped softly at the door jamb. "Are you needing anything?" I asked. "Drink of water? More quilts or a foot warmer?"

"Sorry to wake you," Nation said.

"You didn't."

Prairie spoke from shadows so deep I could barely see her. "I can't wait until morning. I have to say it. Mary Pearl, we know about your problem."

I caught my breath. Forced myself to smile again. Even laughed a little. "What problem could I possibly have that keeps my friends up at night gossiping about it?"

William said, "It isn't heartless gossip. It's concern. It's about your sister's baby. And the way she stole away your betrothed fiancé. Is she upstairs listening in?"

Even Nation chimed in. "Really sorry, kiddo. But you shouldn't be carrying that load the rest of your life. Why don't you just sue the blackguard and take him for every cent he's got?"

"Sue him?" I asked. "For what?"

William spoke again. "Breach of promise. It's completely justified in your case. You had an agreement of marriage. He broke the agreement, possibly because your sister got herself in a compromising situation while you were at college. He felt obliged to rescue her. Prairie told me when he jilted you he sent you money. That was to keep you from thinking of him as liable for a lawsuit. But breaking a woman's heart is definitely an offense against society. He could be made to pay a great deal more. You should see a lawyer."

I whispered the word again. "Pay?"

Nation said, "He should be living in a poke barrel, and you'd be rich. You'd be free to come with me."

"I . . . I'll think about it," I said.

Prairie hugged me. "You're the cleverest, sweetest person I've ever known. Please think about it. No one should have treated you like he did."

Aubrey had done me wrong, though not for the reason they believed. I couldn't tell these friends. I felt lying and mean, like a lowdown cur. Prairie was the one who was sweet. She wasn't like anyone I'd ever known, and in a way, I could see she had more bravery and orneriness than me and I liked her for it. She reminded me of my dead sister, Esther. I was heartbroken to say "so long" to them the next morning.

CHAPTER EIGHTEEN

In January of 1909, Rebeccah married Dr. Pardee. She moved away to Benson to live and the house felt empty of women with just me and Mama.

Monday, the first of March, Rachel and Aubrey made another trip out to our farm. They must have left before dawn to arrive before noon. Harvest was long past, but the shelling machine was running, and when they drove up, Zachary ran to the barn where Pa and Clover and I were working. The din from the barn stopped as sudden as pulling a blanket over my head. Everything came to a standstill, like the whole farm was waiting for a thunderstorm. Clover calmly quit shoveling the mountains of pecans from one area to another, and Pa washed his forever brown-stained hands and face. Just like they'd been waiting for a visit, I waited, maybe I should say "hid," in the barn as the two men walked out and talked to them. I knew Ma was probably already hard at work fixing up some dinner for them. I should be in there helping. Rachel should, too, for that matter. I don't mind at all fixing meals for Pa and my brothers, but I wasn't going to raise a finger to feed those two. Then I heard my brother's voice, extra loud, saying, "She's gone down to see Granny. Won't be home until late."

After some time passed, the pair of them decided they weren't going to stay to dinner, and they took off back to town, a good seven hours' hungry drive.

When I came into the house, Ma had dinner on. Pa pointed to a folded paper on the kitchen table, thick as a block of adobe. "That there's for you."

I loosened the string and unfolded the wrapper. It was a pile of money. Dropped it on the table. I jumped when I saw it like it had been a rattlesnake's head.

Pa said, "He said it was two thousand dollars. He's acoming back next Monday with more until you give in. Rachel was acting real sweet."

I couldn't help but sneer at the packet, especially with its being dressed in the words, "Rachel was acting real sweet." My thoughts went right away to wearing a pistol under my apron and carrying a knife in my boot. I said, "At least they gave us fair warning. Next Monday I'll be ready. Wait. Give in? To what?"

"They want to adopt Remington."

"They wanted to buy my baby?"

"Well, he didn't put it like that."

I stared at that stack of bills. Left them lying there while we ate and then I did the dishes. As I moved through the kitchen working, the sight of that cash started an angry train of thought, a train that felt full to bursting with a head of steam I could barely control. And then an idea came to me just when the clock in the parlor chimed five; I said aloud, "He's not the only lawyer in Tucson. I could sue him with his own money."

Ma looked up. "What, honey?"

"Just daydreaming, Ma." I wiped my hands and stacked those bills the way they had been, carefully pulling that paper wrapper tight around them before I tied it with string. It looked like a gift. It made me shudder. I left it on the table between the salt cellar and the fruit bowl that had only a single dried-up lemon in it.

Remmy fussed that evening during supper and although I was hungry, too, it took me two hours to calm him down so I could have a bowl of cold stew. Zachary washed the dishes and Clover dried. Pa slept in his chair with an open book on his lap. If I sued Aubrey Hanna, I wondered how low I could bring him, and what he'd pay to stop me. What would it do to his reputation in town? Maybe he'd have to move somewhere else, like Morocco or Prague? Or perhaps he'd just be wearing a barrel on ropes and living in an arroyo eating nopales with javelinas for neighbors? That meant Rachel, too, would suffer from the scandal and starvation. Well, mad at her or no, I couldn't do that. How could I hurt him and not her? And then, even if I could convince Clover or Pa to take me to town to sue that polecat, what would they think of me? Even less than now, I believed. If I won, I'd break Ma's and Pa's hearts. If I lost, I'd break my own again.

Maybe I would just keep the money and not let him have Remmy. I peered at him, sleeping in his little bunk. What a treasure he was. How perfect and beautiful. Aubrey owed me the money, that was certain. Trying to keep me from suing him? Trying to exact some kind of truce maybe, too? I'd be willing to gamble that he'd no record of that cash anywhere. No one could know, legally, that he'd laid it on our table. There'd be no trace and I could just keep it.

Everyone but me had gone to bed when the clock struck nine. I spoke aloud again, saying, "If he had this kind of money lying around, where was he when we needed it to save my brothers?" If he'd given up this cash for them, Ezra might have been well and whole, and gone on living a good life, instead of being barely himself. Aubrey was willing to put out what amounted to five years' wages for anyone else, to get my child, but he hadn't done any more than buy Clover's courting buggy when we needed the cash. It was Clover who'd gone without, and didn't even get what he paid for that buggy. Aubrey could have easily purchased back the Wainbridge land he'd bought for me. I didn't want it. I wanted it sold, but he'd claimed there were no buyers. Sure as the sun rises in the east I wasn't going to live there and wait for him to come slithering in some night. He'd had unspeakable wealth all along, but not for when my family needed it.

We should keep it. Aubrey Hanna should hang. Those were just facts. Then I stayed awake at least another hour, thinking of what that money could buy. Boots and hats and coats for the family, a house for myself and fine furniture. Rugs and gilt-framed mirrors like at Prairie's house. In this Territory, I could go a long way using that much cash. It was a pleasant dream, but even as I thought it, I knew it would be stealing. Taking anything you didn't earn or make with your own hands was thieving, plain and simple.

The following week and the next, when my sister and her husband drove up, I kept myself in the barn or the well house or the chicken coop with my baby. Although I carried a pistol at all times, I was afraid of either of them getting their hands on him in a way I can barely describe. As if they'd snatch him off like trolls in a fairy tale, carried off to a castle or a dragon's lair, and raised to be something other than I want him to be.

New packets of money appeared on the table between the fruit bowl and the salt cellar. I didn't open the new ones because they were larger than the first. Every time I passed the pile of cash, it felt like I was stoking a fire, like my insides had turned to a steam engine and that stack of greenbacks was coal. If that man walked in here while I was cooking, he'd better bring a doctor with him, I thought. One who knows how to sew up a knife wound. I stood them all on top of each other, set that hard, brown, dried-up old lemon on the stack, and turned the bowl upside down over it all. At least I wouldn't have to look at it.

· · ·

Of course, when Aubrey and Rachel had said they'd come every Monday, there was no reason for them to keep their word. On a warm Wednesday when I was hanging diapers on the line, I heard the familiar sounds of horses and trap, greetings from Ma and Pa. I dried my hands on my skirt and dipped my finger into the lard can by the back door. My hands were so cracked and split from washing that the grease sunk in like a camera flash. I walked around the side to the front of the house where we had a fire pit going with half a calf on a spit. We were fixing to have a roasted dinner because it was Ezra's birthday. All the folks were coming.

My heart sank and my breath stopped. Standing before our porch was Aubrey's buggy. We had not invited Rachel and Aubrey, but I believe she knew what day it was. Zachary nearly knocked me down, running so fast toward me. "Rache is back with that skunk. They got your boy. They got your boy! I'll get my gun," he said.

"Zack, no. There won't be a need to do that."

"They ain't taking my cousin, Imp. They ain't. If I don't *need* my gun, I won't *use* it, that's all."

There sat Ma next to Rachel who was holding Remington, bouncing him happily on her knee and talking silly to him. My little baby cooed and drooled on her in return, smiling his one-tooth smile. A new packet of money laid on the table next to the upside-down fruit bowl. Rachel lifted the corner of it and recognized the other packets. She was just saying, "You should put this cash somewhere safe, Ma."

Pa asked, "How long you all gonna stay? You want us to make you up a bed?"

"Sure, Pa. We brought Ezra a gift for his birthday. Thought we'd spend the night and then head back. Give everyone time, you know."

Aubrey Hanna stood up and drew a large sleeve of folded paper from his coat front. I waited by the parlor door, just listening. Remmy saw me and squealed, holding up his little hands. Rachel did not put him down nor bring him to me. She just held on to him as he squirmed.

Ma said, "I have to check on the meat outside," and left that kitchen like she'd been stung. I was about to follow her when I heard Aubrey say something that included my name, so I looked back to pay attention. Remington started to cry, but Rachel held him fast. I ran outside to the porch again and rang the dinner bell. I didn't ring the usual, though, I beat and clanged that iron a hundred times so everyone would know we had trouble and to come early.

Pretty soon Charlie, Gilbert, and Brody came to the back door and washed up at the barrel. Then they all paraded straight through the house and sat in chairs on the porch. I stayed by Ma, out by the meat, and pretended I was busy, but stayed where I could see Rachel holding my baby at all times.

Aubrey cleared his throat as if he was about to give an oratory. He stood in the doorway so he'd be taller than everyone else. "Folks, this is a great gift that I propose to present to my lovely wife, your daughter, dear sister, and sweet friend. While Mary Pearl here has created a sad episode of shame for this family, Rachel and I come here to grant you all this blessing. I have here a writ from the central court in Tucson. All we need is a *single* signature on one document, by the named herein Mary Pearl Prine, relinquishing all rights to, and custody of, the newborn babe Rachel now holds, and who shall be henceforth known as David Aubrey Chester Hanna. Rachel and I will adopt the child and become his legal parents, taking on all responsibilities and bearing all costs of the child's rearing, education, and care." He slithered over toward me, holding the packet of papers in my direction as if I'd take them from his hands and sign over my baby to a devil without a second whim.

I felt my face grow hot and then my hands and feet grow cold. I searched the faces around the table, wondering where each person would stand on his "offer." Then at last I said, "Why don't you find some other poor orphan to adopt? Why must it be Remmy? Rachel, give me my baby. Can't you see he wants me?" Remington had gone from whining and reaching and squirming to full-fledged yowling. He twisted and turned, then spit up on her skirt.

Rachel came and stood next to Aubrey with Remmy in her arms, saying, "I could be happy with any baby, of course. But you *need* us to take him. You will be better off, and we're family. It's the best thing for everybody. I promise you I will love him with all the love any mother could give. Aubrey is ready to be his father. Now, stop that, Davy, honey. Be a good little man for your mama."

That was the last I could bear. Just then Aunt Sarah and Udell drove up and took chairs, and it was enough of a diversion to draw Rachel's attention. I shoved my hands between Remmy's belly and Rachel's, and wrenched him loose, twisting away. He came free with a handful of Rachel's hair. I screamed to be heard over his frantic cries, "Mama? Papa? Did you know about this? Do you agree with this? Do *you* think I should give up my baby? What about you other boys?" I asked, glaring at my brothers and cousins. As if he knew he was back in loving arms, Remmy relaxed from his terror fit and nodded sleepily against my bosom. I held him tight, hugging his head to my shoulder as he hiccupped.

No one said a word. Brody stared at me like I was on fire and he wasn't sure he wanted to put it out.

"I demand to know where you all stand," I said. "I thought all was well here. Maybe you'd rather I took off to Albuquerque like I'd planned? Maybe I should just leave in the morning?"

"No, honey," Mama said. "We didn't know Aubrey and Rachel had planned this. I don't speak for your pa, but for myself, right now I was considering what might be best for the child."

"Papa?" While I waited for him to speak, the days of holding watch over Duende, hoping for the best, preparing for the worst, played out in my imagination. Having to do what was just and kind to the horse, not what I wanted—which was for him to get well and go back to being wonderful and beautiful, a spirited, fiery stallion. I marched straight to Rachel and stared hard into her face without speaking a word, stealing myself for the impact of Pa's words.

At last, Pa said, "Mary Pearl, I didn't know about this before now. You are neither too young nor too foolish to have anyone else make this decision for you. It *might* be better for the baby. We sure don't want you to take off to some strange town thinking we'd not stood by you."

I said, glaring into Rachel's eyes, "He wants this baby, all right. He's crazy to get this baby. He'll do anything to get this baby."

Pa said, "Don't you think Aubrey is thinking of the good of your child?"

My jaw felt like it had turned to iron. Hard to move, painful to get my lips to make words. I hollered with every ounce of breath I owned, "He wants this baby, Pa, because it's *his!*"

Silence filled the outdoors as if a heavy quilt had dropped from a ceiling.

Rachel burst into tears. "Mary Pearl, how could you say that? How could you accuse Aubrey, of all people?"

Aubrey said, "You have no proof of that. You played fast and loose, off by yourself in that eastern school. Harlots don't get to *choose* what happens to their children."

I stared at Rachel, but spoke as loudly as I could to the crowd. "Papa, it was never you who failed in protecting me. It was her. My sister. Rachel." I spit out her name. "She took me to her house to introduce me to her friends, but I'd caught Granny's cold. I spent most of those three days in bed, sniffling and feverish. Rachel was mad at me—well, you know you were—because she wanted to have a tea and a dinner party and had to cancel them. Then she took off to tell her friends not to come, and Ezra went out to look around town."

"That was me," Ezra broke in.

"Yes, it was, honey," I said.

"Maypoe came and said 'I sleep wi' you 'cause I scared.'"

I went on, "But Ezra was gone and I was asleep. Sick. And who came home unexpectedly in the middle of the day? Who let himself into the room where I slept?" I turned toward Aubrey, looking straight into his eyes. "And who here is wearing a scar from the slice of my hunting knife that goes from his belly to his eyebrow? You ran to your bedroom and threw the mirror on the floor, to pretend that's what slit you from one end to the other."

Rachel shrieked and put her face in her hands. Then she lowered them and screamed, "Liar!"

"You didn't even notice the trail of blood from my room to yours, did you?"

Aubrey's face darkened a shade of purple I'd never seen on a living human. The muscles in his chin worked, his jaw flexed; his eyes glowed like they'd been lit on fire.

Aubrey's pa, Udell, sitting next to Aunt Sarah, stared at him like he'd just grown horns out of his head, but he didn't say anything.

That's how it goes, I thought. I've read about it. No one supports or believes the girl. She should have fought more or screamed louder or should have just brushed it off because boys will be boys. No harm done to them. Just the girl who is ruined and a baby who must be raised. It was no wonder more girls killed themselves than lived in a situation like this. Surely my family would believe in me. Surely.

Aubrey said in a low voice that sounded to me for all the world like a puma murmuring before it leapt, "Let's see you produce said knife. Let's see you stand up and swing it like you were defending yourself. If you were lying down as you claim, you can't even reach my forehead, much less cut my face with a knife."

I hissed, "You were still bending over me. I could reach just fine."

"And where is the supposed knife?"

"I left it in the leg of the dirty campesino who'd captured my brothers. Long gone." I knew, however, full well that it was even now in the side of my right boot.

Rachel wailed, "Papa, you know this isn't true. She's just saying this to keep the baby from me. We have a legal right to him. We have the adoption papers ready, and I want him. Don't you want *me* to be happy? I'm not the one who sassed around in some school in Illinois. Don't you care about our future? *She* isn't *married*, Pa. She got herself in a fix after she ran off."

Papa turned from her to me and back to Rachel. Mama just bowed her head and wept. Papa said, "How can I say I believe one daughter and not the other? If I take your word, Rachel, I lose Mary Pearl forever. If I take Mary Pearl's word, I lose Rachel forever. Either way, Mr. Aubrey Hanna, what you have brought to my home with this document you carry has torn our family apart for all time."

Aubrey shook the papers at me. "Just sign it. You'll see him now and then, as long as we judge that you've left off all of your questionable ways."

I had tried to remain firm and steadfast before his accusations, but that last statement broke all my reserve. I felt so hurt I could barely breathe. I held Remmy close, rocking him on my shoulder, and said, "Go away and never come back, Aubrey Hanna. I would not give you my child to raise if you were the last man standing on this earth. I wouldn't let you raise a goat. Get out of my presence. Get off this land."

"I've got a legal right," he said.

"Why's that?" I asked. "Are you admitting he's your baby?"

Aubrey stammered just a bit, then closed his mouth.

Brody leapt forward, snatched the papers right out of Aubrey's hand, and held them up. With a voice I'd never heard him use, he hollered, "Are you agreeing to any of this or no, Mary Pearl?"

"No," I said. "If he comes after me he'll never find me or my baby! We'll be gone where no one will know."

Brody took two strides and tossed the sheets into the fire pit. The fancy velum flared red and yellow in less than a heartbeat. He said, "Ezra, buddy, fetch me a rope."

My eyes widened. I believed Brody meant to hang Aubrey.

"Burning the papers will do you no good. I've already filed a copy with a circuit judge. He and the sheriff are already on their way here. Rachel? Fetch your child."

Brody Cooperand stood and twisted a lasso into that rope faster than I could see it. He made it to the doorway in about three long steps. "Mary Pearl, get in the house. That baby is Mary Pearl's, and none of yours," he said. "You gave up all right to him when you deserted her. I never hog-tied a lawyer before, but I'm fixing to learn how."

I did what he said, running in and closing the door, leaning against it as I slipped the big bolt into place. Just like Aunt Sarah listening to Brody's "paying a call," I could hear everything, but I moved to the window to see what would happen between them.

Aubrey demanded, "Get out of my way, cowboy."

"No, sir. I won't." Brody, standing on the porch, was head-to-head even with Aubrey. Aubrey was a tall man, but at that moment I doubted whether his height was any match at all for the level of pure scrap and grit contained in the shorter stature of Merle Brody Cooperand. In a few seconds, Charlie, Gilbert, Clover, and even Zack and Ezra joined Brody on the porch.

Charlie said, "Fella, you've married into this family by your own choice. In case you didn't know, even though my last name's Elliot, we're every last one a Prine. We stand together by one another's decisions. Mary Pearl has got a right to do what she's chosen. If you aren't the one took liberties with her, then you are just a bystander and you've come up with a real twister of a plan to get your way. If you *are* the one, you are a *pendejo cabrón* of the first water, and I won't have you stinking up this dinner, nor trying to weasel that baby away from his mother. I think you and Rachel there ought to just get back in your buggy and drive all night and get home before I decide to yank a knot in your tail so tight you won't soon see the end of it. There's a good moon out. Use it."

Rachel cried out, "Papa? Mama!"

No one moved.

Ezra came limping up, holding the reins of the horses tethered to Aubrey's buggy. "Food you!" he called.

As I watched from the window, Aubrey almost forcibly hoisted a crying, wretched Rachel into the buggy seat. He snapped the whip too hard, taking out his anger on the poor horses, and they drove away leaving a string of dust hanging in the air.

I laid my sleeping baby on the settee and stepped back outside.

Mama came to me and hugged me. She whispered, "You did what I would have done."

Nothing could have made me more proud.

Later that afternoon, Mama took to her bed. She slept long and hard, and when she woke, she didn't get up. She said she was tired to the bone. I reckoned her heart plumb broke in two from what happened. She couldn't catch her breath, she said. Felt like a horse was sitting on her chest. Clover rode to Benson to get Pardee, but he was out making calls and no one knew when he'd return. He'd left Rebeccah in charge of some patients, and she was still mixing cough syrup when Clove left, but said they'd come the next day.

Mama's heart gave out later that week. Oh, the loss of her firm love and warmth. It felt as if a wide arroyo had opened up in the land, the sky, our hearts. They dug her grave in the rocky ground, next to the rest of the family in the plot on Aunt Sarah's place. As Pa worked, pale and sweating, the sky opened up with a harsh, windy rain. It was hard work and I feared he'd join her in the hole if he didn't slack up a little, but he wouldn't hear of slowing. Mama was our sure foundation, everybody agreed. I felt so alone and blowy. Felt like a curtain in a window with no one home, just drifting with the wind.

It didn't take me long afterward to make up my mind about living out my days with a man who had all the character I wanted to teach my baby son. I wasn't interested in being smitten and crazy with love ever again. I'd done that and it was horrible. Nation might have been plenty of fun, but standing over Mama's grave, I pledged my troth without even telling him to Merle Brody Cooperand instead, knowing he was a genuine gentleman, a gentle man. Made up my mind I'd have to ask Brody if he still had a hankering for me when the funeral was over and my heart didn't feel so like a shattered plate of glass.

After the funeral, I came to the parlor and found Brody in a chair with Remington asleep across his chest and his hand holding the baby's head. He nodded at me and said, "Little feller was crying and I figured just to let you say your farewells to your ma. He went right back to sleep. No bigger'n a lamb."

"Thank you." Though I'd planned to speak to him, I found myself mute. Just too full of thoughts and tears, I believe, to say anything more, so I said, "Thank you," again.

The pot of daffodils I'd given her withered and drooped that same week.

Brody walked to our house one afternoon not a week later, cleaned up some, with the same shine on the toes of his boots as before. It would be difficult to pin down and describe the flutter in my heart I felt when I saw him riding up. It was excitement and peace at the same time, as if he brought with him a gentle calm, along with a deep longing. He asked if he could call on me just then. "Well," I said, "yes, if you could talk a little louder." Remington was slurping his fill and hiccupping against me under a shawl.

Brody laughed and smiled, looking sheepish. Then he said, "Miss Mary Pearl, I just want you to know something. That, well, that day when ol' Aubrey came with his papers and was fixing to take that little feller, I had my eyes on you. I saw you was full of fight, but trying to think what was better for the baby, like you did with your horse. I took them papers away from him, just to watch what you did. It was only when I saw your face that I thought of throwing them in the cook fire. If you'da paused, or claimed to want to think it over, I'da got on my horse, and rode off to the ranch I want to build up north, and never seen you again."

That statement filled me with a dread. Until that second I had never considered not seeing him again if I moved to Albuquerque. Never thought he'd not be here when I came home. I didn't rightly know what to say, so I just waited. Remmy fell asleep. Was I smitten with Brody? Not at all. Did I feel desire? Only a little. I just plumb admired the man. Respected him. Felt comfortable with him like I would with a hug from my pa. What I felt was longing, just like longing for home. And when I was near him, I felt as if I'd come home. As if I needed him.

He went on, "It was because you wanted no part of it, could never give up that boy, that I knew you was the girl for me, if only you'd be convinced of it, too. It all came real clear to me in less than a shake."

"I was proud of you for doing it. No one else even thought to get rid of his papers." It was too clumsy with this baby on my shoulder to reach out, pat his arm, or any of the endearing things I felt I wanted to do.

"Paper burns."

"Yes, it does," I said.

"And so, are you? Convinced, I mean?" he asked in a whisper.

I asked, "That I am the girl for you? Or that you are the man for me?" When I'd thought the sentence in my head, it seemed sweet and charming, but the look of dismay and doubt on his face told me it was not. I wanted to swallow my words and change his expression.

"Well"—he started rolling his hat in his hands—"I reckon both."

I took a deep breath. "I had only thought you were being brave when you asked me before, trying to save me from having a child without a pa's name. But, yes. I hope I'm the girl for you. I pray you're the man for me. I believe you don't even know that the M in Remmy's middle name stands for Merle. I feel a fondness for you that has grown every time I see you. I believe I'm *well* convinced, Brody. No fooling. I can't imagine living without you."

He clasped his hand to his face and kind of grunted like he was squelching a holler, and said, "Well, shoot," then he scratched his ear and put his hat on his head and took it off again in about the length of a single breath.

I said, "Tell me about that ranch up north."

"It's got a little rock house that has a stairway to the ceiling in case you wanted to add on a second story. There's no cookstove yet, but a good fireplace indoors. And fields of good grass, and a couple hundred miles of fence, but some's falling down. The best thing is, there's always water. Snows in the winter, if you don't mind the cold."

As he talked, I imagined the fine place we could build with the money lying on the kitchen table. And then I felt so troubled I began to weep. Brody was so honest and kind. He deserved to know I was capable of killing and cunning and thievery. When he asked me why I looked so sorry, I told him about the money, and how much I wanted it, including how much of it there was and that I'd wished Aubrey dead.

Brody's face didn't hide his disappointment. "What you fixing to do with it?"

I flexed my toes and felt how inside my boots one big toe was always swelled more than the other. Damaged forever by the venom it once had touched. There could be nothing Aubrey Hanna could give me that wasn't poisoned. "Leave it there," I said, surprising myself. "When we're gone from here, Clover can give it back to them. I don't want to touch it." I felt as if I could breathe easier than I had in weeks. That glowing hot steam engine in my lights slowed and let out its whistle.

He nodded. "That's the best thing."

"When do you figure to head north?"

"Couple weeks. That's enough time for you, isn't it?"

It seemed like enough time, but just two days later, the new county sheriff, John Nelson, showed up with more papers from Aubrey and Rachel Hanna. Sad enough for me, I was rocking Remmy on the front porch when he rode up and I couldn't hide. He tipped his hat and introduced himself. Even though I was afraid of him, I let him have a merry smile, hoping to warm his heart. He admired my baby and said good morning to Pa and Clover, who came running when they saw the stranger dismount at our porch. I let Pa do the talking, but I kept my ears open and eyed my line of escape should this fellow pull a gun or lay hands on my baby or me.

After a while, Sheriff Nelson said, "Young lady, you know I can't advise you to break the law. The people of this county have placed a debt of trust in me, you see, to carry out the law. I've got to serve you these here papers. This here's a court order signed by a judge." He read from the page. "Mr. Aubrey Hanna has vouched that he is the bona fide father of an illegitimate child known here as Remington Prine, being less than one year of age." The sheriff looked up. "If you had another place to live, say, out of this county, where I'm not obligated to see you again, nor testify what exactly happened to these here papers, it might not bother the voters too much."

Pa said, "It might bother Mr. and Mrs. Hanna."

I liked the way the sheriff thought a minute before he said anything. He pulled his hat back on and straightened it. "You say Mrs. Hanna is your daughter, sir?"

"Yes, she is."

"Possibly she'll be blessed with a child herself soon enough, and leave off this here."

"That'd be my hope."

"Yes, sir. Good day to you, sir. And miss or missus," he said, tipping his hat to me. "Just hate to see families quarrel like this. Sure do." With that, he mounted up. He turned his horse but stopped and took off his hat again. "Mr. and Mrs. Hanna are acoming this direction on Saturday. They'll want me to come along so they can take possession of that baby. Probably won't get here until after noon," he said. "If I don't see you, you take care now." Then he rode toward Tucson.

Pa looked at me, his face sad and pulled down. "I'm sorry for Rachel, but she's got a husband. I feel like it's my duty to take care of you, Mary Pearl."

"Yes, sir?"

"We need to have a family talk. You go get your aunt Sarah. I want to settle out some things. I have a half-day's work to do. If you'll take the baby with you, Clover and Zack can help me in the barn so we can finish that last load."

"Papa, Brody asked me to marry him and move away."

"I know that. He asked my permission. Made some promises."

"Are you against it?"

"No. He's all right. Just fetch the family and him, too, and let's lay out everything we have got before us so no one is in the dark."

I took up Remmy and laid him on my shoulder. He barely stirred. I set off walking.

Up the road came Brody and Gilbert, trying to get ahead of three ornery strays. The cows kept getting off the side of the road and wouldn't turn around. For a moment or two, I just admired the way both men stuck in the saddle, whistling soft, cutting their horses this way and that, circling the steers like they'd been born in the saddles as part of the horse. I waved and once they got all the animals pointed in the same direction, back toward their corral, Gilbert followed them while Brody got down and came toward me, leading his horse.

"Brody," I said, "I know we were going to wait to marry. What would you say if I told you I want to leave a week or two early? Get married right away?"

"I don't mind if we marry this very day," he said. "I just need time for a bath."

"I don't mind, either. But that's too quick to get my family here. I'll send Zack to the station to telegraph Rebeccah. Right now, I'll take Remmy and say so long to the rest of the family who live down this road. Pa wants everyone to come and talk in a while. For the wedding, they can gather after morning chores tomorrow."

"Climb up. I'll carry you down there."

"No, that's all right. I'd feel better if you stayed behind me and watched over us where you can see if any polecats are nosing around. He could just as easy have been following that sheriff."

Brody frowned. He took his gun belt out from his saddlebag and hung it on low, tying the holster to his thigh. "He's looking for a case of lead poisoning."

"Maybe," I said.

"He might find it. You head up the road. I'll just rest here a spell and watch."

"Thank you."

"We're really getting hitched tomorrow?"

"Yes."

"M-mind if I give you a little kiss?"

I wrinkled my nose and smiled. "Nope. I don't mind."

Brody leaned toward me and planted a soft kiss on my cheek, as gentle as a butterfly. "It's us against him and everything else," he said. "Nothing before, none of it matters. I never in my life thought someone like you could think on me at all. I ain't much of a prize. You've been to college and I ain't never read a book."

I touched his face tenderly. "I think on you plenty. I think how nice it'll be to wake up beside you all the days of my life, that's what I think. I'd go with you wherever you go, to the ends of the earth, Brody Cooperand."

He shook his head and covered his face, as if the blush pained him.

I whispered in his ear, "Reckon I could give you a little kiss, too?"

He smiled, staring hard at the desert ground, then gave a boyish little shrug.

I gave him a little buss on the cheek like he'd given me. Then I said, "I'm going to say good-bye to my aunt and my granny now."

I walked away, and in a few steps I heard Brody shout, "Whoo-hoo!" and, turning around, saw his hat fly straight up in the air over his head. I grinned and waved at him. My heart felt as if it swelled into the sky with joy.

I hurried with my sleeping boy on my arm toward Aunt Sarah's old place, stopped and told Charity to bring Gilbert in the morning, and then went further on to Udell Hanna's, where Granny stayed with Aunt Sarah and Udell now that all the troubles were done. Udell had built Granny a special room which she liked very well, and that was as it should be. Aunt Sarah could tend her needs better than Pa, who was not a bad nurse when Ezra needed help, but he would have been embarrassed to give his ma a bath if she needed it.

I knocked on the door and hollered, "Hello!" and then just walked in and found Granny in the parlor. "Morning." I was feeling every ounce of Remmy's twenty pounds, and was happy he fell asleep in my arms so I could lay him across my lap to talk to my grandma.

"Ain't you cold, girl?"

"No, Granny. I've walked all this way and I'm warmed through and through. I got something to tell you though."

"I reckon you're going to Kentucky with that boy."

I stared at the sky through the window glass. There was no reason to correct her. Kentucky was just some distant place, far away, back in time, in the recesses of her great supper table set with all the pieces of her life. "I believe so."

"It's cold there."

"I know. Better than roasting alive most of the year here. I met up with a jackrabbit the other day who asked me to please throw him in the fire so he could cool off."

"It's only April."

"Yes'm."

"When you leaving?"

"Couple of days. Wedding's tomorrow."

"You got my memories hid good?"

"I do. No one has seen them, although Rebeccah told me she was jealous and wished you'da given her something like it."

"Secrets is heavy things. I gave her a gift by her not having to carry it. You're the one toting the heavy load."

I let out a chuckle. "I agree."

"You a woman now."

"Yes'm, I believe." I listened to her rocking chair moving, memorizing the squeaks of it. "I'm gonna marry Brody Cooperand."

"That's fine, girl. He's straight up and square all around."

"Papa is coming with us. Ezra and Zachary, too, so I can take care of them as I always have. It seems like a good thing. Zack is already setting his sights on schooling, but until then, I'll send away for mail-order books. Clover is gonna keep up the pecan farm."

"That so?"

"I . . . I want you to come with me, too."

"Ah, that's no good. I'm too old for gallivanting. You got a new life to live and a new family to start. Taking care of the old, that's not your job now. Kentucky's a wild place. What town you heading fer?"

"Springerville."

"Good farming there?"

"Yes'm. Brody thinks so. Ranching, too. They run cows up there mostly. He's got a place between two mesas overlooking a settlement called Eagar. There's plenty of people speak Spanish there, so I can talk to everybody. He's going to set me up a room for my photographs."

"Pish. You're gonna be running after little ones and chickens too much for that, likely."

"Maybe so. But I do want you to come. I'll miss you so much. I can't bear the thought—"

"That I'll pass on while you're gone? Listen, honey. That's how it will always be. My ma and grandma passed without me being near. It's a blessing if you get to hold your loved ones as they cross over, and don't be thinking it's not. But you see, you got all my wishes and dreams and thoughts with you. Anytime you miss me, you just open it and read a spell. That'll likely bore you to sleep, but there I'll be right beside you, just like when I first told it to you."

"Ah, Granny."

"I won't mind if you write in it some, too. Add some pages to it when you get a chance. You know, back in the days of your great-great-great-grandmother, a lady always kept a book. You *should* keep a book. Your aunt Sarah has kept a book since she was younger than you. How else would I know about all her secret wishes?"

"You mean, you read it?"

"'Course."

"I thought you couldn't read."

"Well, that's only sorta true. I can read when I want to enough."

I grinned at her. "Granny, you're a rascal."

"When I want to be, I reckon. Now hug me and don't break my old bones. I feel like I'm strung with spiderwebs, not a bit of iron left in me."

"I believe there's some iron left," I said. "You've made me want to be a better person. I'll never forget that."

"Write some, too. You best do it or when I die I'll come haunt you."

"Ah, Granny!"

We both laughed. We both cried.

Aunt Sarah came out to the porch and handed me a large bundle full of pans and towels and a set of bed linens. She said, "I'll drive you back home. You can't carry all this and that little buster of a boy, too. I got a bone to pick with you, too. You know I'm not happy to be losing my best hand."

"I know. But you're running sheep now, more than horses. It only makes sense you give a job to a good sheep man."

"Reckon so. You know I've always thought of you as my girl? More like me than my own daughter April has been. We'll be there tomorrow morning for the happy day."

"I'm not gone for good. We'll visit, and *our* door will always be open. It's only six hours by train. North to Holbrook and then east to Springerville. I'll always love you, Aunt Sarah. And always be beholden to you, for giving me the schooling you did."

The next morning, Brody and I held hands in Ma's best parlor and pledged before my family to stand by each other all our days. I was surprised that he'd come with a gold band for my finger. He couldn't have gotten to town and back so quickly, so he had to have bought it before now.

Aubrey's father, Udell, begged forgiveness for his son's actions, saying he and Aubrey's mother had been separated for decades and he had nothing to do with the boy's upbringing, and he would have liked to see him trained to know right and wrong. I don't believe a person can ask or accept forgiveness for someone else, just like they can't say someone else is sorry for what they did. But I told him I was forgiving everything and determined to be happy, and not to worry, but plan to visit us at our ranch.

We packed up our wagon that afternoon. We spent the night in it, on a little bunk, but so cold we wrapped up like blanket rolls and huddled together for warmth. Two burritos, side by side. Too cold to uncover, too embarrassed as well, knowing my family was just steps away, and even if we'd stayed in the house, it would have been in separate rooms for the same reason.

It was a frosty morning in that wagon on that hard bunk, and I turned to look toward Brody. My hair was all tangled over his face, and he swept it back, touching it like it was something new and rare. He said, "I thought I was dreaming. I wished for this morning so many times before now, it don't hardly seem real."

"I have to admit I never before expected to see you beside me in the morning. Not until that day you came to propose. I had to try on the idea several times before I thought it would fit."

Then he wrapped one arm around me and pulled me close to him. "There ain't nothing better in the whole world," he said, "than to wake up next to you. The rest of my days, you'll be the first thing I see every morning and the last thing I see every night. Being married to you is better than a cool drink of water."

I smiled. That was the second longest speech I'd heard from him. I nestled into his arms and laid my face on his chest. "I can count on you. I trust you. That's everything in the world to me. I have come to love you, Brody. Very much."

He inhaled sharply and pulled me tight. "You do, really?"

"You think I'd have married you for less?"

"You can draw us up a brand and I'll get it made for our stock."

"I still want to hear you yodel."

"Someday, I reckon. Maybe I'll teach Remmy. Meanwhile, I'll build you a home."

"I'll cook your suppers. And have your children." I smiled.

He pulled his head back and raised his eyebrows with a grin. "That sounds like a fine bargain." Then he kissed my forehead. I sighed. Felt like I should say something but I paused, waiting for him to speak. All he did was nod. After a long time, he said, "We need to get a move on and make some tracks, but there's a little while until folks are up."

"Then we can stay in here a little longer, I believe."

By that afternoon there were six of us heading north. Pa, Ezra, Zack in one wagon, Merle, Remmy, and I in the other. A few hours ahead of the sheriff and my sister and her polecat husband. It took five days to get north through the mountains, and though we watched behind, there was never any sign we were followed. I hung my painting of Ma's daffodils in my little kitchen on the wall over our bed. Remmy's little bunk was a shipping crate with padding I made, and it sat at the foot. A month later I sold half of my Wainbridge land to Clove for a dollar, and the rest I sold to the railroad for many more dollars, although they've done nothing with it. Brody and I used the cash to build up the herd.

We left Clover at the pecan farm, happy enough, I suppose, working away his years as boss of the place. Six months after that day, Rachel came to visit Clover, driving the buggy that had once been Clove's, loaded with trunks and valises full of her fine clothes and a single china teapot. She put the matched set of palomino mares in Pa's barn, walked into the house and took off her bonnet, made herself a pot of coffee, and never left. Acting as housekeeper and cook, she stayed even after Clover married a girl named Bess McAdams from Pomerene.

Rachel wrote me a couple of times, asking forgiveness for Aubrey's actions. She said that Dorothy and the other two maids she'd hired left her house abruptly, and she was at a loss to know why. I suspected that was her way of telling me between the lines that Aubrey was after those ladies as well, and no woman had been safe in her house. I wrote back and told her all was well between her and me, but I did think at the time she should have asked forgiveness for her own actions, even if her reason was that they were swayed by a slick talker like Aubrey Hanna. Still, I sent her a photograph of Ma's daffodils in bloom. She sent me a scarf she knitted.

EPILOGUE

Seven, nearly eight years have passed.

Our little line shack now has five rooms, a porch, and two more rooms upstairs. One of them is my art and portrait studio.

Merle and I have four boys, with another baby on the way. This one feels different. Lighter. I'd sure like to have a girl this time. I'd like to sew a pinafore and curl her hair instead of patching knees and making fishing poles. I hope it is a girl. We have a spread outside of Eagar, Arizona, where I can see a wide valley from the road to my house. Pa lives on our place in his own house as foreman.

Ezra lives pretty well, does chores and grooms horses, sometimes when they've just been groomed, but the horses don't mind. He'll never be able to live on his own. Sometimes he gets dreadful headaches and can't breathe, and I fear he's lived his last every time he catches a cold. Zachary has gone through the university in Tucson. He studied agriculture and is planning to farm cotton in the Phoenix area, but said he'd visit us up here in the cool country come June.

Meanwhile, my studio hangs with photographs of people from Springerville and Holbrook, dead children and loved ones, and a number of wandering elk, bears, horses, dogs—especially Checkers, who is quite the photographed dog—and other critters, plus plenty of my family and my children. We'll have the most photographed children in Apache County in what is now the state of Arizona as of February 1912. The best part of that is that when people come from town to have a portrait done, everyone who sees my photographs of all my boys lined up like stair steps always remarks on how like their father they all look. While I am thinking that they probably just look like *me*, I smile and say, "It's more important they act like him."

I have a good income making plates of people and their children, even their dogs and other animals, too. I am known for always setting up a big mirror next to my flash pan to add extra light. When I take images of people's dead loved ones, sometimes I set up a nice mirror not just to bounce the flash, but to catch a loving mother or father in the image, so there is a portrait of two people, the child and the grieving parent. It's a unique photograph and most people buy the one parlor card but also a small print of the one that includes their own face as they look down at the baby in the coffin. It's all about the light and the way it paints halos around the faces in that moment in time, almost like that lovely painting in the Wheaton library.

Aunt Sarah and Udell Hanna still live outside of Tucson, and the new people running Maldonado's place are good neighbors again. Charlie wanted to go back to West Point, but after all that happened that year, he decided to learn to fly an aero plane instead. He's barnstorming the whole country now, and takes a little box camera along. He wrote to say he's thinking about taking a job as a deputy sheriff up on the Mogollon Rim and selling that aero plane. He won't be far away, just a day or two on horseback.

Prairie and I write often, although I have not seen her since the day she visited. Last time I got a letter from her it came with a photograph

of her along with her husband and three children all in fancy clothes
and kid leather shoes with thirteen buttons apiece. I'm glad she has
that life. Gladder still that I have mine. Rawhide boots are better pro-
tection from a rattler than high-button shoes. She said she heard Calvert went to bed one night in the Wheaton library and didn't wake up
in the morning. He was found wearing my old roping hat and holding two apples. That library won't be the same without its being
haunted, I suspect.

Nation Hollingsworth went to China three years back and
hasn't been heard of since. I'm sad, but I believe he was doing what
he loved to do. The *Chicago Tribune* published a book of his photographs, and his aunt sent me a copy of it. Inside the back cover was
the print he'd made of me that had got me so riled up back then. I
considered keeping it, but I have the other uncolored version of it,
and so I relegated that tainted-looking image to the fireplace. As
Brody said once long ago, "Paper burns," and he meant that it flamed
with satisfaction.

I planted Mama's daffodils by my front porch. This place grows
them fine, and there are no javelina. The bulbs have multiplied from
five to eighteen last I saw them in full bloom. Every day when they are
blooming I walk out there and just listen, quietlike, for Mama's whisper. Merle is outside right at this moment building a swing for the
children. He took extra care that they can run to it and not trample
their grandma's flowers, even though most of them never had laid
eyes on her, for it is all they have of her and she was a good woman, he
tells them. Pa nods and tears fill his eyes.

I keep my Granny's memoirs safely hidden, but she's given permission for all of us to read them. Merle has built a secret second room
in our cellar, just like she told me.

Rebeccah and her doctor husband, along with their two little girls, are visiting at our house. I'm leaving all my children, other than the one I'm carrying, that is, with them and Pa and Ezra for six days, and Merle has bought us tickets for the train from here across Flagstaff to Williams, Arizona. From there we will take the spur north.

My reticule holds a receipt for reservation of two nights at the brand-new El Tovar Hotel (with convenient indoor plumbing) on the south rim of the Grand Canyon. Room has been given to extra luggage for my camera and plates. I'm so excited I could bust. This trip is going to be something I'll remember all my days. I'm going to write about every minute of it to Granny. She's gone blind, so someone really will have to read it to her, the rascal.

Standing breathless at the edge, on our last day at the canyon, arm linked with Brody's, I held *Pride and Prejudice* in my free hand, ready to pitch it into the Colorado River. Some people believe that nice girls don't read novels. I don't think it made me turn bad, but I do think it gave me ideas about what was important in life. Even my mama was of a different mind after she read one. A girl needs to have her wits founded on the real things around her, not some made-up world. There is a much better recipe for life than what was in Jane Austen's book. She was wrong writing that happiness came with a man with money. At least, none of that held water out here in Arizona. In the end, I left the book on a table in the lobby, as if forgotten.

Before this little girl—I hope—is born and could possibly be swayed by a novel into loving the wrong man, or thinking that looks and money are reasons enough to devote herself to someone, I want to teach her that love is not handsomeness or promises of adventure; it is not wealth or fine clothes or sashaying around society parties eating petit fours. Someone who loves you doesn't ask you to be something you aren't already, nor make you believe you'd never amount to a thing without him. Love is building a little cart for our boys to pull. Digging a hole for another apple tree. Fixing my stirrup at dawn. Putting up a shelf for my photographic plates.

A day later, Brody clicked his tongue to the team pulling our buggy and as we turned toward home, I shielded my eyes from the sun. He saw me do it and pulled the shade a little lower for me. I smiled at him and fingered my gold wedding band. Love isn't about looks or money or even accomplishments. Love is a million little promises kept.

ACKNOWLEDGMENTS

Warm thanks to my editors, Sam Zukergood and April Osborn.

NANCY E. TURNER was born in Dallas, Texas, and currently resides in Pinetop, Arizona, with her husband, John. She started college when her children were full-grown. With a degree in fine arts from the University of Arizona with a triple major in creative writing, music, and studio art, Turner went on to become the bestselling author of many novels, including *These Is My Words*, *Sarah's Quilt*, and *The Star Garden*.